Praise for *Hemlock*

"A clever mix of fun and frightening, *Hemlock* had me biting my nails with anticipation. I can't wait for more!"
—Kimberly Derting, author of *The Body Finder*

"A riveting romance and a thrilling mystery, *Hemlock* is the werewolf story done right. I devoured it in one sitting and am ravenous for more! A fantastic start to a compelling new trilogy." —Sarah Beth Durst, author of *Enchanted Ivy* and *Ice*

"A werewolf tale filled with hurtling action, searing emotion, and enough twists to keep readers glued to the page until the final breathless scene." —Sophie Littlefield, award-winning author of *Banished* and *Unforsaken*

"Seamless writing and plenty of action mark this intelligent, dark paranormal debut. Older teen paranormal fans will likely clamor for the next book in this planned series."
—ALA *Booklist*

"Jacob fans rejoice: Peacock's debut is loaded with were-wolves both creepy and hot. Mac's smart and believable voice will leave readers looking forward to more."
—*Publishers Weekly*

"Intriguing. The book is full of twists, and . . . the major revelation at the end of the story is unexpected and well-crafted. Mac and the other characters explore serious issues such as trust and betrayal, prejudice, and identity in ways that teens will recognize. A good purchase for fans of the supernatural."
—*VOYA*

". . . Peacock hold[s] readers with an intense love triangle. . . . Will be enjoyed by fans of Maggie ... Meyer."

KATHLEEN PEACOCK

LOCK

 KATHERINE TEGEN BOOKS
An *Imprint* of HarperCollins*Publishers*

Katherine Tegen Books is an imprint of HarperCollins Publishers.

Hemlock

Library of Congress Cataloging-in-Publication Data
Peacock, Kathleen.
  Hemlock / Kathleen Peacock. — 1st ed.
    p. cm.
  Summary: High school senior Mackenzie attempts to solve the mystery
of her best friend's murder in a town affected by the werewolf virus.
  ISBN 978-0-06-204866-0
  [1. Werewolves—Fiction. 2. Murder—Fiction. 3. Mystery and detective
stories.] I. Title.
PZ7.P31172He 2012   2011027327
[Fic]—dc23   CIP
                                                                  AC

Typography by Torborg Davern
13 14 15 16 17 LP/RRDH   10 9 8 7 6 5 4 3 2 1
❖
First paperback edition, 2013

FOR MY FAMILY—
THOSE STILL HERE AND THOSE WHO
ARE NEVER FAR FROM MY THOUGHTS

April

BLOOD RAN DOWN MY HANDS IN THIN RIVERS. I YANKED on the chain-link fence, ignoring the pain, desperate to widen a gap at the bottom where someone had cut the wire. Puddle water soaked through my jeans as I kneeled on the filthy pavement. Small things—*don't think about mice and rats*—scurried in the darkness.

It was no use. The blood made my hands slip, and even after throwing all of my weight against the fence, I wasn't strong enough to stretch the hole by more than a few inches.

A cat could have squeezed through. Maybe. If it were starved and held its breath. There was no way I'd make it.

I let out a ragged yelp of frustration and immediately clamped my bloody hands over my mouth, trying to recapture the sound.

Too late.

I glanced at the opening of the alley just as he stepped inside. Like before, he stayed in the shadows, using them to hide his face. There was no way in or out unless it was past him.

I was trapped. As effectively as if I were in a cage.

My breath came in small gasps.

I was going to die. Just like the others. Tears blurred my vision; I blinked them away.

No!

Not taking my eyes off him, I used the fence to haul myself to my feet. I licked my lips and tasted the tang of copper; it made my stomach roll.

I was *not* going to die like this.

I would not die scared and alone in a dirty alley.

There was a broken hubcap near my feet. I picked up one of the jagged halves and clutched it like it was some sort of *Kill Bill* weapon. Panic crushed my chest and I knew I looked ridiculous—worse than David facing Goliath with a slingshot. . . .

Laughter echoed down the alley, sending shivers down my spine.

I tried to remind myself that David had won.

David had won and I was not going to die here. I was stronger than that. I was . . .

He rushed forward, a blur so fast I barely had time to slash out. He grabbed my wrist and broke it as easily as someone snapping a twig.

I screamed and dropped the hubcap as waves of pain radiated up my arm.

In one smooth move, he was behind me, pinning my arm behind my back.

There was a popping noise followed by white-hot agony. I screamed a second time as I felt my shoulder dislocate.

Despite the pain and the black spots swarming at the edge of my vision, I fought to twist free. I wasn't going to die here. I didn't want to die here. I couldn't die here.

There was a sound like a knife being dragged across a whetstone. Pain exploded across my torso as blades sliced my skin and—

"No!" A choked sob was ripped from my chest as I sat bolt upright and fought against my blankets.

For a horrible moment, the image of the alley was super-imposed over my bedroom and I wasn't sure where I was. Slowly, reality reasserted itself as the sights and sounds of my nightmare faded away.

Every muscle ached—as though I really had just been fighting for my life.

With a shuddery breath, I turned on the bedside light. The bulb flickered to life and illuminated my room—the burgundy bedspread and matching curtains, the ginormous bookcase I'd found at a yard sale and stained cherry-red, the posters and pictures. An ordinary room. Not a dark alley off Windsor Street.

I was safe. I was home.

I pulled my knees to my chest.

"Just a dream," I whispered, throat hoarse.

Almost involuntarily, my eyes were drawn to a framed picture across the room: two girls who couldn't look, or act, less alike. Me with my messy blond ponytail, ruler-straight hips, and a bemused but aloof expression on my face and Amy—my best friend—with ink-black hair, an hourglass figure, and a come-hither smile.

"Just a dream," I repeated.

But it hadn't been a dream. Not for Amy.

I squeezed my eyes shut as the first tears started to fall.

The wind had a bitter edge that made my eyes sting and slipped through the gaps in my coat. I shivered and Kyle draped an arm over my shoulder. So far, April had been colder than anyone could remember, almost as though the ever-present gloom that had settled over Hemlock was affecting the weather.

The minister paused. "It's almost over," murmured Kyle. At six one, he had the better view. We stood ten rows back, hovering on the edge of the crowd. It was the best I could manage. Any closer and it was hard to breathe.

Ten rows back was safe. All you could catch from here were glimpses of waxed wood and polished brass under a mound of white flowers.

Even if I had wanted to get closer, it would have been difficult. An impossible number of people—more people than had known Amy in life—had crowded into the quiet corner of Fern Ridge Cemetery that was the final home to Hemlock's wealthy and powerful.

I leaned into Kyle. For once I didn't care if people mistook us for a couple. The urge to turn and run was less overwhelming with an arm around me. With Kyle's arm around me.

"Can you see Jason?" I asked. Jason was Amy's boyfriend and had been best friends with Kyle forever. The

4

four of us—Amy, Jason, Kyle, and I—had been a unit for years, ever since I moved to town.

Given how hard this was for me, I couldn't imagine what he must be going through.

Not that I could get him to talk about it. When Jason was upset or hurting he did one of two things: he shut down or he exploded.

Kyle squinted and craned his neck. His thick, chestnut-colored hair fell over his eyes and he absently pushed it away. "I can see the back of his head. That's about it. Wait—they're turning around."

The minister had finished the final dedication. Ashes to ashes.

At some signal I couldn't see, the crowd started moving back across the grass to cars that would take them to Amy's house. Once there, they would drink tea, eat small sandwiches, and talk about how beautiful she had been.

I just wasn't ready for lukewarm tea, finger foods, and a roomful of people all struggling to say the right thing. I felt the pinprick of tears and I bit the inside of my cheek until I was sure they wouldn't fall.

I hated crying in front of other people. Even Kyle. Besides, I had to be strong for Jason.

We walked away from the surge of mourners, stopping when we were underneath a large elm. I kicked at the dead grass with one black shoe. "Do you think the reporters are still at the gate?"

Kyle's shoulders tensed. "Definitely. They'll probably

tail people back to the house."

I swallowed back a wave of anger, the effort almost choking me. It wasn't like I was surprised. Amy's death would have made headlines even if she hadn't been young, beautiful, and rich. In the week since the attack—since the murder—the story had been splashed all over the news. It was the ninth attack in Hemlock in five weeks and the third to result in death.

But that wasn't what had turned things from media frenzy into full-blown circus.

Amy was Amy Walsh. As in granddaughter of Senator John Walsh.

I placed a tentative hand on Kyle's forearm. "They'll probably leave you alone today." With Amy's family finally out of seclusion, the reporters had more interesting game to hunt than her friends.

Kyle let out a short, skeptical snort. "Everyone thinks I'm somehow responsible, that she wouldn't have gotten attacked if I had just picked up the phone when she called. For all I know, they're right."

I shook my head. "You didn't do anything wrong. Besides, they could just as easily blame Jason or me."

After all, I was the one who had blown off plans with her so I could study. If I hadn't done that, Amy and I would have been sitting in a movie theater at 10:37 p.m. She would never have called Kyle, because we'd be eating pop-corn and making fun of some lame horror flick.

She wouldn't have been out by herself.

She wouldn't have been attacked.

She wouldn't be in a heavy, wooden box. . . .

I shuddered and slammed a door shut on the thought.

Fern Ridge was on a hill, and we were close enough to the edge of the grounds to see the town stretching out around us. I concentrated on that, trying to pick out the peaked roof of my apartment building and pretending I was there instead of inside the cemetery gates.

Kyle touched my arm and nodded toward the crowd. Jason had broken away and was headed in our direction.

"Hey guys." His eyes were bloodshot and his blond hair—normally so perfect—looked like it hadn't seen a comb in days. The suit was designer, but he slouched like he was wearing rags.

I gave him an awkward hug and then stepped away quickly in case there were any reporters hiding among the mourners. "Are you okay?"

Jason shrugged. "Better than Stephen. He flew all the way in for the funeral and then couldn't make it through the gates."

I scanned the faces in the crowd as they passed. Sure enough, I didn't spot Amy's brother, but I did see her grandfather. I'd always thought Senator Walsh looked young for his age, but today, every minute of his sixty-odd years had been etched onto his face. He seemed smaller than I remembered—thinner and not as tall—almost as though Amy's death had somehow compressed him. But there was nothing weak in his gaze as it swept the three of us; it was hot enough to scorch.

I knew what he was thinking.

It was our fault Amy was dead. All of our faults.

The best friend who had bailed; the boyfriend who had been running late; the guy who hadn't answered his phone.

Six days ago, a werewolf had killed Amy and we were each to blame.

1

I IGNORED A TWINGE IN MY SHOULDER AS I WIPED DOWN another table. My back was paying the price for too many hours spent waitressing at Mama Rosa's Fine Italian Eatery this week. Not that I was complaining. Though I had the coming weekend off, tonight was my last shift before I switched to working just Saturdays and Sundays. School had started two weeks ago, and it was already getting hard to keep up. So much for Amy's theory that seniors just coasted and classes would be the things that happened between parties.

She had been so full of plans for our last year at Kennedy, but she had never considered a scenario in which I'd be going through it without her.

I straightened and bit my lip. It had been five months since Amy's funeral, but I still kept expecting her to burst into the restaurant like the whole thing had just been a gruesome joke. There were days when I picked up the phone and got halfway through dialing her number before remembering it had been disconnected.

A familiar tightness closed around my chest. I walked past the checked tablecloths and cheesy votive candles in glass jars and signaled to one of the other waitresses that I was stepping out for a minute.

Outside, I leaned against the corner of the restaurant's brick facade, hoping the fresh air and last lingering rays of sunlight would clear my head. Things were slowly getting better, but there were still times when I missed Amy so badly it was like a physical ache.

And it didn't help that there seemed to be a reminder of her around every corner.

Take the shop across the street. It was empty now—its windows lined with yellowing newspaper and a For Lease sign hanging in the door—but it used to sell vintage clothing and accessories. It had been one of Amy's favorite places.

The owner had closed the shop and left town after her fiancé was killed by a werewolf. He had been the first victim. Amy was the third. For two months—March and April—the town had lived in a near constant state of terror as a werewolf went on a rampage, killing four people and infecting eight others with lupine syndrome.

I tugged my hair out of its ponytail and twisted it back up again as I spared the street one last glance. The stores that had survived the drop in tourism—because nothing kept visitors away like a killer werewolf—all had cheerful window displays and colorful awnings. Huge, round flower planters lined the street at regular intervals, still over-flowing with greenery and bright blooms, while Riverside

Square was just visible on the next block.

If I didn't know better, I would have thought Hemlock was the perfect small town; I'd have thought nothing bad could happen here.

Sometimes I really wished I didn't know better. That I could just forget.

Pushing that thought away, I headed back inside.

I checked on my tables, refilled drinks, and brought a slice of chocolate cheesecake to a woman doing paperwork in a back booth. I was just bringing a large pepperoni pizza to a table of four when the restaurant door opened and my cousin—and legal guardian—Tess blew in like a hurricane. She was working later and dressed accordingly: sort of a mix between rocker chic and a bird of paradise. Tess waited tables at the Shady Cat, a microbrewery/restaurant that was just off the college campus and known for its eccentric staff and a decorating scheme so zany that it could have been yanked straight out of Tim Burton's head.

Every couple of weeks, Tess would radically overhaul her look. Judging by the purple and pink in her hair—which had been blond when I left for school in the a.m.—that time had come and gone while I'd been in class. I felt a small twinge of envy: it looked great, but was something I'd never be able to pull off. I wouldn't even be brave enough to try.

She flopped into a booth—one that hadn't been cleared—and made a face at the half-eaten food in front of her.

I shook my head and tried to suppress a grin as I walked over. She wasn't in my section, but I hadn't seen her all day. Besides, the other servers were used to Tess's lack of respect for the table chart.

"There were six perfectly clean booths," I pointed out, scooping up plates and paper place mats. I laughed at the absolutely revolted look on her face as she spied a lipstick stain on the rim of a glass. "Why'd you pick this one?"

Trying for a mobster accent, she said, "You know I like this booth. It's my booth. The one I always sit in. It's my office. Where I do business." She'd clearly been bingeing on the *Sopranos* DVDs I'd borrowed from the library.

"Caesar salad, hold the croutons?" I guessed, ignoring the accent.

Tess leaned back and rubbed her nonexistent belly. "I was thinking pasta."

"What happened to the blood oath you took to swear off carbs?" Tess's diet was the only thing that changed faster than her hair. The bell in the kitchen rang. One of my orders was up. "I'll be right back," I called over my shoulder.

Eight minutes and three table checks later, I returned to Tess, salad in hand. I set the plate in front of her. "Here, eat this. The chicken gives it protein and I got them to hold the bacon bits." We'd watched *Charlotte's Web* on cable last week, so I knew it'd be at least a month before she would eat pork again.

Tess grinned and shook out a napkin. "You're so good to me. So responsible." A devilish smirk crossed her face. "You're seeing Kyle tonight, right?"

I leaned against the booth and rolled my eyes. "Don't start."

"What's she up to now?" asked a deep voice from some-where over my left shoulder.

I jumped as Tess's boyfriend, Ben, slid past me and took the seat across from her. I hadn't seen him come in.

Ben shrugged out of his battered leather jacket and smiled. College girls hung out at the Cat for hours just to get a glimpse of that grin. Add in the blond hair, tanned skin, and Hollywood looks and Ben was officially walking eye candy. I sometimes wondered, a little guiltily, if those same love-struck girls would still swoon if they got a good look at the web of scars that crisscrossed his torso, sou-venirs from a car wreck that had killed his mother and brother when he was fifteen.

He was staring at me, waiting for a reply.

It took me a second to remember what he had asked. "She's lecturing me on my love life."

He laughed. "Should have known. Tess, give the kid a break."

"Kyle stopped dating that clingy train wreck." Tess pouted for a moment. "Mac has to strike while the iron's hot." She raised her eyebrows suggestively and stuffed a forkful of croutons and lettuce into her mouth.

I glanced around the restaurant. It was still quiet. No one would say anything if I loitered at table four. "It doesn't matter if he's dating Heather or not. Kyle and I aren't like that." It was a conversation I'd had with Tess so many times that I had my lines practically memorized.

Did I ever think about what was under Kyle's indie rock T-shirts and jeans? Well, yeah. He was good-looking and

I had a pulse. But thoughts weren't action. Besides, some things were too important to mess with. "Kyle is my best friend. Why would I risk screwing that up?"

"Mackenzie Catherine Dobson, have you learned *nothing* from romantic comedies? Do I need to make a trip to the video store?" Tess set her fork down and sighed. "'We're just friends' is the oldest plot device in the book. All it really means is that you're just friends until one of you gets the balls to do something about all that unresolved tension."

Ben stifled a laugh and I felt my face flush.

Oblivious, Tess slid out of the booth and dropped a couple of bills on the table, even though she'd barely touched her food. "I'll be home late. Don't wait up." She tugged on my ponytail. "We need to do something about your hair." She was out the door before I could respond.

Ben paused to put a hand on my shoulder. "Don't worry. I'll find some way to embarrass Tess at work." He winked and headed after her.

It was hard not to like Ben—though I'd worried when they started dating. Ben was twenty-two—four years younger than Tess—and before getting a job with her at the Cat, he'd been part of a work crew renovating this huge farmhouse the Walsh family owned. I'd wanted Tess to be happy, but the idea of her dating someone who worked for Amy's family had been one more reminder that my best friend and I weren't really equal.

I glanced down at the empty salad bowl and scooped up the crumpled bills. The Caesar had cost eight dollars and Tess had left me twenty. Talk about an epic tip.

Not that any tip was enough to get her off the hook for teasing me in front of Ben. I might have to delve into the very large vault of embarrassing Tess stories as payback.

I wondered if Ben knew about the time she'd jokingly handcuffed herself to a police officer boyfriend only to find out he'd left the key back at the station. Humming to myself, I cleared the table.

The phone rang just as I finished punching two orders of tortellini into the computer. "Rosa's," I said, pressing the receiver to my ear.

"I can't pick you up tonight." Kyle's voice came through with a burst of static.

"No big."

"Will you get a cab?"

"Sure," I lied. After five months without a single werewolf attack, life in Hemlock was starting to get back to normal. Kyle, however, seemed permanently locked in overprotective mode.

"Are you lying?" he asked.

Of course I am, I thought. The last time I'd gotten a cab, the driver had spent the entire ride hitting on me. I wasn't spending seven bucks to be trapped in a car with a lech. "Nope. I'm a safety girl. Wait a sec, why can't you pick me up?"

"Heather is freaking out. I have to head over there and I don't know how long I'll be."

I twisted the phone cord around my finger and tried not to say the first few things that came to mind. This was the third time in the last month that Kyle had been subjected to one of Heather Yoshida's meltdowns. It was total over-kill—even if they had dated for almost a year. Why did the Heathers of the world always get great guys like Kyle?

"You know," I said, trying to keep my tone conversational and light, "one of the perks of breaking up with someone is that you no longer have to deal with their drama."

"And if anyone would know about breakups . . ."

"That's such a cheap shot." It wasn't my fault that I'd had only one real boyfriend. Or that he had been a jerk who accused me of being an emotional iceberg when I wanted to take things slow.

I glanced up. The night manager looked pointedly from me to her watch; I wasn't supposed to use the phone for personal calls. "I gotta go," I told Kyle. "I'll talk to you tomorrow."

"Cab."

I sighed. "It's gone, Kyle. No one in town thinks it's coming back." As much as I wanted them to find the thing that had killed Amy, I was starting to accept that it had left Hemlock.

Kyle didn't say anything for a minute, then, quietly, he said, "No one really knows what happened, Mac. There's no guarantee it won't start again."

"Fine, I'll take a cab," I lied.

"At least be careful when you walk home." He hung up before I could retort.

An hour later, I grabbed my jacket and backpack from the staff room, left a share of my tips for the guys in the kitchen, and pushed my way out through the heavy employees-only entrance at the back of the building.

The cool breeze coming off the river felt good against my face—especially after an evening spent wandering in and out of a hot kitchen with trays of heavy Italian food. Rosa's, like most of downtown Hemlock, was only two blocks from the waterfront. When I glanced to my right, I could see the lights from the other side of town reflected on the water like falling stars.

Movies and books always talked about the wrong side of the tracks. There hadn't been a train through Hemlock for almost six decades, but we did have the river. People with money—people like Amy and Jason—lived on the north side. Even Kyle's family lived over there, though in one of the more modest neighborhoods.

The south side was home to the rest of us, and I actually preferred it to the stuffy atmosphere across the bridge.

I passed a couple in their twenties who were laughing just a bit too loudly and holding hands a little awkwardly. Probably a second date. Despite the gorgeous September evening, they were the only other ones on the street.

Though people were starting to go out again, they usually drove after sunset. Almost everyone believed that the werewolf that had terrorized the town had either been killed or had left—but the uncertainty made it hard to feel completely safe. Multiple werewolf attacks were rare, and the number of attacks in Hemlock was unheard of—even if you didn't count the eight victims who had survived only to develop lupine syndrome and be shipped off to the rehabilitation camps that were mandatory for anyone carrying the virus.

I shuddered and quickened my pace until I finally reached Elmwood Avenue. A century ago, Elmwood had been home to the nicest digs in town, but most of the old, sprawling houses had been gutted and converted into apartments—like the one Tess and I shared.

I noticed a group of figures in the shadowy gulf between two streetlights a block away and felt a momentary spark of fear. I slowed my pace, wondering if not calling a cab had been a mistake. Then I recognized them.

With a population just shy of 160,000, Hemlock was a little too quiet for gangs, but the town did have its own group of stereotypical bad boys.

They could be a complete pain in the butt, but they wouldn't hassle me. Not really. Most of them were fairly harmless—though there was one guy who was doing a jail stint for slipping a girl GHB at a kegger.

As I got closer, I realized they had someone surrounded.

Whoever it was, he was already on the ground and must have taken at least a few hits. I caught a glimpse of a black jacket and broad shoulders, but then someone stepped in front of me, blocking the figure from view.

"Need someone to walk you home, Dobs?" Trey Carson gave me a lopsided grin, revealing the dimples in his dark cheeks. He wasn't wearing a jacket, and his gray T-shirt strained over the muscles in his upper arms and chest, almost as though he had bought it a size too small. Knowing Trey, that was probably exactly what he had done. If he'd spent half as much time on school as he did on his pecs, then he wouldn't have been doing a replay of senior year.

The guy on the ground groaned, but there wasn't anything I could do for him—at least not at the moment. I could call the cops when I got home. If I had to. If it looked bad enough.

I was really hoping it wouldn't look that bad. For one thing, I was friends with Trey's sister. For another, I'd spent my formative years around people who'd had very strong opinions about the police and rats.

Trey raised an eyebrow, waiting for my reply.

"Thanks but I'm good. Besides, it looks like you've got your hands full." I stepped around him just as the figure on the ground looked up.

The guy they were pounding was Jason.

2

I RAN TO JASON AND CROUCHED AT HIS SIDE. BLOOD trickled from the corner of his mouth, and he was going to have one heck of a bruise on his cheek.

"Are you okay?"

He reached into his jacket pocket and hauled out a slim bottle of Jack Daniel's. "I'm having a blast." He tried to laugh and ended up coughing. "Don't be like that," he complained as I snatched the bottle from his hands. "It's medicinal."

I ignored him and stood. Six months ago, the sight of Jason bleeding on the ground would have had me crazed. Now I just wondered what he had done to deserve it. There was a limited amount of trouble you could find in a town the size of Hemlock, but Jason kept doing his best to sink to new depths. I was starting to worry it was some sort of passive-aggressive suicide.

I tossed the bottle to Trey. "What did he do?" Trey shrugged, uncomfortable, and I shook my head. "You wouldn't be using him as a punching bag if he hadn't done *something.*" Despite the trouble he was always getting into and the scams he was always running on the side, Serena's brother was weirdly honorable; he never hit anyone without a reason.

Jason spat on the sidewalk and tried to stand. It took him two tries. "Gentlemen's disagreement, Mac. Don't worry your pretty head about it." The corner of his mouth quirked up in a condescending grin.

If anyone else had used that tone with me, I'd have walked away and let Trey go to town. But it was Jason and that made a difference. It was impossible to know exactly what Amy would say or think if she were here, but I did know one thing: she'd want me to take care of him.

I stared at Trey and repeated my question. "What did he do?"

Trey sighed and tugged on his earlobe. "He lost on a bet and hasn't paid up."

I couldn't believe Trey had been stupid enough to take a bet without collecting cash upfront, but the way he ran his high school gambling ring wasn't any of my business.

Jason coughed. "It's not my fault you don't take AmEx."

I glared. "Shut up, Jason." To Trey I said, "How much does he owe you?"

"Eighty and an apology."

Eighty dollars. The thirty-seven I had made in tips, plus almost all the cash I kept in my wallet for emergencies— enough to cover the power bill if Tess forgot again. I shoved my backpack against Jason's chest. "Hold this," I spat, too livid to look at his face.

"Mac . . ."

"Don't say anything." I unzipped the front pocket and yanked out my wallet. I spoke in deliberate, clipped tones, hauling out bills a few at a time to punctuate each word. "You. Are. Going. To. Pay. Me. Back."

I handed the cash to Trey.

"Sorry, Dobs," he said, taking the bills and slipping them into his back pocket. He probably was. Taking money from his kid sister's friend was different from taking it from a guy like Jason. Besides, Trey probably knew how hard I had worked for it, something Jason—who'd always had everything handed to him—would never get.

I glared at Jason. "Now tell the nice man with my money that you're sorry."

He spat again and handed me my backpack. "I'm sorry," he told Trey as he squared his shoulders. "It must suck, knowing you fight like your mother."

This time, when Jason hit the ground, it took him longer to get up.

I pressed a damp washcloth to Jason's face, gently trying to wipe the blood away. "Well, you're certainly going to turn heads tomorrow." I frowned as I examined the massive bruise that was just starting to rise on his cheek, a bruise that roughly matched the size and shape of Trey's knuckles. "I'll say this much: Serena's brother knows how to land a punch."

Jason shrugged. "Might as well give everyone something new to talk about. Besides, chicks dig men with battle scars." He took the cloth from my hand and tossed it onto the coffee table.

I almost pointed out that it would leave a water mark, but honestly, the coffee table was so battered that one more blemish would never make a difference. "Yeah, well, next time you get into a fight, try *not* bringing up the guy's dead mother."

Jason flushed. "I forgot." He actually looked genuinely embarrassed—something that didn't happen often. He cleared his throat. "I'm sorry about the money. I'll pay you back."

I made a noncommittal noise. I wasn't ready to forgive him yet. Getting him to walk the block and a half to my apartment building hadn't exactly been fun, and getting him up the winding staircase to the third floor had been nearly impossible. When we hit the second-floor landing, he had turned slightly green and I could have sworn he was about to puke all over my new pink Chucks.

"Are you sure you don't want to go to the hospital? You were walking like they hurt your ribs." I reached for his T-shirt and started to haul up the blue cotton, trying to get a good look at the bruises on his torso.

"First she invited me up to her apartment, and then she tried to undress me. . . ."

I rolled my eyes. "Don't flatter yourself," I muttered, letting his shirt fall back into place.

He shook his head. "I'm all right. Besides, if I go to the hospital, they'll call my dad. He already dragged me to the shooting range on Sunday, so I think I've used up my allotted quality time this week."

I sighed. "Why is it that quality time in your family always seems to involve injuries or guns?" I never could figure out why Jason's father was so obsessed with firearms when he could afford to pay people to conceal and carry for him.

"Not entirely true," corrected Jason. "Some quality time involves making piles of money and having torrid affairs with the household staff."

He caught my hand. "Thanks for taking care of me, Mac," he said, giving me a small grin. It wasn't his old smile; it was the sad half smile he sometimes wore after he had been drinking. Lately, it seemed like the only time Jason smiled was when he was at least a little drunk.

And that was becoming more and more of the time.

Everything was messed up without Amy around.

I bit my lip and fought back the sudden urge to cry. Amy was the one who had died, but I sometimes had the feeling that she wasn't the only one I was losing. "Jason . . ." I gently freed my hand. "She wouldn't want—"

He cut me off. "Don't, okay? We can talk about her tomorrow, if you want. Just not tonight." He rubbed his temple. "All right?" He shivered, even though it was warm in the apartment. Any time I tried to bring up Amy, Jason started shaking.

I nodded, though I knew we wouldn't talk about her tomorrow. We never did.

Jason rolled his shoulders, trying to work out the kinks from his fight with Trey. "Don't suppose you have anything to drink?" The half smile was gone, his expression locked down and inscrutable. "You tossed my JD."

"Sorry. Just water and soda." There actually was a bottle of vodka—Ben's and safely tucked away behind a box of cereal—but I wasn't about to let him have it.

Jason's green eyes narrowed. "It's not nice to lie."

I wondered what had given me away. "Whatever. Besides, haven't you had enough?" I was seriously starting to worry that Jason was going to end up in some sort of rehab facility, right down the hall from a celebrity catastrophe. Only the best for a Sheffield.

"Am I still conscious?"

I nodded, not sure I liked where this was going.

"Then I haven't had enough."

"Jason . . ."

"A reporter called the house today, Mac. He wanted to know if I had heard about the attack last night and if I had a comment." Jason watched my face, waiting for me to get it, then shifted his gaze to the floor. "There was another attack. A werewolf with white fur. The police are keeping it quiet so people don't start panicking."

I felt like I had just been doused in cold water. The beginnings of a headache danced along my skull and I was suddenly freezing. What if it was starting again?

It took me a while to find my voice. "It might not be the same one," I said slowly, uncertainly. White was a rare color among werewolves—like naturally redheaded humans— and white fur had been found at each murder scene in the spring. Amy'd had white fur clutched in her fist—or so the *Dateline* special had said.

25

A thought occurred to me, and I reached out to tilt Jason's chin up, forcing him to look at me. "It can't be the same wolf—this is the first attack in months."

The wolf that had gone after Amy had probably been suffering from bloodlust—a condition that was sort of like rabies. Less than 2 percent of people infected with LS developed it. Not all werewolf attacks were committed by wolves suffering from bloodlust, but multiple ones almost always were. And once a wolf with bloodlust starting killing, it didn't just stop. It craved it.

No way could that same wolf have gone all summer without attacking anyone. *Unless it left Hemlock and came back*, whispered a small voice in the back of my head; I tuned out the thought.

"I guess . . . ," said Jason uncertainly. He sighed and rubbed his cheeks roughly, like he was trying to sober up a bit. "I should call a cab or something. Get out of your hair."

"Why don't you crash here tonight?" I knew the cramped two-bedroom apartment I shared with Tess would be preferable to the huge house across town. Besides, I didn't like the thought of Jason hitting up his father's liquor cabinet. Not tonight. He shouldn't be on his own. "We can watch a movie and you can sleep on the couch." The sofa was a lumpy, plaid hand-me-down Tess had gotten from someone at work, but given how much Jason had been drinking, I didn't think a few broken springs would bother him.

He looked up. "Tess won't mind?"

I rolled my eyes and stood. "You know she won't. She probably won't even notice." Truthfully, she might not even make it home before Jason left in the morning.

Ben lived one floor below us, and Tess, reasoning that she was still in the same building and therefore still being a responsible guardian, had started spending some nights at his place.

"Tess the mess," Jason muttered. He let his head fall back against the couch. "Thanks." That one word was filled with relief.

"Do you think you should call home?"

He closed his eyes. "What for? It's not like they'd care."

I wanted to argue, but it would have meant lying. On the surface, Jason had everything—money, connections, a house that was better suited to 90210 than Hemlock—but the picture underneath wasn't that pretty. Most of the time his parents barely remembered they had a son.

"It's all right," he said, somehow picking up on the things I wanted to say and couldn't. He sat up straighter and opened his eyes. "You don't have to lie for them. They are who they are." The words were empty, almost totally free of inflection or recrimination, but I knew Jason cared more than he let on.

"I'm going to hop in the shower and get the smell of pepperoni out of my hair," I said, tugging my ponytail out of its elastic. "You can find us a movie on cable."

Jason reached over and grabbed my hand again, tugging me back down, a serious, thoughtful expression on his face. I crouched so we were at eye level. "Do you think everything will be all right?" he asked, leaning forward until our faces were inches apart. His eyes were full of shadows and storms.

I suppressed a shiver. Jason had this uncanny way of looking at a girl—an intensity that could leave you disorientated and a little lost. He did it without even trying. After three years, I still wasn't completely immune to it.

"Do you?" he repeated, softer this time.

How was I supposed to know?

I stared into Jason's eyes, and for a split second I had that feeling you get when an elevator drops too quickly. You know there's a floor underneath your feet, but it feels like you're falling. I nodded and my hair fell over my face. Without missing a beat, Jason brushed it back, his fingers lingering on my cheek just a second longer than necessary.

"Everything will be all right," I lied, and then I headed for the bathroom before the confusion could show on my face.

For an instant, I'd had the impossible feeling that Jason had been about to kiss me.

I wiped the steam from the mirror and stared at the person looking back at me. Plain and pale with dishwater blond hair and guilty brown eyes. Nothing special. Nothing like Amy had been. I leaned forward, gripping the edge of the sink. I couldn't stay in the bathroom all night.

"It's okay," I whispered to my reflection. "She would understand. You didn't mean to think it."

Sometimes, thoughts just popped into my head—like the ones I occasionally had about Kyle. None of those thoughts ever meant anything, and neither had this particular thought.

It was nothing. Less than nothing.

Thinking that Jason had been about to kiss me didn't mean I wanted him to or that he had actually been contemplating it. It was exhaustion and stress and the smell of alcohol on someone else's breath. It wasn't want or reality.

Amy wouldn't need to forgive me, because there was nothing to forgive.

I shut off the bathroom light and opened the door.

Jason was snoring softly on the couch. He was still wearing his jeans, but he'd tossed his shirt onto the coffee table, knocking over one of Tess's pillar candles in the process. CNN flickered on the TV. So much for a movie.

With a sigh, I turned off the television just as a story about Senator Walsh came on. Lately, it seemed like Amy's grandfather was always on the news.

Jason rolled onto his side. I cringed a little as I noticed the dark smudges on his skin. Trey really had done a number on him.

I watched him for a minute, holding my breath and waiting to see if he'd wake up. Asleep, he looked younger. His face lost the hard edges it had developed over the past five months and he didn't look as haunted.

Dozens of girls at Kennedy High would have killed to have a shirtless Jason Sheffield stretched out in their living room. I could probably have taken pictures and auctioned them off. I couldn't really blame them. Kyle was lean and athletic through years of playing soccer, but Jason had the kind of body that came with personal chefs and trainers. The kind of body that cost money.

Practically every girl at school had, at one point or another, spent a boring Spanish class fantasizing about kissing Jason. Including me. Before I knew Amy—before I knew Jason was *with* Amy—I had daydreamed about him, too.

It wasn't like Amy and I had been friends from the moment I stepped into town. I knew who she was—everyone knew who she was—but we'd never spoken. Not until we collided outside of Starbucks and both ended up wearing her mocha latte. Considering her shirt cost about three times the value of everything in my closet—including sneakers—she'd been remarkably cool about it. I bought her a replacement drink, and despite the fact that wearing frothy beverages wasn't exactly fashionable, we ended up walking down to Riverside Square, sitting on the ledge of the fountain, and talking for hours. Amy had grilled me about every city I'd ever lived in and told me how she couldn't wait to get out of Hemlock.

The next morning, she was waiting for me by my locker. For reasons I never quite understood—especially given all the advantages she had—Amy seemed to have just as much trouble making friends as I did.

The next time I saw Jason, the daydreams were history. They had to be. Amy was the first friend I'd had in years, and that was important to me.

Looking back, it had probably been strange. Amy was the rich granddaughter of a US senator, and I was a foundling who lived with a cousin who waited tables.

I knew people couldn't figure out how poor, parentless Mackenzie Dobson had ended up as part of a group that included kids from the two most powerful families in town, but Amy, Jason, Kyle, and I just seemed to click. It was like we had known one another our whole lives.

I turned my back on Jason long enough to grab a faded patchwork quilt from the hall closet. He didn't stir as I tucked it around him.

"You're such a disaster," I whispered, gently touching the bruise on his cheek. "I wish I knew how to help you."

Half the girls in school wanted Jason, but they didn't know him. Not really. He was spoiled and could be arrogant. He was often careless and had become disaster personified. Hell, he practically needed his own federal response team.

But he could be really thoughtful and kind. And he hadn't always been a mess. He'd started getting into trouble last year, and then Amy's death had just made him spiral further out of control.

The girls in town thought Jason was tortured and broken, and that made him sexier in their eyes. I didn't care about that. All I wanted was to figure out how to fix him.

Before he completely self-destructed.

3

"YOU KNOW, HE'S ACTUALLY A PRETTY GOOD KISSER."
Amy perched on the edge of my bed, her pale, heart-shaped
face turned away so that I could see only her profile, half-
hidden behind a curtain of black hair. "I don't blame you for
thinking about it."

I struggled against the bedclothes, trying to sit up. "I
wasn't. Thinking about it." Amy didn't say anything, and
the silence was heavy and oppressive. "Okay," I admitted.
"I thought about it for a second, but it was an accident. It
didn't mean anything."

She grunted and stared at her lap. "I thought it would
take you longer."

My heart thudded in my chest. "Amy, I swear. Nothing
happened."

"Maybe not yet. But it will. You'll forget about me." She
paused and then added, "You both will."

I reached for her hand. It was cold, like ice. "Never," I
promised.

"Liar." Her voice was suddenly sharp and frigid, like a

burst of arctic air. She squeezed my hand so hard that I heard something crack.

"Amy," I whimpered.

"You did this," she said and turned toward me. The other half of her face was a ruined mask, like red candle wax that had melted. The left side of her body was covered in gashes and blood. "You did this," she repeated, squeezing my hand until my bones shattered and I screamed.

"Shhhh."

I lashed out and shoved the figure kneeling by my bed. Strong hands caught my arms, holding them so I couldn't do any real damage.

"Mac, shhhh. It's all right."

It took me a moment to recognize Jason's voice, his familiar shape, and the way his eyes glinted in the faint light from the street lamp outside. I stopped struggling and tried to catch my breath.

"You were having a nightmare."

I swallowed. I felt like I had just run a marathon. "Thanks," I mumbled. "Figured that out."

Jason sat on the floor next to my bed. He'd pulled his shirt on at some point during the night, and I was oddly grateful. "What were you dreaming about?" he asked.

What could I tell him? Not that Amy had shown up with her skin hanging off her face and blood soaking her clothes. Not when that was probably how he had seen her.

Jason had been there, in the alley. He'd been looking for Amy and had arrived moments after the police. There was a rumor it had taken two officers to drag him away from her. I didn't know if it was true; I'd never worked up the courage to ask.

That was why he had become so much more self-destructive. He felt guilty for not finding her sooner, for not saving her.

What if the attacks were starting all over again?

I shivered and tried to convince myself that the attack last night was an isolated incident, the unrelated work of another wolf. There were tons of infected people hiding all over the country. There could easily be another werewolf in Hemlock. Maybe even another white one.

The color of a wolf's coat was a trait passed on with infection—a constant, visual reminder of the animal that had bitten or scratched you. The attack could have been the work of someone who had been infected in the spring and hadn't turned themselves in. There were twelve attacks that the police knew about, but that didn't mean there couldn't have been more.

"Mac?" Jason was waiting for an answer.

I didn't want to talk about the dream, so I lied. "There was a fire and stuff. Burning."

He glanced at me, then away. "You said her name."

"Oh."

"I miss her," he admitted, his voice almost a whisper. Always "her" now. Never "Amy."

"Me too."

"I'm not ready to talk about it."

"I know." The way he shuttered everything inside wasn't healthy, but I was scared of pushing him. Jason had been so

34

unpredictable over the last few months that sometimes he seemed like a stranger. "I miss you, too," I admitted, and let out a nervous breath.

Jason laughed—a low, bitter chuckle—and tilted his head back to stare at the ceiling. "Not much to miss. I was only ever good when I was with her." He scrubbed a hand across his eyes. "The rest of the time, I was just another tool with a trust fund."

It wasn't true, and I hated that he thought it. I propped myself up on one elbow. "Do you remember the first time we met?"

He shook his head.

"I'd only been in Hemlock for a couple of weeks. There was no way Tess was going to turn me over to the state— she kept telling me that—but . . ." I trailed off and tried to swallow past the lump in my throat.

Other girls had moms who made them peanut butter sandwiches and dads who read bedtime stories and checked under the bed for monsters. I had a mother who skipped out on me sometime before my first birthday and a father who was wanted for everything from gunrunning to selling peyote out of the trunk of his car.

"Mac?" Jason reached out and touched my hand, just for a second.

"Sorry," I said. It was easy to get lost when thinking about the first fourteen years of my life. Hank and I had been in Hemlock for my grandmother's funeral when he finally ditched me. He went out for a pack of cigarettes and never came back. No phone calls. No letters. No explanation or reason to think he even remembered, or cared, that he had a daughter. "I just know how lucky I was Tess took me in. It's not like having a teenager to look after was on her to-do list."

Jason closed his eyes, but I could tell he was still listening.

"Anyway, I was so far behind in school. Hank had us moving so fast and so often that half the time he didn't even bother registering me for classes. We were in math and Mr. O'Leary asked me to do something simple—multiply, I think—and I couldn't do it."

"He was making you do a problem on the board." Jason's voice had a far-off quality. "I remember your clothes didn't fit right. Your sleeves didn't cover your wrists."

"Thrift store fashion." I smiled a little. "Something you'd know nothing about."

"Touché."

"Anyway, he made a big deal of the fact that I couldn't make it past the first step. I just stood at the front of the class while everyone stared." I blushed at the memory of dozens of kids watching me, all knowing they were smarter than the girl with the messy hair and threadbare clothes.

Jason opened his eyes and grinned. "And I rode to your rescue like a knight on a white horse."

I nodded. "You called him fat and bald and a bully. It was the first time I'd ever seen anyone stand up to a teacher. You didn't even know me."

"He deserved it." Jason watched as I settled back against my pillows. "The guy was a jerk." He said it causally, like it was no big deal.

I wished I could tell him how much it had meant to me without sounding like a Hallmark card. Instead, I said, "You should get some sleep."

"What if you have another nightmare?"

I shrugged, trying not to let on how much the thought unnerved me. "I'm a big girl."

Jason frowned. "Would it be okay if I stayed until you fell asleep?"

Something about the thought of Jason watching me sleep made me uncomfortable in a way I couldn't quite pin down. I opened my mouth to refuse, and a shadow of disappointment slid over his face. To my surprise, I found myself saying, "All right."

I tried not to think about how Tess would react if she found out. She wouldn't care about Jason staying over, but she'd definitely draw the line at him being in my room at three thirty in the morning—despite her constant teasing that my love life needed some, well, life in it.

"Thanks," he said, a hint of relief in his voice.

I had the sudden suspicion that I wasn't the only one who'd had a bad dream.

It took me a while to get comfortable. I wasn't used to having another person around while I tried to sleep. The faint sound of Jason breathing and the rustle of cloth as he shifted positions made it hard for me to completely relax. Eventually, though, I started to drift off.

"Mac?"

"Mmmhmmm?"

"Do you think it's my fault?"

"No."

"If I had been there . . . with her . . ."

It was the what-if game. We all played it. We couldn't get away from it.

Even though it was warm in the room, I drew my blankets a little tighter around myself. "It's not your fault."

"Okay."

Jason was quiet for a few minutes, and I started to drift off again.

"I'm going to find it."

"Uh-huh." I struggled against the current of fatigue that was dragging me under. "Wait. Find what?"

"The wolf that killed Amy."

"Jason . . ." Even if the new attack meant the wolf was back, Jason couldn't go after it. Not on his own; he'd get himself killed. "I hear vendettas are going out of style," I said, reaching out and fumbling until I found his hand. His skin was cold, almost as cold as Amy's had been in my dream.

"Not for everyone. There are people who will help."

Something in his voice set off warning bells. I started to sit up, but he gently let go of my hand and pushed me back down. "Just go to sleep, Mac. You're exhausted."

"But . . ."

"Forget I said anything. I was only talking." He stood. "Actually," he said, "I think I will go back to the couch."

"Jason . . ."

He paused at my bedroom door. "Night, Mac."

I swallowed. "Night."

When I was certain he was settled on the couch, when I could no longer hear him moving around the living room, I grabbed my iPod from the nightstand and scrolled through the videos until I found one that had been taken last November fourteenth. I needed an image of Amy, something to wipe out the nightmare.

I turned the volume down low enough that Jason wouldn't hear and hit play.

Amy's hand reached toward me. "Put the camera down, birthday girl."

"No way," came my voice from somewhere offscreen. "The second I stop taking pictures, you're going to make me play kid games."

Amy rolled her eyes. "That's the point, Mac. We're at Chuck E. Cheese's. Games are mandatory."

I hit pause. Amy's face filled the screen, whole and perfect and not at all like it had been in my dream. Her grin was huge, and a temporary glitter tattoo of a star adorned her cheek. I'd worn a matching one at her insistence.

She'd talked Tess into letting her throw me a birthday party at Chuck E. Cheese's when I turned seventeen. She said it was to make up for all the nonbirthdays I'd had when I was with Hank. It had been lame and embarrassing and, somehow, just right.

With a shaky breath, I turned off the iPod and wiped my eyes with the corner of my sheet. Then I prayed.

Are you there, Amy? It's me, Mac.

She didn't answer.

4

Shrill buzzing cut through my sleep, leaving my dream in tatters. I threw back the covers, gasped as my bare feet hit the cold hardwood floor, and stumble-dashed to the intercom.

I hit the button to trip the downstairs lock and glanced around the living room. There was no sign of Jason. I grabbed a white hoodie from the laundry basket Tess had left near the door and pulled it on over the tank top and shorts I had worn to bed.

I opened the door, wrinkling my nose at the smell of stale cigar smoke from the apartment across the hall. "I overslept!" I called. "I totally forgot to set my alarm."

"You didn't. I'm early."

I surveyed the sight before me as Kyle hit the top of the stairs. "Wow," I said, crossing my arms to ward off the chill from the hallway. "You look horrible." I stood to the side and Kyle walked in.

He shrugged and headed for the kitchen. I followed

and watched him search for coffee. "Second cupboard," I reminded him.

Kyle's clothes were rumpled. He had dark circles under his eyes, and he was moving stiffly. His shaggy, brown hair was a mess and he hadn't shaved. Kyle usually looked slightly disheveled in a vaguely sexy way—like an artist or the bassist in a band—but right now he looked as though he had slept in a ditch.

"You weren't in a fight, were you?"

"No."

"Did you go over to Heather's?"

"Yes." He spooned coffee into a filter without looking at me.

"Care to elaborate?"

"Not really." He raked a hand through his hair and met my eyes. "That all right?"

If it had been a fight with his ex, it was probably best if I knew as little as possible. Heather hated me. With a vengeance. Kyle's girlfriends always did.

I squinted at the clock on the microwave: 6:45 a.m. "Didn't you go home at all?"

"Mac . . ."

"All right. Dropping subject." I leaned tiredly against the counter and tried not to shiver. Living in a building that dated back to the 1880s might be great for atmosphere, but it was drafty. Plus, every muscle in my body was crying for more sleep; it wasn't like I had gotten a lot of rest with everything that had happened last night. Not that I was in

41

a hurry to tell Kyle about Jason and Trey—especially since it already seemed like he was in a bad mood.

"Did you at least call your mom?"

Kyle shrugged. "I told her I'd be out late."

I knew the rules were different for guys—less chance of them getting jumped at 3 a.m. and no chance of them getting knocked up in the back of a Honda—but I also knew Kyle's mom still worried, especially after the werewolf attacks last spring. And I liked his mother. Unlike Jason's parents, Kyle's had always been really nice to me.

"Call her," I insisted. "I've got to get dressed, anyway." I headed to my room before he could argue. As comfortable as I was around Kyle, I drew the line at hanging out in my PJs.

Not that the sight of me in a tank top and boxers would have any effect on him. Kyle was only peripherally aware that I was a girl. That was one reason we'd always be strictly platonic. Even if I wanted to go there—which I didn't—Kyle didn't seem to realize there was a "there" to go to.

Ten minutes later, I was fully dressed with deodorant under my arms and a freshly washed face.

"Cereal?" I asked.

Kyle nodded.

I moved around the kitchen, splitting the last of a box of Cheerios between two bowls and dousing each with a generous amount of milk as I tried to figure out how to tell Kyle about the new attack. "I saw Jason last night," I ventured, cautiously, as I set the milk back in the fridge.

Kyle grunted.

I turned and passed him a bowl. "You're still not speaking?"

"Not so much."

"It was an accident." Last Saturday, Jason had gotten drunk and picked a fight. If Kyle hadn't jumped in, Jason probably would have ended up in the ER. They hadn't spoken since. I, of course, was stuck in the middle.

Kyle shrugged and walked over to the small, two-seater breakfast table. "Scratching a CD is an accident. Dragging your best friend into a brawl against three varsity football players is practically manslaughter."

"At least they weren't linebackers," I pointed out, taking the seat across from him.

"Why do you keep making excuses for him?" Kyle sounded tired. "It doesn't help him, you know."

I traced patterns in my cereal with my spoon. "I'm just trying to cut him some slack. It's not like I've given him a permanent 'get out of jail free' card."

"No. That's what his father's money is for." It was hard to frown with a mouthful of Cheerios, but for the next few minutes, Kyle managed. Eventually, he said, "It's not like he was the only one who cared about Amy."

"You know it's different." Suddenly, I wasn't very hungry. I couldn't think about Amy and do something as mundane as eat. I pressed my hands to my abdomen and focused on the faux wood grain of the tabletop, trying to quell the sick feeling I still got whenever I talked about how Amy had died. "He saw her body. Anyone would be messed up after that. Think about how you'd feel if a werewolf killed Heather."

Kyle's spoon clanged to the floor and I looked up, startled. "I mean . . . if you and Heather were still together," I clarified, not entirely sure what I had said to freak him out.

And he was definitely freaked. In fact, Kyle looked like he had been sucker punched.

Before he could say anything, the front door opened and Tess slumped into the apartment.

"There's coffee," I said.

She shook her head. "Too tired," she mumbled. "Just want my bed." She tossed her jacket over the back of the couch, dropped the morning paper onto the kitchen table, and stumbled down the hall to her room.

I waited until I heard the noise from the small TV Tess kept in her bedroom. She always needed background noise to help her sleep.

"There was another werewolf attack," I said, figuring there was no good way to say it. I gave Kyle the CliffsNotes version of what Jason had told me.

He stared at the ceiling, like he expected it to open up and give him answers. "It could just be someone who was infected last spring and who didn't turn themselves in. The attack could have been an accident. A wolf who just lost control."

Back when werewolves were just creatures in scary stories—back before the government announced the existence of lupine syndrome—everyone always said they transformed during a full moon. Real werewolves could shift any time, at any place. Fear and anger were two big triggers. The better a person was at controlling their emotions, the better they were at controlling the shifts. Supposedly, control got easier with practice.

Kyle met my eyes. "Or else the wolf is back."

I shook my head. "I'm not sure I can even think about that." I wanted them to find the wolf that had killed Amy, but I didn't want the attacks to start again. I didn't want anyone else to go through what we had.

I reached for the paper Tess had left on the table, hoping there'd be something about the attack in its pages despite Jason's theory that the police were keeping it quiet. A ball of lead settled into my stomach as I scanned the front page. Everything Jason said to me when I was half-asleep came crashing back. *I'm going to find it. The wolf that killed Amy. There are people who will help.*

"What is it?" asked Kyle.

I handed him the paper and swallowed. "The Trackers are in Hemlock."

Kyle pulled into the school parking lot and found a spot behind a BMW with a Go Coyotes! bumper sticker. Next to the BMW, Kyle's ancient Honda looked severely outclassed. Almost everyone from the north side of town went to Kennedy, even though their rich parents were always complaining about the need for another high school in that part of town.

I climbed out of the car, slung my backpack over my shoulder, and glanced up at the hulking, three-story building. KHS had been constructed out of plain, light-brown bricks and had been designed by someone who obviously felt straight lines and neat blocks were an architectural religion. It had about as much personality as an IRS office.

"Promise me you'll talk to Jason," I said as we navigated our way toward the front steps through a sea of American Eagle.

Kyle opened his mouth to object, but I cut him off. "The Trackers are seriously bad news and you've always been the best at talking sense into him."

The Trackers claimed to be the ultimate community watch for the werewolf age. They proactively went after people infected with LS, rounding them up and shipping them off to government-run rehabilitation camps.

But the werewolves didn't always make it to the camps alive, and even regs—regular humans—had a habit of getting hurt when the Trackers were around.

People jokingly called them exterminators. If only they knew.

I slid an elastic off my wrist and pulled my hair into a messy bun at the nape of my neck. The September morning was chilly and overcast, but a trickle of sweat ran down my spine. Amy wasn't the first person I cared about who had been murdered.

We couldn't let Jason get involved with them.

Kyle shoved his hands deep into his pockets. He looked better than he had when he'd turned up at the apartment; I'd made him comb his hair and shave. He hadn't been thrilled with the idea of using a pink Classic Lady Bic, but he did it to shut me up. "Jason and I are barely speaking. He's not going to care about anything I have to say. Not for a while."

"Please, Kyle. Hank always used to say that small warning signs paved the way for big trouble."

Kyle snorted. "Mac, your dad was probably talking about knocking over liquor stores and grand theft whatever."

I opened my mouth to toss back a snarky retort, but the words died on my lips. Three men—too old to be students—were hanging around the main doors. One of them was surreptitiously snapping pictures of the crowd with his phone.

He turned his head to say something to the man on his left, and I caught a glimpse of the tattoo on his neck: A red *T* over a black dagger. The official Tracker crest. The last time I had been this close to one of those tattoos, I'd been nine and living with Hank. Eight years later, I still had nightmares about it.

I could think of only one reason they'd be hanging around the school and taking pictures: they were searching for students infected with LS. Every muscle in my body tensed as my pulse started to race.

Somehow, I made it past them and through the doors. The familiar sights and sounds of the main lobby surrounded me—the glass wall of the administration office, the bank of pay phones, the academic pennants hanging from the rafters—but it was almost like another image was overlaid on top of everything: a block of run-down tenements surrounded by cracked pavement and broken glass.

Our street in Detroit.

Leah had lived down the hall from Hank and me. She was a photographer who had come to the city to work on a yearlong photo series about urban landscapes. She slipped me food when my father forgot to buy groceries—which was often—and she let me hide out in her apartment and flip through her art books when his friends were over. She was pale and small and her Norwegian accent had made her seem exotic and magical. I used to pretend that she was the princess of a frozen kingdom, stripped of her possessions by an evil witch and exiled to America.

When the Trackers found out she was infected, she'd been dragged, kicking and screaming, out of our apartment building. . . .

I jumped as Kyle's fingers skimmed my hand.

"Detroit?" he asked, his brown eyes dark with concern. Kyle was the only person I'd ever told what had happened.

"Yeah." I let out a deep breath and forced the memories out of my head.

The Trackers were in Hemlock, and I couldn't afford to freak out every time I saw one. If I did, I'd probably find myself on a list of suspected werewolves and—infected or not—that wasn't a safe place to be.

5

SERENA CARSON WAS WAITING FOR ME BY MY LOCKER. We had started hanging out after her best friend moved away last year. It was right around the time Kyle and Heather had gotten serious and I'd begun feeling like a fifth wheel in my usual group.

Serena firmly believed that a lack of height could be compensated for by a larger-than-life wardrobe. Today it was a pink leather trench coat that looked ultrabright against her dark skin and knee-high boots over jeans so tight they probably came with a warning label. Her shoulder-length curls were held back by a turquoise scarf. She was the only person I knew who could compete with Tess in terms of brightly colored clothing.

"Did you see the goons outside?"

I nodded and spun my combination. "I guess it was inevitable that they'd turn up."

Serena hated the Trackers as much as I did. Before someone had stepped in and whipped them into shape, they'd been a motley offshoot of a couple of white supremacy groups—a fact most people conveniently forgot.

She bit her lip. "It's a little late, though. I mean, where were they five months ago?"

It *was* kind of strange timing—the attacks in the spring were the type of opportunity they should have been all over—but maybe the Trackers had been waiting for an opening in their busy schedule. Political lobbying, mob violence, and bake sales didn't just plan themselves.

"I don't know," I admitted. "Jason said there was an attack a couple of nights ago that the police are keeping quiet. Maybe that brought them." I swallowed. "I'm worried Jason is thinking about joining."

Serena snorted. "What a surprise. That boy doesn't have the sense God gave a cactus."

I grabbed my books and shut my locker.

"Werewolves did kill his girlfriend," I reminded her as we started toward chem. I cringed as soon as the words were out of my mouth. It shouldn't have been an easy thing to say and yet it had slid from my throat with almost no thought or effort.

"I know." Serena's expression softened. "And I did actually hear the rumor about an attack. One of my brother's friends knows someone's sister or something." She absently pulled one of the gold bangles she was wearing off of her right arm and slipped it onto her left. "So what did the Trackers promise him? Wait—let me guess: retribution for Amy?"

Jason hadn't actually told me, but what else could you offer the guy who could buy practically anything he wanted?

"Probably." Even to my own ears, the one word sounded miserable.

It wasn't like I couldn't understand the temptation. Not knowing what had happened that night, never learning who had killed her . . . it was like being stuck in limbo.

"You're worried about him." It wasn't a question. Serena had watched me worry about Jason all summer.

"Yeah," I said. "Speaking of which . . ." I took a deep breath and hitched my backpack a little higher on my shoulder. "Trey and a couple of his friends beat up Jason last night."

Serena glanced over, her gaze darkening. "And . . . ?"

If I wasn't so determined to save Jason from an early grave, I'd kill him for putting me in this position. Her brother's extracurricular activities weren't Serena's favorite subject. The words came out in a rush. "IwassortawonderingifyoucouldaskTreytobackoff."

She raised an eyebrow. "Was that supposed to be English?" But the edge of her mouth quirked up in a slight smile.

"Could you ask Trey to stay away from him for a bit?"

We turned into chem class, and the faint smell of old science experiments made my nose itch. Serena tossed her bag onto the black lab table we shared and gracefully flopped into her seat. "I hate to be the one to break it to you, but if Trey is hassling Jason . . ."

"It's because Jason deserves it. I know." I sat down and took out my books.

Serena frowned and dug through her bag. "I'll mention

it to Trey, but I wouldn't get your hopes up; it's not like my brother ever listens to me."

The bell rang and the surrounding lab tables quickly filled up. Mr. Harris—who'd probably been teaching chemistry when my father went to Kennedy—asked us to take out our books and turn to chapter three.

I flipped through the pages, barely registering a knock on the classroom door.

"Mac . . ."

Serena tugged on my sleeve and I looked up as the three men who'd been hanging around outside the school strode into the room.

"Excuse me," objected Mr. Harris, looking like a disgruntled owl as he was pushed aside, "you can't just barge in here."

The oldest of the three men handed Mr. Harris a piece of paper. He looked more like a lawyer than some sort of thug. There was a hint of silver in his dark hair and he was actually wearing a suit. "We're here with the full support of the Hemlock police department," he said, voice loud enough to carry across the room as his two companions began walking down the middle aisle.

They definitely didn't look like lawyers. In fact, they looked like the kind of guys lawyers sprung on technicalities.

I held my breath as they passed our table. There were holsters on their belts, and one of them smelled as though he had bathed in a vat of AXE body spray.

Serena made a slight gagging sound and clamped a hand over her mouth and nose.

Mr. Harris argued with the man at the front of the room as the rest of us stared, mesmerized, at the other two Trackers, waiting to see where they would stop and what they would do.

They stepped up to a table at the back. A scrawny freshman who was taking the class because he was some sort of science genius glanced up. He looked like he was on the verge of puking.

"Riley Parker?" asked one of the Trackers in a deep rumble.

The kid nodded.

Without warning, they hauled him to his feet, sending his chair and books scattering to the floor.

Mr. Harris shouted for them to stop and rushed to the back of the room.

He reached for one of the Trackers only to be shoved roughly away. Off balance, he stumbled and collided with a lab table, his arms sweeping a tray of beakers and test tubes to the ground with a crash that elicited shrieks from the two girls who were sitting there.

The rest of us sat frozen—too stunned to do or say anything.

The Trackers dragged Riley Parker toward the front of the room. When they were halfway to the door, Riley began struggling. One of them reached for the holster at his hip, and my heart stopped, certain he was going for a gun. He pulled out a thick, boxy instrument and thumbed a button on the top. Twin darts shot out, piercing Riley Parker's back.

Riley's entire body convulsed as he was tased. After thirty seconds that seemed to last an eternity, he went limp.

Without a word, the three Trackers carried him out of the classroom.

After Riley Parker had been dragged away, Mr. Harris asked us to stay in our seats and limped out of the room. Ten minutes later, face pale, he came back and informed us that Riley was being detained on suspicion of having LS. He spent the rest of the period just sitting at his desk, not saying anything, while the rest of us exchanged worried whispers.

I couldn't find Kyle during break, and English seemed to stretch on forever while speculations about Riley passed from desk to desk. I heard at least a dozen different stories ranging from genuine infection to a publicity stunt. People even added Amy to the mix—saying the freshman had confessed to murdering her.

As soon as the bell rang, I bolted to the second floor, where Kyle had poli-sci.

"Are you all right?" he asked, scanning my face as I tried to catch my breath. "I heard what happened in chem."

"I'm kind of freaked," I admitted, wiping a bit of perspiration from my forehead and trying to ignore the way my hand shook. "It was pretty horrible. They actually tased the guy and dragged him out of the room. How is that even legal?"

Kyle shrugged. "Werewolves don't have rights to violate, remember?"

I shivered. Somehow, that thought made it worse. "I looked for you on break."

A faint blush swept across Kyle's cheeks. "I had to talk to someone."

I knew "someone" was code for Heather and I felt a brief surge of irritation that he had been talking to her instead of checking to see if I was okay. Not to be a drama queen, but I had seen a boy get jolted with fifty thousand volts. Surely that outranked a manic ex-girlfriend.

I started walking toward the cafeteria, and Kyle fell into step beside me, adjusting his pace to compensate for my shorter legs.

"Did you at least talk to Jason?" I asked as we took the stairs down to the first floor and followed the smell of cardboard pizza and mystery meat loaf.

Kyle shot me a wary, sidelong glance at the tone in my voice. "Yeah. He invited me to a Tracker youth meeting tomorrow night."

"Seriously?" My heart sank.

"You thought he was going to join," Kyle reminded me. "You can't be surprised."

"I was just hoping there was still time to talk him out of it."

"Well, now's your chance."

I glanced up. Jason was leaning against the wide archway that led into the cafeteria, arms crossed, one knee slightly bent, looking as cool and composed as a *GQ* model—until you got to the eyes. They glinted like bits of broken glass, like he was looking for a fight. The bruise on his cheek added to the effect. He didn't look hungover, but then, Jason rarely did.

"Hey." He uncrossed his arms and pushed away from the wall.

"Hey," said Kyle.

Even though I had food in my backpack, I followed Jason and Kyle to the lunch line and stood between them.

"You know," said Jason, after a few moments of increasingly awkward silence, "if you were worried about me, you could have talked to me yourself." He watched me out of the corner of his eye, waiting for a response as the line inched forward.

"I thought . . ." I glanced at Kyle, but he just shrugged: it had been my idea to stage an intervention, and now I was on my own. "I didn't think you'd listen to me."

Jason added a bottle of water to his tray. "Look, Mac, I know you've got some sort of issue with the Trackers, but they're the good guys. I heard about what happened this morning. It's all over school. If they hadn't identified that Parker kid, he could have bitten or scratched anyone in that room."

I wasn't stupid: I knew not all werewolves were good. Some of them did attack and kill people. And one of them had killed Amy. But Charles Manson, the kids from Columbine, that guy with the Kool-Aid—regs did horrible things to each other, too.

And plenty of werewolves, like Leah, never hurt anyone. "Even if Riley Parker is infected, there's no proof that he was a threat. You didn't see the way they hauled him out of class. It was like he was—"

"An animal? That's what they are, Mac." Something cold slid behind Jason's eyes, and he leaned toward me, invading my personal space. "After everything that's happened, I can't believe you care about a filthy fleabag." The last word came out low and harsh, practically a curse.

"Lay off, Jason. She's just worried about you."

"Then she should have talked to me herself instead of making you do it."

Kyle snorted. "Right. Because you're being so calm and rational."

I shook my head. Kyle didn't have to defend me—not against Jason of all people. "Hemlock doesn't need the Trackers. The police—" I stopped, suddenly remembering the remark the Tracker had made to Mr. Harris about having the support of the police department.

"Who do you think asked the Trackers to come?" Jason's voice dropped to a fierce whisper. "Amy's grandfather made a call and the police invited them in the next day. He wants the Trackers to find Amy's killer, and after that last attack, the police want some answers." His green eyes bored into mine. "Why don't you?"

The words were like a slap. Kyle said something to Jason, but I couldn't hear him over the roaring sound in my ears. I stepped out of the line and tried to keep from shaking as I crossed the cafeteria and dumped my knapsack onto a random table. I sat down and stared out the bank of windows that overlooked the parking lot, waiting for the urge to yell and/or cry to pass.

"Mac?"

I looked up. Ethan Cole was staring down at me. The bright smile on his face clashed with his spiky, blue hair, Goth clothes, and multitude of piercings. A group of his friends hovered a few feet behind him, like moths around a streetlight.

He handed me a yellow flyer.

"'RfW Counter Rally'?" I asked, reading the large, black letters across the top of the page.

Ethan nodded. "The Trackers are having a recruitment meeting tomorrow night, and we're going to stage a peaceful protest outside. We want to show them that not everyone in town wants them here."

Regs for Werewolves—RfW—was a national network of werewolf rights activists. It was mostly made up of regs who opposed the rehabilitation camps and the lack of civil rights for people infected with lupine syndrome. They tried to draw attention to facts like how there were fewer annual werewolf-related fatalities than murders committed in, say, the state of California. And they tried to raise awareness about attacks on wolves and conditions in the camps—not that anyone really knew much about what went on behind the fences.

"I'm not really sure the words 'peaceful' and 'Tracker meeting' go together," I said, folding the flyer and slipping it into my backpack.

"Someone has to try, right? Look at what happened this morning." With another small smile, he headed to the next table, friends in tow.

I watched them try to hand out more flyers. Most people wouldn't take them. When they tried to give one to Trey Carson, he actually laughed.

I liked Ethan, but I was pretty sure attending a RfW rally while the Trackers were in town was tantamount to running across a shooting range wearing nothing but a bull's-eye duct taped to your butt.

At best, most people thought RfW was a joke. At worst, they thought the members were fleabag-loving traitors. Twelve years ago, the government announced the existence of lupine syndrome, and the whole world got scared. No matter how many pamphlets RfW handed out—no matter how many rallies they organized or statistics they quoted— that fear wasn't going away.

Giving my head a small shake, I rummaged through my bag until I came up with a granola bar and a banana. It wasn't a diet thing, just a Tess-forgetting-to-buy-groceries thing.

I glanced back at the lunch line. Jason paid for his food and then turned to scan the cafeteria. His eyes locked on mine—just for a moment—before he walked to another table.

Kyle slid into the seat across from me. The slice of pizza on his tray made my stomach growl. "He's not mad at you. Not exactly."

I frowned and peeled back the wrapper of my granola bar. "Then why is he sitting over there?"

Kyle took inventory of my practically nonexistent lunch. "Do you want me to get you something?"

I shook my head. "No thanks."

I watched a junior claim the seat next to Jason and crank up the charm. "I don't get why he's mad. All I did was ask you to talk to him."

"He wants you to have faith in him, I think."

I opened my mouth to say that I did, but the words wouldn't come out. "I just don't want him to get hurt."

"You can't save someone who doesn't want to be saved," said Kyle with a shrug.

Three minutes ago, my lunch hadn't looked nearly big enough; suddenly, I didn't have an appetite. "You can't really think that. He's your best friend."

"I know. But things aren't always as simple as you think they should be." He started in on his pizza.

"If I were in trouble, wouldn't you try to help me?"

A blush I didn't understand swept across Kyle's cheeks. Across the room, the junior was leaning so far into Jason that she was practically on his lap. "I mean, the three of us are best friends. If I thought you were in trouble, I'd try to help."

"Just like you would for him?"

There was a strange note in Kyle's voice. Something almost possessive that didn't fit the cafeteria or the conversation or the person he was talking to. Me. "Of course I would. Why would you even ask that?"

He didn't answer.

"We're going to go and keep an eye on him, right? Tomorrow night?"

Kyle shook his head. "Can't. I have other plans." He studiously avoided my gaze.

I knew that note in Kyle's voice—the half beat of hesitation and the quick inhale of breath that meant he was lying. "What plans?" I asked suspiciously.

Something caught his attention and he ignored the question.

Annoyed, I turned to see what he was staring at.

Not what. Who.

Heather Yoshida stood in the middle of the cafeteria, watching Kyle like the rest of the world didn't exist. She looked almost as bad as he had this morning. Normally, Heather looked like she had stepped out of a fashion magazine, but today she was wearing a baggy T-shirt—one that looked suspiciously like something out of Kyle's closet—and jeans that were only one step above sweatpants. Her long, jet-black hair hung limply over her shoulders, and she wasn't wearing a single scrap of jewelry.

I turned my gaze back to Kyle. He looked lost and tired and, maybe, a bit angry. After a moment, he seemed to remember I existed.

"Is everything okay?" I frowned, remembering how Kyle hadn't wanted to talk about his ex earlier. "Is something going on with Heather?"

He flinched slightly at the sound of her name. A flashing neon sign lit up my brain: PREGNANT. The word felt like a knife sliding into my chest—oddly painful for something I didn't have a direct stake in.

"I'm okay," he said. Two words that had never sounded less convincing. "I just remembered that I've got someplace to be."

Confused and worried, I watched Kyle stand and walk out of the cafeteria. He used the door that led to the gym so that he wouldn't have to walk past Heather.

If he was avoiding her, it didn't work: five seconds later, she trailed after him.

A prickly feeling crept up my neck, and I glanced around the room. Four tables away, Jason was watching me, completely ignoring the girl who was giggling and clutching his arm.

6

"I CAN'T BELIEVE I LET YOU TALK ME INTO THIS," MUT-
tered Serena as the number 16 bus rumbled over the bridge
connecting the north and south sides of town.

"I didn't talk you into anything," I reminded her as we
reached Jason's neighborhood and began passing a string
of progressively nicer—and larger—houses. "You invited
yourself along."

"Okay, then I can't believe you didn't talk me out of
this." Serena reached across me and tugged the pull string,
signaling that we wanted off at the next stop.

The bus slowed to a halt and we followed a line of nan-
nies and housekeepers to the doors. Public transit in this
part of town was for the people who supported the big
houses, not the people who owned them.

I checked the display on my cell phone as we started
walking toward the community center. We weren't late.
And Kyle hadn't called.

I'd tried twice to convince him to come, but he used
the same vague excuse—the same lie—both times: He had

plans. Plans that did not include babysitting Jason.

It wasn't like this was how I wanted to spend my Friday night—especially not after the things Jason had said to me in the cafeteria yesterday—but someone had to keep an eye on him.

I glanced at Serena. She had a resigned and slightly apprehensive look on her face.

"You really don't have to come."

She shook her head. "No. I want to go. Trey heard that Riley Parker wasn't even infected, that they let him go this morning. Apparently, he was so traumatized that his parents won't send him back to Kennedy and are talking about suing. If the Trackers are going to start randomly dragging people away without proof, I'd like to know as much about them as possible."

Unofficially, the Trackers had no authority of any kind. They were a civilian group and subject to civilian laws. But a lot of police departments let them have free rein when they came to town. It was easier that way. Besides, it wasn't like werewolves had any rights to violate. If Riley Parker had been infected, his parents wouldn't be talking about suing anyone.

We turned onto a winding road lined with thick hedges and gated driveways.

"Explain to me, again, why this part of town needs its own community center when they already have a country club?" asked Serena as the offending building came into view.

I opened my mouth to answer but was shocked silent

by the sight of a dozen people hovering at the edge of the parking lot, all carrying bright signs.

RfW had actually shown up.

"They're either really ballsy or incredibly stupid," whispered Serena as we passed.

I spotted Ethan and said a quick prayer of thanks that he was facing the other direction. I didn't want to see the flash of disappointment on his face when he realized I was there for the meeting and not the rally.

We climbed the center's wide, granite steps, and I took a deep breath. How bad could it be? I'd probably have to shake a few hands and listen to a few speeches. Two hours and I'd be out of there—hopefully with a promise from Jason not to join. I could handle two hours.

Besides, I might even learn something about the latest attack. Though I'd told Jason it was probably a different white wolf, the fear that I was wrong—that maybe the wolf was back or had never left—had steadily gnawed at me over the past two days.

In the months after the attacks ended—as it became clear that the police might never find the person responsible—I had convinced myself that I could be okay without any answers or closure. Now there was doubt, and suddenly I wasn't okay at all.

A smiling man in crisp blue jeans and a white T-shirt handed us each a pamphlet as we stepped through the doors. "Welcome," he said. "You're just in time."

"Thanks," I muttered, taking the piece of paper and trying not to look at the Tracker crest tattooed on his neck as we walked past him and into the small gymnasium.

We navigated our way around the dozens of teens sitting on the floor and found a free space along the back wall.

Jason stood near the front, talking to people I didn't recognize. Just beyond him was a row of pictures: poster-sized images of the four people who'd been killed last spring. In between photos of a smiling twenty-something girl and a serious middle-age man was Amy's last yearbook picture.

I felt a pang in my chest as I stared at the photo. The morning it had been taken, Amy had swung by my place early so she could do my hair and makeup. She even called Tess the night before and had her confiscate all of my elastics so I couldn't wear a ponytail. "It's our second-to-last yearbook photos," she'd said. "In twenty years, I want us to flip through our yearbooks and marvel at how fabulous we looked."

"Wow," whispered Serena as she scanned her pamphlet. "This is pretty heavy for a teen recruitment drive."

I glanced down at my own folded sheet of paper. *WHY THE CAMPS DON'T WORK* was printed in large, red letters across the top.

Twelve years ago, when the government announced the existence of lupine syndrome, they passed an emergency bill and built seven rehabilitation camps. There were only two ways to catch LS—a bite or a scratch from a fully or partially transformed werewolf—and there was a thirty-day incubation period before the disease was full-blown and people actually started shape-shifting. After those thirty days, all newly infected people were supposed to turn themselves in for lifelong internment. Their assets were seized and they lost all of their constitutional rights. There were no appeals and no second chances.

Not surprisingly, plenty of people tried to keep their condition a secret. They didn't turn themselves in and they spent their lives constantly looking over their shoulders, ready to run at any moment. There was an LS tip line you were supposed to call if you suspected someone was a werewolf in hiding.

I turned the pamphlet over. *Thou shall not suffer a wolf to live* was printed in old-fashioned script on the back.

The words sent a jolt through me.

I'd been nine on the day a group of men with tattoos on their necks beat Leah to death while our neighbors cheered them on. I hadn't seen the whole thing—not even most of it—but I had *heard* it. I hadn't been able to squeeze my way through the crowd, but I'd heard Leah scream and beg and, at the end, howl.

And when Hank had found me, when he swept me up in his arms, I'd clung to him and buried my face against his jacket and called him "Daddy." It was the only time I could remember doing any of those things.

"Isn't that Amy's grandfather?"

I looked up, startled out of my thoughts. Senator Walsh was indeed walking to a podium at the front of the room. At Amy's funeral, he had looked shrunken and weak. Now he looked energized—like the years had fallen away and he was ready to take on the world.

I wasn't sure about the world, but he'd definitely been

making waves in Washington. Before Amy's death, he'd been one of the most vocal supporters of increased werewolf rights. Two months ago, he had held a press conference to publicly throw his support behind building additional camps and implementing more aggressive procedures to target werewolves.

It was a complete turnabout and beyond major news. A Hollywood ghostwriter was supposedly working on a book about it.

But that didn't explain what he was doing here. This was just a local Tracker meeting and he was a US senator.

He cleared his throat and the room fell silent. "For those of you who don't know me, my name is Senator John Walsh. Amy Walsh was my granddaughter." His gaze swept the crowd. "Until last year, I believed—as some of you might—that werewolves were unfairly persecuted in our country. Unfortunately, it took tragedy here in Hemlock to show me how wrong I was. If stricter measures had been in place to proactively apprehend people infected with lupine syndrome, then my granddaughter might still be here today." He gripped the edge of the podium. "I can't change the past, but I can work toward a safer future. For Amy's memory and for all of you. With that, I'd like to turn the floor over to someone who *is* working toward that safer future: Branson Derby."

Chirrups of disbelief broke out around the room, and Serena let out a low, surprised whistle as a man strode forward and clasped hands with the senator.

Six years ago, Branson Derby had taken a bunch of

loosely affiliated, ragtag groups from across the country and organized them into one united force—with himself at the helm. He was behind the spin doctors and the public service campaigns and the dozens of initiatives the Trackers were undertaking in their war against werewolves.

At first glance, he looked unimposing. He had a hawkish nose, sharp cheekbones, and sandy-brown hair that was going gray. Like an understuffed scarecrow, he was tall and thin and his faded blue jeans and brown leather jacket seemed to hang on his frame, their colors blending with his tanned skin.

Then he turned to the room and smiled, sending shivers down my spine. If sharks could smile, they'd smile like he was now.

Voice smooth and southern and filled with authority, he said, "I want you to turn your head and look at the person on your right." Heads swiveled around the hall. "Now picture that person's throat gaping open, torn out by a werewolf. Like Amy Walsh's throat was torn out."

He was using Amy's death like a stage prop. I was going to be sick.

Derby continued. "Now turn your heads to the left." Automatic compliance from the spellbound audience. "Anyone in this room could be infected. The person you're looking at right now might be one of them. You can never let down your guard."

The lights dimmed and Derby raised his hand, a small remote held loosely in his palm. A picture suddenly filled the white wall behind him. A smiling redheaded woman and a young boy with light-brown hair and gray eyes. A family portrait.

Click.

A ripped jacket, the bend of a knee—those were the only clues that what we were looking at had once been a person, that it wasn't just a pile of mangled raw meat. My stomach rolled.

"This, of course, is the woman from the first photograph." Derby's voice was calm and level. The glow from the projector cast sinister shadows across his face. "A group of werewolves broke into her home, killed her two sons while she watched, and then killed her."

"I think I'm going to be ill," whispered Serena. She closed her eyes.

"Now," Derby said, "let's talk about the attack that occurred three nights ago."

7

"So do we catch the next bus or do we try and find Jason?" asked Serena as we stood on the community center steps, surrounded by a restless crowd of pre-Trackers. Derby had done a great job of stirring everyone up, but without an outlet for their energy, people were just hanging around, reluctant to go home but not having anything to do.

I shivered. The sun had set while we'd been inside, but on the edge of the grounds, the RfW rally was still going strong—or as strong as a small group of people with poster board signs could be.

I didn't see Jason anywhere; it was like he had vanished the second the meeting ended. "Do you mind if we check for his car?" Even though he lived just a few streets away, Jason had been raised in a house where the phrase *oil crisis* was considered obscene—probably because his dad owned a chain of auto dealerships.

Serena shrugged gracefully. "Sure. Though we may need a battering ram to get to the parking lot."

We started pushing our way through the crowd.

"Traitorous fleabag lovers," said someone behind us.

I turned my head, but I couldn't see who had spoken.

"No right to be here," added a second, female, voice from the front of the crowd.

A girl and three guys—two of them in varsity jackets—broke away from the throng and strode across the parking lot. They walked up to the man who seemed to be in charge of the protest—a guy with a gray ponytail who looked like he had been at the original Woodstock.

"This can't be good," I muttered.

The girl said something and the protester shook his head. Even though we were too far away to hear the exchange, the people on the steps all seemed to hold their breath.

And then, in the space between one heartbeat and the next, one of the varsity guys threw the first punch.

The response was almost instantaneous. Half the crowd on the steps bolted, yelling anti-werewolf slurs as they ran for the protest like they were storming Normandy.

Without thinking, I grabbed Serena's hand and started running with them—not because I wanted to join the RfW slaughter, but because we'd be trampled if we didn't move.

It was like being in the mosh pit at the world's most out-of-control concert. Serena gasped out a curse and held my hand in a death grip as we were shoved from all sides. It was impossible to know which way was out.

Around us, punches flew, and then someone collided with me hard enough that I lost my grip on Serena.

I yelled her name as we were swept in opposite directions.

Trying to force my way to where I had last seen her, I bounced off shoulders and elbows like a pinball. People were screaming and bleeding and crying and I felt like I had fallen into one of those war movies Kyle's dad was always watching.

For a second, I spotted Ethan, normally so calm and kind, as he punched a Tracker in the face.

Someone shoved me and I stumbled forward, barely catching my balance before I was pushed again and again. I had the horrifying thought that I was going to fall and be crushed, but then, suddenly, I was knocked to the outer fringe of the crowd.

I staggered a few feet away and began running along the perimeter of the mob, trying to catch a glimpse of Serena as I frantically yelled her name.

The sea of bodies parted—just for an instant—and I caught sight of her pink coat as a boy hauled her to her feet.

Jason.

He half dragged, half carried her away from the surge and toward the relative safety of the parked cars.

Sirens blared and a police cruiser swerved around the corner. Everyone scattered—the way they did when the cops busted up drinking parties out by the lake. Everyone who could run, that is.

So quick that it was almost dizzying, it was over.

A few people crouched on the ground among the

wreckage of broken signs and debris, too stunned—or wounded—to flee.

Slightly shell-shocked and shaking, I headed for the cars.

Jason and Serena were standing next to his SUV. When he spotted me, his shoulders relaxed and his breath came out in a rush. He shook his head. "Well," he drawled, "that wasn't in the program."

I ignored him. "Are you okay?" I asked Serena as I scanned her for bruises. Her cheeks and forehead were covered in a light sheen of sweat and she was trembling, but only her clothes seemed to have suffered any real damage.

She nodded. "Just very, very rattled." She slid her phone out of her purse and hastily sent a text. "Trey," she explained, catching my curious look. "I asked him to come pick me up."

Jason leaned against the SUV. "I can drive you home."

Serena shook her head and tried to brush some of the dirt and grass from her coat. "No offense, but I've seen how you drive. I think one near-death experience is enough for tonight. Besides, didn't you lose your license?"

Jason hesitated a second too long before saying, "I got it back."

I made a mental note to check his wallet the first chance I got.

"Jason!" A guy I didn't recognize strode toward us. He looked about nineteen or twenty, with sun-bleached hair and bronzed skin. The collar of his faded denim jacket just grazed the unmistakable tattoo on his neck.

"You're going to Tuesday's meeting, right?" the guy asked.

I blinked. It was like he was completely oblivious to the riot that had just taken place. Then again, he was a full-fledged Tracker. Maybe this sort of thing happened wherever he went.

He spared a quick grin for Serena and me. He looked a bit like Ben—the same sort of blond hair and build—but the smile didn't reach his eyes and there was something a little mean about the turn of his mouth that kept him from being attractive. He focused back on Jason. "I know you're not big on public speaking, but we really need you on the program next time. Your story would really help drive home how dangerous these fleabags are."

Jason nodded and they walked a few feet away to talk.

Serena frowned. "Is it just me, or are we the only ones freaked out by the fact that the evening just went totally *Gangs of New York*?"

"It's not just you."

A knot twisted in my stomach as I watched Jason talk to the Tracker. They didn't look like two people who had only met in the past couple of days. In fact, it looked an awful lot like they'd known each other for a while. I had the sudden suspicion that maybe Jason had been talking to the Trackers long before they arrived in town.

A second police car reached the community center, and two more cops joined the ones who were questioning stragglers and kicking at broken signs. A handful of people were standing watch over a couple of girls who had gotten trampled and were waiting for an ambulance.

On the other side of the street, Trey pulled up in the orange rust bucket he and Serena shared. It couldn't have been more than ten minutes since she had texted him; he must have already been on this side of the river.

"Do you want us to drive you home?" Serena asked, eyes darting to Jason and the Tracker.

I shook my head. "No thanks. Jason can take me."

She gave me a quick hug. "I'll call you tomorrow, okay?" She broke away and crossed the parking lot. She wasn't limping or moving stiffly. I guess she really was okay.

Jason returned just as Serena reached her car. I tried to ask him how long he'd known the guy in the denim jacket and if he was really going to join the Trackers, but the questions wouldn't come out.

I was too scared of what the answers might be.

"Jason, can we go somewhere and . . ." My voice trailed off as goose bumps swept along my arms. Branson Derby was headed our way.

"Jason," said the older man, nodding as he reached us. "Sir."

The undisguised respect in Jason's voice took me aback and I tried not to stare. I couldn't remember Jason ever sounding that respectful to anyone.

Up close, Derby appeared older than he had looked onstage. Fine lines had begun to snake their way outward from the corners of his eyes and mouth. His skin looked like parchment—like he had spent too much time in hot, dry climates. He was probably in his mid- to late forties, but he wasn't aging gracefully.

"I haven't met your friend," he said.

"This is Mackenzie Dobson. She attended the meeting." Jason swallowed. "She was friends with Amy."

Derby offered me his hand. After a moment's hesitation, I reached out and shook it. His grip was sure and firm, just this side of being too firm for comfort. I withdrew my hand and resisted the urge to wipe my palm on my jeans. The man made my skin crawl.

"Such a tragic loss," he said. "I've become quite well acquainted with Senator Walsh and the family." He glanced at Jason and there was something disturbing and proprietary about the look, almost as though Jason was a horse he was thinking about buying. "I assume, like Jason, you'll be joining our teen chapter."

I smiled and kept my eyes carefully blank. "I'm not much of a joiner."

Derby didn't return my smile. "In times like these, Miss Dobson, pure citizens need to stand together."

He shifted his attention to the police and to an ambulance that had pulled up for the injured girls. "If you'll excuse me," he said, turning and striding purposefully toward the flashing lights.

"I can't believe those idiot fleabag lovers had the nerve to show up here," said Jason, once we were alone.

The nerve? Had he seen the same fight I had? "The crowd rushed them."

Something flashed in Jason's eyes. "The crowd was *provoked*."

"By twelve people carrying flimsy signs?" I watched Derby as he shook hands with the police. "He gives me the creeps," I said, voice low.

"Derby? He's great—as long as you're not a werewolf." Jason shoved his hands into his pockets. "They killed his family, you know. A gang of wolves in Nevada. That picture he showed at the start of the meeting—the woman and boy? Those were his wife and son. They killed his other kid, too. His whole family was wiped out."

He cleared his throat. "Derby . . . understands. He knows what I went through. What I'm going through. I can really talk to him."

Hurt and not thinking, I said, "Maybe the two of you can form a support group. Lord knows you won't talk to Kyle or me."

Jason took a step back, annoyed and out of reach. "I don't get you, Mac. Werewolves killed your best friend and you're upset because I've been talking to Derby? The Trackers are the only ones doing something—really doing something—to prevent attacks. It's like you don't care that she's dead. Like you don't want to find the freak responsible."

I reeled. "Of course I care that . . ." I couldn't make myself say the rest, say that Amy was dead. Before he could hurl any other words at me, I turned and strode out of the parking lot.

I walked past iron gates and ridiculously large houses

that were lit up like birthday cakes. I wasn't sure how long I would have to wait for the next bus, and I didn't care. I crossed my arms over my chest as I walked, curling around the sting of Jason's words. Tears blurred my vision and threatened to spill over. I sucked in a deep breath and concentrated on not letting them fall.

Crying wouldn't bring her back. I had figured that out the first week she was gone.

Yes, a werewolf had killed Amy. But I couldn't blame an entire group of people—even if that would have been easier. The only person to blame was the one who had killed her. One person. One werewolf.

A werewolf that someone had to find. The police or the Trackers or . . .

Me.

I tripped over a crack in the pavement, barely aware of where I was going.

What if *I* could find the wolf? It was crazy—borderline ludicrous with a side of suicidal tendencies—but what if it was possible? After all, it wasn't like I was some sheltered teenager from suburbia. I had spent my childhood being raised by a man who made flying under the radar an art form.

Whatever else the wolf was, he was just another flavor of bad guy. Scarier and more dangerous than the ones Hank brought home for a beer, but still . . .

A car approached slowly, from behind.

"Mac, get in."

I kept walking.

"Come on, Mac. You heard what they said about walking alone at night. It's not safe."

I snorted. Like anything bad would happen in this part of town. When the attacks had started last spring, Hemlock's wealthiest residents had pooled their resources and hired twenty-four-hour security for their neighborhood and the surrounding area. None of the attacks had occurred on this side of the bridge.

I quickened my pace. I heard the car roll to a stop and the sound of a door opening and closing, but I didn't look back, not even when I heard footsteps running to catch up with me.

Jason made a grab for my sleeve and I shook him off. "Go to hell." My voice was thick and the words weren't entirely convincing, but I still put everything I had into each syllable.

He stepped around me, trying to block my path.

I turned and strode the other way.

Jason followed and I whirled. "She was my best friend!" I spat, choking on each word. I put my arms behind my back, scared that I would hit him, never wanting to hit anyone as badly as I did right then. "Don't you think I want them to find the thing that did it? Do you think it was easy for me? Sitting there and wondering if the Trackers really could do something when I hate them?"

I sucked in a deep, ragged breath. Behind my back, the muscles in my arms trembled. It felt like my entire body was shaking. "Don't you *ever* say that I don't care that she's gone."

He reached for me a second time and I shook my head. "I swear to God, Jason, if you touch me, I'll hit you." My voice was small and quivering. Not my voice at all. A nine-year-old scared of the dark and not sure if her father would ever come home. "I swear to God I will."

Ignoring me, Jason reached out and gently drew my arms forward. He slid his hands over mine, holding them for a dozen heartbeats before letting go. "I'm sorry." His green eyes searched my face, waiting for it to soften. When it didn't, he said, "I wouldn't have blamed you if you had hit me."

Without a word, I walked to the car and slid into the passenger seat. I quickly wiped my eyes with the heel of my hand, not wanting Jason to see how close to crying I was.

He had accused me of not caring. If he only knew what thoughts were running through my head.

I couldn't save Amy, but maybe I could find the thing that had killed her—maybe I could do that one last thing for her. And save Jason while I was at it.

If someone found Amy's killer—if *I* found Amy's killer—then the Trackers wouldn't bother sticking around.

We'd all get closure, and Jason would never turn up with a black-and-red tattoo on his neck.

8

I LEANED FORWARD AND RESTED MY ELBOWS ON THE small, round table Jason had managed to snag for us. I grimaced as my arm came into contact with a sticky substance that I hoped was spilled beer. "Ugh. This place is disgusting." I had to yell over the din of the crowd and the bad dance music pumping out of the speakers.

Jason started in on another beer.

"Maybe that should be the last one," I suggested, already having resigned myself to the role of designated driver— despite not being sure if I could talk a drunken Jason into the backseat. At the rate he was downing drinks, I wasn't sure he'd even be able to walk out of the club.

I should have known he'd start getting tanked as soon as we were through the door. After sitting through Derby's slideshow of death, I could understand wanting a little oblivion. No, the only real surprise was that I'd let him convince me to go out after the fight we'd had.

Part of it had been my need for a distraction. For a second, when I had wanted to hit Jason, I'd reminded myself of my father. Hank had never laid a hand on me, but I'd seen him hit plenty of other people. Guys who owed him money. Dealers who pissed him off. Crooks who screwed him over. He hadn't always needed an excuse—though he'd always been able to think of one later.

Hank practically lived for that feeling he got when he swung a first punch. Facing down Jason, just for an instant, I had wondered what that feeling would taste like.

With a shake of my head, I locked the thought away and focused on the present.

As usual, Bonnie and Clyde was far more crowded than it had any right to be. The duct tape on the seat of my chair kept sticking to my jeans and a glance at the floor in the blinking lights showed years' worth of grime. This was one club where girls never visited the washroom to check their makeup or gossip. Serena and I had gone in once—on a dare. It was not an experience I ever wanted to repeat.

At least the main part of the club was dark and crowded enough that the smaller vermin kept out of sight. Despite its flagrant health code violations and habitual serving of minors, B&C was never raided or written up by the health inspector—just one of the perks when the owner's brother was the chief of police and cops always drank free.

Tess would kill me if she knew I was here—though it was hardly the first time.

The guy who had spoken to Jason after the Tracker meeting approached the table with a girl in tow. When I realized he was with Alexis Perry, I stifled a groan.

Without waiting for an invitation, they both pulled up chairs.

Alexis looked like a punk pixie—her petite build and heart-shaped face were accompanied by a pink bob, combat boots, and a jacket that was held together with safety pins—and her dad was about as racist as they came. If you wanted proof, all you needed was a glimpse of the ink covering his chest and arms. The guy's body was like a walking white supremacist billboard. Even though Alexis lived with her mom, she'd embraced his beliefs with a zeal that had gotten her suspended from school eight times in the past two years. No wonder she was trailing after a Tracker like a puppy in love.

"Mac, this is Jimmy Tyler," shouted Jason. Even shouting, he slurred his words.

Jimmy gave me a little salute with his bottle and dragged his chair closer as Alexis glared. "I saw you in the parking lot," he said. He shrugged off his jacket, revealing a T-shirt that said *Hunt or be Hunted* across the front.

I nodded and pushed my chair back a few inches, giving him my best "not interested" look.

He didn't take the hint. "I'm Branson Derby's nephew."

This night, literally, could not get any worse.

I tried to catch Jason's attention, but he was watching the crowd on the dance floor. I noticed a button on Alexis's jacket—a caricature of a severed wolf head—and shivered, a slight movement that Jimmy mistook for interest.

He leaned forward and placed a hand on my knee. "You know, I've been hunting wolves for the past five years. Since I was fourteen."

He waited for me to make some small noise of appreciation. Instead, I said, "I have to go talk to someone." It wasn't a lie—not exactly. I very much felt the need to talk to someone else. Anyone else.

Jason looked up as I stood, but I ignored him. It hadn't bothered him that Repulsive Tracker Boy had been hitting on me.

I pushed my way to the bar and ordered a Coke. Shoulders hunched, I stared into my glass and wondered if I should just go home and leave Jason to fend for himself.

"Wow. Coke. Hard-core."

I straightened. "Very."

Ethan Cole slid onto the bar stool next to me. "You don't look like you're having much fun," he observed. If another guy had said that, it might have been a come-on, a hint that they could make my night better. Not from Ethan.

"Nice bruise," I remarked, noting the smudge on his cheek. "What happened to it being a peaceful protest?"

"Hard to remember you're a pacifist when someone's fist is connecting with your face." He ran a hand through his disheveled blue hair. "Anyway, I got hit defending Eric Johnson. It was terribly romantic—or would have been if he hadn't just ditched me for some random college guy."

I took a sip of my Coke. "And you're crushed, I assume."

"Devastated."

I swiveled around to scan the rest of the bar, looking for Eric and his random college conquest.

"You can do better," I said after I spotted them. "Easily."

Ethan shrugged. "Of course I can. But sometimes I like to slum it." He grinned.

I caught sight of Jimmy Tyler. He had abandoned Alexis and was making his way toward the bar. Great. "I've got to go make a call," I told Ethan, sliding off the stool and slipping away before he could ask what was going on.

There was a narrow, dank hallway to the left of the bar that led to the washrooms. It was the only place quiet enough to make a phone call without going outside. There was a couple making out against one of the graffiti-covered walls, but they were too wrapped up in each other to notice me as I passed.

Halfway between the couple and the washrooms was a busted pay phone. I leaned against it as I tried to call Kyle. Voice mail. Great.

I left a message telling him I was at the bar with Jason and to call me. I could probably deal with getting Jason home, and Derby's nephew would eventually get tired of hitting on me, but still . . .

I slipped my phone into my pocket as raised voices drifted down the hall. The tonsil pals had left—gone somewhere more private or less private—and been replaced by Jimmy and Alexis. Jimmy was leaning in toward a third figure while Alexis hung back and kept an eye on the rest of the bar.

"You were part of the protest," said Jimmy, his voice filled with barely veiled threats.

The figure shrugged. "Yeah. And?"

Ethan.

This so wasn't going to end well.

The pay phone was in its own little nook and no one had noticed me, but there was no way for me to get out of the hall without walking past them. No way for me to try and get help without drawing attention to myself.

Jimmy shoved Ethan into the wall. Ethan was tall but as skinny as a rake; Jimmy had at least fifty pounds on him.

Jimmy cocked his arm back, drawing out the moment, waiting for a reaction.

"He's not worth it," I said, pushing away from my hiding spot and ignoring the vaguely wounded look Ethan shot me. I walked forward and put a hand on Jimmy's arm. He was an idiot, but a strong one: there was a perfectly good set of muscles under the fabric of his shirt.

Alexis stared at my hand as though she'd like nothing better than to cut it off.

"Don't tell me you actually feel sorry for this twerp."

I shrugged. If I answered, it would only make Jimmy go harder on him.

Jimmy shook his arm free and then nuzzled my hair. I repressed the urge to step back. Oblivious to my revulsion, he said, "Why don't you let me take care of him, and then I'll meet you back in the bar."

"Jimmy," whined Alexis, "you said we would go somewhere after you took care of him."

Jimmy ignored her, and a crushed look swept across her face. I would almost have felt sorry for her—if she had been anyone else.

"Why don't you and I just go back to the bar now," I

said, hoping Jimmy would agree and I could ditch him after Ethan slipped away.

Ethan was staring at me like I had lost my mind.

Jimmy shook his head. "The guy's a member of RfW. He needs to be taught a lesson."

So much for luring him away. I glanced at Alexis. She acted tough, but she had been in my gym class last year. She practically cried every time a volleyball grazed her.

No, Alexis wasn't the one I had to worry about.

Nerves stretched as tight as piano wire, I took a deep, shaky breath.

"I won't be long," Jimmy soothed, misreading my every gesture as disappointment. "I'll meet you in a few minutes."

I shook my head. "I don't think you will."

He was still trying to make sense of my words when I kneed him in the crotch.

9

JIMMY CLUTCHED HIS PRIVATES AND CRUMPLED TO THE ground as he tried to find the breath to curse me.

"Oh God," I muttered as Alexis turned and ran—probably to get reinforcements.

Ethan lunged forward and started kicking Jimmy.

"Not now!" I yelled. Grabbing his arm, I dragged him toward the main part of the club. We had to find Jason and get to the SUV before Jimmy was able to stand or Alexis rounded up a squadron of drunken Tracker recruits.

I pushed my way through the crowd on the dance floor, losing my grip on Ethan as I crashed into, and was shoved by, dancer after dancer. I had to get back to the table. I had to get back to Jason. The music and lights and people made it hard to breathe.

Empty. The table was empty. I scanned the crowd, trying to distinguish Jason from the churning masses. I heard a shout behind me and whirled. Jimmy was on his feet and he wasn't alone. They hadn't spotted me yet, but they were starting to fan out. Six in all—two of them kids I went to school with who wouldn't have any trouble recognizing me.

I turned back to the spot where I had lost Ethan. Three Trackers were between us. Great. Excellent. Fanfrikintastic. They hadn't seen us yet, but they would.

Ethan took a step toward me. I shook my head and he froze. The blue glow from the spotlights near the dance floor made his face look strange and ghostly. We'd attract less attention if we weren't together. The Trackers were looking for a pair; they wouldn't expect us to separate.

I pointed from my chest to Ethan's and made a splitting-up motion. He shook his head, but I nodded. As if to prove my point, the Trackers started walking toward his end of the club, forcing him to step back into the shadows.

I couldn't stay here and I couldn't afford to keep looking for Jason. Trying to use the crowd as camouflage, I skirted the outer edges of the room, darting from group to group until I could see the exit. There was a shout and I didn't wait to see whether it was me or Ethan they had spotted. I just ran.

To the door and out the door.

Across the parking lot and past Jason's empty SUV.

Down the block and around the corner.

Wheezing like an old man on a treadmill, I stumbled to a clumsy stop, fished out my phone, and punched in the number of the Stray Cat.

One ring. C'mon, Tess.

Two. Please, Ben.

I counted the rings as I walked past a darkened pawn-shop and a piercing parlor that had been shut down for health-code violations. Technically, Bonnie and Clyde was located downtown, but this was a part of the strip that most people avoided after dark. Though there were a few shops, the majority of the buildings were warehouses and self-storage units.

There was a whooping yell behind me. I didn't know how many of them there were or if Jimmy was with them, and I didn't take time to check before breaking into another run.

I'd never been more aware of the absence of people, of the way shadows and dark buildings could press in on a person. I stretched my stride as far as it would go, trying to increase the gap between us. Each breath sliced my throat and chest.

I heard Amy's voice in my head. *Run, Mac, faster.* I wanted to tell her that I was trying, but I knew that trying wasn't good enough. I fumbled with my cell as I ran, desperate to key in 911 but too frightened to slow down enough to hit the right numbers.

My foot caught the edge of a pothole and I went sprawling, hitting the ground with a thud that knocked the air out of my lungs and left me stunned. My phone skidded across the pavement, and the granite curb dug painfully into my stomach. My right arm had taken the brunt of the damage and was muddy and scraped. *That's going to hurt*, I thought, dimly, as rough hands yanked me to my feet. Before I could get my bearings, someone slapped me. Hard. Then again.

"You said we were just going to scare her." The voice was high-pitched and anxious. I knew that voice, had heard it recently. Alexis.

I looked up—straight into Jimmy's face.

"We are scaring her," he said. "You're scared, aren't you? What's your name? Mac?" He dug his fingers into my arms. "You're scared, right, Mac?"

When I didn't answer, he shook me.

I couldn't find my voice. Stupid. I had been so stupid back at the bar. I should have found the bouncer or stayed out of it or . . . Someone was breathing in ragged little gasps. I realized it was me.

Jimmy started dragging me away from the edge of the street.

When I realized where he was taking me—an alley between two vacant buildings—I fought back. I kicked. I yelled. I used my nails on his arm and cheek. Sometime during the struggle, I lost my jacket, the fabric ripping from my shoulders as he fought to get me under control.

I couldn't let them take me into that alley.

Horrible things happened in alleys.

Amy had died in an alley.

I pushed and pulled and screamed. Hot tears ran down my cheeks and blurred my vision.

"Help me!" Jimmy ordered Alexis, his sour breath coming out in a rush and clinging to the insides of my nostrils and the back of my throat.

Despite looking decidedly unenthusiastic, Alexis helped drag me, still kicking and screaming, to the mouth of the alley.

No. No. No. No. Think. I couldn't think. I needed to

think. It was impossible to think. Tears and snot ran down my face. Jimmy pushed me against a brick wall and my stomach heaved. I was on the verge of throwing up on him, but he didn't seem to notice.

Alexis glanced at the street. She looked frightened, like she had suddenly realized things were rapidly spiraling out of control. "Jimmy, she's scared, all right? Let's just go."

"Not nearly scared enough," Jimmy muttered. He shot a glare at Alexis. "You were the one who said you wanted a future with us. This is part of what we do." He focused back on me. "We teach lessons."

I twisted away and he hauled me back, moving his hands to my shoulders so he could get a better grip. The look in his eyes turned every drop of blood in my veins to ice. I started shaking, shivering so hard that I bit my tongue and tasted blood.

"Do you like werewolves?" Jimmy snarled. "Is that why you tried to help that little RfW punk?"

I tried to turn my head, to look away, but he grabbed my jaw and forced my face back to him. "Do you have any idea what Trackers do to traitorous regs who like fleabags?"

Out of the corner of my eye, I saw Alexis take a step back. "Jimmy, she'll tell the cops."

He laughed, his breath ruffling my hair. "No she won't," he said, sounding so sure of himself that I almost believed him. "You won't go to the police, will you?"

He shook me. Once. Twice. The back of my skull knocked against the brick wall.

"No," I stammered. "I won't go to the police." And I

meant it. In that moment, I would have promised anything if they'd just let me go. My eyes burned and my chest hurt and it was hard to get enough air.

And he was laughing at me.

He leaned forward and brushed his lips across my cheek, whispering, "It wouldn't matter if you did. As long as the Trackers are in town, we *are* the police."

I couldn't breathe.

Had Amy been this scared the night she died? Had she known what was going to happen beforehand?

Fresh tears filled my eyes, distorting Jimmy's face. He brushed them away—a cruel, mocking parody of a caring gesture—and, over his shoulder, I saw a fourth person in the alley.

10

KYLE.

I tried to turn my head, to see if he really was there or if he was just a hallucination conjured up by my battered psyche.

"Stop that." Jimmy shook me until it felt like my brain was sloshing against the sides of my skull. My head bounced off the brick wall and sharp pain radiated out in waves. If he kept it up, I was going to have a concussion.

There was a low growl from the front of the alley. "Jimmy . . ." Alexis's voice came out a frightened squeak. A heartbeat later, something huge and dark slammed into Jimmy.

He was still gripping my arms. We both flew through the air and landed in a tangled heap. One of his knees caught me in the stomach and I retched, vomit clinging to my hair and clothes. My abdomen throbbed, and it felt like I had been split in two. I tried to breathe in shallow, hiccup-like breaths as I rolled off him. Jimmy had taken the brunt of the impact and was stunned.

I pushed myself to my hands and knees.

Alexis stared at me, her mouth open in a small, horrified O. She backed toward the street and then turned and ran.

Something soft and warm slid across my skin. Fur? I held my breath and turned my head. A werewolf was sniffing the blood on my arm.

The wolf gave a small yelp and shook its head. I started crawling backward, slowly, watching it for any sign it was about to leap for my throat.

I'd thought I had seen Kyle. I'd thought someone was going to save me.

There was no one.

I was going to die. Just like Amy.

I made it four or five feet and my strength gave out, my arms buckling beneath me. I waited for the wolf to crash into me, to split my body open with claws and fangs.

The werewolf padded over to me and I recoiled. It gave a sharp growl of displeasure and then licked my hand with its large, wet tongue before nudging my leg with its head. It was brown, I realized. Not white. It wasn't the same wolf that had killed Amy and attacked someone three nights ago.

I got back onto my hands and knees and weakly began to crawl, turning to the street even though it put the wolf at my back. The werewolf gave my legs another nudge of encouragement. It wanted me out of the alley.

It was herding me toward safety.

I made it six or seven more feet and then my strength gave out a second time. I was close enough to reach out and touch the sidewalk, but I couldn't cover that last bit of distance. I lay on my stomach, my cheek pressed to the dirty pavement. Small pebbles dug into my skin, but I couldn't raise my head.

Behind me, Jimmy swore and the wolf growled—not the displeased, impatient growl it had given me but a low, dangerous sound that raised the hair on the back of my arms and neck. Something flew past my head and shattered on the wall. A chunk of glass bounced off the brick and sliced my forehead. A beer bottle. Snarling erupted. Behind me, someone screamed.

I had to move, had to make my way out onto the street, where a passing car might spot me, but I couldn't budge. I was either too broken or too scared, and at that point I couldn't tell the difference.

Something thick and warm ran down my face. Blood.

"Our Father who art in Heaven. Hallowed be thy name . . ." The words stuck in my throat. Hank had been an atheist and Tess went to church only at Christmas and Easter.

"Thy kingdom . . ."

A particularly loud scream echoed behind me and I choked on a sob.

"Thy kingdom come."

Tears streamed down my face. Battered, bruised, and terrified, I struggled to curl into a ball. Blackness rose up. There was another scream behind me, and then, mercifully, I passed out.

Someone shook my shoulder. "Mac? Come on, Mac. Open your eyes." The voice was low and insistent. It was keeping me from oblivion and I resented it.

I turned my head away from the words. I need to find the dark place. The dark place was safe. Things couldn't hurt me there. I could hide. Why wouldn't the voice let me go?

"C'mon, Mac."

Eventually, I forced my eyes open.

Kyle was kneeling next to me. He sighed and leaned back.

Shock forced the air out of my lungs and cut through the fog in my head.

"You're naked." My voice cracked on the last syllable. Not just naked—covered in blood. It stuck to his chest and arms, sickly red-black in the moonlight. I stared past him at the broken shape in the shadows. "Why are you naked?" The words came out high and unsteady.

Kyle stared down at me, a mixture of fear and sadness on his face. "I won't hurt you."

Of course he wouldn't hurt me. Why would he? Why was it even a question? "Why is there blood on your arms?" I whisper-asked, my voice quaking.

He cringed and stared at the ground.

"Kyle?"

He shook his head.

I pressed my hands to the sides of my skull, trying to keep my thoughts from splitting me in two. He couldn't be infected. Not Kyle. "What did you do?"

He reached for me and I cringed away, scooting backward on my butt. "Is he dead? Did you kill him?"

Kyle shook his head. "He's alive."

"But you attacked him? You're infected. Oh God." I doubled over, fighting the urge to retch.

Faster than was humanly possible, Kyle was on me. My whole body stiffened as he cradled me against his chest.

"I had to." His voice was thick and I realized he was crying. Kyle never cried. It wasn't Kyle. "I had to save you. Please, Mac."

His bare skin was tacky with blood; he was covering me in it. I tried to push him away and everywhere our skin touched, mine came back red.

"Lemme go." My hands were sticky—I didn't realize blood could be so thick and sticky. "Kyle, let me go!"

He dropped his arms, hugging himself like he was the one who needed protection. "I would never hurt you."

"You're covered in someone else's blood!" The alley swam in and out of focus.

Kyle glared into the shadows where Jimmy was lying like a broken tin soldier and a low growl rumbled in his throat. "I didn't have a choice."

Kyle didn't growl. Couldn't growl.

It wasn't Kyle. This wasn't real.

I scrambled to my feet. Not a good idea. The alley tilted. The walls caved in and the ground rushed up. Blackness claimed me again.

11

"WOW. JASON REALLY LET YOU DOWN, HUH?" AMY SAT next to me, resting her back against the brick wall. "He does that. More than you'd think."

I wrapped my arms around my legs and pressed my chin to my knees. I didn't answer.

There was a spot of blood on my hand. She reached out and dipped her finger in it, then grimaced. "These things are always so messy."

Strange noises and scents drifted into the alley. Steady beeping. Bleach. The crackle of an intercom.

Amy sighed and rolled her eyes. "Guess we'll just have to talk later." She pushed herself to her feet and rippled. Her image and the alley walls swirled together and became bright light.

Light that was accompanied by pain.

Sharp and immediate and threatening to crack my skull like an eggshell. I let out a low moan.

"She's waking up."

A white room swam into focus. Beds with railings and

thin cotton blankets. A hospital. Someone leaned over me and I cringed away, instinctively, until the rainbow hair and frightened hazel eyes registered.

"Tess?" My voice came out a croak.

She brushed the hair back from my face, her touch feather-light. "It's okay, Mac. You're okay. You're all right now. You're safe."

She turned away and I realized she was crying. She wiped her cheek with her hand and took a deep, shaky breath. When she looked back at me, I noticed ghostly trails of mascara running around her eyes and over her cheeks.

"Ben just went to the apartment to pick up some clothes for you. He'll be back soon. We weren't sure how long you were going to be out."

I tried to remember what had happened, why I was in the hospital, but it was like a thick mist had taken up residence inside my brain, obscuring everything. I couldn't decide what hurt more: my head or my throat. I tried to swallow. "Water?"

Tess glanced over her shoulder and I heard footsteps, the squeak of rubber soles on linoleum.

I struggled to sit up, but she gently pushed me back down. Even though she was being careful, it hurt when she touched my shoulders. "Easy. You've been out of it for a few hours. The doctors said it was shock. . . ." Tess reached for a small, white switch. With the push of a button, the bed raised itself to a sitting position.

Kyle came into view, standing in the door to what was probably a washroom, a paper cup in his hand.

My stomach lurched. Something about the way he was framed by the doorway tugged at my memory.

An alley. Brick walls. Broken glass. Rough hands on my skin.

"I'm going to get the doctor, tell him you're awake." Tess bent down and brushed a light kiss across my forehead, but her words and exit barely registered.

Memories dragged me under. Textures and sounds and sights and smells. And blood. I couldn't get enough air.

"Mac?" Kyle took a hesitant step toward the bed. He set the cup on a small, wheeled table.

"Can't. Breathe." I squeezed my eyes shut, but that was worse: Jimmy Tyler's face leered behind my eyelids, like an image projected on a movie screen.

"Should I go after Tess?"

I wanted to answer, to tell him no, but the word wouldn't come out.

Strong hands cupped my face. "Mac, open your eyes." Kyle's voice was calm but insistent. Almost commanding. *"Mackenzie."* I opened my eyes. "You're having a panic attack. You're okay. Take a deep breath."

I shook my head. How could I breathe when there wasn't any air in the room?

Kyle leaned forward until all I could see were his eyes. Brown and warm and bottomless. "You can do it, Mackenzie," he said firmly. "Just one deep breath."

My eyes watered and Kyle's face splintered, like I was looking at him through a broken lens.

Mackenzie. He never called me that.

I sucked in a breath and let it out. Then another.

Kyle lowered his hands. Once I stopped shaking, he reached for the paper cup and handed it to me.

A bit of water spilled onto his hand as his fingertips brushed mine. "Sorry," I mumbled and took a sip.

He stepped away and crossed his arms. "For what?"

"Falling to pieces." It was hard to look at him.

"For being human, you mean." There was a strange hitch in Kyle's voice. He smiled but it was obviously forced. "Don't apologize for that. Otherwise, I'll have to start apologizing for being . . . you know . . . not."

Panic tugged at me again, but I squashed it down. I could deal with this. I was always saying that not all werewolves were bad, that LS shouldn't be some sort of black mark. But saying that—even believing it—didn't mean I wanted Kyle to be infected. "Tell me it's not true."

He sighed. "Fine. It's not true."

He looked normal. Perfectly normal. He was wearing the Elliott Smith T-shirt I'd bought him at a thrift store, and his dark hair was wavy—the way it got when he didn't dry it after a shower. The expression on his face was exasperation with a tinge of bemusement—his mom called it his "Mac" look. And yet . . .

"Are you lying?"

He rolled his eyes. "Of course I'm lying."

"Not cool," I muttered.

Kyle shrugged. "I didn't want you to start hyperventilating again." His hair fell over his eyes and he brushed it aside. "I figured annoying you was safer than admitting anything." He was joking, but there was something dark and worried in the way he watched me.

I shifted on the bed, closer to the edge, and he stepped away, even put his hands behind his back. Almost as though . . .

Oh. Oh!

The realization hit me: Kyle thought I was scared of him.

Was I? It was normal to be scared of werewolves—even people in RfW admitted sometimes being afraid—but this was *Kyle*.

I pulled back the thin hospital blankets and swung my legs over the side of the bed. I looked down. Great. Hospital chic. At least I had shaved my legs yesterday morning.

"What are you doing?"

"Nothing." I stood, testing my balance. A little wobbly, but not too bad. I tugged on the hospital gown, trying to preserve a little dignity and modesty.

For a split second, I could have sworn Kyle checked out my legs.

I took a step forward and he backed into the wall. "Mac . . ." His voice came out high and uneasy, and I flashed back to what Kyle had been like when we first met: a gangly mess of elbows and knees with a voice that hadn't broken.

"Shhh," I said. "I'm testing something."

Kyle frowned. "Testing what?"

"Myself." I took a deep breath as three years of memories rushed through my head and strengthened my resolve.

There was a draft from the hall and I really wished I had pants. Or at least shoes.

I shivered and Kyle, thinking I was reacting to him, started to move away. I reached out and touched his chin with two fingers, turning his head so that he was looking at me. "The floor is cold, idiot." My pulse thundered in my ears. I was touching a werewolf. I gave my head a small shake. No: I was touching Kyle.

"You're scared of me. I can tell." He licked his lips. "I can smell it."

Okay, that was a little creepy. "What's your next trick gonna be: predicting my period?"

Kyle shook his head and let out a nervous laugh. "Trust me, Jason and I figured that out years ago—totally out of self-preservation."

Jason . . .

"He's all right," Kyle said, catching something in my face that made his own expression harden. "I called the house. I was going to tell him you were here, but his mother claimed he was . . . *indisposed*." He said the last word like it sliced his throat on the way out. He looked like he wanted to say more, but he just shoved his hands into his pockets and muttered something too low for me to catch.

Tess's voice echoed down the hall and Kyle turned away. "I'd better go. She lied to get me in here. It's supposed to be family only."

Before I could argue—before I could ask him to stay—he was out the door.

Ms. Fisher was in her midthirties, wore too much makeup, and spent way too many hours in tanning booths. The police had called her a "werewolf consultant," but when she turned her head to the side, the hilt of the dagger tattoo on her neck peeked out from underneath her pink silk scarf.

"Mackenzie, no one is denying that you've been through a terrible ordeal." She crossed her legs and leaned toward me. "It's normal that you would be confused. We just want to find out what really happened."

I shook my head. "I'm not confused."

Across the hospital room, Tess's expression was stormy as she leaned against the wall and listened.

We had been going in circles for thirty minutes, me trying to tell a modified version of the truth while Fisher did everything she could to twist my words and discredit me. The two police officers she was with hung back and took notes. I couldn't tell which one of us they believed. After all, it was strange that a werewolf would attack a grown man and leave a girl completely unharmed.

But it was the truth. Every mark on my body had been left by Jimmy: a sprained wrist, a gash on my forehead, and the bruises on my upper arms and shoulders where he had gripped me hard enough to leave behind bluish imprints of his hands.

I also had a minor concussion, which wasn't making the interrogation—sorry, the *interview*—any easier.

"Jimmy Tyler and Alexis Perry followed me out of Bonnie and Clyde and assaulted me. The werewolf drove them off. I don't know who it was or why it helped me, but it did." No way was I telling them that the wolf had been Kyle.

He had saved my life.

He was my best friend.

Since neither Fisher nor the police brought up his name, I was fairly certain Alexis hadn't seen him before he shifted. She had, after all, been watching Jimmy and me.

Ms. Fisher sighed and tucked a strand of bottle-blond hair behind her ear. "Mackenzie, I'm here to help you, but I need you to think very hard about what really happened."

I struggled to appear calm despite the anger that was raging through me. Losing my temper wouldn't help anything. "I know what really happened."

"I've already spoken to Jimmy Tyler and Alexis Perry and they told a very different story. They both said that they followed your screams to the alley and that Jimmy tried to drive off the werewolf while Alexis ran to call 911. We have her phone call."

I swallowed. "They're lying."

"Mackenzie, that is a very serious accusation to make." She glanced down at her notes. "Bonnie and Clyde is a bar, is it not? Do you want to tell us what an underage girl like yourself was doing there?"

"All right, that's enough." Tess pushed away from the wall and strode over to where I sat on the edge of the bed. She put an arm around my shoulders and glared at Fisher. "Mackenzie has been extremely patient with your questions, but you're acting like she's on trial."

One of the officers cleared her throat. "Perhaps we could discuss this in the hall?"

Tess nodded. "Let's." She flashed me a reassuring smile, but the look on her face as she followed the others outside reminded me of a lioness preparing to fight.

She was back a few minutes later, sliding a business card into her back pocket. "They want us to call if you remember anything else."

"They're really gone?" Though I'd tried to stay calm while they were in the hall, part of me had been terrified that they'd come back and haul me down to the police station to ask more endless questions.

Tess nodded and brushed the hair back from my forehead, frowning at the stitches in my temple.

"Can we get out of here now?"

She gave me a tired smile. "Definitely. Why don't you wait here while I take care of the paperwork and find Ben? He's probably still hanging around the lobby."

She headed for the door.

"Tess?"

"Yeah?"

"Can you pull the privacy curtain? I just want some quiet. . . ." Even with the door closed, anyone from the hall could look in as they walked by. I was feeling twitchy and exposed.

She nodded and pulled the curtain around my half of the room.

Once she was gone, I stretched out on the hospital bed and stared at the ceiling. So Kyle was a werewolf. I reached up and touched my cheek, remembering the way he had cupped my face during my panic attack. My stomach tightened in a way it usually didn't—not when it came to Kyle.

I forced myself to think of something else, to replay

what the police and the Tracker—sorry, werewolf consultant—had asked and said. Ms. Fisher had seemed way more interested in protecting Derby's nephew than finding out the truth.

At least that had made it easier to lie about Kyle.

The door creaked open and I heard footsteps. I started to sit up but put too much pressure on my wrist; I fell back against the mattress with a sharp hiss of pain.

A hand snaked around the edge of the privacy curtain, drawing it aside just far enough for Branson Derby to slip past. He let the curtain fall back into place, hiding us from view.

I scrambled for the call button, but he was faster. He grabbed my wrist—the one wrapped in an elastic bandage—and started to squeeze, gently at first, then harder. Tears leaked from the corners of my eyes and black spots filled my vision.

"If you scream or try for the call button, I will make your life very difficult. Do you understand?"

Branson Derby had come to ask about his nephew. Panic welled in my chest, and I tried not to let it show on my face as I nodded.

"I took the liberty of peeking at your chart," he confessed. "A sprain can be so painful—some people say almost as bad as a break." A slow smile curved his lips and he squeezed harder, digging his fingers into the soft spot just over my pulse.

I gasped, then clenched my teeth, determined not to give him the satisfaction of seeing me in pain.

He let go of my wrist and I cradled it against my chest.

"Good girl." Derby sat on the edge of the bed. Leaning forward, he brushed his fingertips across the gash on my temple. He smelled liked Old Spice and wood smoke and something else—a faint scent worked into his worn leather jacket: sweat mixed with blood.

I pressed myself as far away from him as I could. If the rails hadn't been up on the far side of the bed, I would have fallen to the floor.

"What do you want?"

"I just spoke with Ms. Fisher. She said you were rather *insistent*. That you seem to think my nephew attacked you and that you were saved by a werewolf."

I didn't say anything.

"I want you to recount your story. You were savagely attacked. No one will blame you for being confused. It's best not to muddy public opinion with ridiculous stories about benevolent werewolves."

"For the Trackers," I said, trying to wrap my head around the man in front of me. His nephew had nearly been killed and he was thinking about damage control. Cause above family.

Derby's gray eyes glinted. "For everyone." He stood and crossed to the window. "People count on my group to keep the wolves in check. The police can't do it—they don't have the resources and they're constrained by the law. That's why they called us in. We're here on the personal invitation of Senator Walsh."

He stared down at the parking lot. "I understand you're

claiming not to have seen the wolf before it shifted. That really is quite unfortunate. And difficult to believe."

A chill swept up my spine. I had the distinct feeling that very bad things happened to people who withheld information from him.

"I didn't see anything."

Derby turned and crossed his arms. "Miss Dobson, I have a problem. And I do not like problems. I can't keep the media from reporting that there was an attack last night and that my nephew was bitten and infected, but I can keep the details to a minimum. And I can make it so that your name stays out of it. Completely. Alexis Perry has already agreed not to tell anyone what she witnessed." He frowned. "It really is unfortunate that she wasn't more observant."

He sighed and shook his head. "But that is neither here nor there. The point is, I can keep the press away from you—provided you keep quiet. Do you really want them constantly hounding you, asking you to relive last night over and over?"

Bile rose in the back of my throat. "And your nephew?"

"There's nothing I can do for him. It was obvious to both the police and the hospital staff that he was bitten. He'll be sent to a rehabilitation camp."

My surprise must have shown on my face because he added, "Nephew or not, he's one of them now." His mouth twisted around his next words. "A werewolf."

Derby shrugged. "In a way, you actually did me something of a favor—or that wolf did. My nephew has been difficult to control. Now I'll no longer have to worry about his lack of judgment."

Jimmy would spend the rest of his life behind a fence. It was a harsher sentence than he'd get from the regular justice system. And I was betting that very bad things happened to Trackers who found themselves on the inside of the camps.

Of course, nothing would happen to Alexis. I'd still have to see her every day at school.

It wasn't right, but maybe Jimmy being locked away could be enough. Maybe it had to be.

The way Derby shrugged off his nephew's interment made me certain he wouldn't hesitate to hurt anyone standing in his way. Besides, if my name got out to the press, there could be a chance I would accidentally say something that could endanger Kyle.

"Fine," I said, throat dry. "Keep my name out of it and I'll keep quiet."

Derby raised an eyebrow, surprised, probably, that I hadn't argued. "Very good, Miss Dobson. Unfortunately, I wasn't finished."

A hundred-pound weight dropped into my stomach.

"I also want you to keep last night a secret from Jason Sheffield. I know he was with you prior to the . . . incident. When he asks you about last night—and he will—tell him you went straight home."

I bit my lip. Lie to Jason? About being attacked?

Derby's eyes bored into me. They were cold and hard, like shale slick with rain. "I have plans for Jason Sheffield. I don't want any childish affection he has for you to cloud his judgment, to make him question his place with the Trackers."

I swallowed. "I think you're overestimating how much he'd care."

Derby shook his head and moved toward the bed. He stared down at me the way cruel boys studied flies before pulling off their wings. "Actually, I think you're one of the few things he does care about. Maybe almost as much as revenge." He shrugged. "As I said, I have plans for Jason. If his feelings for you were to get in the way of those plans, he'd be useless to me. He might even become a liability."

Derby leaned down, so close that I could smell stale coffee on his breath. "Do you know what I do to losses and liabilities, Miss Dobson?"

I shook my head.

"I cut them loose. Permanently."

The curtain was suddenly thrust aside and I let out an embarrassingly loud shriek. I had been so intent on Derby that I hadn't heard anyone else enter the room.

"What's going on?" The glare Ben leveled at Derby was hot enough to scorch. Like everyone in the country, he knew who the man was. His gaze flicked to me. "Are you all right, Mac?"

I nodded. "Mr. Derby was just leaving."

"Of course." Derby gave my hand a small squeeze, carefully twisting my wrist in just the right way to exert pain. To the casual observer, it would have looked like a caring gesture.

Ben was not a casual observer. He read the pain in my eyes and took a step forward.

I gave a small shake of my head—I could stand a little pain and I didn't want Ben to get on the wrong side of the Trackers. It was bad enough that I had managed to end up on it.

Derby increased the pressure for a heartbeat and then released my hand. "I just wanted to check on the girl who was lucky enough to survive a werewolf attack." He turned and walked out of the room, calm, confident, certain that I wouldn't contradict him.

All of the air burst out of my lungs in a relieved rush.

I swung my legs over the side of the bed and tried to stand. Not good. Ben darted forward to steady me before I fell. "What did he want?" His voice was laced with anger and the look in his gray eyes sent a chill through me. Ben almost never got angry.

"Nothing," I lied, steadying myself and stepping away. "He just wanted to follow up on some of the questions the police asked me."

Ben weighed my answer and then nodded, swallowing the lie.

Lying to Ben was easy. Lying to Jason was going to be harder. Much, much harder.

But I didn't have a choice.

I was pretty sure Derby had just threatened Jason's life.

12

"So that was Branson Derby. He was shorter than I thought he'd be."

My stomach clenched. It was night and we were back in the alley.

Amy shivered and wrapped her arms around herself. "Relax. This isn't your place. It's mine."

She was right. The walls were closer together and the color of the bricks and the shapes of the puddles were slightly different. There was a chain-link fence blocking off the back of the alley from an adjacent vacant lot. The graffiti on the walls suggested doing several things I was pretty sure were physically impossible.

I had been avoiding this part of town for months. I knew people left flowers and teddy bears in the alley as a makeshift memorial—Tess had even suggested that going might give me some closure—but I hadn't been brave enough to visit the place where Amy died.

"It's okay," she said as she kicked a bottle cap. She was wearing a short, gray dress over a pair of pink leggings and black high-tops. It was what she had been wearing when I canceled our plans so I could stay home and study.

"What's okay?"

The bottle cap went flying down the alley and made a soft ping as it bounced off the brick wall. "You not coming here sooner."

I swallowed. "How did you—?"

"Doesn't matter. Anyway, the whole murder-scene-memorial idea is kind of morbid. Kyle comes, you know." She was quiet for a moment. "I wish he'd stop. All it does is make him sad."

I did know. Kyle's mom had told me because she was worried about him: she thought he was still blaming himself for not answering Amy's call the night she died.

"Derby won't find it, you know. Him." Amy glanced up at the stars, just for a second, and let out a frustrated sigh. "If he finds the wolf too soon, it'll be game over."

"He'll be a hero."

She shook her head. "He'll be obsolete. He's playing the long game, and round two hasn't even started yet."

I took a deep breath and counted to ten, praying for patience. "I have no idea what you're talking about."

Amy smiled. It wasn't a happy smile. A small line of blood trickled out of the corner of her mouth. "You will."

And then I was staring at my bedroom ceiling, at the small spot where paint had begun to peel away.

In life, Amy had liked keeping secrets. She loved knowing things other people didn't. My dreams were magnifying that quality, turning her into a nightmare version of the Cheshire cat.

I rolled over and glanced at my alarm clock. Noon. Almost exactly. I had three seconds' worth of panic before I remembered it was Sunday.

It took me two tries to climb out of bed, and my body kept trying to convince me it was too stiff and sore to move as I walked to my closet. I pulled on a pair of ancient jeans—washed so many times that they were almost as comfortable as pajama bottoms—and a green-and-white long-sleeved T-shirt that had the Kennedy Coyote on the back.

I tugged the sleeves down to hide the bruises on my arms and the bandage wrapped around my wrist. Out of sight, out of mind.

Ben glanced up from a paperback when I walked into the kitchen. "Hey, comatose girl."

I rolled my eyes. "Teenagers are supposed to sleep late. We're kinda known for it." The rest of the apartment was weirdly quiet. It was never quiet when Tess was around.

Guessing my thoughts, Ben said, "Tess figured you'd be up soon. She went to get you a new cell phone, and then she was going to swing by the deli to grab sandwiches."

I felt a small pang of guilt: I was the one who had lost the phone. She'd probably come home with something about ten times better than what I'd had—Tess always let sales-people talk her into things—and she probably wouldn't let me pay her back.

"I'm not sure I feel like eating," I admitted as I slid into the chair across from him. "So you're my designated baby-sitter while she's gone?"

Ben shrugged. "If I say yes, you'll tell me that you don't need a babysitter and kick me out. So, no, I'm not your designated babysitter. I'm a guy whose apartment has no running water."

"Again?" There were a few nice things about living in a building that was practically a historic landmark. Reliable plumbing was not, unfortunately, one of them. "Did you call the super?"

With impeccable timing, Ben's phone went off. He took it out and glanced at the display. His face darkened and he let it go to voice mail.

I raised an eyebrow.

"Family stuff," he said.

"Oh." I didn't push. I knew Ben didn't get along with most of his family. He'd been in Dayton for a funeral the week Amy died. When he got back, he'd been quiet and withdrawn for days. All he'd tell Tess was that he'd fought with his father.

The intercom buzzed. "Wow," I muttered, "we're more popular than a pretty girl at a *Star Trek* convention."

I started to get up, but Ben waved me back down. "I'll get it."

I tugged at a thread on my jeans, praying it wouldn't be Kyle. I knew I was going to have to talk to him—I wanted to talk to him—but first I needed to figure out what I was going to say. Before heading to bed last night, I'd looked online for a FAQ that told you how to have the "so you're a werewolf" conversation with your friends. The first page of search results had been filled with links for Tracker blogs and articles about Amy's grandfather and his new anti-werewolf stance.

My head snapped up as Jason's voice came over the intercom.

I opened my mouth to tell Ben not to let him in—that I didn't want to see him—but I was too late: he had already pressed the button to unlock the main door.

"I'm gonna run down to my apartment for a minute, okay?"

I nodded, fighting the urge to beg Ben to stay. He opened the door and I heard him greet Jason and tell him I was inside.

And then Jason was in the apartment. It had been a day and a half since I had seen him, and the bruise on his face from the fight with Trey had taken on a yellowish-green tinge. He was wearing a gray coat that made his pale skin and blond hair look almost ghostly. His eyes were bloodshot and I was pretty sure he was hungover but not catastrophi-cally so.

For a second I wondered if he had gone out again last night and how he had gotten home.

Then I told myself that I didn't care.

I pushed my chair back and stood. The movement was a little too fast and I had to grip the edge of the table to steady myself.

Where were you?

How could you have left me alone?

Do you have any idea what happened to me?

The questions tried to force their way out, but I shoved them down. All but that first one. "Where were you Friday night?"

Jason crossed the living room. "I'm sorry. I saw you talking to Ethan at the club and . . ." His voice trailed off as he got closer. He closed the remaining distance in three quick strides.

He reached out and I froze, my heart pounding like a bird beating itself against the bars of a cage. His fingertips traced the gash on my temple, his frown deepening as he touched each stitch.

"What happened?"

The two words were so full of concern that I almost crumbled. But then I remembered the empty table at Bonnie and Clyde and the feeling of Jimmy's hands on my shoulders and the smell of Derby's breath as he leaned over me in the hospital.

I knocked his hand aside and stepped back. "Nothing. I fell."

He glanced at my neck. The collar of my shirt had slipped down just far enough to show the edge of the bruises, bruises that looked like fingerprints. I tugged the collar back up.

Not fast enough.

Jason swore under his breath. "Did something happen at the club?"

I struggled to keep my voice steady, but it cracked around the edges. "Nothing happened. I tripped and fell."

"Right." Jason's cheeks flushed as though he had a fever, and he unfastened the top two buttons of his coat. "Is that why you haven't answered your phone and Kyle told me to leave you alone for a couple of days? Because you fell?"

The anger in his voice brought mine rushing to the surface. He didn't have the right to be angry, not when he had disappeared. I was the one Jimmy and Alexis had followed and hurt. I had woken up in the hospital and had had to listen while that Fisher woman implied that I was weak and confused. And I was the one Derby had gone to with his threats.

Nothing had touched Jason. Nothing ever touched Jason.

My vision blurred and I closed my eyes. I would *not* cry in front of him. If I did, he'd never let this go. He'd find out the truth and Derby would come after the both of us. In that moment, I hated him.

I opened my eyes.

Voice low and earnest, Jason said, "If something happened, you can tell me. I can help."

I choked back a bitter laugh. The idea of Jason helping anyone was ludicrous.

"Mac . . ."

I shook my head. "Where were you? Friday night, at the club, where were you?"

He sighed and pushed his hair back with both hands, leaving it sticking up in little peaks and valleys. "I saw you talking with Ethan and I went to the guys' room to—"

"Puke your guts out?"

He blushed. "I blacked out. When I came to, you were gone."

"And you didn't go looking for me." *Kyle would have gone looking for me. Kyle did go looking for me. Part of this is your fault. You wanted to go to Bonnie and Clyde. You weren't there.*

My head pounded with the effort of holding the words back. And all to protect him from Derby—even after he hadn't protected me.

Masochistic friendship at its best.

And I was so tired of it.

Jason spread his hands. "I'm sorry, all right? Be mad if you want, but at least tell me what happened."

I crossed my arms. Uttering each word slowly and distinctly, I said, "I told you. I. Fell."

"*Mac,*" he breathed my name like a curse. His face looked haunted, the way it had in the weeks after Amy's death. "Whatever happened, you can tell me. If someone hurt you, I'll . . ." He clenched his fists at his side. There were scrapes on his knuckles, ones that hadn't been there a day and a half ago.

For a moment, my resolve shook. I wanted to believe in Jason. I wanted to believe he could be strong and capable and someone I could turn to when I was in trouble.

I wanted to believe he could be the way he used to be.

"I can help you. Let me help you."

I stared into his bloodshot eyes and then glanced at the slight bulge on the left side of his jacket, the telltale bulk of a bottle. A slow, painful ache built in my chest.

Maybe the old Jason would have been able to help me.

Not this one. Not this wreck who had slowly replaced my Jason over the weeks and months until it was hard to remember a time when I counted on him for anything. I took a deep breath. "When was the last time you were able to help anyone?"

For a split second, he looked stunned, and then his face slid into a cold, impassive mask. He looked like his father: handsome and cruel. "Fine," he said, turning and heading for the door. So softly that I almost didn't catch it, he added, "You're worse than Amy when it comes to secrets."

Amy.

I remembered what she had said in my dream, the hints that Derby might not want her killer to be found right away. And I remembered the thought I'd had after the Tracker meeting, the idea that maybe I could do something to find the thing responsible for her death.

A year ago, one of Jason's uncles had been arrested for fraud. One call from Jason's father and it had all been swept under the rug. At the time, people complained that the police department would do anything for a Sheffield.

Jason reached for the knob.

"There is something you can do for me." The words came out in a rush and left an acidic taste in my mouth.

He froze. "What's that?"

"I want the police report on Amy."

Jason turned and gaped. "I don't have it."

"But you can get it." I was very certain of that. He just had to find the right person—or ask his father to get it for him.

123

He shook his head. "No."

"Please, Jason. I've never asked you for anything."

"Don't ask me for this. Ask me for anything else and I'll do it—just don't ask for this." His hands shook at his sides, just the slightest tremble. "Why do you even want it?"

I couldn't tell him the real reason. He wouldn't get it for me and he might tell Derby. I shivered, imagining what Derby's reaction would be if he thought I was meddling in the Trackers' business. And he would definitely consider Amy's death their domain.

"I just want to know more about what happened that night. I think it would help me deal with things."

Jason turned back to the door. "It wouldn't. Trust me. If I could forget everything about that night, I would."

Before I could argue, before I could ask again, he was gone.

13

"Mac?" Tess poked her head through the bath-room door. "Serena is on the phone. Do you want me to take a message?"

I put down the scissors I was holding and turned around.

Tess's eyebrows shot up so far that they were practically in orbit. "What in the name of all things holy did you do to your hair?"

I scrunched up my face and tugged on my new bangs. "It's not that bad, is it? I was trying to hide the stitches." The stupid gash on my forehead stood out like Harry Potter's lightning bolt. Even Jason, as oblivious as he was to everything, had noticed it right away.

"Hon, it looks like you were mauled by a Weedwacker."

Scowling, I held out my hand. Wisely, Tess passed me the phone and retreated without another word.

I glanced in the mirror as I pressed the phone to my ear. The bangs didn't look *that* bad. The art teacher I'd had last year was always going on about asymmetrical compositions. That's what the bangs were. Not crooked. Asymmetrical. "Hey, Serena."

"Good. You're alive. Now you can tell me why you haven't answered any of the texts or messages I've left you since Friday. Where have you been?"

My stomach knotted.

I couldn't tell Serena the truth. I trusted her, but I couldn't risk that she might accidentally let something slip to Jason. Besides, I had a feeling that the less people knew about my interaction with the Trackers, the safer they'd be.

I had even lied to Tess about Derby's visit.

"Jason and I went to Bonnie and Clyde and I lost my cell phone."

"Let me guess: you dropped it while rubbing soothing circles on Jason's back as he puked."

I sighed. "Something like that."

"Someone needs to tell him that the drunken and tragic antihero isn't all that sexy in real life. I ran into him last night and he was wobbling like a human dreidel. And the guys he was with—"

"Serena?"

"Yeah?"

"I really, *really* don't want to talk about Jason right now." I leaned against the bathroom sink and took a deep breath. I stared at my reflection. My eyes were dry, but they were red-rimmed and bloodshot. It had been hours since Jason had left, but I was still feeling shaky.

The silence on the other end of the line was heavy. I was pretty sure Serena was trying to figure out if she could pry without technically mentioning Jason's name. Finally, she said, "Do you want to do something tonight? There's a horror movie playing across the river."

I laughed. I couldn't help it. The idea of paying ten bucks for a scare right now was kind of hilarious—in a vomit-inducing way. "Rain check? I'm seeing Kyle later."

It took five minutes of promising Serena that she could pick the next two movies we saw, but I finally got off the phone.

Tess looked up as I walked into the living room. I perched on the arm of the couch and grimaced as the muscles in my back objected. It was nearing Advil time again.

She shuffled her Tarot deck—a gift from an ex who had tried to cultivate a new age streak she didn't actually posses.

"What are you doing with those things? You don't even know how to read them."

She shrugged and drew a card at random. "I just think they're pretty. Plus, I like to make up my own rules for them." She held up the seven of cups. "Like this one? Means they're totally going to be swamped at the Cat tonight."

"I don't need you to stay home," I said for the eighth time. I took a deep breath. "But I do need a favor."

Tess tucked a strand of pink hair behind her ear. Her eyes narrowed. "I hope you're not going to ask me if you can go out tonight."

"Just to Kyle's." There was no need to tell her that I wasn't entirely sure Kyle would let me in. I hadn't exactly lied when I told Serena that I was seeing him later: I was determined to see him—it was just that he had been ignoring my calls and texts all afternoon.

I tried to look sweet and angelic and responsible. "I was hoping I could borrow Dragon." Dragon was Tess's mostly green Toyota. The car was so old that they'd stopped making the right shade of touch-up paint, so every time Tess scratched the car—which was often—she just used the first tube of paint she came across.

"Mac . . ." Tess struggled to find the right words, her face more serious than I had ever seen it. "I know you don't want to talk about what happened, and I'm trying to respect that. You're tough—I get it—but I think you should take it easy and stay close to home for a few days. I can call the school tomorrow, see if you can miss some classes—"

I shook my head. "If I skip school, I'll go crazy. I need the distraction. And I want to see Kyle. Seeing Kyle is normal. Safe." Or it would be if he weren't a werewolf.

"Maybe I could go with you. I don't like the idea of you going out on your own." On a good day, Tess could pass for nineteen. She almost never looked over twenty-one. But the past forty-eight hours had left dark circles under her eyes and there were faint lines on her face that I'd never noticed—not wrinkles, not exactly. Worry lines, maybe.

I felt a twinge of guilt for putting her through so much. Part of me wanted to tell her that I'd stay in and we could order pizza, watch *Pretty in Pink,* and make fun of Molly Ringwald's prom dress. But I had to talk to Kyle.

The longer I waited to see him, the more awkward and tangled things would get. And the fact that he wasn't answering my texts or calls worried me. A lot.

"I'll be fine. Really. I'll go straight to Kyle's and I'll keep the car doors locked and I won't drive over twenty miles an hour."

Tess bit her lip and studied my face. After a very long minute, she asked, "Do you really need to see Kyle tonight?"

I nodded. "Yeah. I really do."

She sighed and stood. "Okay. You can borrow Dragon. But first we have to fix the mess you've made of your hair."

Tess almost always parked on the street. She told Ben she did it to save time, but I knew it was really because the pigeons that hung around the back of the building freaked her out. We'd watched *The Birds* last year, and ever since, she claimed the pigeons were just biding time before making their move.

For some reason, 90 percent of Tess's fears seemed to come from movies we watched on cable.

I walked down the crumbling stone pathway that led to the street and passed a black sedan with tinted windows and Tennessee plates. It looked too nice to belong to anyone in the building, but there were a few college students living on the first and second floors; maybe someone's parents were visiting.

I unlocked Dragon, slid behind the wheel, and adjusted the seat to compensate for the fact that Tess's legs were practically a mile longer than mine.

"You'd so better be home," I muttered as I started toward Kyle's. I'd sent a dozen texts and left at least six voice mail messages over the last four hours. Unless there was something wrong with his phone, he had some serious explaining to do.

My wrist ached slightly as I gripped the steering wheel, but it was bearable. I hardly noticed it after the first few minutes.

I turned off Elmwood and glanced in the mirror. The sedan was behind me.

Coincidence. Had to be.

I took the next right. The sedan was still there, an ominous, black blot in my rearview mirror.

I swallowed and tried to ignore the way the muscles in my chest tightened. I wasn't being followed. That was off-the-charts paranoid. Why would anyone want to follow me? All I was doing was going to Kyle's.

And Kyle wasn't important. He was just . . .

The werewolf who had saved my life and infected Branson Derby's nephew.

Fighting the urge to floor the gas pedal, I took the next two lefts and then another right, driving in a large, circuitous route that didn't actually go anywhere. The black car copied every turn.

I nudged the car up to thirty. The sedan didn't speed up—almost like whoever was driving knew they had spooked me—but it still followed.

Another turn put me squarely in the upscale part of downtown, the three-block stretch that was occupied mostly by small galleries and boutiques. Being Sunday evening, the stores were empty and dark. Even the coffee shop was closed.

Gripping the steering wheel so tightly that my knuckles

turned white and my wrist throbbed, I debated my options. I could go home. I could go somewhere completely random, like the mall. But I couldn't lead them to Kyle. Maybe they weren't Trackers. Maybe there was nothing to worry about. Maybe—

Without thinking, I hung a left so suddenly that horns blared and tires squealed. Potter's Lane was little more than a passageway connecting two streets—used exclusively by pedestrians—but I knew it was just wide enough for Dragon to squeeze through. Jason had tried it the one time I'd been stupid enough to let him drive Tess's car.

I heard an ear-grating crunch and hit the brakes just long enough to safely look in the mirror. The sedan had tried to follow, but it was too wide to fit between the brick buildings. The front of the car had crumpled like tinfoil.

A cacophony of horns sounded behind me as I headed for Kyle's.

The sun was just starting to dip below the horizon as I shifted my weight from one foot to the other and rang Kyle's doorbell a second time.

I glanced nervously up and down Salinger Drive. The Harper house was the last door on a sleepy, dead-end street. The homes in this neighborhood weren't as large or as new as the ones by Jason's place, but they were still a far cry from the apartment I shared with Tess. A lot of them were owned by people who worked in Hemlock's medical research industry, like Kyle's parents.

A few lawns down, a group of kids chased one another

in a game that looked like a cross between tag and hide-and-seek, but otherwise, the street was quiet. Still, I was filled with so much nervous energy that my skin itched. I kept expecting another black car to roll down the block, and I couldn't shake the feeling that someone was watching me, even though the only eyes I saw belonged to the three slightly creepy garden gnomes that hung out in Mrs. Harper's flower beds.

A shadow moved toward the door, just visible through the frosted glass, and then, suddenly, Kyle was in the open doorway, staring down at me with an expression that hovered between surprise and annoyance.

"Are your parents home?"

He blinked, like it took him a second to process the sentence, before saying, "No. They're out."

I breathed a sigh of relief. "Great. I need to stash Dragon in your garage." Before Kyle could ask me why or object, I was down the driveway and behind the wheel. After a couple of minutes, the garage door slowly rolled up.

I left the car in the spot usually occupied by the Subaru Kyle's dad drove and walked through the door that connected the garage to the kitchen.

Kyle was waiting inside. Arms crossed, he leaned against the stainless steel refrigerator. The last rays of orange light filtered through the window, throwing highlights over his hair and casting his face in shadow. "And the Toyota had to be in the garage because . . . ?"

I bit my lip. "There was a car hanging around outside my apartment building. I think it was following me."

The change in Kyle was instant. One second he was the boy I had been friends with for years, and the next he looked like someone hard and dangerous. He pushed away from the refrigerator and started for the door, tension rolling off him in waves.

"It's okay." The anxiety emanating from Kyle made it hard to find my voice, made me a little breathless. "I lost them on the way over. I just didn't want anyone to spot Dragon in your driveway."

I tried to say it matter-of-factly, like this was the sort of thing that happened to me every day. I didn't want to feed Kyle's anxiety with my own when his was already thick enough to choke on.

"Why would someone be following you?"

I pushed my hair back from my face, not missing the way Kyle's eyes darted to the stitches on my forehead. "Derby showed up at the hospital. I told the police that I didn't know the identity of the wolf that saved me, but he didn't believe me."

Kyle cursed under his breath. "They were following you because of me. Because they thought you'd lead them to a werewolf."

"Maybe not." It was cold in the kitchen, but that had nothing to do with why I was suddenly trembling. Even just talking about what had happened in the hospital set my pulse racing. "Derby didn't just ask me about the werewolf." I realized I was talking about Kyle in the third person and shook my head. "About you," I amended. "He also warned me not to tell Jason what happened to me after I left the club. Derby has some sort of *plan*"—the word was like cotton in my mouth and I had to struggle to spit it out—"for Jason, and he's worried I'll screw it up. He made it sound like he'd hurt Jason if I told him."

Kyle's eyes blazed. "What sort of plan?"

I sighed and leaned against the kitchen counter. That was the worst part: not knowing why Derby was so interested in Jason. "I have no idea, but I don't think he wants to start a bowling league."

Despite the gravity of the situation, I waited for the ghost of a smile to cross Kyle's face. It didn't.

"Are you going to tell him?"

"How can I?" My stomach twisted. If I told Jason, and Derby followed through on his threat, I'd never forgive myself.

Kyle stared intently at a spot on the wall just beyond my shoulder. "So Jason gets off scot-free. He doesn't have to deal with any guilt, because he'll never know what happened to you or that he could have stopped it." Kyle clenched his fist, like he wanted to hit something, and let out a low, mirthless chuckle. "That's just great."

I took a hesitant step toward him. "Kyle—"

He shook his head. "Forget about it. It doesn't matter."

It obviously did, but not knowing what to say, I stupidly said the first thing that popped into my head. "Where are your parents?"

"They went to my aunt's. They won't be home until late."

"Oh."

"Yeah."

"Were you avoiding me?" I asked just as Kyle said, "It's okay if you don't want to be alone with a werewolf."

"I was trying to give you space," Kyle answered just as I said, "I'm not worried about being alone with you."

"Sorry."

"Sorry."

He looked so miserable and lonely that, suddenly, all I wanted to do was find a way to make it better. Make him better. I crossed the few feet that separated us. "Ummm, Kyle?"

"Yeah?" he muttered.

"You're kind of a bonehead." He opened his mouth, but I rushed on before he could say anything. "If I'm seeking you out—like, you know, say, *calling you*—I don't need space." Then, before I could change my mind or worry that he'd pull away, I hugged him.

Every muscle in his body stiffened and my heart stutter-skipped, but I didn't let go. I turned my face so that my cheek lay against the cotton of Kyle's shirt, and I pressed my palms flat to his back.

It's still Kyle, I told myself, breathing in the scent of his deodorant and the laundry detergent his mom used and the slight cinnamon smell from his favorite gum. Underneath that was a new scent—something that reminded me of forest earth and cedar trees—but I didn't let myself dwell on that.

I didn't let myself think of brick walls and brown fur and bright red blood or the way Jimmy Tyler's screams had echoed in my ears.

After a long moment, Kyle put his arms around me and rested his chin against the top of my head.

"I've missed this," I admitted, voice slightly muffled against his shirt. When Kyle and Heather had started getting serious, we'd imposed a mutual ban on things like hugging. Even after they'd broken up, the ban seemed to have stayed in place.

Kyle pressed a kiss to the crown of my head and my face inexplicably flooded with warmth as something fluttered in my stomach. "What was that for?"

He shrugged against me. "For not bolting," he said, voice rough.

Kyle pulled away and I felt unsteady and a little lost. He headed for the door but I stayed rooted to the spot.

"C'mon," he said softly. "No use standing in the kitchen all night."

I followed him downstairs but stopped with my foot on the last step. *What's wrong with you?* I asked myself. *You've been in Kyle's room hundreds of times.*

Kyle turned. "Mac?"

I shook my head. I couldn't explain that my hesitation had nothing to do with the fact that he was infected and everything to do with the fluttery feeling I'd gotten when he wrapped his arms around me.

Mutely, I followed him to his room.

Kyle switched on the desk lamp. The bulb flickered and then cast a warm glow over the familiar wood-paneled walls, plaid curtains, and movie posters. A year ago, Kyle had convinced his parents to let him turn the basement rec room into a bedroom. His bed and desk were near the door. He'd set up the other half of the large room as a sort of lounge with a forty-two-inch TV—the predecessor to the flat-screen upstairs—and a sofa that was probably older than he was.

I sat on the edge of the unmade bed and suddenly thought of Heather. I'd never asked for details, but she must have been down here. The thought of Heather and Kyle in his room—on his bed—made my stomach twist in a way I didn't totally understand and definitely didn't like.

Kyle grabbed the swivel chair from his desk and rolled it toward the bed. "You must have questions." He sat down and leaned forward, watching my face intently, like he was the one looking for answers.

It took me a minute to realize he was talking about the fact that he was a werewolf. Not exactly an easy thing to forget—at least it shouldn't have been.

"Have you told your parents?" I asked, forcing myself to focus.

He shook his head.

"Are you going to?"

He hesitated. "I don't know," he admitted eventually.

"How did you get it? And how long have you had it?" I swallowed. *How long have you been keeping things from me?*

Kyle took a deep breath, like he had picked up on the question I hadn't asked. That was one of the differences between him and Jason: Kyle always gave just as much weight and consideration to the things I didn't say as to the things I did.

"I got it from Heather. About five weeks ago. I didn't know she was infected and we were fooling around and then arguing and then she . . . sorta . . . she started to shift and she . . ." He ran a hand through his hair.

I blushed. "Bit you? Scratched you?" It took thirty days from bite or scratch to first change. In a way, though Kyle had contracted LS over a month ago, he'd only been a full-fledged, shape-shifting werewolf for about a week.

He nodded. "Scratched." He spun in the chair and slowly pulled up his shirt. "She picked it up in Seattle when she was visiting her cousin."

I clenched my teeth and sucked in a sharp breath at the sight of five livid scars running from his upper back to the waistband of his jeans. Without thinking, I reached out and touched one of the marks. I gently ran a finger down it—almost the same way Jason had traced the gash on my temple.

"Does it hurt?" I asked, voice coming out strangled. I was going to kill Heather Yoshida.

"It did. Not so much now."

I stared at Kyle's scarred, ruined back, and my eyes filled with tears. Someone should have protected him. I should have protected him. Angrily, I brushed the tears away. It wasn't fair to cry when he was the one who had been hurt. "Did she do it on purpose?"

Kyle let his shirt fall back down. "I don't know," he admitted.

He turned to face me and his eyes widened. "Are you *crying*?" He sounded a little panicked, like the sight of a crying girl was scarier than anything that had happened over the past forty-eight hours.

I dropped my gaze to my knees and clenched my fists.

Kyle rolled the chair closer, so close that my legs were between his. "Mac?"

I shook my head. So far, the tears hadn't fallen, but if I looked at him—if I thought about how much it must have hurt and how scared he must have been—it would be like a dam breaking.

Kyle reached out and gently tilted my chin up, forcing me to meet his eyes. The expression in them was sad and a little broken.

He swallowed. "Don't cry for me, Mac. Please don't." He leaned forward and rested his forehead against mine. "I'm not worth it."

My heart skipped several beats and then raced to catch up. I felt like I had stepped off a cliff and was plunging forty thousand feet. "Kyle, I—"

I was still fumbling for the right words when he pressed his lips to mine.

It wasn't hesitant or awkward or the way you'd kiss your best friend. It was soft and sure and full of heat. And it was the easiest thing for my lips to part, for me to reach up and pull him closer as his hands gently cupped my face and then trailed down my neck and along my shoulders.

Somehow, we both ended up on the bed, my back pressed to the mattress and Kyle leaning on his elbows so he wouldn't crush me. A low growl trickled from his throat—a sound that had nothing to do with his being a werewolf.

"I have," he said, between kisses, "been wanting. To do that. For two years." He gently brushed the hair back from my face, caressing my temple with the pad of his thumb.

It was ridiculously hard to think when he kissed me. I swallowed and tried to get my pulse back under control. "You never said anything."

He gazed down at me and the spark in his eyes sent shivers—the good kind—along my spine.

"I thought you'd freak and bolt."

I blushed. Would I have freaked? Maybe. I'd always been so busy insisting that Kyle and I were just friends that I had never stopped to ask myself—really ask myself—if I wanted more. Sometimes, though, when I was half-asleep and too tired to self-edit, I wondered what kissing Kyle would be like.

My imagination hadn't come close.

"Well," I said, head spinning, "I've neither freaked nor bolted. Your move."

I expected him to kiss me again—wanted him to kiss me again—but a dark, almost pained look slid across his face.

He pushed himself away from me and sat on the edge of the bed. Icy tendrils spread through my chest, killing all the warmth that had been building. "Kyle?"

"This was a mistake," he said, voice so low that I had to strain to hear. "I shouldn't have . . ." He took a deep breath. "It was a mistake." He stood and walked away from the bed.

I sat up and grabbed Kyle's pillow. I hugged it to my chest. It took me three tries to get a single word out. "Why?"

He turned and stared at me, eyes wide and full of dis-belief. *"Why?"* he echoed. "I'm a monster, Mac. In what scenario *wouldn't* this be a mistake?"

I set the pillow aside and started to push myself to my feet, but he stopped me with a single, cutting word. "Don't."

"You're not a monster, Kyle."

"Do you remember that night in the alley? Do you remember what happened before you passed out?"

I shook my head and looked away from him. I didn't want to remember. I felt a phantom grip on my arms, a ghostly throb on the back of my skull where it had hit the brick wall. "You saved me," I whispered.

Kyle was in front of me in an instant. Out of the corner of my eye, I saw him sink to his knees, but I couldn't look at him.

"After that," he prodded. "What happened between Jimmy letting you go and you passing out?"

"It doesn't matter," I said as I squeezed my eyes shut and tried not to remember the color of the werewolf's fur— Kyle's fur—and the way Jimmy had screamed. "Why are you doing this?"

Kyle touched my cheek and my eyes sprang open.

"Because you need to understand," he said. "Whatever else I was—whoever I used to be—I'm one of the monsters."

"Not everyone infected with LS—"

The desperation on Kyle's face stopped the words in my throat. "Is a monster. I know. But I nearly eviscerated a man. I wanted to kill him, Mac. I think I would have if you hadn't started coming to. That isn't very human."

He stood in a fluid, graceful movement and looked down at me. "Anyway, it doesn't matter. I'm turning myself in. I'm going to the LSRB."

Before I could make my throat work, before I could argue, Kyle walked out of the room. I heard his feet on the stairs, but I didn't follow. I couldn't stand. I felt like I was being ripped apart.

The LSRB.

The Lupine Syndrome Registration Bureau.

It was like a cross between the CIA and the CDC. It was the government organization that ran the tip lines, investigated potential infections, and oversaw the camps.

I pushed myself back on the bed until my shoulders were against the wall, and then I pulled my knees to my chest. He wasn't serious. He couldn't be serious. If Kyle walked into the local LSRB office, they'd send him directly to a camp. He'd be cut off from everything and everyone.

Once you walked through the camp gates, you were dead to the rest of the world.

And the camps themselves were horrible. The government did a good job of keeping the conditions secret, but everyone had heard the rumors of overcrowding and food shortages and killings. Anything could happen to Kyle in a place like that.

Tears slid down my face.

I had to talk him out of it. The LS tip line didn't take calls on Sundays, so Kyle would have to wait for the local LSRB office to open in the morning before he could do anything stupid.

That gave me one night to change his mind. Panic swelled in my chest, but I pushed it down. There was no reason to panic, because I was going to fix this.

There had to be a way to fix this.

I wiped my face on my sleeve. I'd keep watch on him twenty-four/seven. I'd even find some way to lock him up if I had to. I wasn't sure how you could restrain a teenage werewolf, but I'd find a way. Jason could help. With a sinking feeling, I remembered Derby's threat. Maybe there was some way to tell Jason that Kyle was infected without telling him *why* Kyle wanted to turn himself in.

He would help, wouldn't he? A decade of friendship had to outweigh a few Tracker meetings. It just had to.

The rest of the house was quiet. I wondered if I should go upstairs and check on Kyle or if he was going to come back down. Maybe I could—

With a noise like splintering ice, the window above me exploded.

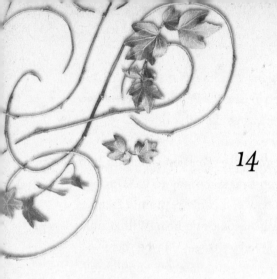

14

I threw my arms up, instinctively covering my head as shards of glass rained down. When I was sure it was safe, I looked up. There was a ragged, gaping hole where the window above the bed had been. The night breeze tossed the curtains, and bits of glass were everywhere: in my hair, lodged in the folds of my clothes, covering the sheets.

"Mac!" I heard Kyle's shout and the sound of feet pounding across the kitchen. Then, suddenly, there was a defending crash followed by silence.

The Trackers.

They had managed to follow me.

They knew Kyle was infected.

I had led them here.

I had led them to Kyle.

Nicking my arms and hands on bits of glass, I scrambled off the bed and raced for the door. Halfway there, I tripped and looked back. One of the garden gnomes from the front yard was lying in the middle of the carpet, its head severed by the impact.

There was a huge thud upstairs. Heart seizing in my chest, I took the stairs two at a time and threw myself over the landing and into the kitchen.

I was prepared for a crowd of Jimmy Tylers; instead, I got 105 pounds of furious ex-girlfriend.

Kyle's eyes—wide and panicked—flicked to mine, just for an instant, and then locked back on Heather.

"You have to calm down." He reached toward her and she jerked back.

A low sound trickled out of her throat, more animalistic than human. The broken remains of the Harpers' kitchen table were piled at her feet, and the French doors that led to the backyard were hanging off their hinges.

"I saw you." Heather's voice was usually annoyingly musical and sweet. Now she sounded like someone who had just smoked two packs of cigarettes and chased them down with a thimble of turpentine.

Tears ran down her face and she didn't make any effort to wipe them away. "I saw you, Kyle. Through the window."

Every ounce of blood in my body rushed to my face as I was flooded with embarrassment and fury. "You were watching us?" I took a step forward, forgetting—or maybe just not caring—that Heather was infected.

She made a lunge for me, but Kyle was suddenly there, blocking her path. "You have to leave." His voice was a low snarl.

Heather tried to force her way past him. Her eyes were the wrong shape—too large and too far apart. Her jaw jutted out the way a jaw shouldn't, and her cheekbones were in slightly the wrong place. Her face was changing in small, horrific ways as I watched.

I stepped backward, and my hip collided with a plant stand. A pot of ivy went crashing to the ground, scattering shards of clay and clumps of dirt across the tile floor.

Heather swiped at Kyle with a hand that was no longer human. It was long and twisted and tipped with thick claws that sunk effortlessly into his shoulder.

Kyle let out a howl of pain as he staggered back. He clamped one hand to his ripped and bloody shirt as he fell to his knees.

Heather stared at her own hand in dismay, like she couldn't quite believe what she had done.

I ran forward and reached for Kyle, but his spine bowed and he let out a ragged yell. "Keep away!"

I backed up until I reached the far wall and then watched, powerless, as Kyle's body tore itself apart with the sound of hundreds of twigs snapping at once. I pressed my hands to my ears, trying to block out the sounds as bones shattered, muscles shifted, and fur replaced skin.

When it was over, the boy I had kissed was gone, replaced by a large, brown wolf.

Heather shook her head and stared at Kyle. "I'm sorry," she said, the words coming out twisted because her mouth was no longer the right shape.

She reached up to wipe the tears from her face and my stomach lurched in disgust and rage as she left a trail of blood—Kyle's blood—on her cheek.

The wolf advanced on her, teeth bared and hackles raised.

"Please, Kyle." Her gaze darted to me and she snarled.

Kyle let out a furious bark and continued his slow advance, herding her toward the broken doors.

"I didn't mean to hurt you," Heather said. "I . . . I love you."

Kyle kept pressing forward, and she didn't resist—not even as he forced her out into the yard.

Heather shot me one last, hate-filled glare and then turned and ran.

I stood in the ruined kitchen and stared, dazed, at the werewolf in front of me.

Kyle.

The wolf turned away from the gaping door and regarded me with its animal eyes.

Still Kyle, I reminded myself. *It's still Kyle.*

The air around the wolf seemed to shimmer as fur flowed back into skin. Muscles and bones straightened, the process somehow less terrifying in reverse. After a moment, Kyle was Kyle again.

Completely Kyle.

Every. Naked. Inch.

He climbed unsteadily to his feet, facing away from me.

I had seen Kyle in the pool at Jason's plenty of times. But this wasn't the pool. And Kyle was not wearing swim trunks. Given what we had been doing twenty minutes ago, the blood rushed to my face.

"Are you all right?" He sounded exhausted.

I swallowed. Cleared my throat. "Yeah."

"Could you turn around?"

My face burned with enough heat to destroy a small forest. "Um. Sure." I turned my back and crossed my arms. Wow. It was suddenly 120 percent easier to think.

"Give me three minutes," he said.

I waited until I heard him cross the kitchen and head down the stairs before I turned around. I walked over to the broken kitchen table and prodded the wreckage with one foot.

I wanted to be far, far away when Kyle tried explaining the mess to his parents.

Figuring my three minutes were up, I headed down to Kyle's room, gripping the banister because my legs felt unsteady. What would Heather have done to me if Kyle hadn't been here?

I paused in his doorway. Kyle was standing in front of the closet. He'd put on a pair of jeans and his black Vans, but he was shirtless.

He turned and I gasped.

I crossed the room and lightly pressed my hand to Kyle's shoulder. The skin was smooth and perfect, like Heather had never touched him. I knew werewolves healed superhuman fast, but there was a difference between knowing something and seeing proof.

Kyle closed his eyes, just for a second, and let out a slow breath. "She could have scratched you. Or worse."

I shuddered and let my hand drop. My muscles trembled with the aftereffects of an adrenaline rush. I felt like I had just downed a pot of black coffee after pulling an all-nighter.

Glancing around the room, I said the first thing that

entered my head. "She killed the garden gnome."

Kyle stared at me like I had lost my mind.

I pointed at the headless gnome. "It's what she used to break the window. Maybe you could glue his head back on." A high, slightly manic laugh bubbled in my chest. There were a hundred things to be worried about, and I was babbling about a tacky lawn ornament. I clamped a hand over my mouth, worried the laugh would turn into sobs if I let it escape.

My life hadn't felt this out of control since I'd lived with Hank.

Who was I kidding? Things had never felt this out of control.

"You can't turn yourself in."

"Mac—"

"No." I shook my head. "I lost Amy to a werewolf. I'm losing Jason to the Trackers. I can't lose you, too."

Kyle put a hand on my arm. "You'd be okay."

He couldn't possibly think that. Not really. "I'd spend the rest of my life not knowing if you were all right and wondering if you were still alive. Okay isn't even a remote possibility."

Kyle dropped his hand and stepped back. "You should head home," he said, voice completely blank, like the last hour had never happened. "My parents will be back soon."

I clenched my fists. "I'm not leaving until you promise not to turn yourself in."

"Mac . . ."

Knowing it was playing dirty but not knowing what else

to do, I said, "If you turn yourself in, Derby will assume I knew you were the one who saved me. I'll become a target. Besides, Heather might try to kill me. You know how competitive she gets. She can't stand losing a parking space."

Kyle stared at me, a stricken expression on his face, and I felt slightly sick at how I was manipulating his protective nature. I reached for his hand, but he moved away. I tried not to feel hurt and failed.

"I need some space. A few days to figure things out."

I opened my mouth to argue, but he cut me off. "Please, Mac."

"Promise you won't turn yourself in, and I'll give you space."

"I promise I won't do anything without telling you first." The expression on Kyle's face was hard and resolute. It didn't leave any room for argument.

It was the best I was going to get. "Okay," I said—even though it wasn't really okay at all.

Kyle glanced out the broken window. "You really should go home. It's getting late and Tess will be worried."

I felt like an invisible door was slamming shut between us.

I bit my lip. "Kyle. About what happened before . . . about what Heather saw . . ." I trailed off, unable to find the right words and scared of saying the wrong thing.

He exhaled slowly. "Mac. I meant what I said. It was a mistake."

I had been caught off guard by the kiss. I hadn't asked for or expected it. There was absolutely no reason to feel like something important was being ripped away. Kyle and I would go back to normal—or as normal as we could be— and I'd try to forget the way he had held me and pressed his lips to mine.

"Are you all right?" he asked warily.

"Sure," I lied as I turned and headed for the stairs. So softly that only a werewolf could hear, I added, "You can't lose what you never had."

I managed to make it across the bridge before the tears got so bad that I had to pull over. And then, sitting in the dark car on a deserted street, I cried like my heart was breaking.

15

THREE DAYS IN THE REAL WORLD IS PRACTICALLY nothing. It blends together and is over quickly and soon forgotten. But time passes differently in high school—especially when you're not talking to either of your two best friends.

Kyle wanted space and I was trying to give it to him. And Jason . . .

I couldn't talk to Jason. The text messages he kept sending me made it clear he thought I was ignoring him because he had refused to get me the police report. That was part of it—a big part—but there was also Derby.

If I didn't talk to Jason, I couldn't put him in danger.

Twice I'd spotted a dark sedan outside of school and I'd seen Trackers hanging around the parking lot and hallways. They didn't make any effort to cover their tattoos or blend in. A few times I'd seen them talking to Jason.

Even Derby himself seemed to be taking an unusually high interest in the students. They had let him hold an information session yesterday afternoon about the Trackers' new incentive program: hand over the name of a werewolf and—provided they turned out to really be infected—you'd get a thousand-dollar reward. It was rumored that Senator Walsh was putting up the money, although, publically, he denied it.

I hadn't gone to the info session, but Serena said the gym had been packed.

There was only one reason the Trackers would be so interested in Kennedy after what had happened with Riley Parker: they still thought there were werewolves on campus.

My stomach knotted as I spotted Alexis Perry.

She slammed her locker door shut. "Happy?" she asked.

I looked away and kept walking, trying to ignore the sensation that things were crawling over my skin. She had been there. She had watched—had helped—Jimmy drag me into that alley.

"They sent him away because of you," she hissed, just loudly enough for me to hear.

A scathing reply flew to my lips and I almost stopped, but then I saw Jason. He was leaning against the door-frame of an empty classroom, talking to some girl who had transferred at the beginning of the year. She was wearing a ridiculously tight red T-shirt with the words *Hunt or be Hunted* across the front. Hmmm. Skanky and she shopped on the Tracker website. What a keeper.

I couldn't say anything to Alexis without it turning into a fight. And I couldn't start a fight without Jason finding out what had really happened. I closed my mouth and kept walking.

Jason called out my name as I passed, but I just stared at the floor and quickened my pace, anger and frustration radiating off me in waves as a roaring sound filled my ears.

Three days of this. I so wasn't going to make it through the week. I bit my lip and wished—for about the millionth time—that Amy was here. Not the dream Amy who'd been haunting me at night but the real one. She'd know what to say or do to take my mind off things, to make them seem bearable.

Of course, with Amy around, none of this would be happening.

I rounded a corner and practically steamrolled Ethan Cole. He tried to ask me something—I didn't even register the words—but I just mumbled an excuse and kept going. Up the stairs. A right. Through the glass doors. Into the library.

The quiet hum of the air-conditioning and the musty smell of reference books enveloped me and I sucked in a deep, calming breath. Since it was noon, the library was dependably deserted, save for a few die-hard geeks who were sharing gaming strategies at one of the long study tables.

I walked past the new computer stations—donated by Jason's father to keep him from getting suspended last May—and headed for the nonfiction section at the back.

The health books were in the third aisle. I scanned the titles, looking for anything on LS. I needed more information on lupine syndrome than they gave us in health class—both to try and figure out anything I could about

the werewolf that had gone after Amy and to try and understand this whole new part of Kyle's life. A part of his life
that I could probably never fully comprehend.

There would be more books at the public library, but
they had one of those detectors at the door that beeped
when you tried to take things without checking them out.

Maybe it was extra paranoid on my part, but if I were
a creepy hate group dedicated to finding and eradicating
werewolves, I'd try to get the library records and see who
had checked out the books on LS.

If the Trackers really did have the full support of the
police department, that probably wouldn't be too hard.

Ideally, I wouldn't need books at all, but searching for
information about lupine syndrome online had proved to be
insanely frustrating. I'd found some stuff on the CDC and
LSRB websites, but a lot of it was slanted toward the risk
of LS and the reasons to report infected people. When I'd
tried using a search engine, the results had been even more
useless.

Giving my head a small shake, I crouched down to scan
the bottom shelves.

A wave of dizziness hit me and I had to grip the nearest
shelf to keep from toppling over. My dreams of Amy had
been getting steadily worse. The one last night had been so
bad that I'd been scared to go back to sleep. I had downed
cup after cup of coffee and watched infomercials until dawn.

The dizziness passed and I peered at the books in front
of me. There were only two on LS: *The Wolf Inside* and *Managing an Epidemic*.

I unzipped my backpack and slipped both books inside—right next to the thick stack of notes and computer printouts I'd gathered on the Hemlock attacks and murders. Jason might not have gotten me Amy's police report, but that didn't mean I couldn't find out things on my own. Unlike reliable information on LS, details about the Hemlock attacks had been pretty easy to find online.

"Umm . . . Mac?"

I looked up. Serena was standing at the end of the aisle, frowning.

"Why are you stealing those books? The library doesn't charge for them, you know."

She walked over to me, her heels clicking against the tile floor.

I raised an eyebrow. "Since when do you hang out in the library at lunch?"

"Since I saw Alexis Perry try to melt the flesh from your bones with only the power of her cross-eyed, inbred stare. Which was remarkably like the death glare Heather Yoshida was shooting you all through English. Which all comes on top of the sprained wrist and the stitches in your forehead—neither of which you'll explain." Tucking a strand of hair behind her ear, she fixed me with a no-nonsense, "spill it" gaze.

"I told you, I—"

"Fell. Right." Serena frowned. "*Which I told you* is the most cliché excuse in the book."

I sighed and shifted my weight so that I was sitting on the floor with my back against the shelves. There really wasn't a better place to have a private conversation at lunch.

Most people had accepted the falling story, but Serena had been relentlessly trying to get the truth out of me. I didn't want to tell her—I figured she'd be safer if she didn't know—but I couldn't keep dodging the same questions over and over.

Following my lead, Serena sank gracefully to the floor, smoothing down the orange skirt she was wearing so that she wouldn't flash anyone who happened to wander past.

"You have to swear you won't tell anyone. *Seriously* swear."

She nodded.

"You heard about Derby's nephew, right?" It was a rhetorical question. Everyone had. Of course, they'd heard only the story the Trackers were putting out, the one that painted Jimmy as the tragic victim of another werewolf attack.

"Before he was attacked, I had a run in with him at Bonnie and Clyde. He hit on me and I embarrassed him. He followed me out of the bar and shoved me up against a wall. That's how I got the sprain and the cut." I couldn't tell her the rest—the parts about Kyle—so I added, "Some guy coming out of the club saw and stopped him."

Serena's eyes glinted. "But you were with Jason?"

I shook my head. I didn't want to tell her that Jason had passed out and abandoned me—admitting the truth hurt too much. "I didn't feel like babysitting him, so I went outside to call a cab."

She didn't look convinced. "It doesn't sound like something you'd have to lie about."

I gently rubbed my wrist. "Derby asked me not to tell anyone—asked and implied it would be very bad if I refused the request. I think he was worried people would feel less outraged about the attack if they knew his nephew had roughed up a girl earlier in the evening."

Serena's eyes narrowed. "That's evil."

You don't know the half of it, I thought. "Anyway, Alexis had a crush on the guy. She was angry when he flirted with me. Hence the glaring."

"And Heather?"

Heather had been absent Monday and Tuesday. English was the first I'd seen her since her meltdown at Kyle's. I'd spent the entire class gripping the edge of my desk, convinced she was going to leap across the room and go for my throat.

I couldn't tell Serena that Heather was a werewolf—or about everything that was going on with Kyle—but take *werewolf* out of the equation, and I did have a boy problem. Serena was good at boy problems.

I'd had a grand total of one relationship, which had lasted all of five weeks. I was so out of my depth.

Staring at a crack in the tile floor, trying to ignore the warmth flooding my face, I said, "Kyle and I kissed. And Heather saw us. And then Kyle said he needed space." The words tripped over each other, each leaving me feeling worse than the last.

"So that's why I haven't seen you and Kyle together since last week?"

"Yeah." I looked over to gauge Serena's reaction.

She studied me thoughtfully. "Who kissed who?"

"He kissed me." I remembered the way Kyle had pressed his lips to mine, so sure and steady, without the slightest bit of hesitation. My stomach knotted.

"And did you want him to kiss you?"

"I wasn't expecting it. But I didn't want him to stop. And I definitely kissed him back. It felt . . ." I trailed off, not sure how to articulate it.

Serena summed it up in a single word. "Right?"

I nodded. "Until Heather showed up." I thought about it. "Or I guess it went wrong before that. She saw us through his window, but before she rang the doorbell"—*busted through the back door and destroyed the kitchen*—"Kyle said it was a mistake."

Something twisted deep inside my chest and my voice got oddly thick. "He kissed me. And then he said it was a mistake."

Serena wrapped an arm around my shoulders. "Normally, I'd quote that copy of *He's Just Not That Into You* I picked up at a yard sale, but—Heather or no Heather—you and Kyle have been simmering for years. You have to talk to him."

"He was the one who said it was a mistake and asked for space," I reminded her softly.

"Trust me. Forget what he said and just talk to him." A

thought flickered past her eyes. "Have you told Jason yet?"

I shook my head. "No. Why?"

Serena gave my shoulder a squeeze before climbing to her feet. "You might want to tell him before he finds out from someone else."

I nodded. That made sense. The three of us had been friends for so long, and Jason didn't handle change well. Of course, telling him would mean talking to him—if I could even get him away from his new Tracker friends.

With a sigh, I stood and brushed the dust from my jeans. There was no point in telling Jason anything until I talked to Kyle. There might not be anything to tell.

"You won't say anything about Derby's nephew to anyone, right? Not even Trey?"

Serena looked mildly insulted. "Of course not." She started for the end of the aisle. "My brother let me have the car today. Why don't we go get pizza—real pizza instead of the cardboard they serve in the cafeteria—and you can tell me why you were stealing library books."

I turned a page in *Managing an Epidemic* and studied a picture that had been taken halfway through the construction of one of the camps. I had told Serena that I wanted the books because I'd been thinking about Amy a lot and was trying to understand why a werewolf would have hurt her—in other words, exactly half the truth.

I flipped back to the previous chapter and took another look at a series of maps showing the spread of lupine syndrome. They went back only twelve years—to the six months before the US government had announced to the world that werewolves really existed.

For at least two years before that, werewolf sightings had been steadily on the rise—especially in larger cities. And the reports weren't just coming from crazy people or junkies tripping out. Upstanding citizens were calling the police with stories about humans turning into animals, and ordinary people were walking into emergency rooms claiming they'd been attacked by wolves.

Even though I'd been only five, I could dimly remember sitting cross-legged in front of a battered television and watching the president make the announcement. It had been replayed on every station hour after hour for days. The government urged calm, and everyone panicked, and Hank—in a rare moment of decent parenting—had promised he wouldn't let anything get me.

Old people asked each other where they'd been when JFK was shot; my generation asked each other if they could remember the day werewolves officially came out of the closet.

"All right. What's going on?" Tess sat on the edge of the coffee table.

"You've asked me that three times already." I glanced up. "I'm fine, really. I'm just doing homework."

I'd planned on reading the books in my room, but with Tess peering through the door every half hour, I'd eventually given up and sprawled out on the couch.

She shook her head. "You only had one egg roll with supper and you barely touched your rice. You love Chinese takeout night." She reached out to touch my forehead. "Are you getting sick?"

I ducked. "Tess, really, I swear on the stack of self-help books next to your bed, I'm fine." A hurt look flashed across her face, and I felt like I had kicked a puppy. She was just worried about me. I sat up and marked my place in the book with a scrap of paper.

"It's been five days since"—I fumbled the words—"since the hospital. You've got to stop watching me like a hawk." I squinted at the clock in the kitchen. "You're going to be late for work if you keep hovering."

There was a knock on the door and I jumped, dropping my book.

With a concerned shake of her head, Tess stood and went to answer it.

Kyle.

All the muscles in my chest contracted. Serena had said to talk to him—like that wasn't the hardest thing in the world to do—but he hadn't been in school this afternoon, and each time I picked up the phone to call him, my hand trembled so badly that I could only dial the first three numbers.

He stepped into the apartment. "One of your neighbors let me in."

Tess slid her feet into a pair of pink, Prada-wannabe shoes that she'd be cursing in less than two hours and grabbed her purse.

"Maybe she'll tell you what's wrong," she said to Kyle as she shot me a sad, troubled look. "God knows I can't get anything out of her."

She slipped out the door, shutting it softly behind her.

I bent over, grabbed my book from the floor, and clutched it to my chest.

Over the past three days, I'd practiced dozens of conversations with Kyle in my head—lying in bed, washing my hair in the shower, walking to school—but now, when he was in front of me, the words I had so carefully constructed toppled like a house of cards.

He pushed his hair back from his face. There were shadows under his eyes, like he hadn't been sleeping. "I guess you didn't tell her that I'm the thing that's wrong." He shrugged off his jacket and set it over the chair next to the door. He hesitated, almost like he was debating something with himself, and then he walked across the room.

I stood, still clutching the book like it was some sort of shield.

"You were right about the camps. I can't just turn myself in. People might assume you or my parents knew. With the Trackers in town, it's not safe to have a werewolf in the family. Especially with them offering reward money for turning us in." Before I could feel any sense of relief, he added, "But I am leaving Hemlock."

I dug my fingers into the cover of my book. "You can't."

Kyle shook his head. "I have to. It's safer for everyone if I go. I don't want the Trackers to have an excuse to hurt my parents. Or you."

"I can take care of myself."

His eyes flashed. "Like you did that night at Bonnie and Clyde?"

Without thinking, I hurled my book at his chest. He deflected it, easily, and I stalked to my bedroom.

I stared out my window, so hurt and angry that it felt like a physical ache.

The loose floorboard near the door creaked as Kyle stepped over the threshold. "I'm sorry. I should never have said that."

"No," I said. "You shouldn't have." Despite the anger in my voice and the hurt coiling in my stomach, I didn't pull away when Kyle walked up behind me and gently put his hands on my arms, standing so close that his chest brushed my back.

The truth was, I did kind of blame myself.

Everything that was happening to Kyle was my fault. Maybe not him getting infected, but a lot of what had happened after. If he hadn't hurt Jimmy, Kyle might never have wondered if he was a monster.

"If you hadn't saved me," I said, "you wouldn't have considered turning yourself over to the LSRB. And you wouldn't be thinking about leaving town now. This whole mess is my fault."

Kyle exhaled, a soft rush of breath that stirred my hair. "No. Half the school showed up for Derby's information session. It's not safe for anyone with LS. I've spent the past three days trying to convince Heather to go stay with her grandparents for a while. She's leaving on Saturday." He gently squeezed my arms. "I'd be thinking about going even if I hadn't . . ."

Even if he hadn't hurt someone.

I leaned back against him, and after a moment, he slid his hands down my arms and placed them lightly on my waist.

"What happened that night wasn't your fault."

I wanted to believe him. "I didn't have to confront Jimmy," I whispered.

"You were trying to help someone. And you couldn't have known what would happen. What he did . . . there was no excuse. Life in a camp is too good for him."

I turned around. "I don't want you to go."

Kyle brushed a bit of hair back from my face. "None of this is about want. It's just better for everyone if I leave. And it'll be easier on you if I don't complicate things before I go."

"Complicate . . . ." I stared at him, eyes wide, suddenly getting it. "That's why you said kissing me was a mistake?" My voice rose with the lunacy of the idea. "Because you think it'll make things harder on me if you go?"

He shoved his hands into his pockets and backed up a step. He stared out the window, like the view of the fire escape and parking lot was riveting. After a moment, he nodded.

I closed the gap between us. "Kyle David Harper, sometimes you are supremely stupid."

His eyes darted to mine.

"It doesn't matter whether you kiss me or not. When you leave, it's still going to kill a part of me to lose you."

Then, before he could object, I stood on tiptoe and firmly pressed my lips to his.

Kyle used the wall as a backrest and I curled up next to him, my head on his chest. I listened to his heartbeat, trying to ignore the fact that it was beating much faster than a human heart would. Werewolf fast.

"Saturday is so close," I said softly. It was *too* close.

He pressed a kiss to the top of my head. "I know."

"Maybe . . ."

"No," he said. "No maybes. It's the way things have to be."

"But—"

He twined his fingers around mine. "What would you do if our roles were flipped? If I was still human and you were infected?"

My hand looked small in his.

I turned my face into his chest, caught off guard by the sneakiness of the question. "I don't know," I lied.

"Of course you do. You'd try to protect me. And Tess. And Jason. You always try to protect everyone. Even when they don't deserve it. Even when it hurts you."

I thought about Jason and how I kept trying to pick him up off the ground even when it felt like it was breaking my heart. And then I thought about the stack of papers in my backpack and my theory that the Trackers would stay in town only until Amy's killer was found.

If the Trackers left, Kyle wouldn't have a reason to disappear. There were werewolves hiding all over the country—some people said there were tens of thousands of infected people running around outside of the camps. Why couldn't he just keep hiding in Hemlock?

My heart raced and I pushed my hair back nervously. "I have something to tell you." I reached over the side of the bed and grabbed my backpack. I unzipped the bag and took out my computer printouts and notes. "I've been looking up stuff on the werewolf attacks," I confessed, handing Kyle the stack of paper.

His brows knitted together as he flipped through the pages. "Why?"

I took a deep breath. "The Trackers are only in town because Amy's grandfather asked them to find her killer. I thought that if I found the werewolf first, they'd clear out." I wrapped my arms around myself, suddenly cold. "I just have this feeling that they're not doing everything they can—like Derby wants to draw out finding it so he can stay in town longer and generate bigger press or something."

Kyle pressed his fingers to his temple like he had the mother of all headaches. "Don't you have any self-preservation instincts at all? Derby already threatened you once. What do you think he'll do if he finds out you're sticking your nose into the murder case he was brought here to solve?"

I sighed. "You could try giving me some credit. I *can* be sneaky, you know."

He didn't look convinced.

"Anyway, if the Trackers leave Hemlock, you wouldn't have to."

"Mac . . ." Kyle closed his eyes, just for a moment, looking suspiciously like he was praying for patience, and then climbed off the bed. "I'd still have to leave. Even if the Trackers were gone."

He paced. "All it would take is for me to lose control at the wrong time, for the wrong person to get suspicious. At least if that happens in another town, you and my folks will be okay. If it happened in Hemlock, everyone would assume you knew. So you going on an insane chase after Amy's killer won't make a difference. And if this is something you're doing because you think it'll somehow protect Jason—"

Heat rushed to my face. "It's not an insane chase," I said as I climbed to my feet. I struggled to keep my voice steady. "And it's not something I'm doing just for you. Or for Jason."

I walked over to Kyle. "I keep dreaming about Amy. Bad dreams. If they never find out who did it—if I don't at least try to figure it out on my own—I'm going to keep having them. This is something I have to do." I crossed my arms. "This is something I *am* doing."

He stared down at me. "How can I make you change your mind about this?"

I shook my head. "You can't."

Kyle let out a low, frustrated groan. "I can't leave," he muttered. "Not if you're going to go after a killer werewolf on some crazy crusade."

A wave of hope hit me and I tried to keep it from showing on my face.

Kyle walked out of my room and headed for the apartment door. My fragile hope turning to apprehension, I followed.

"I'll stay and I'll help—it's the only way I can keep an eye on you. Besides, if there is something to find, I owe it to Amy to at least try."

He looked so desperate that my heart twisted and I wondered if telling him had been the right thing to do.

He grabbed his jacket from the back of the chair and pulled it on. "But after this—if we find the thing responsible or the Trackers do—I really am leaving."

I swallowed and nodded.

It was only a reprieve, but I would take it. I'd take it and try to figure out a way to make it permanent.

"Where are you going?"

"I promised my mom I wouldn't be out too late. A couple of Trackers showed up at the house this morning. One of the neighbors is a member and he told them about the noise coming from our place Sunday night. The whole thing really unnerved her."

A knot formed in my chest as I remembered the damage Heather had done to the Harpers' kitchen. The idea that there had been Trackers at Kyle's house was *way* too close for comfort. "What did she tell them?"

"The same thing I told her and dad: it happened when no one was home and was probably a bunch of kids messing around. Incidentally, they think I was over here that evening." He reached into his pocket and took out his car keys. "Anyway, the Trackers asked if they could take a look around, but since the mess had already been cleaned up, there wasn't anything for them to find. It was lucky it took the neighbor a couple of days before he thought of mentioning it."

Lucky. Right. It could have been worse. So much worse.

Kyle frowned. "Mom wanted to call the police when they got home Sunday night, but Dad said there wasn't any point."

"Do you think he knows?" Maybe it wouldn't be the worst thing if Kyle's father figured things out. Maybe he could help, somehow.

"I don't think so. I hope not." Kyle opened the door and stepped into the hall.

Like usual, the smell of cigar smoke hung heavy on the landing.

I followed Kyle out of the apartment and down to the street. His Honda was parked in front of the building.

I sniffed my T-shirt. "I swear, living across the hall from the guy in three A is going to leave me permanently smelling like a smoke shop."

Kyle grinned. "It's not that bad. Trust me. Superior nose and all."

Superior nose. "Kyle . . ." I bit my lip. It couldn't be that easy, could it? "Can you smell other werewolves?"

He shook his head. "Only after they've started to transform. The rest of the time, they just smell like regs."

I tried not to look too disappointed. It would have made things a whole lot easier if Kyle could have just spent an afternoon at the mall, picking werewolves out of the crowd.

It would have at least given us something to start with.

Kyle watched me, a slightly worried expression on his face. "I'll pick you up for school tomorrow, okay?"

I nodded and fought off a yawn.

He reached out and stroked my cheek with the back of his hand. "Are the dreams really that bad?"

Shivering, I nodded. "I've never had nightmares like these before." Sometimes there were moments when Amy was herself—when it seemed like we were just hanging out—but the dreams always took horrific turns. Last night, I had been the one attacked by a wolf while Amy recorded the whole thing on her phone and provided a running commentary. I'd woken up gasping and crying, convinced that my sweat-damp sheets were soaked with blood.

"You can call me, you know. If they get bad and you can't sleep."

I smiled. "You're going to protect me from my subconscious, too?"

In response, Kyle brushed his lips against mine. The kiss was soft at first—almost chaste—and then deepened.

When he finally pulled away, I had to put a hand on the car to steady myself.

"Good night, Mackenzie Catherine," he said softly, before walking around to the driver's side.

I stepped away from the curb and watched as he drove away. I waited until the Honda's taillights were swallowed by darkness, and then I turned back to the apartment building.

I had told Kyle that his leaving would hurt just as badly

regardless of whether or not we "complicated" things. I hoped I was right.

A tear slid down my cheek and I brushed it away. I felt like I had just entered the ultimate zero-sum game. Kyle would stay, but only until Amy's killer was found. Gain one thing and lose another.

A car door slammed, jolting me out of my thoughts.

I glanced back at the street. A car I hadn't noticed was parked in the shadows under a large elm. My stomach lurched as Jason stepped into a pool of light cast by a street lamp.

The look on his face reminded me of an animal on the verge of striking. I'd seen that look directed at other people—usually when he was so drunk that he itched for a fight—but he'd never looked at me that way before.

He stepped onto the curb, balance failing him a little as he swayed slightly between one step and the next. "And here I thought you were avoiding me because you were mad."

I licked my lips; my mouth was suddenly dry. "I haven't been avoiding you." All right, so that was a complete lie. I was totally avoiding him, I just couldn't tell him why.

"So how long have you and Kyle been going at it?" Jason's tone was fake casual, venom under velvet.

"We're not—" I started to deny it, but movement on the street caught my attention. Two other guys had gotten out of the car and were leaning against it, watching us like we were a movie at the drive-in.

I shook my head. I hadn't done anything wrong and I

172

wasn't going to put on a show of defending myself in front of his new friends. "You know what? Believe whatever you want. It's none of your business, anyway."

Jason let out a short, scathing bark of laughter. "You're right. It's none of my business. I don't care who you hook up with."

The hostility in his voice was like a slap. I may have been avoiding him, but I didn't deserve this. I started for the apartment building but made it only three steps before I turned, too furious to just walk away. "Why do you do that? Why do you try and drag other people down with you?" I looked at Jason and saw what everyone else probably did. A pathetic rich kid who destroyed everything in his path. "Do you think this is what Amy would want? Do you think she'd want you to hurt yourself and anyone who cares about you?"

Jason reached into his jacket and took out a thick, brown envelope. "You know what I think?" he asked, tossing the package at my feet. "I think she'd find it kind of poetic. Not that you would understand."

He turned to leave and the collar of his jacket slid down, exposing a black dagger on the side of his neck.

16

IN THE SPACE BETWEEN ONE BREATH AND THE NEXT, I was at Jason's side, frantically yanking back his jacket. Trackers were marked in two stages: first the dagger, and then later the *T*. I had to see if he had the full tattoo.

He grabbed my wrist—thankfully the one that wasn't sprained—and roughly pulled my arm away from his neck, his grip tight enough to hurt. I tried to wrench free, but it was like forcing your way out of a pair of handcuffs.

"What did they do to you?"

Jason shook his head. "Nothing I didn't ask for."

"Having trouble with your girl, Sheff?" One of the Trackers stepped onto the lawn. His cheeks were rutted with acne scars and his head was shaved. Some guys looked okay without hair. This guy was not one of them.

I tugged my wrist free.

Jason didn't take his eyes off me. "No trouble, Less. I'll be done in a minute."

Bald Less took a long—insultingly appraising—look at me and then shrugged. "Whatever, man. Just hurry up. Alexis is getting restless."

Sure enough, Alexis Perry was leaning out the passenger-side window, talking to the Tracker who'd stayed by the car. "Come on, Jason," she yelled as Less strode back across the street.

"Great company you're keeping," I muttered, rubbing my wrist.

"I'm not looking for your approval." Jason kicked the envelope over with the toe of his shoe. "Enjoy the reading. I figured, since you already seemed to hate me, you might as well have a decent reason."

I didn't know how to reply. I couldn't do anything other than watch, dazed and befuddled, as Jason walked back to the car and climbed, a little clumsily, into the backseat.

With the squeal of tires and a chorus of shouts, he was gone.

I bent to retrieve the envelope he had tossed at me and clamped a hand to my mouth to muffle a strangled sound that tried to force its way out of my chest.

I'd been worried Derby would get his claws into Jason—I just had never expected Jason to bare his neck and welcome it.

Operating on autopilot, I managed to make it back upstairs and to my room.

I sat cross-legged on the bed and stared at the envelope. Every nerve in my body hummed like a power line and my pulse seemed to skip beats. Part of me wanted to call Kyle, to ask him to come back so I wouldn't have to do this on my own, but another part of me didn't want anyone watching while I pored over the last few moments of Amy's life.

It felt oddly private—like the things she whispered to me while I slept.

Hands shaking, I fumbled with the flap and ripped the envelope open.

The file slid out easily. A plain brown folder with Amy's name and the date of her death printed on a white label. Feeling like I was standing on a high ledge, I opened the folder.

Photos.

Why hadn't I realized there'd be photos?

Amy's black high-tops. Her hair. Her blood. One brown eye staring sightlessly at the camera.

Another photo. Amy's hand wrapped in a bag, preserving the white fur that had been clenched in her fist.

Her torso, which didn't look human at all. Just a mess of shredded fabric and things—*don't think about organs and insides*—glistening in the dark.

I dropped the photos and bolted for the bathroom. My shoulders shook as I knelt on the ceramic tiles and threw up into the toilet. I retched over and over—long after there was nothing left in my stomach—as tears streamed down my face.

The phone rang in the kitchen, but I couldn't get up. I couldn't make my legs work and my throat was on fire.

I pressed my cheek against the edge of the bathtub, letting the cold porcelain draw some of the heat away from my face. Someone—some*thing*—had done that to Amy, and none of us had been there to keep her safe.

After a while, when I was sure I could stand, I got to my

feet and flushed the toilet. I washed my hands and splashed water on my face. I avoided looking in the mirror. I couldn't look at my own face—whole and alive—after seeing those pictures of Amy.

I turned off the bathroom light and went back to my room.

I kept my eyes on the *Les Mis* poster on the far wall—a souvenir from a trip Tess and I had taken to New York the summer before last—and sat on the bed. Going by the texture of the paper, I separated the photos and slid them out of the police folder and back into the envelope.

I'd look at them again—if I had to—but not right now.

My stomach knotted. Jason had seen Amy after the attack. He'd seen her like this, and I couldn't even look at the photos.

I forced myself to start reading the file.

The detective leading the case—Mike Bishop—had been pretty thorough. There were witness reports and locations where Amy had been spotted, even her cell phone records. It was almost like an episode of some prime-time cop show.

I scanned the phone records, zeroing in on the hour just before her death. Kyle's number had been highlighted—the last number she'd called—as had two calls to Jason. A third number was highlighted in blue. I didn't recognize it, but Amy had called it seven times during that one hour.

I frowned and turned the page over. The number belonged to Trey Carson. Why would Amy have called Serena's brother? I leafed through the rest of the papers, eventually coming to a statement from Trey.

He'd been working at the video store and had forgotten his cell at home. He had no idea why Amy had called him. I flipped back to the phone records. Each call had lasted about ten seconds—just long enough to hang up after you'd gotten someone's voice mail.

One wrong number might have been a mistake, but no way could Amy have called the same wrong number seven times.

Something clicked.

Jason was supposed to pick Amy up at the mall that night, but she'd been found in an alley off Windsor Street. Windsor was just about halfway between the mall and the video store.

It didn't make much sense—I'd never even seen Amy talk to Trey—but what if she'd been on her way to see him the night she died? It seemed unlikely, but so did all those phone calls.

I went back to the statements. There was one from a woman who'd seen Amy walking with a blond man of medium build and height. The police had shown her a photo of Jason, but the woman couldn't be positive that he was the man she'd seen: it had been dark and she'd only glimpsed him for an instant and from behind.

I knew it couldn't have been Jason. He'd been late picking Amy up. He hadn't seen her until he found her in the alley.

The apartment door creaked open and my heart tried to jump out of my chest. I'd been so upset after seeing Jason that I had forgotten to turn the dead bolt.

"Mac?"

My shoulders sagged in relief at the sound of Ben's voice.

"In here," I called, hastily shoving the police file behind the small mountain of pillows at the head of my bed.

I tried to look calm and normal as Ben appeared in the doorway.

His hair was damp, like he'd just gotten out of the shower, and his clothes were rumpled. The jeans he was wearing had the beginnings of holes over both knees.

"You're not working tonight?" The Cat had a pretty relaxed dress code, but they drew the line at denim.

Ben shook his head. "Business has been down again since those two new werewolf attacks. My shifts got cut back." He glanced around my room. "Tess asked me to come upstairs and check on you. She called and didn't get an answer."

I couldn't tell Ben that I had been heaving my guts out in the bathroom, so I shrugged and said, "I was doing laundry downstairs."

He nodded and his eyes locked on the green-and-white Coyotes pennant on my closet door. An odd expression crossed his face, almost like he was somewhere else.

"Are you okay?"

He blinked. "Yeah. Sorry. Usually you have your bedroom door shut when I'm over."

That was true—though it wasn't anything personal. Tess had a habit of ransacking my room and never putting anything back. I liked Ben, but I didn't want him to see the contents of my underwear drawer scattered across the floor just because Tess thought one of her bras had gotten mixed in with mine the last time she'd done laundry.

He walked over to the pennant, pushed it to one side, and watched it swing back into place. "My little brother would have been your age by now. He'd be a senior. He'd be going to basketball games and dating girls and saving up for his first car."

I swallowed. It was the most Ben had ever said to me about his brother. "What was his name?"

"Scott." Ben turned away from the pennant. "His name was Scott."

"Does it ever get any easier?" I asked, thinking about Amy.

He leaned against the wall and crossed his arms. "In some ways. After enough time passes, you realize that maybe a whole day went by where you didn't think of them. Then you feel guilty because you're not supposed to forget—even if it is just for a day."

"Ben, you can't . . ." I struggled to find words that wouldn't sound empty and cliché. "You can't spend your whole life blaming yourself for an accident." Tess had told me that Ben had been in the backseat of the car when it crashed, that a truck had blown through a red light, pulverizing the front of the car and killing his mother and brother almost instantly. She'd also told me that he still dreamed about it, that there were nights when he woke up screaming. "It wasn't your fault."

He shrugged. "I survived and they didn't. That's fault enough."

I knew Ben was twenty-two—only five years difference between us—but he seemed so much older sometimes. "Is that why you don't talk to your family very much?"

He shot me a piercing gaze and I felt guilty for asking. After all, I hated it when people asked me questions about Hank. "You just never really say much about them," I stammered. "I didn't even know you had any family until you left for your aunt's funeral last April."

Ben shrugged. "It's complicated. I remind them of what they lost and they remind me of all the memories I've spent years trying to walk away from."

I wondered if it would be that way with me and Jason and Kyle. Maybe someday, instead of needing one another, we'd just see each other as painful reminders. I thought about the tattoo on Jason's neck and a dull ache spread through my chest. Maybe we'd somehow already reached that point.

Ben was watching me. "Are you okay?"

I nodded. "Yeah. I've just been thinking about Amy a lot lately."

His cell phone rang and he slipped it from his back pocket. "Tess," he said, glancing at the display. His thumb hovered over the talk button. "Are you really okay?" he asked.

I nodded again and grabbed a book from the stack next to my bed. "Yup. Tell her I'm staying in and doing homework."

Ben flashed me a small, slightly sad smile and answered the call. "Hey, Tess. No, Mac's fine. She's just studying . . ."

I waited until I heard the front door close behind him, and then I gave him an extra two minutes to get down to the second floor. Once I was sure he was gone, I got up, walked across the apartment, and turned the dead bolt.

No more interruptions.

Back in my room, I pulled Amy's police file out of its hiding place. I finished the page I had been reading and flipped to the next.

Jason's statement.

I skimmed—after all, I knew most of it—until I reached the fourth paragraph.

We broke up and Amy got out of the car. I didn't think she'd go far. I was just trying to give her a few minutes to calm down. I was going to go after her and drive her home. But I couldn't find her. It was like she disappeared.

I read the paragraph a second time. Then a third.

I struggled to make sense of the words.

I'd spent the past five months thinking Jason felt guilty for being late picking Amy up on the night she died; instead, he was the reason she'd been out there on her own.

My stomach rolled and my vision blurred. For an instant, I thought I was going to throw up again. Then the moment passed and I wiped my eyes with the back of my sleeve.

How could Jason have lied to me about something this big? How could things have been so bad between him and Amy—bad enough for them to break up—without me having the slightest clue? Anger and confusion washed over me as I flipped through the rest of the file, looking for any more bombshells.

A sticky note fell onto my lap. *Bishop removed from case June 8th*. It wasn't anything official-looking, just a three-by-three-inch scrap of yellow paper.

I set the report down on the bed. I rubbed the wrist Jason had gripped so tightly, and I remembered what he had said: *I figured, since you already seemed to hate me, you might as well have a decent reason.*

17

JASON'S PHONE WENT STRAIGHT TO VOICE MAIL. JUST
like the other fourteen times I'd called.

I glanced up as Kyle rounded the corner. "Anything?"

He shook his head. "His car's not in the lot and he wasn't
in bio. He could just be too hungover to bother showing
up." He crossed his arms and leaned against the locker next
to mine. "It wouldn't be the first time."

My stomach twisted. I needed to find Jason. I needed
him to explain the things in that report and the tattoo on
his neck and . . . everything. I just needed him to explain
everything.

"You didn't see him last night, Kyle. He's hanging out
with losers like Alexis Perry. He let the Trackers brand him
like he was a piece of cattle. And—" I immediately stopped
talking as two muscular men wearing T-shirts emblazoned
with the Tracker crest strode down the hall, their arms
weighed down with boxes.

One of them paused. "Which way to the main office?"

"Straight to the end of the hall and then a right followed

by a left," said Kyle. My heart thundered in my chest, but he didn't even look nervous.

The Trackers moved on.

"Now what?" I mutter-asked, knowing Kyle didn't have an answer any more than I did.

I gathered up the threads of what I had been saying. "Jason gave me the report knowing that I'd find out about the breakup. Why would he do that after keeping it secret all summer? Even by Jason standards, that's self-destructive and messed up."

Kyle frowned. "I could drive over to his place. He might not let me in, but I could try." He didn't look too enthusiastic about the idea.

I shook my head. "And if a bunch of Trackers are over there? No way." I slammed my locker door. "I just don't understand how he could have lied all summer. Why didn't he just tell us the truth?"

"Maybe he didn't know how. Or maybe," Kyle said, voice oddly detached, "he was worried he'd lose you if he told you the truth."

I wondered, suddenly, how much it had scared Kyle to tell me he was infected.

"Wouldn't have happened," I whispered, and I wasn't just talking about Jason. "You guys are both stuck with me."

I picked up my backpack and slung it over my shoulder. "You didn't know Jason was thinking about breaking up with Amy, did you?" Kyle and Jason had been best friends forever, but I was sure he would have told me if he had known.

"I knew they were having problems." He shrugged and

looked away, watching the crowd milling in the hall. "I didn't know it was serious."

The bell rang, signaling the end of the morning break. Kyle pressed a quick kiss to my lips. "I'll catch up with you after class, okay?"

I watched him head for the stairs, and then, on a whim, I turned and headed away from English, toward the south entrance. Kyle had checked the parking lot, but sometimes Jason parked on the street—despite the fact that the entire block in front of the school was a no-parking zone.

Sheffields never got parking tickets.

I suddenly thought of my father. Hank used to say that the smartest crook could be brought down by a single ticket. He always fed the meter plenty of change, and the only time he drove above the speed limit was when he was trying to outrun something. Or someone.

"Skipping class?"

I whirled at the familiar, musical voice.

"I'm surprised Kyle lets you wander around by yourself. You know, since he's so protective." Heather brushed a non-existent speck of dust from her skirt. She looked up and the hatred in her gaze hit me like a blast of wind.

I glanced up and down the hallway. Except for the two of us, it was completely deserted.

She stalked forward and I backed up. I tried to keep my voice steady. "What do you want, Heather?"

She titled her head and sniffed the air. "You don't sound scared, but I can hear your heartbeat and smell the sweat leaking out of your pores. You kind of reek."

"Yeah, well, you're a werewolf." I trailed my hand along the wall as I backed up, not taking my eyes off her. There was a short hallway a few feet behind me that led to the gym. There wasn't a class in there this period, but there was a door that led to the cafeteria.

If I could make it to the cafeteria—to other people—she might leave me alone. I let my backpack slide to the ground. If I had to run, it would only slow me down.

Heather grinned and it reminded me of Derby. Completely feral.

"I'm not going to fight you over Kyle." I struggled to keep my heart from leaping out of my chest as a trickle of sweat ran down the side of my face.

Heather laughed. "Please, like you could." The muscles in her torso started to widen, and a button popped off her shirt as the fabric strained over bulk that hadn't been there a moment ago. "I would have torn you to pieces Sunday night if he hadn't stopped me." She smiled and her teeth were suddenly sharp and pointed. "That's why he's making me leave town, you know. He's worried about poor, fragile Mackenzie Dobson."

Kyle was *making* her leave?

Before I could process the information, Heather's back twisted and she doubled over. "You messed up everything," she panted. "Kyle belongs with me. He's the same as me." She lost control and shifted completely.

I ran.

I heard the wolf behind me as I yanked open the gym door and threw myself inside.

Racing for the other end of the dark, cavernous room, I tripped over a discarded baseball bat and went sprawling. I felt Heather sail over me as I hit the ground.

She collided with the bleachers, the force of the impact enough to wrench a small, high-pitched whine out of her.

If I hadn't tripped, she would have torn out my throat. I remembered the pictures of Amy from the police file and was flooded with panic. That's what Heather wanted to do to me. That's what she *would* do to me.

Shaking, I grabbed the bat and scrambled to my feet.

Heather paced in front of the cafeteria door. She looked like Kyle when he transformed; she had the same color fur and was just a little smaller.

There was no way out. I couldn't get past her, and she'd overtake me before I could make it back the way I had come in. I was completely trapped. The realization roared through my head, obliterating every other thought.

An announcement about yearbook photos came over the loudspeaker and Heather glanced up toward the rafters, baring her teeth like the noise hurt her ears.

And that's when I noticed the equipment closet.

Taking advantage of Heather's distraction, praying I'd be fast enough, I raced for the door. I pushed myself harder than I had ever pushed myself before—harder, even, than the night Jimmy had chased me.

I hurtled inside and slammed the door shut a nanosecond before she hit it from the other side.

Lock? Where was the lock? With a sinking feeling, I remembered that the lock was on the outside.

I could hear Heather growling through the door. How long would it take her to realize that all she had to do was shift back and open it with her hand? She collided with the wood again, and the hinges groaned.

Light filtered into the small room through a dirty window high on the wall, but there were bars over the glass. There was no way out.

Heart hammering, I dropped the bat and pushed the wooden horse they used for gymnastics against the door.

It wasn't enough.

She was going to get in.

The muscles in my chest ached as I sucked in panicked breaths. I didn't want to end up like Amy in those photos. I couldn't end up like Amy in those photos. *Please, God, don't let me end up like Amy in those photos.* I bit my lip to cut off a strangled cry.

Help. I had to get help.

I reached into my pocket and hauled out my phone. I didn't think, I just dialed. I wasn't even sure what keys I was pressing.

Jason picked up on the first ring.

I yelped as Heather collided with the door again, so hard that the wood splintered around the hinges.

"Mac?"

"I'm in the gym." My throat didn't want to work, and I had to force the words out. On the other side of the door, Heather's growling had gotten louder. "In the equipment closet. Heather Yoshida is outside the door and—"

Thud!

The top hinge gave way.

"Heather's infected and she's breaking down the door, and oh, God, Jason, she's going to get in."

"Hang on." Jason's voice was rough and desperate. "I'm pulling up to the school now." I heard the slam of a car door followed by the sound of Jason's labored breathing as he raced for the building. "Call Derby!" he yelled to someone. "There's a wolf inside the gym!"

The second hinge went flying and the door started to topple. "It doesn't matter," I said, my voice a whisper-sob. "It's too late. She's in."

I retrieved the baseball bat and I heard Jason yell my name as I shoved the phone into my pocket and backed up to the far wall.

The wolf leaped over the wooden gymnastics horse and landed on a huge stack of gym mats, the ones that were too ratty to use in class but never seemed to get thrown out.

She stared down at me, hackles raised and teeth bared. I tried not to think about the way Jimmy had screamed in the alley as I moved along the wall, holding the bat out in front of me.

Sharp pain sliced through my arm and I glanced down. I had gouged myself on the edge of a battered set of metal shelves.

Heather leaped at me and I threw myself forward, hitting the stack of gym mats with enough force that they fell to the ground—fell on top of me—in a heap.

The wolf plowed her way through them, teeth snapping for any part of me she could reach. I tried to ram my baseball bat down her throat.

She yelped and shook her head, then dove at me again, twice as determined.

I was going to die. Icy certainty filled me.

Suddenly, Heather let out a high-pitched whine and fell, twitching, to the ground.

Hands dug through the mats, tossing them aside, and then Jason was there, pulling me to my feet, saying something that I couldn't hear over the pounding of my pulse.

He half carried me out of the closet and to the bleachers, even though I tried to tell him I could walk.

The overhead lights flickered to life and I blinked. There were shouts from the equipment closet and I stiffened.

"It's all right," said Jason. "It's just the two Trackers Derby assigned to protect the school. You're lucky they started today." He lifted my arm and gently turned it so he could examine the cut. He pressed his lips into a hard line.

Three Trackers, trailed by Alexis and wheeling some sort of folded metal contraption, burst into the gym.

"Where is it?" asked a burly man in worn flannel who looked like he wrestled grizzly bears in his spare time.

"In there," said Jason, jerking his thumb toward the equipment closet.

Alexis glared at me suspiciously, but followed the three men.

Jason waited until they were out of earshot and then

gripped my shoulders. "Did Heather scratch you?"

I felt disorientated and dizzy. My head throbbed and my heart wouldn't stop racing.

Jason tightened his grip. "Did she scratch you?" His eyes were bright and manic.

I started to say no, but what came out was "If she did, it'd be stupid to tell you."

Jason's fingers dug into my skin. "Mac, I swear to God, I am not joking. You have to tell me if she scratched you."

I pushed him away. "No, all right?" I hissed. "I cut myself on the edge of a shelf in the closet." Jason stared at me, like he wasn't sure if I was telling the truth. "Go check the shelves if you want. One of them should have a smear of my blood on it."

I tried to stand and swayed on my feet.

If Jason hadn't caught me, I'd have been kissing the waxed gym floor.

I closed my eyes for a moment, concentrating on breathing in and out.

Heather had tried to kill me.

At the sound of footsteps, I opened my eyes.

Branson Derby strode toward us, the expression on his face hardening as he zeroed in on the way Jason's arm was around me. He raised one eyebrow, almost as though to ask if I remembered our conversation in the hospital.

Like it would be possible for me to forget. I bit my lip as I gently pushed Jason's arm away and put some space between us.

The expression on Derby's face didn't soften. "Miss

Dobson. I knew there was an attack on campus, but I had no idea you were involved."

Something in his tone made me think that if he had known, he might have held the Trackers back and let Heather kill me. At least then there'd be no chance of me telling Jason what really happened last Friday night.

Derby's gaze locked on my arm, and I tugged the sleeve of my shirt down.

"She cut herself on a piece of metal," explained Jason, before Derby could ask. "It's not a scratch."

"And you think she'd tell you the truth?"

Jason flushed and met Derby's eyes. "I believe her."

Derby stared at him until Jason dropped his gaze. "Sir." He cleared his throat. "I believe her, sir."

The look Derby turned on me was about as friendly as the look a constrictor gives its prey before squeezing the life out of it. "Did you know the werewolf?"

I nodded. "We have a class together."

"Its name is Heather Yoshida," supplied Jason.

It, not *her*.

Five Trackers—the two Kyle and I had seen in the hall and the three who had showed up after Jason—trooped out of the equipment closet, maneuvering a wheeled metal cage between them. The cage couldn't have been any larger than four cubic feet, and a brown wolf lay unmoving inside.

Alexis had found the baseball bat and was trailing behind the cage, periodically poking the wolf through the bars.

I knew it was Heather, but she looked so much like Kyle

that it was entirely too easy to imagine that it was him in the back of the cage—that he was the one Alexis was taunting.

"What's going to happen to her?" I asked.

"She'll be processed and sent to a rehabilitation camp," said Derby. "Where she belongs. Where they all belong."

"Where she won't be able to hurt anyone," added Jason.

Derby shot him an approving glance and then focused back on me. "Why did it attack you?"

Jason stared at me, waiting for me to answer. He had seen Kyle and me kiss. Werewolf or no werewolf, it didn't take a genius to figure out why two girls would have a catfight at school. It was practically a cliché. And it was a cliché that would put Kyle on Derby's radar.

Jason opened his mouth, but before he could say anything, I collapsed.

This time, his reflexes weren't fast enough to catch me. I hit the floor with a bone-jarring thud, and my mouth filled with the copper taste of blood. I had bitten my cheek.

"Mac?"

Jason bent over me, trying to help me sit up. I did my best to look dizzy and sick—it didn't require much acting.

He glanced at Derby. "She was under a pile of gym equipment when we found her. I think she hit her head. I'd better get her to the school nurse."

Derby nodded once, curtly, and strode off.

Jason helped me to my feet and tugged my arm over his shoulder. He wrapped his own arm around my waist. Stooping slightly to compensate for the difference in our heights, he led me out of the gym.

I tripped over my own two feet, and Jason tightened his hold around my waist.

We crossed the empty cafeteria, the smell of overcooked food making me slightly nauseous. No matter what the time of day, there were usually a few students in the caff, but it was completely deserted. Even the lunch ladies seemed to be gone. "Where is everyone?"

"The school's on lockdown. Standard procedure for a werewolf on campus."

I stopped walking. "Since when does Kennedy have procedures for werewolves?"

"Since last week. Derby realized the school wasn't doing enough to protect us. That's why Mike and Doug—the two guys who neutralized Heather—were put on campus. It's part of a pilot program he's working on with schools and colleges."

Great. Trackers on every campus. A small voice in the back of my head pointed out that I might be dead right now if they hadn't been here. I pushed it aside.

Jason let go of me and stepped away. Under the bright cafeteria lights, I finally got a good look at the tattoo on his neck. He had the black dagger but not the full tattoo, not the red *T*.

Trackers were marked in two stages. The black dagger indicated their pledge to join and the oath of allegiance they swore. The red *T* came later, after some sort of initiation. Jason wasn't fully part of them—not yet—but I still wasn't sure if I could trust him.

The taste of blood lingered in my mouth.

Jason crossed his arms. "Are you going to tell me why you faked fainting? I've seen *SNL* sketches with better acting." He searched my face for an answer. "Did Kyle know Heather was infected? Is that it? Were you trying to protect him?"

He was so close. Way too close.

He watched me, warily. "What are you hiding?"

My father always said the trick to lying convincingly was to blend in a certain amount of truth. If you found the right mixture, you could scam almost anyone.

"I saw Heather on Sunday." *Truth.* "She wanted to talk to me about Kyle." *Sort of true—if ripping my throat out counted as talking.* "She lost her temper and started to shift. I didn't know what to do, so I kept quiet." *Truth.* "Kyle doesn't know." *Lie.*

Jason ran a hand over his face. "You can't protect them, Mac. They're not people. If we hadn't gotten there in time . . ."

He looked like he was torn between hugging me and shaking me. "I was running faster than I've run in my whole life and I could hear you on the other end of the phone and I *knew*. I knew I wasn't going to get there in time." He swallowed, roughly, the Adam's apple bobbing in his throat. "I thought I was going to have to listen to you die."

He looked the way he had before everything had gotten so messed up. Strong. Dependable. The hero of a story rather than the punch line of a joke.

For a moment, he was the Jason I kept waiting to come back.

But then he turned his head and the fluorescent light

hit the tattoo on his neck, and the illusion was shattered.

"What would you have done if she had scratched me?" My voice was barely a whisper, but it seemed to echo in the empty room. "If I had said yes when you asked?"

Jason shook his head. "Don't ask me that."

He was slipping so far away, and there wasn't anything I could do to stop it. I felt like something inside me was breaking. "You would have turned me over to them, wouldn't you? You would have let those people drag me off in a cage."

His green eyes flashed. "*Those people* just saved your life. If they let Heather out, how long do you think it would be before she attacked you again? Or someone else? They're animals, Mac. That's what they do. That's what they did to Amy."

I thought of the police report and the lies and omissions that had gone on for months. "And whose fault was it that Amy was out there that night?"

"Don't make this about her." There was a warning note in his voice, sharp, like jagged metal.

I suddenly felt sad and tired and alone. "How could this ever be about anything else?"

Jason's hand twitched toward his jacket, to the flask or bottle that was probably tucked inside. "If you would just come to a few more meetings, if you would give the Trackers a chance, you'd see that they're not the bogeymen you think they are. Maybe, if you weren't so busy lying to protect werewolves, you'd learn something."

Anger surged through me. "You're going to talk to

me about lying? Seriously? You're the one who didn't tell me the truth about what happened the night Amy died. Don't compare lies, because mine aren't even in the same league."

"Mac . . ."

He reached for my arm and I stepped back. Black spots hovered at the edge of my vision. "You let me find out what happened from the police report. From a piece of paper."

"You don't understand—"

"You're right. I don't. Why didn't you just tell me?"

Jason glared, his eyes glinting in the overhead lights. In an eerie echo of Kyle's words, he said, "Because I didn't want to lose everything."

Without another word, he turned and strode back toward the gym. Back to the Trackers.

Jason hadn't been exaggerating about the school being on lockdown. The lights were off in all the classrooms and each door was locked. It was the same thing they told us to do if there were ever gunshots on campus.

Turn off the lights. Huddle near the back. Pray that whoever was prowling the halls would walk past your door without stopping.

I sat on the floor a few feet from Kyle's class and waited. The blood from the scratch on my arm dried as I counted the seconds and minutes until the announcement that it was safe to start exiting the classrooms.

I expected the principal to give the all clear. Instead, Branson Derby's smooth, southern voice filled the school and sent shivers down my spine as he told the students of Kennedy that a werewolf had been trapped in the gym and that classes had been canceled for the remainder of the day.

I climbed to my feet as students flooded the hall.

Kyle pushed his way past them, cell phone in hand. He walked right by me, then froze and whirled, the relief on his face so acute that it made my chest ache. "Thank God you're okay," he breathed.

He reached for me, but I shook my head and walked into the now empty classroom.

After he was inside, I shut the door and turned.

Kyle stared at my arm. He inhaled, and I realized he could smell the blood. I tried to tell myself that it wasn't a big deal, but my stomach twisted and I wondered what my blood smelled like to him.

He raised his eyes to mine. "Was it Heather?" He swallowed and it took him two tries to get a second question out. "Did she scratch you?"

I bit my lip. "Yeah. It was Heather. And she didn't scratch me."

He reached for me, but I stepped back and crossed my arms. I told myself that I was just spooked, that I wouldn't let anyone hug me right now. It didn't have anything to do with the fact that Heather and Kyle looked almost identical when they shifted.

Hurt flashed across Kyle's face. It was there for barely an instant before he buried it, but it was impossible to miss.

I closed my eyes, just for a second, and saw Heather crouched above me, teeth bared, ready to spring. My heart raced and I took a deep breath to try and slow the beats as I opened my eyes.

Kyle shoved his hands into his pockets. "How did you get away?"

"The Trackers showed up. And Jason."

"How did they know?" he asked, his tone suspicious.

I felt a brief surge of guilt, but then wondered why I felt as though I had done something wrong. As much as I hated the Trackers, Jason had been right: they were the reason I wasn't dead. I raised my chin. "I called Jason. Heather had me cornered in a closet and she was breaking through the door."

"I would have—"

"Done what? If I had called you, you would have charged out of class and someone would have found out you were infected." It was true, though I hadn't been thinking that clearly when I called Jason. I hadn't thought at all; I had just dialed.

"So you called the Trackers." Kyle's voice lashed out like a whip.

I wasn't going to feel guilty. I refused to feel guilty. "I called *Jason*. And if I hadn't, I'd probably be dead."

Kyle flinched. "I didn't think she'd go after you. I told her to leave you alone."

He had *told* her? "Before she shifted, Heather said you were making her leave Hemlock. Is that true? Were you forcing her out of town?"

Kyle's expression twisted, becoming something cold and bitter. He suddenly reminded me of Jason—Jason when he was teetering on the edge and looking for a fight. "I told her that if she didn't leave, I'd report her to the LSRB. Is that what you wanted to hear?" He clenched his hands into fists so tight that the muscles in his forearms looked as though they had been carved in stone. "I didn't trust her not to go after you, so I threatened to completely destroy her life."

Pain and loathing flashed across his face, naked and raw.

"Kyle . . ." I took a step toward him and then stopped, not sure what to do or say.

"Forget it," he muttered. "I can't expect you to trust me when I'm not even sure who I am anymore." He strode past me and out the door.

Feeling like a coward, I let him go.

18

I spent three hours in my room, poring over the police report and reviewing my notes on the other attacks. Besides the fact that all of the attacks had taken place on the south side of town, there didn't seem to be any connection between the victims. Which made sense. It wasn't like werewolves suffering from bloodlust had motives for what they did—they were like rabid animals.

Unfortunately, that meant that Amy's killer could have been anyone. The white wolf was a needle and Hemlock was my haystack.

With a sigh, I slid my notes into my backpack and grabbed my phone. I needed a break and I'd had the thing for almost a week without really setting it up.

I added some music and changed the ringtone, then I transferred some photos from my computer. I flipped through the images until I came across a picture of Amy, Jason, Kyle, and me at fifteen. Amy had her arm slung over my shoulders, and Kyle was making rabbit ears behind her head. Back then, Amy's curves were just starting to make an appearance, and half the time she dressed more like a tomboy than a Hilton heiress. She stared up from the picture with a cocky, challenging grin, almost like she was saying, "Come *on*, Mac. Figure this thing out already."

Suddenly desperate to make some headway—any headway—I slipped the phone into my pocket and grabbed my jacket. I scribbled a note for Tess and then headed downtown.

Amy had called Trey Carson seven times the night she died. I was going to find out why.

Halfway to my destination, a light rain began to fall. I shoved my hands into my pockets and kept my head down as I turned right at the music shop and walked past a brick wall that was plastered with posters for garage bands and open mike nights.

Two girls—one short with mousy brown hair, the other leggy and blond—were struggling to put up a large, red-and-black poster before the rain really started coming down. I almost asked if they needed help—the poster was really too big for two people to manage, especially in the rain—but then I noticed the tattoo on the blonde's neck and got a good look at the poster itself. It reminded me of the war propaganda we had looked at in history class. The illustration showed a wolf menacing a mother and child underneath the words *YOUR DUTY TO REPORT*.

A shiver crept up my spine as the rain slipped past the collar of my jacket and dripped down my back. I broke into a light jog, trying to get away from the girls and their poster and reach shelter before I got completely soaked.

A half a block later, I tripped to a clumsy stop under the striped yellow-and-brown awning of Java Coyote—so named because most of its customers were students at Kennedy and its owner had been cocaptain of the Coyote cheerleading squad in her glory days.

I found an elastic in my pocket and pulled my damp hair back into a ponytail as I pushed my way inside. It took a minute for my eyes to adjust to the dim glow of the coffee shop.

Java Coyote was the sort of place that barely broke even. Most of the armchairs and couches were ancient and threadbare—a fact the coffeehouse tried to hide with an abundance of bright orange throw pillows. The pillows—combined with the dim lighting and deep burgundy walls—always made me feel like I was in a genie's lamp.

Half the seats were occupied. For a weekday, that was practically unheard of. As I walked past clusters of students, I heard Heather's name over and over. My skin itched as I tried to ignore the sensation of people staring at me. By now, everyone knew Heather was the werewolf the Trackers had caught on campus and that I had somehow been involved.

It wasn't hard to spot Serena. She was at her regular Thursday table, engaged in her regular Thursday activity: watching the college-age barista boy she'd been crushing on since summer.

I waved and got in line for a coffee and tried to figure out how I was going to casually ask her about her brother. Serena could be fiercely protective of Trey—even though she hated some of the things he did and the guys he hung around with.

People continued to stare as I waited. I resisted the urge to turn to the nearest tables and say something snarky. Any reaction would just fuel whatever stories were going around.

I turned, paper cup in one hand, impulse cookie in the other, and stifled a curse. Trey was sitting at Serena's table, leaning so far back in his chair that the two front legs hovered above the ground. I wondered, suddenly, if there was some cosmic affidavit that said nothing in my life was allowed to be easy.

"Hey, Dobs," he said, letting his chair fall back to the ground and kicking out a second seat for me as I approached the table. Despite the weather, Trey didn't have a jacket. I guess it was easier to show off his muscles in shirtsleeves.

I tried to smile as I sat down, hoping the grin didn't look as fake as it felt. "Hey."

Serena frowned. "You weren't in English. Did you hear about Heather?"

I guess no one had filled her in on the whole story. "I skipped," I said, remembering the sound of splintering wood as Heather forced her way into the closet. I stared down at my cookie; suddenly, I didn't have much of an appetite. "And, yeah, I heard about Heather. Jason told me." I knew Serena would find out the truth—probably sooner rather than later—and that she'd probably be upset with me for lying, but I just wasn't up to talking about it.

Trey snorted. "Let me guess, Jason was playing toy soldier with his Tracker friends and was in the heart of the action?"

I glared at Serena. "Did you tell Trey about Jason joining the Trackers?"

She opened her mouth, but it was Trey who answered. "Ree didn't have to," he drawled, "what with the new ink he's been flashing."

"Oh." I stared at my hands and felt my face flush. Of course. I wouldn't be the only one to notice Jason's neck. "Sorry."

Serena reached over and patted my hand. "It's okay," she said. "What did Kyle say? Has anyone told him?"

I swallowed, remembering Kyle's face in the classroom. "He knows. I think he just wants to be by himself for a while. You know, to process things."

She sighed. "Mac, if you and Kyle are going to be—"

I cut her off. "Serena, I'm pretty sure there is no me and Kyle. We're not an us." The words left a bitter taste in the back of my mouth. They felt true and final and sad. Forget the fact that he was a werewolf and planning on leaving town, how could there ever be an "us" after the way Kyle had looked at me just before walking out of that classroom?

A chair scraped back against the linoleum floor and I glanced up as Trey stood. "I have a feeling I have too much testosterone for wherever this conversation is heading. Anyway, I said I'd meet someone."

"What someone?" asked Serena sharply.

Trey flexed the muscles in his arms, almost like a nervous tick. "Not Cecil." He glared at his sister reproachfully. "I remember my promise."

Before Serena could say another word, he turned and strode out of the coffee shop.

"Promise?" I asked, playing with the paper band on my coffee cup.

She rubbed the back of her neck, like she was trying to work out tension. "Cecil Bell. That guy who got arrested over the GHB thing in March. He got out last week."

I bit my lip. "Trey is still friends with him?" As much trouble as Trey got into, I couldn't see him hanging around with a guy like Cecil—not after finding out that he had drugged a girl.

Serena snorted. "No. He hasn't had anything to do with him since he found out." She took a sip of her coffee. "After Cecil got arrested, the police asked Trey some questions. Someone told the idiot about it, and he's been going around talking a lot of trash about Trey being a rat."

"And the promise?"

She shrugged. "I asked Trey not to beat the shit out of him. Lord knows someone should, but I don't want my brother getting in trouble for it."

Trey had talked to the police about Cecil. It was kind of the perfect opening. I took a deep breath. Kyle and Jason were already mad at me; I might as well see how many other people I could alienate. "Did you know the police also talked to Trey about Amy?"

Something slid behind Serena's eyes, almost like a vault door slamming shut. "Yeah," she said. "They kept hassling him even though he was at work when she was killed."

"You never told me." I tried not to let the hurt and

suspicion I was feeling leak into my voice. Judging from the way Serena tensed, I failed.

"I didn't think it mattered. They only talked to him because she called his cell. It was just a wrong number."

"That's what Trey told you?"

Serena sighed. "Yeah. So?"

I leaned forward. "Amy called his number seven times. You don't think she was smart enough to realize it was the wrong number the first time she got his voice mail?"

Serena stood and pulled on a yellow raincoat, shoving her arms through the sleeves with such force that I half expected the seams to rip. "Look, we're friends, so I'm going to give you the benefit of the doubt and assume you're not implying my brother knows anything he didn't already tell the police." The anger on her face turned to disappointment. "And you know what? You could have asked Trey about the calls yourself instead of waiting for him to leave."

She didn't give me a chance to reply—which was just as well since I didn't know what to say.

I watched as Serena wove around the other tables and then pushed her way past a group of java junkies and out through the door.

Her purse was still slung over the back of her chair. I hesitated for a minute, then scooped it up and ran out of the shop.

Outside, the rain had stopped. My sneakers slapped the wet concrete and puddle water splashed the bottoms of my jeans as I raced after Serena's yellow raincoat.

I caught up with her at the end of the block, just by the entrance to Riverside Square. She glanced over her shoulder, then turned and crossed her arms. For a minute, she almost looked like Trey, like someone to be scared of.

Wheezing slightly, I held out the purse, and her expression softened marginally.

"I'm sorry," I said. "I wasn't trying to imply anything. I just thought it was strange that Amy would keep calling Trey and I thought, I dunno, that maybe he knew something that he forgot to tell the cops."

Serena took her purse and frowned. "How did you even find out they talked to him?"

"Jason got a copy of the police report." For some reason, maybe the look on Serena's face when I asked about Trey, I didn't want to tell her that Jason had gotten the report at my request. "So far, all it's given me is lots of questions."

"Can I tell you something? As your friend?"

I nodded.

"If you dig into Amy's life, you might find out things you'd rather not know. She wasn't perfect."

I blinked. "You barely knew her."

"I knew enough." Serena glanced at her watch. "Look, I've got to go. Dad's out of town at a pharmaceutical convention and I promised I wouldn't let my little brother walk home from the bus stop by himself. All this werewolf and Tracker stuff has my father kind of freaked. He tried to cancel his trip, but his boss is a total jerk."

She turned and strode across the square, startling a bunch of pigeons into flight as she passed the fountain in the center. I could just make out her car parked on the far side of the park.

Not knowing what else to do, I let her walk away—even though part of me desperately wanted to shake her until she told me why Amy had called Trey. Because I was pretty sure she knew more than she had told me.

I felt a familiar ache in my chest.

Serena was just the latest in the line of people who had kept things from me. Life with my father had been a whole series of fabrications. Kyle had hidden the fact that he was infected. Jason hadn't told the truth about what happened the night Amy died.

People lied. That's just what they did.

"Worst. Breakup. Ever." Amy stared up at the night sky, hands clasped behind her head, ankles crossed as she lay on the hood of an old, black Chevy that was missing its tires and doors. Abandoned cars stretched in all directions and hubcaps dotted the ground like giant silver snowflakes. We were in the junkyard on the edge of the Meadows—a place we used to go on dares.

"Aren't you cold?" I asked. Amy was wearing a short, yellow sundress with spaghetti straps. I didn't see how her bare arms and legs could be very comfortable against the cool metal and glass of the car.

"Nope." She popped the word, making a clicking noise with her tongue. "You don't feel things like cold when you're dead. In fact, you don't feel much of anything. I don't even feel angry at Jason anymore."

Death had made her a bad liar.

"Why did he break up with you? And why didn't he tell anyone?"

"Didn't you ask?"

"I asked him why he didn't tell me. He wouldn't answer."

Amy let out a soft snort. "Figures you'd be more interested in why he didn't tell *you* than in why he broke up with me in the first place." She examined her nails and chipped away at the polish. "You'll have to work things out for yourself. Though smarts have never exactly been your strong suit. No wonder your dad left you behind. He couldn't afford to let himself be dragged down." Amy's voice took on a sickly, singsong tone. "You were just an inconvenient mistake that was always in the way. Garbage he couldn't wait to toss."

I closed my eyes, not wanting them to reflect how badly her words hurt me.

Amy cursed and my eyes snapped open. She shook her head. "Sorry. It gets all jumbled up in here."

"Here?"

"In your head. It's hard to separate my thoughts from yours. It's like knights and bishops moving around a chessboard, and sometimes I'm not sure which one of us has control of the pieces." She sat up and hugged her knees. "You have some *serious* self-esteem issues."

I saw something move out of the corner of my eye, a dark shape that I couldn't quite make out. As soon as I looked directly at it, it disappeared and all I could see was rusting metal and overgrown grass.

"It's okay," said Amy. "It won't hurt you. It's looking for Kyle."

My heart leaped into my throat and every muscle in my body tensed. I spun, trying to pin down the shadow, eyes desperately sweeping the junkyard. "How is that okay?"

Amy shrugged and slid off the car. She was moving oddly—like her bones and muscles didn't quite want to work. "I'm lonely," she said. As I watched, her skin pulled back until it was waxy and taut. Her hair became thin and straggly. Her brown eyes misted over, covered by white spiderwebs. She became a dead thing.

I stumbled back and tripped on something in the dark. I fell to the ground.

She stared down at me with sightless eyes. "It's cold and lonely here, Mac. I need Kyle more than you do. Besides, you took Jason."

Tess pulled up to the school. "Are you okay? You've barely said two words since you got out of bed."

I nodded and jumped a little as a roll of thunder peeled. It hadn't started raining, but the weather forecast was calling for severe thunderstorms and they'd looked imminent enough when I'd gotten up that I had accepted Tess's offer of a ride to school.

She sighed. "I wish you'd just tell me whatever's going on with you." She looked tired. She'd only gotten home from work around six, and instead of crashing, she had stayed up so she could have breakfast with me and give me a drive. She rubbed her eyes. "You're not in some kind of trouble, are you? Like maybe the kind that takes nine months?"

I burst out laughing. "Tess, I think I'm a pretty unlikely candidate for Immaculate Conception."

She didn't so much as smile. "What about the kind of trouble your dad used to get into?"

I tried to squash the rising sense of guilt. If Tess was thinking about the sort of stuff Hank used to pull, then she was beyond worried. I hated keeping things from her—especially things that were so epically big—but her knowing about Kyle or Derby was dangerous. I couldn't tell her.

Underneath the guilt, though, was a small spark of anger. Did she really think I'd risk turning out like my father? Just because he had tried to teach me how to hot-wire a car when I was eleven didn't mean I was going to go out and steal one.

"I swear: nothing's going on." I unbuckled my seat belt. "Thanks for driving me."

Tess scanned my face, but whatever she saw didn't seem to reassure her. "Ben's not working tonight. If you need a ride later, just give him a call."

"Okay," I said, climbing out of the car and shutting the door behind me.

Fat raindrops began hitting the ground and a flash of lightning split the sky as Tess drove away. I counted the seconds before the thunder rumbled.

Just as I reached the school door, I heard the low roll, still far off. I blinked and headed inside, turning right instead of left at the main corridor.

The not unpleasant scent of gas and motor oil wafted through the hall as I passed the shop classes. I remembered Serena saying something, just after school started, about Trey having his locker down here.

I figured Serena had told him that I'd been asking about the phone calls. He'd probably lie about them, but at least he'd have to look me in the eye while doing so.

As far as plans went, it was pretty abysmal; I just didn't have any better ideas.

I waited long after the first and second bells had rung and the hallway had emptied. Trey never showed.

Eventually, I gave up and headed to chem.

No Serena.

I sat at our usual lab table and stared at her empty seat.

Serena maintained a practically 4.0 GPA. She didn't skip class and she almost never took sick days.

Trey had a solid alibi that was backed up by store sur-veillance footage—but he was hiding something and Serena was covering for him. I was sure of it. I just didn't under-stand why. He couldn't have killed Amy, so what was Serena trying to protect him from?

I fidgeted through class and tried not to listen to the jocks behind me as they speculated on who else at school might be infected.

"She was dating Kyle Harper. Do you think he could be a furball?"

I clutched my pen so hard that the plastic cracked and blue ink smudged the side of my hand.

"Nah," said one of the others. "Harper's friends with Sheffield and I heard Jason was the one who ID'd the Yoshida chick. He'd know if Kyle was infected."

"I've been thinking about that reward money the Trackers are offering," said a third. "Could make for a decent party fund. All we'd have to do is find a couple of fleabags."

"Right," snorted the guy who had spoken first. "Like finding fleabags is that easy."

I was on my feet a half second before the bell rang and I had to force myself to walk to Kyle's class and not run.

I got there just as the teacher opened the door and students started streaming out. Kyle wasn't one of them.

I checked his locker.

Nothing.

Panic closed around me like a vise as students pushed past me. The jocks in chem had dismissed the thought that Kyle might be infected, but would everyone else?

I headed toward the main doors at a normal pace, not running, not giving anyone a reason to notice me. With everyone talking about werewolves, today was not the day to stand out. I pulled my cell from my pocket and dialed Kyle as I walked. No answer.

If he was screening his calls, I was going to kill him.

I stepped outside and stood in the sheltered alcove of the doors as I scanned the parking lot. The rain was coming down hard, but I didn't have any trouble spotting Kyle's car or seeing that it was empty.

He hadn't been in class, but his car was in the lot; he was here, somewhere.

I spun on my heel and headed back inside. I spotted Ethan Cole coming out of the administration office. He had practically the same class schedule as Kyle.

"Ethan!" I jogged to catch up to him.

He smiled. "Hey, Mac." He ran a hand over his spiky, blue hair as a faint blush tinged his cheeks. "I've been meaning to talk to you—I tried, the other day, but you were in a hurry."

"Huh?" I shook my head as a dim memory of giving Ethan the brush-off floated back to me. "Oh, right. Wednesday. Sorry."

"It's okay." He looked desperately uncomfortable. "I just wanted to thank you—you know, for what you did at Bonnie and Clyde."

"Oh." I felt my own cheeks grow warm. "That's okay. I mean, I'm sure you'd have done the same for me."

Ethan nodded but he still looked uncomfortable. His gaze darted to my forehead, to the stitches that were just barely visible underneath my bangs. He fidgeted with his lip ring. I didn't know if he had heard the falling story that I'd given everyone who asked.

"Listen, I was just wondering if you've seen Kyle around. His car's in the lot, but I can't find him anywhere."

"I saw him on the third floor," said Ethan, looking relieved at the change of topic. "I think he was headed for the drama room. It can't be easy—you know, having everyone talk about your ex like she's a bloodthirsty monster instead of a person with a disease."

Normally, I'd agree—if it weren't for the fact that the ex in question had tried to rip my throat out.

The bell rang and Ethan automatically glanced at the big clock on the other side of the lobby. "I've got to get to class."

I nodded. "Yeah. Me too."

He seemed on the verge of thanking me again, but then he just gave me a small smile and headed down the hall. I was glad I had helped Ethan at the club, but I was really hoping things wouldn't be awkward every time I saw him. Otherwise, I'd be paying for my good deed until graduation.

I headed up the stairs and turned left at the third-floor landing. Glancing around to make sure the coast was clear, I slipped down the small hallway that led to the drama room. The school had canceled the theater classes last year—not enough students ever signed up—but they hadn't repurposed the space.

Some enterprising then-senior had broken the lock so he and his friends could sneak up here with girls. Somehow, Amy had found out about it.

I pushed open the door and wrinkled my nose at the stale, slightly musty smell in the room. The overhead lights were off, but gray morning light filtered through a row of windows that hadn't been cleaned in ages. Rain pelted the glass, the *rat-tat-tap* oddly soothing.

Kyle was sitting on the edge of the small stage that ran along the right side of the room, his sneakers dangling a half foot off the floor. He didn't look up when I walked in.

"What do you want, Mac?"

I swallowed. "How did you know it was me?"

He glanced up. His hair fell over his face and he brushed it away. His eyes were cold and empty. "Werewolf, remember? Heightened sense of smell."

I walked forward until I was standing just a few feet from him. "Are you saying I stink?" I joked, trying to break the ice.

Kyle didn't smile. "What do you want?"

"You weren't in class." I crossed my arms. It felt like the chill in the room was seeping through my skin. "I was worried."

"Everyone was talking about Heather and shooting me looks like they wondered if I knew. Like they were wondering if I was infected."

I wanted to reach out and touch his arm or hug him or do something, but instead, I said, "I heard some of the jocks talking. Most people don't know how much you and Jason fought this summer. They think your best friend is a Tracker and they'll assume that means you're not infected."

Kyle grunted. "My best friend *is* a Tracker. At least until he figures things out. Then he'll probably watch while they throw me in a cage and drag me off. Hell, he'll probably help."

"Maybe you should have a little more faith in him," I said softly.

Kyle's eyes locked on mine and I was the first to look

away. I ended up staring at a faded poster that someone had taped next to the door.

"Maybe you need to grow up and stop thinking you can save everyone."

The words on the poster blurred together. It was for last year's Harvest Dance. It had been right before Kyle started dating Heather, and the four of us—Kyle, Jason, Amy, and I—had gone together. Amy had drunk too much before the guys picked us up. Once in Jason's car, she had thrown up on his shirt and told him that she loved him more than anything—even more than her designer sunglasses or the vampires in the romance novels she kept under her bed. Jason had patted her head and told her that he loved her, too, and asked her to please stop trying to kiss him—at least until we could stop somewhere and buy her a toothbrush.

Kyle had captured the whole thing on his phone.

"I don't think I can save everyone," I said, forcing myself to look at him. "But I have to believe Jason can walk away from them."

Kyle rubbed a hand over his face. "The tattoo—"

"He hasn't gotten the whole thing, only the dagger." Even to my own ears, it sounded like the world's flimsiest hope. "I'm sorry I called him instead of you. I'm not even sure I knew who I was dialing until he picked up."

"I know why you did it," said Kyle. He stood and then, gracefully, stepped off the stage and landed lightly on the balls of his feet. "I know why you called him instead of me."

A moment ago, the room had felt like it was filled with frost. Now, suddenly, the air felt too hot, like it was super-charged.

Kyle's brown eyes were full of shadows and fire. He cleared his throat. "Jason's human."

19

I SHOOK MY HEAD. "KYLE, THAT DIDN'T HAVE ANY-thing to do with it."

Kyle wiped his palms on his jeans, like there was dirt on his hands he was trying to brush off. "I saw the way you looked at me afterward, Mac. Like I was danger-ous and you finally got it. Like Heather made you finally understand what I am." He glanced away. "I wanted you to understand—I was worried you were in some kind of denial about the whole thing—I just didn't expect it would hurt so much when you did finally get it."

My throat went dry and my pulse pounded too loudly and too fast. It was true. I had looked at Kyle and seen, for an instant, Heather—Heather as she crouched and pre-pared to rip my throat out—but Kyle was nothing like her and I knew that. I'd just been shaken and frightened and not thinking straight.

I opened my mouth to explain, but he cut me off. "Any-thing you say right now is going to be a lie."

He closed his eyes for a handful of heartbeats. When

he opened them, it was like someone had kicked dirt over the fire that had been raging. "Things have to go back to the way they were between us. I'm going to stay just long enough for us to resolve things with Amy—either until we find something or give up—but after that, I'm gone. Until then, things have to stay platonic. It's better for both of us."

I let out a choked, skeptical laugh. "We can't just go back to the way things were. We can't pretend nothing's happened." There were cigarette burns on the carpet and I scuffed at them with the edge of my Skechers as I let out a deep, shaky breath. "I'm sorry for the way I acted after Heather. I was freaked out." I looked up and met his eyes. "But that doesn't mean I want to go back to the way things were. Even if I thought it was best—which I don't—I couldn't. I can't just hide how I feel, like there's a faucet I can turn on and off."

"Why not?" asked Kyle, his voice sharp, like a piece of wood snapping under too much weight. "I've been doing it for years."

"And whose fault is that?" I tossed back, suddenly defensive. He couldn't choose to keep his feelings secret and then blame me for the pain it caused. "If you had told me how you felt two years ago, then maybe none of this would be happening right now."

Kyle looked as though he had been struck.

For a split second, I felt a horrible sense of satisfaction, but then it was gone and I somehow felt worse. "I'm sorry. I just . . ." I swallowed. "What if I don't give up? What if we go through everything in the police report and I still keep going? Will you stay?"

Kyle grabbed his backpack from the floor and slung it over his shoulder. "If we get to the end of the police report and don't find anything, then I don't think there's anything to find. If you want to spend the rest of your life chasing ghosts, I can't stop you." He took a deep breath. "But you'll have to do it without me."

"Do you think I can just forget about Amy?" I demanded, suddenly so angry. "Not all of us are as good at tossing people aside as you are."

He froze. "That's not fair."

"But it's true." My pulse thundered in my ears and the words came out rapid-fire, like bullets. "First, you kiss me. And then you tell me it was a mistake. Then you show up at my apartment to tell me that you're going to leave town—oh, but maybe you'll stay for a while because you're worried I'll get into trouble." Tears filled my eyes and spilled over. I didn't bother wiping them away. For once I *wanted* someone to see me cry. I wanted Kyle to know he had hurt me. "And then you're suddenly okay with being some sort of quasi-friend-with-benefits as long as I know there's an expiration date. And before I can even get used to that, you get mad because I called the wrong person during my near-death experience and had trouble dealing afterward." My voice broke. "You keep picking me up and putting me down. Why is it so easy for you to throw me away?"

The door to the drama room opened.

"Did it hurt?" a giggling, female voice asked.

I wiped my eyes with the sleeve of my shirt and turned toward the interruption.

Jason stood in the door, the light from the hallway bouncing off his blond hair like a halo. The girl I'd seen him with on Wednesday—the one with the *Hunt or be Hunted* T-shirt—was draped over him, one finger tracing the tattoo on his neck.

"Ooops," she said, catching sight of Kyle and me. "I guess the room is taken."

Jason brushed her hair back and murmured something in her ear.

She went completely still and then shot a murderous glare in my direction before turning on her heel and leaving. She slammed the door on her way out.

For a moment, none of us moved and the air seemed to grow thick. Then Jason strolled across the room.

There was nothing in his walk to give him away—he didn't weave or lurch—but he was wearing sunglasses. Inside. At noon. He slipped them off, revealing eyes so bloodshot they looked as though they'd been sandblasted. He squinted in the dim light, like even that much illumination was enough to make his head hurt.

He glanced from me to Kyle and grinned. I had the feeling angels probably smiled like that—right before they fell. "Uh-oh. Trouble in paradise already?"

Great. It was probably obvious that I'd been crying. "Don't start." I glanced at Kyle. His posture, his expression, the curve of his mouth—they were all hard, like he was steeling himself for a fight.

"I mean, if you two crazy kids can't make it work, then—"

"God!" I whirled on Jason. "What part of 'don't start' do you not get?"

He held up his hands and backed away. "I was just making an observation."

"No, you were being a jerk," said Kyle, the faintest hint of a growl in his voice.

Jason snorted as he reached into his jacket pocket and slid out a bottle. "At least I didn't just make her cry." He peered at my face as he unscrewed the lid. "I've always wondered what you looked like when you cried. Actually, I've sort of always wondered if you had tear ducts." He took a swig from the bottle. "Even at Amy's funeral, I didn't see you shed a single tear."

I saw a blur of movement out of the corner of my eye, and then Kyle slammed Jason into the wall, balling one hand in the front of Jason's shirt.

The bottle Jason had been holding hit the carpet with a dull thump, and the amber contents spilled over the floor. He made a choking noise as the collar of his shirt dug into his neck.

The muscles in Kyle's arms trembled, not with the effort of pinning Jason to the wall, but with the strain of holding back, of not crushing him. "You don't get to talk to her like that. Not after everything you've put her through."

"Stop it, Kyle!" I ran forward and put a hand on his arm. His skin was damp with sweat and his muscles writhed under my touch. Jason was too intent on staring Kyle down to notice, but the primitive parts of my brain—the ones that told me to hide during thunderstorms or not reach out and touch fire—screamed at me to back away from the angry werewolf.

"Everything I've put her through?" Jason's voice was hoarse with the effort of speaking. "Wasn't it your fleabag ex who attacked her yesterday?"

"Shut up, Jason." I pulled on Kyle's arm. "Please, Kyle. Just let him go."

"Did you know what Heather was?" Jason rasped. "Because if you knew what she was and didn't report her, then you're the reason Mac almost got hurt."

Kyle let go and stepped back so quickly that Jason slid to the floor.

"At least I tried to protect her. Why don't you ask her how she really got that cut on her forehead or that bandage she's been wearing around her wrist?"

"Kyle!" If he told Jason the truth about what had happened, Derby might come after all of us.

Jason pushed himself unsteadily to his feet. "What are you talking—"

I cut him off. "Did it ever occur to either of you that maybe *Mac* doesn't need protecting? That maybe *Mac* finds your he-man acts both insulting and chauvinistic? In case you haven't noticed, *Mac* is pretty good at taking care of herself."

Kyle cleared his throat. He looked exhausted and wary. "Why are you talking about yourself in the third person?"

"I don't know," I admitted, gaze darting from one to

the other. "I thought it lent a sense of gravity to what I was saying."

Jason straightened his shirt. "What's 'chauvinistic' mean?"

"It's in the dictionary next to a picture of your father," muttered Kyle.

I threw up my hands. "What? So next time I'm just supposed to let you fight?" Never mind that they were best friends or that Kyle could have shifted right then and there.

Jason nodded. "Yes. Preferably with your cell out and recording so we can post it to YouTube."

Kyle almost cracked a smile. He opened his mouth to say something, but the drama room door suddenly opened and Alexis Perry stepped inside. Her pixielike face lit up when she saw Jason, but her smile slipped when she noticed Kyle and me.

"Derby sent me to find you. Your phone is off."

Jason shrugged. "I was sick of getting texts every two minutes." He didn't look especially happy to see Alexis, which was a small relief. Given the way she had chased after Jimmy Tyler like some sort of Tracker groupie, it wouldn't surprise me if she turned her attention on Jason.

As if to confirm my suspicion, voice full of concern, she said, "Don't tell Derby that's why it wasn't on, he'll get mad."

Jason rolled his eyes. "Alexis, go downstairs and tell them I'll be there in a minute."

I'd heard that voice plenty of times, but I never thought I'd hear it from Jason. It was his father's voice. Arrogant and dismissive. Like everyone and everything was beneath him.

"Jason—"

"Go."

"Okay," she mumbled, shooting him a wounded look before she turned and left.

"You're going somewhere with Derby?"

Jason glared at me, and the fierceness in his eyes matched the tone he had used on Alexis. "Derby trusts me enough not to keep things from me."

"That's not fair. There are things you haven't told me, either. Like what really happened with Amy."

"I . . ." For a heartbeat, his expression softened; then he gave a small shake of his head. "Forget it. You wouldn't understand."

He pushed past us and headed for the door.

"Where are you going?"

Without pausing, Jason said a single word. "Hunting."

20

I KNOCKED ON THE DOOR OF APARTMENT SIX AND checked the time on my phone: 8:30 p.m. After what seemed like forever, Ben opened the door.

"Mac?"

He stepped aside and I hovered in the entrance. I hadn't been down here very often. Ben spent so much time at our place that Tess had been trying—unsuccessfully—to convince him to just move his things upstairs. After all, it wasn't like they had just started going out; they'd been together for almost a year.

And it wasn't like he had a lot of stuff to move. Ben gave new meaning to the term *spartan*. Most of the furniture he did own all looked like it had come from a thrift store stuck in the 1970s.

"I need a favor." Not the smoothest opening. "Tess has Dragon, and I was wondering . . . if you don't have plans tonight . . ."

"You want to borrow my truck?"

I nodded.

Ben walked over to the kitchen counter, grabbed his keys, and then hesitated. "Does Tess know you're going out?"

"I didn't have a chance to tell her, but I'm just going to the mall. I need girl stuff." I didn't like lying to Ben, but I knew he'd never loan me the truck if he knew where I was really going.

He started to ask a question but thought better of it and tossed me the keys. "It's parked out front."

That was the great thing about guys: mention the phrase *girl stuff* and you could get away with almost anything.

I curled my hand around the keys. "Thanks."

"Don't be out too late. And be careful." Ben frowned, like he was trying to remember if there was anything else a responsible adult—even one who was only five years older—would tell me.

"I'll be fine."

With a shrug, he let me go.

Outside, the rain had stopped, but the wind was starting to pick up. I buttoned my jacket as I headed for Ben's ancient blue Ford.

I heard a shout and glanced across the lawn to the apartment building next door. A group of men were headed up the walkway. Though it was dark, I thought I recognized one of the guys who had been with Jason the night he dropped off the police report.

My stomach lurched as I watched them disappear inside. Maybe it was nothing, maybe they were just meeting someone, but I couldn't help thinking about Leah and the day a group of Trackers had stormed into our apartment building. Jason had said he was going hunting . . .

Even if they were grabbing someone, there wasn't anything I could do—however much I might have wanted to. They had the full support of the police department. Of Amy's grandfather. Of almost everyone.

I practically ran to Ben's truck, as though I thought I could outpace my guilt. I pulled myself up into the cab, trying to use my left wrist as little as possible and barely wincing when I failed. I probably didn't even need the bandage anymore.

I started the engine and headed for the Meadows. Maybe I was cracking up, but Amy had said "knights and bishops" in one of my dreams, and I couldn't get that out of my head. The detective who had started the investigation was named Bishop. Maybe my subconscious had been trying to tell me to go talk to him.

A small voice in the back of my head whispered that I should call Kyle, that I shouldn't go on my own. I ignored it.

He had made it clear that he was staying in town only until we found out something about Amy. If Bishop did have answers, I wanted time to process them before figuring out how much to tell Kyle.

Plus, he had practically bolted from the drama room after Jason left. With a sinking feeling, I realized that I wasn't even sure if Kyle and I were still talking to each other. In three years of friendship, we'd never had a real fight.

No, it was better if I just went on my own—even if the

address that came up when I googled *Mike Bishop* was in the worst part of town.

It only took me ten minutes to get there.

Every place I'd ever lived had one neighborhood with the worst reputation. In Hemlock, that area was a four-by-two-block stretch nicknamed the Meadows—so called because it had almost as many vacant lots as it did ramshackle buildings.

City council was always complaining that the area was an eyesore and a magnet for crime. They should have tried spending the night in some of the places Hank had rented.

I was driving past an abandoned basketball court with cracked asphalt and rotting nets when the truck made a horrible grinding noise and shuddered to a halt.

I tried the ignition. Nothing.

"Please start," I muttered, turning the key a second time.

Not a sign of life.

How was I going to explain to Ben that I had killed his truck? And, almost as important, how was I going to explain that I was not at the mall buying girl stuff but was, in fact, in the worst part of town, across the street from a house that was rumored to be a grow-op.

I suddenly wished I had listened to Tess when she tried to get me to sign up for auto shop.

Deciding I didn't have a choice, I took out my cell and called Ben. No answer.

I tried our apartment on the off chance he was up there, but all I got was voice mail.

Not sure what else to do, I called Tess. She answered on the third ring, and I had to strain to hear her over the background noise of the Shady Cat. "Ben loaned me the truck and it broke down. I'm totally fine but I called his place—and ours—and he didn't pick up."

The Cat must have been swamped, because, miracle of miracles, Tess didn't ask *why* I had needed to borrow Ben's truck. "Did you try his cell?"

"I don't know the number."

She started to recite it.

"Hold on!" I searched the truck's cab for a pen and paper. I found a ballpoint in the visor and an old receipt squashed between the seats. I scribbled down the number and repeated it back to Tess, getting halfway through before the line went dead. She'd forgotten to charge her phone. Again.

I called the number she had given me and counted the rings until it went to voice mail. I waited a few minutes and tried again. Same result.

I closed my eyes and pinched the bridge of my nose. I wondered if Ben had any Tylenol in the glove compartment.

Tap!

I whipped my head around so fast that my skull collided with the driver's-side window.

Kyle stood outside the truck, arms crossed. The ghost of a grin played out across his face.

I pushed the door open. "Didn't anyone ever tell you that it's rude to sneak up on people?" I muttered, rubbing my head.

Kyle rolled his eyes. "You're lucky it's me and not a drug dealer. You do know the only people who park here are the ones looking to buy, right?"

"I didn't park here on purpose." I slid out of the truck, grabbing the piece of paper with Ben's phone number and slipping it into my pocket. I closed the door, made sure it was locked, and leaned against the cab. "The truck died."

I shivered and glanced around at the depressingly dilapidated scenery. "How'd you find me, anyway? No, wait, don't tell me: you followed my scent."

Kyle blushed. "Actually, I was on my way to your place, saw you drive past, and followed." He rubbed the back of his neck. If possible, he turned even redder. "I wanted to apologize. For this morning."

I kicked at a crumpled beer can. "Which part of this morning?"

"All of it." He sighed. "I didn't mean to make you feel like you were something I was just tossing aside."

I shrugged. "Yeah. Well, you did." I wanted to believe him, but part of me couldn't help thinking that both my mother and Hank had walked away from me without any trouble. Why would Kyle be different? Maybe something about me just repelled people.

He shoved his hands into his jacket pockets. "I know. I should have handled things better."

"Understatement."

A flash of annoyance crossed his face. "Before you get too superior, maybe you should tell me what you're doing driving around the Meadows after dark."

Busted.

"Iwasgoingtotalktobishop," I mumbled.

"Figures."

I expected Kyle to rant and maybe yell, to tell me that I was reckless and had about as much sense as an extra in a slasher flick. Instead, he started walking east. "What's the address?"

"Two forty-two Lakeview." I fell into step beside him and studied his profile. Even though Jason was more traditionally handsome, Kyle was good-looking in an offbeat, quirky kind of way—even when he was obviously annoyed. Maybe—if I was being extra honest—especially when he was annoyed. "You're not going to freak out?"

He shrugged. "If I did, you'd just ditch me and go on your own. At least this way I don't have to try and track you all over town."

We rounded a corner and turned onto Lakeview. There were a few less vacant lots and a whole parade of sad-looking duplexes.

"Do you wonder why it's called Lakeview?" I asked as we passed brown lawns separated by rusting metal fences. "I mean, we're not anywhere near the lake."

Up ahead, two men and a woman were walking toward us. They all seemed to be wearing matching white shirts under dark jackets. Despite the chill in the air, they all had their coats unbuttoned.

My shoulders knotted with tension as they came closer. The white shirts each bore a familiar symbol—a larger version of the tattoo each undoubtedly had on his or her neck.

The woman's head was shaved on both sides, and the rest of her long, dark hair was tied back in a ponytail high on the top of her skull. She was tall enough to be an Amazon. Something bounced on her hip and I realized it was a holster—like the ones the Trackers had been wearing that day they hauled the Parker kid out of my chemistry class.

Neither of the two men had holsters, but one looked as though he could bench-press a cow and the other was carrying an aluminum baseball bat.

Kyle brushed my hair back and draped an arm over my shoulder. "Just pretend we're on a date and I'm walking you home," he murmured against my ear.

I leaned into him and slipped my hand under his jacket, resting it at the small of his back. I tried to look like everything was normal, to focus on Kyle and not stare at the three Trackers as they approached.

The man with the muscles nudged the one with the bat and they laughed.

"After I get you home," said Kyle, holding me a little tighter and steering me across the street, "we could order a pizza. I skipped supper."

"Okay," I replied, playing along, "as long as you're paying."

I could feel the Trackers stare as they passed, like an itch between my shoulder blades.

A cell phone went off. "It's Derby," said the woman, her voice turning out to be low and almost sultry. "He wants us to check in."

And then they were around the corner and it was easier to breathe.

I leaned against Kyle. "I saw another group of them by my place."

Gently, he removed his arm from around my shoulders and stepped away. "They're patrols. The news this afternoon said something about Trackers walking neighborhoods where they think wolves might be hiding. They're using what happened with Heather as an excuse."

"They're taking over," I murmured, suddenly wondering if I had been selfish to want Kyle to stay.

Maybe it really wasn't safe for him in Hemlock.

He stopped and nodded toward half of a duplex. "Two forty-two," he said. "Not exactly where I'd expect to find one of Hemlock's finest."

I took in the cracked vinyl siding and overgrown lawn. Cigarette butts littered the crumbling walkway like bits of confetti, and the basement windows were covered with plywood. There was graffiti on the front of the house. Someone had tried to cover it with white paint, but even in the dim glow from a nearby street lamp, you could see hints of the letters underneath.

It was the kind of place you rented when you didn't have anywhere else to go.

"His daughter died two years ago. He was taken off Amy's case in June and put on suspension. His wife kicked him out last month. Respectable housing probably isn't at the top of his priority list at the moment." Catching Kyle's surprised glance, I added, "His wife has a very non-anonymous blog. It came up when I googled him."

I walked to the front door and Kyle followed behind.

When I rang the bell, he stood so close that our shoulders brushed. I counted to sixty, and then pushed the button a second time.

There was a scuffing noise and the click of a dead bolt turning. The door opened half a foot, and a grizzled, bleary-eyed face peered out.

"Detective Bishop?"

The man blinked. "Not anymore." He started to close the door.

"I need to talk to you about Amy Walsh," I said desperately.

Bishop paused, his bloodshot eyes suddenly sharper. "Talk to Branson Derby," he said. "That's why they called him in."

He started to close the door again, but Kyle pushed past me and wedged it open with his shoulder. "We need to talk to you."

"You're trespassing," sneered Bishop.

"So call the police." Kyle's voice came out low and menacing. "We're not leaving until you talk to us."

I grabbed my phone and flicked to the first photo of Amy I could find. "Please," I said, standing on tiptoe and reaching over Kyle's broad back to show Bishop the picture. "She was my best friend."

Bishop stared at the photo. I knew, from my Google search, that his own daughter had been just two years younger than Amy when she died.

"All right," he muttered, stepping back to let us inside. "Ten minutes. That's all I'm giving you."

The smell of rancid takeout containers and empty beer

bottles hit me like a slap as I blinked in the flickering hall-way light. Piles of garbage and dirty clothes were heaped against the wall. Frat boys had better housekeeping skills.

Bishop reached past me to shut the door, and I tried not to breathe through my nose. He needed a pot of black coffee and a shower. Maybe not in that order.

Underneath the three-day beard, dirty clothes, and sour smell of sweat and alcohol, he was so average looking that it was almost comical. A little on the short side, average weight, middle-age, brown eyes and hair—he was the kind of guy you'd forget five minutes after meeting him. He must have been great at undercover jobs.

Without a word, he turned and started down the hall.

I stared at Kyle, who shrugged.

"Detective?" If Bishop heard me, he didn't show it.

Kyle followed him a few feet into the house. "We have a few questions for you about Amy Walsh."

Bishop turned. "Not here," he grunted, eyes darting around restlessly. He disappeared through a swinging door with hinges that screeched like banshees.

"If he goes *Texas Chainsaw Massacre* on us," muttered Kyle, "I'm going to spend the afterlife telling you off."

He reached back and offered me his hand. I took it with-out hesitation.

We entered a kitchen that was, if at all possible, more disgusting than the hall. Kyle gave his head a small shake, and I wondered if the smell of rotting food and unwashed dishes bothered his wolf-sensitive nose more than my human one.

Bishop waited on the other side of the room, holding open a battered screen door.

A trickle of sweat ran down my spine and the smell of garbage made my stomach churn. This suddenly seemed like a bad idea.

Kyle let go of my hand and stepped into the backyard. Quelling the urge to throw up, I followed.

When we were a few feet from the house, Bishop started talking. "Couldn't say anything inside. They're always listening."

"Who's always listening?" I asked, wondering if the former detective was supposed to be on some sort of prescribed medication.

"The Trackers. Derby. Who do you think?" Bishop walked to a small shed in the far corner of the yard.

"You've got to be kidding," muttered Kyle.

Bishop's eyes glinted in the moonlight. "You think I'm joking? They've got the whole house bugged. Except for the yard. They're scared I'll go to the press. Derby has me on his 'liabilities' list."

He disappeared into the small, haphazard structure.

"Mac, we're wasting our time. The guy's certifiable."

I didn't totally disagree, but I wanted to at least give him a chance. "That's what Derby calls people who cross him. He calls them liabilities."

"Mac, anyone could know that. That doesn't prove anything."

Maybe not, but I wasn't going to turn around and go home, not when we were already here. "Stay in the yard, if you want. I'm going to talk to him."

Pretending to be braver than I felt, I stepped into the shed. I let out a small sigh of relief when Kyle followed.

I could just barely make out Bishop in the dark. He leaned over and fumbled with something. A moment later, an electric lamp flickered to life, casting a glow over five feet by five feet of cluttered storage space, broken tools, and cobwebs.

The shed was so small and the smell coming off Bishop so strong that Kyle and I practically stood on top of each other.

Bishop stared at us. Despite his appearance and the fact that he smelled like he had bathed in liquor, his eyes were oddly sharp and focused. "So someone told you I was on the Amy Walsh case?"

"I saw the police report."

The detective raised an eyebrow.

"A friend got me a copy."

I shifted under Bishop's steady gaze and glanced back at Kyle, whose face didn't give anything away. "Jason Sheffield got it for me," I admitted. There couldn't be any harm in telling Bishop that. It wasn't like he was still on the force.

"Ah." Bishop leaned against the dirty shed wall and crossed his arms. "That kid's father owns half of Hemlock—including the police department."

I didn't deny it. Everyone in town knew how much pull Matt Sheffield had. "There was a note in the file saying that you had been removed from the case."

"Removed from the force, more like it. I was put on

leave until further notice." He coughed. "I was having a few personal problems. They claimed emotional stress was impacting my work. They said it was making me *unstable*. Load of BS."

Kyle snorted and I elbowed him in the ribs.

Bishop glared. "I was a good cop. I had the highest case closure rate in the department. Then Derby showed up and I was hung out to dry."

"What does Derby have to do with it?" I did the math in my head. "The Trackers didn't show up until last week, and the note said you were taken off the case in June."

He ran a hand over the stubble on his chin. "The police chief had Derby evaluate the investigations into the were-wolf killings months before the Trackers officially came to Hemlock. Derby read my recommendation that they bring in the FBI and didn't like it. That's the real reason I was yanked off the force."

I stared blankly at him. "Why would Derby care about the FBI?"

"The Trackers don't play well with the Feds," said Kyle. I glanced back. His eyes were locked on Bishop. "They get along great with cops at the local and state levels—and with the LSRB—but the FBI hates them."

"How do you—"

"I've been doing a lot of reading."

Bishop nodded. "Your boyfriend is right." His eyes narrowed. "The department wanted to write off the Amy Walsh murder—all of the murders and attacks—as the work of a werewolf suffering from bloodlust. I didn't think it added up and submitted a detailed recommendation to call in the FBI."

"That wasn't in the file—at least not the file I got."

Bishop frowned. "Do you have it with you?"

I shook my head.

He grunted. "Maybe you'd better tell me what *was* in the file you got."

After I'd listed everything I could remember, Bishop whistled. "Over half of it is missing. Which means one of two things: either half the file is still safely at the department and someone just didn't want anyone outside the force looking at it . . ."

"Or?" prodded Kyle.

"Or someone's destroyed the other half of the file. Probably for the same reason I was put on leave."

"Because you wanted to bring in the FBI?" I tried to connect the dots and came up short. The FBI didn't handle werewolf attacks—they dealt with stuff like kidnappings and serial killers. I stared at Bishop, the pieces clicking into place. "You thought the werewolf was a serial killer?"

My world tilted on its axis. I felt Kyle's hand on my hip. A light touch that was just enough to anchor me.

Bishop watched my reaction. "Before Hemlock, I worked in Miami. Every couple of years, we'd get a wolf suffering from bloodlust. It gets so that you can recognize them real fast. Bloodlust attacks have a distinctive look."

Kyle cleared his throat. "And the attacks in Hemlock didn't match that?"

"Sure they did—if you wanted to believe the easiest

explanation." Bishop turned and rummaged behind a stack of plywood. After a minute, he came up with a crumpled pack of Marlboros. "Knew I had some hidden back here." He dug in his pocket until he found a lighter, and then lit a cigarette. He took a deep drag and exhaled a puff of smoke. "Wolves suffering from bloodlust are like rabid animals. They can't think or process, and when they kill, it's messy."

Kyle's hand tightened on my hip, his fingers gripping the bit of extra fabric where my jeans were just a little too big.

"*Bloodlust* is a good name for it because they mostly use their teeth—it's like they get a rush off the taste of the blood. The attacks in Hemlock were *efficient*. In each case, the medical examiner figured the wolf went for the neck or the abdomen at the beginning of the attack, like it was trying to kill the victims as quickly as possible. With blood-lust, they're not thinking about anything but the taste of the blood. The killings take longer and are messier."

My stomach rolled. It was cool in the shed, but I felt hot, like I had a fever. "I saw the pictures of Amy. Her whole upper body was torn apart."

"You didn't tell me there were photos." Kyle's voice was soft and pained.

"Trust me," I said, "you didn't want to see them." Kyle already had enough issues with being a werewolf. No good would have come from him seeing pictures of what had been done to Amy.

Bishop tossed the remains of his cigarette into an empty coffee can. "The wolf did a good job of messing up the previous victims, but the ME thought it was done after they had already died from a single wound. And there were hardly any bite marks. It mostly used its claws to tear them up. It was almost methodical."

There was something strange about the way he stressed the word *previous*, but I was more concerned with the methodical bit. "So the wolf didn't just lose control?"

Bishop shook his head. "And in the case of your friend, it was an easy kill."

I opened my mouth to ask what he was talking about, but he cut me off.

"Amy Walsh was drugged."

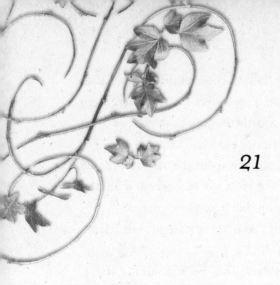

21

I GRABBED KYLE'S HAND, SQUEEZING SO HARD THAT I probably would have hurt him if he hadn't been a werewolf. "What did you say?"

"When we found Amy Walsh, she had a clump of white fur in her hand, but there were no fibers or tissue under her nails."

I shook my head. Tess would probably know what that meant—she was addicted to all those cop and crime-scene shows—but I was lost.

Bishop sighed and looked down at his pack of cigarettes, like he was wondering whether he needed another smoke to have this conversation. "She didn't fight back. If she had grabbed the fur—like someone wanted us to think—there would have been something under her nails. It was too neat, like it was planted. And there was almost no bruising on her arms or legs. She didn't hit or kick or struggle. Rigor didn't set in as soon as it would have if she had fought back. I had them run a toxicology report. The results showed extremely high levels of GHB in her system. High enough that her heart probably stopped just as the wounds to her body were made."

I swallowed. GHB. The date rape drug. The reason you never took your eyes off your drink at a party. "Was Amy . . ." I cleared my throat. "Before she was killed, was she . . ." I struggled to make myself say the word as the walls of the shed pressed in.

Kyle carefully pried his hand free from my iron grip and asked the question I couldn't. "Was Amy raped?" he asked, voice quiet and strained.

"No. There were no signs of sexual assault." Bishop's voice was surprisingly gentle.

I remembered what Serena had said in the coffee shop. "Was it Cecil Bell? Is that why the police were interested in Trey Carson? Because they thought he might know if Cecil drugged her?" Was that why Serena had been protecting him? My head throbbed and my chest ached. I knew Trey was Serena's brother, but would she really try to cover for him if he was hiding something so horrible?

Bishop gave in and lit another cigarette. "Cecil Bell was in prison when Amy Walsh was murdered. A few people on the force thought Carson might have drugged her himself, given his association with Bell, but there was no way he saw the Walsh girl that night." He tossed the rest of the pack into an empty crate. "I shouldn't be telling you any of this, you know."

"Why are you?" asked Kyle. "If you really think Derby has your house bugged, why risk telling us anything?"

Bishop sighed and looked at his hands. The cigarette

shook slightly between his fingers. "I've seen a lot of ugly deaths, but every once in a while, one still gets to you. It gets to be that it's all you can think about. Something about Amy Walsh reminded me a bit of my daughter, Jessica." He glanced up and met Kyle's eyes. "Branson Derby cared more about keeping the Feds out than about solving that case. When I let him bulldoze me out of the force, it was like I let that little girl down." He flexed his hands. "And he took my job from me. It was the one thing I had left and Derby destroyed it."

His words only half registered. I couldn't get past the idea that Amy had been drugged. "A werewolf wouldn't have needed to slip her anything," I said softly. A wolf's body was practically a lethal weapon—that's why people were so scared of them. If one wanted to kill Amy, it wouldn't have needed to slow her down first. "Could the werewolf have stumbled onto her after someone else slipped her the GHB? Maybe it was just a horrible coincidence."

Bishop watched me for a moment, like he was debating something. He took a drag on his cigarette and then asked, "How well do you know Jason Sheffield?"

I blinked, taken aback by the question. "We're friends."

"Been friends long?"

An alarm bell went off in my head and I instinctively moved closer to Kyle, so close that my back was against his chest. "About three years. Ever since I moved to Hemlock."

Bishop glanced at Kyle. "And you?"

I felt Kyle shrug. "Since third grade," he said guardedly.

"And you knew he was having problems with anger?"

"Of course," said Kyle. "Who wouldn't after their girlfriend was killed by a werewolf?"

"One week before Amy Walsh's death, Jason Sheffield was picked up after a fight with a student from the community college. Several witnesses said Jason threatened to kill the kid. The guy ended up in the ER with a broken arm and a busted nose. And Jason was picked up twice before that. Each time, Matt Sheffield stepped in and the incidents just went away."

I knew Jason had been getting into fights, but I hadn't known the police had gotten involved. I struggled to keep the surprise from showing on my face.

"Jason Sheffield was the last person to see Amy Walsh alive. By his own admission, they'd broken up earlier that evening. He has no alibi for the time of her death."

"Because he was out looking for her." I balled my hands into fists. "He found her just after the police did. He—"

"I don't think a werewolf killed your friend."

My mouth dropped open as Kyle said, "Of course a werewolf killed Amy."

"A werewolf wouldn't have bothered drugging her. Maybe whoever did drug her didn't mean to kill her. Maybe they just meant to knock her out. Maybe whoever they got the drug from screwed up the dose. Regardless, Amy Walsh would have died with or without being mauled."

He flicked the ash from his cigarette. "If you murdered your girlfriend in the middle of a werewolf killing spree, wouldn't making it look like a wolf attack be a pretty good way to cover it up?"

"What, exactly, are you saying?" Kyle's voice was sharp, almost threatening.

There was an odd look on Bishop's face, eerily similar to pity. "I think Hemlock had, or has, a serial killer infected with LS. I just don't think that's who killed your friend. Two perpetrators, one using the murders of another to hide his own. I think Amy Walsh was killed by Jason Sheffield."

Bishop's words hit me with the force of a tsunami, and only Kyle's presence at my back kept me from staggering. The meager glow from the lamp seemed to pulse on and off like a strobe light, echoing the pounding of my heart as it beat against my rib cage. It was ridiculous. Insane. Ludicrous with a side of laughable. He couldn't be serious.

Kyle stepped around me. His whole body radiated tension. "Jason can't even remember the rules to *Clue*. He isn't smart enough to think of that."

"Maybe not. But Matt Sheffield is. And he would clean up after his son."

Bishop began ticking off items on his fingers. "Jason Sheffield was with Amy Walsh before her death. He has a history of anger problems and the breakup gives him a potential motive. If your inventory was correct, half the file—including the toxicology report and my recommendation to bring in the FBI—is missing. Not to mention the fact that I was put on leave shortly after openly questioning whether or not your friend really was killed by a werewolf."

He shook his head. "There are only a few people in Hemlock powerful enough to do that, and one of them is that kid's father. Another is Branson Derby—who, according to local gossip, has taken quite a liking to Jason Sheffield. I think the word *protégé* is being tossed around."

A thousand thoughts crashed through my mind, leaving me slightly off balance. Bishop was insane and Kyle and I were leaving—just as soon as I was certain my legs wouldn't give out on me. "If Jason hurt"—I couldn't say *killed*—"Amy, he wouldn't have gotten me the police report."

"The report with pages missing?"

"There's no reason to think Jason took those pages," said Kyle.

"There's no reason to think he didn't."

There were plenty of reasons. I just couldn't think straight enough to list them. I shook my head. Crazy. It was all crazy. "Jason couldn't have done it."

"Jason didn't do it," said Kyle. "And I'm not listening to any more of this garbage." He turned and strode past me, walking across the lawn and disappearing around the side of the house.

I swallowed and started to follow.

"Can I offer you a piece of advice?" Bishop asked.

I paused, one foot on the overgrown lawn, the other still inside the shed.

"You should let all of this go."

How could he tell me everything he just had and possibly think I could do that? "Is that why you told us? Because you've let it go?" I didn't give him a chance to answer.

Kyle was waiting for me on the sidewalk in front of the house.

"The guy's insane." He started walking back the way we had come, his pace too quick for my shorter legs. Each word like a small explosion, he said, "I can't believe we listened to *anything* he had to say."

"You don't think he was telling the truth?" I struggled to keep up while sidestepping broken glass and the debris of the Meadows. "About the drugs and the fur?"

"I don't know. Yes. No. Maybe." Kyle pushed his hair back with both hands as he walked. "The guy's obviously got a screw loose or some grudge against the Sheffields. You heard the way he accused Jason's father of covering for him."

Ben's truck came into view.

"I guess," I said.

Kyle stopped. "What do you mean, you guess? You didn't actually believe any of that stuff he said about Jason." He stared at me, eyes wide. "Mac, tell me you don't believe any of that."

I wrapped my arms around myself. "No," I said. "Of course not." But even to my own ears, I sounded uncertain. Jason *had* changed—and if I was really honest, the changes had started before Amy's death.

"It's just . . . He spent all summer lying about what happened that night. And he let you feel guilty for not answering Amy's call when, all along, it was his fault she was out by herself."

Kyle stared at me like he'd never seen me before. "That doesn't make him a murderer."

I suddenly wished I had never asked Jason for the file, that I had never tried to look into any of this. Better to never have any answers than to wonder—even for a millisecond—if Jason could have hurt Amy. To have Kyle stare at me like I was a complete stranger.

The blighted street blurred and I wiped my eyes with the sleeve of my jacket.

Kyle shook his head and strode away, like he couldn't stand the sight of me. When he reached Ben's truck, he stopped, put both hands on the hood, and stared down at the ground.

After a few minutes, not knowing what else to do, I walked over to him.

He didn't look up. "You were the one who told me I needed to have more faith in Jason," he said softly. He flexed his hands against the hood.

I bit my lip. "I know. And I'm sorry."

"Sorry you wondered if maybe Bishop was right, or sorry that I know you wondered?"

I flushed with shame. "Both, I guess." I felt unbelievably small and wretched. "What do we do now?"

Kyle straightened. "Now we go talk to Trey. After you drop off Ben's keys. My car is parked on the next block."

"You don't have to keep helping me," I said, the words carving a hole in my chest.

"Yeah," said Kyle, "I do." He started walking, slower

this time so I wouldn't have trouble keeping up. "Amy was my friend, too. If Bishop was telling the truth about the drugs and the fur, I have to know."

I opened my mouth to reply, but no words came out. I was struck silent as a white werewolf stepped out of the shadows in front of Kyle's car.

22

THE CRACKED PAVEMENT, RUN-DOWN BUILDINGS, AND
overgrown lots fell away. All I could see was the white wolf.
I didn't move. I barely breathed. I was frozen, pinned to the
spot like a butterfly in a shadow box.

Kyle had parked under a streetlight, and even from a
distance, I could tell the wolf's muzzle was covered in something thick and dark. The pictures of Amy flashed through
my head, the ones where her upper body had been reduced
to a huge, gaping wound.

The wolf bared its teeth as Kyle slowly stepped in front
of me.

He reached into his pocket and then pressed something
into my hand: his car keys and pocket knife.

He was joking, right? Going against a werewolf with a
two-inch blade was like trying to stop a tank by throwing
a pebble.

"I'll draw it away," he whispered, voice pitched so low that
I had to strain to hear him over my thundering heartbeat and
the snarling wolf. "Take the car and get out of here."

"I'm not leaving you."

The wolf began stalking toward us, taking its time like it was playing a game.

Kyle stepped forward and I grabbed his arm, desperately trying to haul him back. "If that's the thing that killed Amy," I hissed, filled with panic, "then it's killed four people."

The muscles in Kyle's arm shifted under my hand, and I stumbled away as bones shattered.

"I'm not people."

With a strangled cry, Kyle fell to the ground. His spine arched as his bones and muscles were forced into new shapes and positions. Nightmarish crunching and tearing sounds came from his body as it ripped itself apart and knit itself back together. His clothing fell away in tattered shreds as fur flowed over his skin.

Taking advantage of Kyle's momentary weakness, the white wolf leaped, trying to fasten its jaws around Kyle's throat before he could complete the shift.

It was too late. Kyle rolled away and was suddenly a brown, snarling wolf.

The two wolves circled each other.

Wolf-Kyle glanced at me and then started backing toward a trash-filled vacant lot.

The white wolf leaped and the two collided in a dizzying blur of fur, claws, and teeth.

I had to do something to help Kyle. Anything.

I spotted a broken brick a few feet from the car and scrambled to get my hands on it. I heard a high-pitched whine from the lot, and when I turned, the white wolf had Kyle pinned. It sank its teeth into Kyle's back, piercing the skin and muscle beneath the fur.

Panic surged in my chest. Kyle was going to lose.

He let out a keening, broken sound and I darted forward.

Neither wolf paid any attention to me.

Hoisting my brick, I aimed at the white werewolf's head and threw as hard as I could. The brick collided with the wolf's skull and then bounced to the ground.

It let go of Kyle and barked out a surprised yelp just as I realized my plan didn't have a step two.

Heart pounding and body flooded with adrenaline, I sprinted to the Honda. Clutching Kyle's car keys, I pressed the button to trip the locks. My fingers skimmed the door handle just as the wolf collided with my side and sent me sprawling.

All the air was forced out of my lungs in a whoosh as I landed on my stomach. My palms stung where they had slapped the pavement. I had dropped the keys on impact.

Gasping, I rolled to my back just as a brown blur of fur sailed over me.

Kyle tried to gain a hold on the white werewolf, but it was no use. The other wolf was larger and better at fighting. I fumbled behind me, trying to find the keys, and watched, helpless, as the white wolf clamped its jaw over Kyle's throat and shook him like a rag doll.

It tossed him aside and Kyle lay, dazed and broken, on the ground.

With Kyle out of the way, the wolf turned on me.

It padded forward, a growl reverberating in its throat that set my skin crawling. The stench of it made my stomach flip. Kyle and Heather smelled kind of like the forest when they transformed; the thing in front of me smelled like something rotten and dead. The fur around its mouth was matted with blood.

My fingers closed around the keys and I pushed myself backward, wincing as my shoulder blades collided with the car door.

The wolf tilted its head to the side and the growl sputtered, like a lawn mower engine that wouldn't catch. Something slipped behind its eyes, some emotion or thought. The wolf shook its head—the way crazy people did in movies when they heard voices.

It took another step forward and shook its head again. The strangest feeling swept over me. I felt like it *knew* me.

But as soon as the thought entered my head, the wolf made a sudden lunge.

Screaming, I covered my face and head with my arms, waiting for claws to tear me to shreds.

Nothing happened.

Cautiously, I lowered my arms.

Wolf-Kyle was struggling to get back up, his hind legs scrambling against the pavement like they didn't want to work. The movement and noise had caught the white wolf's attention, and it had abandoned me to creep toward him.

Shaking, I forced myself to my feet and wrenched open the car door. I threw myself behind the wheel, slammed the door behind me, and jammed the key into the ignition.

I glanced out the window. Kyle, still in wolf form, had made it to his feet and was trying to fend off the white wolf as it circled him and made random lunges, like a cat toying with a mouse.

I yanked on my seat belt, gunned the ignition, and shoved the car into drive.

The Honda's headlights bounced over the deserted street and shone on the two wolves in front of me. I aimed the car at the white wolf and floored it. The werewolf tried to dart out of the way, but I yanked the wheel hard to the left and clipped its hindquarters.

I said a quick prayer of thanks that Tess had dated that defensive driving instructor as the car bounced over the curb. There was a blur of movement on my right: Wolf-Kyle.

I hit the brakes and tried to reach the passenger-side door. It took me two tries before I realized the seat belt was holding me back. I unbuckled the belt, pushed open the door, and then wedged myself as far to the driver's side as possible, giving Kyle enough room to scramble between the seats and into the back.

I glanced in the rearview mirror. The white wolf was unsteadily getting to its feet.

I closed the passenger-side door and slammed the gear-shift into reverse, fully intending to hit the wolf with several hundred pounds of Japanese engineering.

But before I could take my foot off the brake, two black SUVs barreled around the corner at the other end of the block.

Without thinking, I threw the car into drive and sped down the street. I glanced in the rearview mirror just in time to see the white wolf bolt for a vacant lot as the two SUVs screeched to a halt and men with what looked like guns tumbled out.

I didn't ease up on the gas until we were out of the Meadows.

I killed the engine and lights. "I'll be as quick as I can," I said.

Wolf-Kyle raised his head and watched as I slid out of the car and stepped onto the uneven, rocky ground. A year from now, this would be a strip mall, but all the developers had done so far was bulldoze a bunch of rocks and trees.

Across the street, the Walmart sign glowed like a beacon. I could have parked in the lot, but I was feeling extra paranoid. I couldn't remember if there were cameras outside and I hadn't wanted to risk someone catching a naked Kyle on grainy security footage. For all I knew, Derby had put out an all-points bulletin asking local department stores to be on the lookout for suspicious naked people trying to procure discount clothing.

I carefully picked my way across the building site until I reached the road, and then I made a mad dash for the Walmart doors. Hemlock didn't have a twenty-four-hour department store and it was ten minutes until closing.

The guy who rounded up the shopping carts stared as I hurtled past him and into the store. Stumbling to a walk, I tried to brush some of the dirt from my face and jacket as I went in search of the menswear department.

Other customers shot me curious glances and I tried not to shiver. The bright lights, familiar plastic smells, and neatly ordered shelves seemed completely alien after what had just happened.

Guessing at Kyle's size, I grabbed a pair of Levi's and a gray sweatshirt. Feeling slightly evil, I added a pair of boxers adorned with little hearts to the pile. Beggars couldn't be choosers.

A voice crackled over the PA system, announcing that the store would be closing in five minutes.

I darted to the shoes and grabbed the first cheap pair of sneakers I found in size thirteen. Serena had checked Kyle's Vans once, and then made a speculative comment as to the dimensions of something else. Ever since, it had been easy to remember Kyle's shoe size.

Blushing and struggling to hold on to everything, I raced to the small pharmacy section and grabbed a container of baby wipes. Mission accomplished, I headed for the nearest checkout.

I scanned the magazines and tabloids as I waited. There was a copy of *Newsweek* wedged between *Cosmo* and *Star*. The cover advertised an interview with Amy's grandfather—Senator Walsh—and there was a small picture of him shaking hands with Branson Derby. I reached for the magazine, but the line advanced and the cashier started ringing up my things.

I tried not to wince at the total as I swiped my debit card. Then, bags and receipt in hand, I headed back across the road.

Kyle had already shifted. He rolled down the window and I passed him the clothes before walking around to the other side of the car and sliding behind the wheel.

Unable to help myself, I glanced in the rearview mirror and glimpsed a strip of pale skin as Kyle got dressed. "Are you okay?" With a sick feeling, I remembered how the other wolf had torn into him with its teeth.

"Yeah. Shifting speeds up the healing process."

"I thought . . ." I shook my head, unable to get the words out. I had been so horribly certain the other wolf would win. A fine trembling started in my shoulders. I could have lost him. I almost *had* lost him.

Kyle squeezed my shoulder and I grabbed his hand, trying to convince myself that he was solid and real and unhurt.

"I'm okay, Mac," he said softly. "Really."

I nodded and sucked in a deep breath. Then I forced myself to let go of Kyle's hand.

I opened the package of baby wipes, flipped down the sun visor, and then studied my face in the mirror as I tried to clean off some of the grime.

"What about you? Are you all right?"

"Just scraped up a bit." It was kind of miraculous. The wolf could easily have killed me and all I had were a few scratches. It didn't make any sense. It . . . I reeled and gripped the steering wheel as a horrible thought took shape. "Kyle?"

He reached between the seats and snagged a handful of wipes. "Yeah?"

"Do you think . . ." I couldn't get the thought out and had to start again. "Do you think Jason could have been the wolf we just saw?"

"Do I think Jason was the wolf who tackled you and nearly severed my spine with its teeth, you mean?" He snorted. "No."

"Then why didn't it hurt me?" I stared miserably at the bulldozed ground in front of the car. "It was full-on Cujo when it went after you. Something about me stopped it. It was almost like it recognized me."

"Cujo was a Saint Bernard."

"Not the point." I slumped in my seat, suddenly so tired and confused that I was on the verge of tears. "I can't believe you're joking about this."

Kyle climbed out of the car and walked around to the passenger side. He got back in. After a moment, he reached for my hand. "I'm sorry. It's just . . ." He shook his head and traced a circle on my palm with his thumb. "Maybe your knack for saying stupid things when you're worried is rubbing off on me."

"I don't say stupid things," I muttered. "Not always, anyway." I leaned over and rested my head on his shoulder. I wondered if this was a violation of his friends-only rule. Surely there was some loophole for near-death experiences.

He reached over with his other hand and brushed the hair back from my face. After a minute, he gently eased me away, freeing his shoulder and leaving a very platonic amount of space between us. "Not even Bishop thought Jason was actually a werewolf. What makes you think it was him?"

Kyle's voice was careful—almost free of recrimination—but disappointment flashed in his eyes and I cringed.

"I don't. Not really." I wrapped my arms around myself, trying to thwart the chill that pierced my chest as I thought of the way the wolf had stared at me. "At least, I know I shouldn't. I mean, Jason is one of my best friends, and you were right when you said he couldn't hurt anyone. At least the old Jason couldn't. But he hasn't been the old Jason in so long. I just . . . I don't know."

Kyle watched me patiently, waiting for me to make some kind of sense.

"It was willing to go after you, but something about me stopped it. It could easily have torn out my throat"—Kyle flinched—"but it didn't. It was almost like it was fighting itself, the way it kept shaking its head."

"So you think Jason would be willing to kill me and not you? Thanks."

"You guys did seem ready to tear each other to pieces this morning."

"Not even remotely the same thing." He exhaled slowly. "Even if it did recognize you, that doesn't mean it was Jason. Besides, do you really think he would join the Trackers if he was infected? Or that he has the impulse control to keep his temper in check and not shift every time he has too much to drink or someone looks at him the wrong way?"

I blushed. The more he spoke, the stupider it sounded. And the guiltier I felt for saying it out loud. For even thinking it.

"Jason's my friend—even though he's turned into an idiot. He would never have hurt Amy. And no matter what he's done, he doesn't deserve to have you—or anyone—think that. For all you know, Bishop has an ax to grind against Jason's father, or Derby somehow figured out you would go there and put him up to messing with your head."

I stared at the dashboard, stomach queasy with guilt and skin flushed with shame. Kyle was right. He was right and I was horrible. Horrible and disloyal. "Forget I said anything," I whispered. "Temporary insanity brought on by stress and another brush with death."

Kyle didn't say anything. After a minute, I did what felt like the bravest thing I'd done all night: I looked up and met his eyes.

"You know what I think?"

I shook my head.

"I think you were waiting for Jason to really let you down. I think some small part of you was ready to believe what Bishop said, to believe the worst of him."

I sucked in a sharp breath. "That's not true. Or fair. I told him that Jason didn't do it. You were there. You heard me."

"You said Jason *couldn't* have done it, not that he *hadn't*," Kyle clarified. "And I heard the way your voice trembled. I was standing close enough to hear your heart speed up as you listened to Bishop." The expression on his face was impossible to read. "When you expect someone to let you down, it's easier to believe the worst of them."

I swallowed. "And you think that's how I feel about

Jason—like I expect him to let me down?"

Kyle shook his head. "No. I think that's the way you feel about all of us—anyone you let get close."

I blinked, stunned. I felt like I'd been slapped.

"It's okay," he said. "It's just the way you're built. Growing up how you did—it's probably understandable." Frowning, he reached out and brushed his hand against my cheek, wiping away tears that I hadn't realized were falling. "But it does make loving you hard, sometimes."

I opened my mouth to argue, to tell him that he was wrong, but then his last sentence registered. "What did you say?"

Kyle ignored my question and reached for the door handle. "I'll drive us over to Trey's. We should head out before it gets any later."

I unbuckled my seat belt and lunged across his lap, grabbing his hand before he could open the door. I let out a guffaw of pain as I practically impaled myself on the gearshift. "What did you say?" I repeated, voice low and breathless.

Kyle stared down at me. The Adam's apple in his throat bobbed as he swallowed. "That can't possibly be comfortable."

He reached down and gently helped me into an upright position. I ended up sitting on his lap with my legs stretched out onto the driver's seat and my back pressed against the passenger door.

"Did you just say you loved me?"

Kyle blushed and nodded. "Not great timing, I know.

266

Especially after I told you I wanted to go back to the way things were."

It felt like a thousand birds were taking flight inside my chest. "Kyle?"

"Yeah?"

"Shut up." And then I was kissing him, pressing my hands to the sides of his face as his arms strained around me.

I put everything I had into the kiss, all the things I didn't know how to find the words for—the fear that I had almost lost him, the relief that he was all right, the worry that he would leave. I clung to him like I would never let go as Kyle kissed me back with an intensity that made every nerve in my body hum.

"You're still crying," he murmured, moments or hours later, between kisses and breaths.

"It's a girl thing," I whispered, my lips brushing his.

Kyle's hand slipped under my shirt and jacket, tracing circles on the skin at the small of my back. I shivered and he held me closer for a moment, then moved away slightly—just far enough so he could study my face. "I thought it would be easier if I left without admitting it—like if I never said the words, it would stop being true."

The bottom dropped out of my stomach, like I was on a roller coaster that had just jumped the rails.

Kyle sighed and his hand stilled on my back. "But every time I almost lose you, I feel like part of myself gets chipped away. And the thought of leaving just gets harder." He withdrew his hand and pushed his hair back. "I'm probably not making any sense."

I pressed my forehead to his. "You could just stay."

His lips curved up in a sad smile. "You make it sound so easy."

I shook my head and pulled away. "No," I said, and I knew my voice came out desperate and a little lost. "You just always make things too hard."

23

KYLE LOVED ME. KYLE LOVED ME AND HE HAD TOLD ME he loved me and I . . . hadn't said it back. It wasn't that I didn't want to. Sitting next to him in the car, studying his profile in the dashboard light, I *wanted* to say those words.

More than anything.

Because I did love him. I was certain of it. It was in the way I felt when I looked at him and the taste of his name on my lips and how three years of history had brought us to this point.

I was sure.

And I knew—from a thousand books and sitcoms and movies—that the words should be easy to say. Even if I had never said them. To anyone. In any capacity.

But each time I opened my mouth, they stuck in the back of my throat.

We passed a darkened bakery and a gas station where you could buy live fishing bait, and then the houses began thinning out. Trees closed in on both sides and Kyle switched on the high beams as we left the last streetlight behind. Technically, we were still inside Hemlock, though you'd never have guessed it.

I'd once heard Ben tell Tess that he wouldn't mind owning a place out here. He said it was close enough to town to be convenient but far enough out that you had the illusion of quiet. I bit my lip. Ben hadn't been home when we swung by to drop off his keys and explain about the truck. I'd ended up leaving the keys—along with a very apologetic note—on his kitchen counter.

"Why didn't you talk to Trey before Bishop?" asked Kyle, cutting off my thoughts.

I shrugged. "I tried to talk to Serena about the calls yesterday and she totally stonewalled me. Neither of them was at school today. I guess I was hoping Bishop would say something that would give me some sort of clue before I tried talking to either of them again."

"Very Nancy Drew."

"I don't remember Nancy Drew ever having to deal with werewolf murders," I muttered, suddenly gloomy.

Serena's friendship was important to me, and I knew that once Kyle and I showed up there asking questions, it might become a thing of the past. As much as the idea hurt, I was willing to risk it. If it led to answers, I'd risk anything.

"It's the next driveway after this one. On the left."

Kyle slowed and turned.

Serena's house was set at the end of a wide, curving lane and wasn't visible from the road. We rounded the last bend and Kyle muttered a curse. There were two cars and a familiar SUV clustered in front of the Carsons' white, two-story farmhouse.

"Back up," I hissed. "Backupbackupbackupback-
upbackup." Kyle couldn't be near the Trackers. If they
suspected what he was, they'd shove him in a cage. Or
worse. "Oh God, Kyle, back up."

His voice was sharp as he stared into the rearview mirror. "I can't."

I turned and looked out the back window. Another car,
headlights dark, had followed us up the driveway. It parked
at an angle, blocking us in.

They had to be Trackers. Who else would Jason be hanging around with?

"You have to leave me." Kyle started to object and I cut
him off. "Run on foot until you can lose them in the trees,
then shift. You can get away if I'm not slowing you down."

"What about you?"

"I'm human. They won't hurt me." I wasn't actually sure
that was true, but there was less chance of them hurting me
than him.

Kyle's gaze swept the scene in front of the house. "That's
very noble."

"So you'll do it?"

"Not a chance."

A person—too small to be Trey and obviously a girl—was
pushed out of the house. She stumbled across the wrap-
around porch and down the steps. "They've got Serena."

I glanced out the Honda's back window just as two figures emerged from the car behind us.

I gripped Kyle's arm. "No matter what happens, don't

271

lose your temper or shift. Don't give them an excuse to hurt you."

Voice grim, Kyle said, "Of the two of us, my temper isn't the one we usually have to worry about."

A man wrenched open Kyle's door. I recognized him. He was the one we had passed in the Meadows, the guy who looked like he could bench-press livestock. He was holding a Taser. "Out."

"We don't want any trouble," I said as the Amazonian woman he'd been with earlier yanked open my door and grabbed my arm. "We'll just turn around and leave."

Without a word, she pulled me out of the car and started dragging me up the driveway. She was incredibly strong. I tried breaking free, but it was like arm wrestling one of the guys on the football team: completely futile.

I glanced over my shoulder. Kyle was walking calmly in front of the other one. From the way the guy was standing behind him, I was betting the Taser was pressed against Kyle's back.

I swallowed. This so wasn't good.

The Carsons' yard was lit by two small lampposts on either side of the front walkway. As we drew closer, I was able to make out Derby, Trey, Serena, three more Trackers, and Jason.

Serena was kneeling on the ground, trying to help Trey, who couldn't seem to lift his head. Jason watched them with the strangest expression on his face—almost like he didn't know who they were. He was so focused on them that he didn't even notice Kyle and me.

But Derby did. A surge of hatred flashed in his eyes before his hawklike features settled into a fierce grin. Next to the people he had with him—all younger and stronger—he should have seemed weak, but he looked oddly powerful and invigorated. A creature in his element who was completely in control.

We were so screwed.

"Miss Dobson. What a nice surprise." His tone contradicted the words.

Jason glanced over and his eyes widened. He shifted his gaze from me and Kyle to the two Trackers who were keeping us in check. "What are they doing here?" His voice was curiously flat—like that of a telemarketer or someone who had gone into shock. He took a step toward me and stumbled slightly. He shook his head like he was trying to clear it.

"I believe your friends are here for the same reason we are: to talk to Trey Carson. After all, you gave Miss Dobson a copy of the police report."

Jason flinched. Jason never flinched.

"Trey doesn't know anything," interrupted Serena, voice quavering. Her shirt was ripped at the shoulder and tears had made a mess of her mascara.

Derby stared down at her, eyes merciless. "We have reports that your brother is infected."

She shook her head. "He's not."

Trey looked up and I reeled. His face was a mask of bruises and blood, and his left eye was swollen shut. He gently pushed Serena away and staggered to his feet, swaying like he couldn't find his center of gravity. "I didn't hurt Amy," he said, the words coming out halting and choked. "I would never have hurt her."

At a whispered word from Derby, the Tracker next to him went for Serena, dragging her away from her brother.

"Wait!" I tried to wrench my arm free from the woman holding me, but her grip was like a vise.

Derby regarded me coldly. "The Taser pressed to your friend's back is calibrated specifically to take down a were-wolf. I'm not sure what kind of damage it would do to a human, but I wouldn't advise forcing us to test it."

I swallowed and stared at Jason, willing him to look at me. How could he let Derby threaten Kyle?

But he just stood there, shoulders hunched, watching Trey. There was something wrong with him. I'd seen him drunk plenty of times, but I'd never seen him like this. It was like he was somehow . . . vacant.

At a nod from Derby, the Tracker holding Serena shoved her to the ground and leveled a kick at her stomach. She gagged and tried to curl into a ball.

"Ree!" Trey let out a strangled yell and tried to run for-ward, but another Tracker pushed him back.

Black spots hovered at the edge of my vision as my pulse thundered in my ears. I clenched my hands into fists.

Derby turned his attention back to Trey. "Are you infected?"

Trey shook his head, the movement strained and weak. "No. Let her go. She doesn't have anything to do with this."

The Tracker kicked Serena a second time.

"Stop it! Please!" I struggled against the one holding me, forgetting, for a second, Kyle and the Taser. All I could see was Serena. It didn't matter that she had lied to me about Trey. All that mattered was that they were hurting her. "Jason, you can't let them do this!"

Derby passed Jason a silver flask and waited until he took a long swallow before turning back to Trey. "Why did Amy Walsh call you the night she died?"

Trey hesitated but, seeing the Tracker take aim at Serena again, blurted, "She was upset."

Jason tossed the flask back to Derby and strode over to Trey, cold superiority sliding over his face. "Why would she call you if she was upset? You're nothing."

Trey tensed but didn't reply.

Something glinted on Jason's hand—some sort of metal, almost like a knuckle ring. It caught the light as Jason drew back his arm and punched Trey in the stomach.

Trey stumbled but didn't fall. Voice as rough as gravel, he asked, "Why do you care if she called me that night? You didn't care about her any of the nights that came before it."

Jason hit Trey again, full in the face this time. Trey staggered and spat a mouthful of blood onto the grass.

I was going to throw up. I'd seen Jason in fights before, but this wasn't a fight—it was more like torture.

Kyle's voice rang out across the yard. "Jason! Enough!" The Tracker at his back pushed the Taser against him, curtailing anything further he might say.

Derby took in the scene with a small smile on his face. It was like he was watching a rerun or his favorite

play—anticipation for everything that happened but no surprise.

A horrible realization flooded through me: this wasn't
an interrogation; it was an initiation. Derby was going to
push Jason until he did something so horrible that the
Trackers would own him.

Jason flexed his hand. "You don't know anything about
Amy."

Trey tried to laugh, but it came out a broken wheeze. "I
know what you did to her."

It felt as though the ground underneath my feet was
falling away. The Tracker holding my arm let go, but I was
barely aware of it. All I could see was Jason, and all I could
hear were Trey's words, echoing through my head over and
over. "Jason? What did you do?" My voice was so small that
it went unnoticed.

Jason shook his head, dazed. "I didn't do anything to
Amy." But he didn't sound certain.

"Do you really think she didn't know?" Trey looked
oddly strong underneath the blood and bruises as he glared
at Jason. "All those months when you were watching her
best friend? Did you really think Amy was that stupid?"

Trey's eyes found mine, just for a second. "She knew you
had feelings for Mac."

Something hit my shoulder and I gasped. I had backed
away from Jason and Trey without realizing it, backed up so
far that I had collided with Kyle.

It had been me.

I was the reason Jason had broken up with Amy. The

reason she'd run out of his car that night. The reason she was dead.

No wonder she was haunting me.

Kyle murmured something in my ear, but I couldn't make sense of the words as he steadied me with his hands and carefully pushed me so that I was standing to his right—away from the Tracker with the Taser.

Derby walked over to Jason and pressed a Taser into his hand as he whispered something into his ear.

For a moment, Jason went horribly still, and then his face twisted with pain and rage as he took a step toward Trey.

Derby had claimed the Tasers were strong enough to take down a wolf. If Jason used one on Trey and Trey wasn't infected, it might kill him. "We have to stop him."

Kyle tightened his grip on my arm but didn't say anything. Then, without warning, he shoved me.

I stumbled forward, trying to keep my balance. I glanced back just in time to see Kyle's elbow connect with the Tracker's windpipe. The man went down, dropping the Taser and clutching his throat.

I spun and ran for Jason.

There were shouts behind me and I heard Serena yell something, but I concentrated all my strength and energy on lunging at Jason's arm, on getting him to drop the Taser.

For a second, it seemed like I would succeed. I was half Jason's size, but I was desperate and fighting for his future and Trey's life. But then he shoved me and I went sprawling.

I landed hard on my back. For a stunned moment, I

stared up at the stars while I caught my breath and tried to remember how to move.

I turned my head, searching for Kyle.

He was on his knees, a Taser pressed to his neck. Sweat shone on his face and his breathing was ragged. I had no idea how he was managing to push back the wolf.

If he did shift, we were dead. There were too many Trackers. Even with Kyle in wolf form, we'd never get away.

I rolled onto my hands and knees a second before someone grabbed my arm and hauled me roughly to my feet. It was the same Tracker who had dragged me from the car. I was starting to wonder if she took steroids.

Jason advanced on Trey, the Taser shaking in his hand. "Why would Amy have told you anything?"

Trey backed up a step, watching Jason warily.

At some point during the chaos of the past few minutes, Serena had gotten to her feet. "Trey, just tell them!"

One of the Trackers reached for her, but she was faster. She ran for Jason and Trey and threw herself between them. Breathlessly, she gasped, "Amy was sleeping with Trey. To get back at you for Mac. That's why she kept calling him."

Serena's words hit me like a bucket of ice water. *Amy and Trey? To get back at Jason?* My knees threatened to buckle.

Jason shook his head. He turned and stared at Derby. Not me. Not Kyle. It was Derby he turned to. "Amy wouldn't have. Not with a fleabag."

"They're deceptive, Jason. They're not above seducing and preying on human girls. It's a game to them. He used Amy for his own satisfaction and then killed her." There wasn't the slightest trace of hesitation in Derby's voice, no surprise at the news that Amy had been sleeping with Trey.

With a sinking feeling, I realized that he had prepared for this moment, that—as crazy as it seemed—Derby had somehow known about Amy and Trey and had pushed Jason here, to this point, on purpose. And he had known that he would be the one Jason would turn to.

"I didn't kill her," Trey growled. He pushed Serena behind him as Jason's fingers tightened on the Taser.

"Jason, stop!" The Tracker holding me tried to clamp her hand over my mouth, but I ducked my head to the side. "If Trey was infected, he would have shifted by now. Besides, even if he is a werewolf, the police aren't sure Amy's death is connected to the others. They're not sure a werewolf killed her."

Bishop wasn't exactly the entire police department, and he thought Jason was the real murderer—oh, and he was a crazy alcoholic who held secret meetings in tool sheds—but Jason didn't need to know that.

He turned to Derby. "What's Mac talking about?"

"There's a detective who thinks Amy was killed by a human," said Kyle, quickly, before Derby could lie. "We talked to him."

The blood drained from Jason's face at Kyle's words. He stalked toward me. Grabbing my arm with one hand, he yanked me away from the Tracker like I was nothing more than a doll. My heart pounded in my chest as his fingers dug into my skin. His other hand still held the Taser. I was scared of Jason. I had never been scared of Jason before.

Not even after the things Bishop had said.

"I saw her body." His eyes glinted and I realized they were filled with tears. "It was in pieces. *Pieces, Mac.* I couldn't even hold her. When I tried . . ." He made a strangled noise deep in the back of his throat and shook his head.

In that moment, any doubts Bishop had planted about Jason vanished. No one was that good an actor.

He let go of my arm and stepped away from me. "A werewolf did it and Trey is a werewolf."

"Then why hasn't he shifted?"

"Self-preservation, Miss Dobson." Derby's patience for our melodrama was apparently at an end. "Self-preservation and leverage. If he shifts in front of us, his life is over. It's just a matter of tipping the scales enough that he has no choice."

I almost pointed out that beating Serena hadn't done much good, but I really didn't want to encourage them.

Derby glanced at Jason. "There are two canvas bags in the back of my car."

Without being told, Jason turned to get them. Moments later, he was back, one heavy red sack in each hand.

"Set them by the porch," said Derby as he waved one of the other Trackers forward.

The Tracker lifted out a large tank—like the kind exterminators used. He covered his mouth and nose with his T-shirt and began coating the front of the house in a thick liquid. The smell drifted back to us. Not gas, but similar.

It was strong enough to make my nose burn and my stomach roll.

"That, Mr. Carson, is an accelerant. Do you know what an accelerant is?"

"Our little brother's in there!" yelled Serena.

Derby nodded and the Tracker lit a match. "Consider it leverage," he said, as flames roared up the front of the house.

24

Orange light flooded the yard. I ran for Kyle as the Trackers—all but the one covering him—converged on Trey.

The fire seemed to shake Jason out of whatever spell of Derby's he'd been under. He turned on him. "You never said anything about this! This is going too far!"

One of the Trackers broke away from the group surrounding Trey and grabbed Jason's arms, pinning them behind his back.

Derby stared at him coldly. "Remember who it is you're talking to, Jason."

Jason opened his mouth to reply, but the words were lost when two things happened simultaneously: Kyle whirled on the Tracker behind him and Serena ran for the house.

Without thinking, I ran after her.

Serena fell to her knees when she was halfway to the porch. Her spine bent in a way that would leave a human paralyzed. Her bones shattered as her skin split and fur the color of coal dust flowed over her body. I stumble-tripped to a stop, my mind trying to make sense of what I was seeing as a large, black wolf bounded over the flames and into the house.

Two of the Trackers covering Trey raced after her, but they weren't crazy—or dedicated—enough to follow her into the fire.

Serena was infected.

She was infected and she'd been hiding it.

She was infected and she was inside a burning building.

Thoughts ricocheted in my head, each one louder than the last and each one ending with the same four words: Serena was a werewolf.

Forcing myself to focus, I fished my cell out of my pocket. Before I could dial 911, Derby was in front of me. He grabbed the phone from my hand and flung it into the bushes edging the house. He pulled back his arm—to slap me, I think—but Kyle was suddenly between us.

Kyle's hair was damp with perspiration and his breathing was slightly ragged, but he was holding back the shift.

Derby eyed him and hesitated. He was the kind of man who wouldn't think twice about slapping a girl, but a muscular, seventeen-year-old boy was a different story.

There was a shout from one of the Trackers still covering Trey, and everything seemed to move in slow motion as I turned.

Trey was on his knees.

Trey was shifting.

Trey and Serena were both infected and the world I thought I had known was unraveling.

Was everyone in town a werewolf and I just didn't get the memo?

One Tracker was younger than the others. Despite his muscles and tattoos, he couldn't have been any older than nineteen. Eyes wide and frantic, he dodged forward with his Taser, trying to hit Trey before he fully transformed. Without thinking, I ran at him, tackling him from the side.

Jason and Kyle both shouted my name as the Tracker and I fell to the ground and rolled.

He reared up and over me, the expression on his face reminding me of the way Alexis had looked that night in the alley—frightened and in way over his head. A shudder racked my body as I tried to get my arms between us.

A huge, black shape hit the Tracker from the side, its momentum carrying both of them away from me.

Trey.

The Tracker tried to raise the Taser, and the black wolf shredded his arm.

Screaming, the Tracker dropped his weapon and stumbled toward the waiting cars.

I ran forward and retrieved the Taser. It was slippery with blood. Fighting the urge to vomit, I used the hem of my T-shirt to clean the heavy, plastic casing.

A growl swept across the yard and I looked up just in time to see Trey rush Derby.

A Tracker fired his Taser, but Trey dodged the twin darts and circled around, approaching from the other side. He feigned lunges as the Trackers tried to close ranks around their leader.

A look of fear flashed across Derby's face—there and gone so quickly that I wondered if I had really seen it. Before I could process it, tires spun on gravel and head-lights blinded me. I raised my hand to shield my eyes and watched as Derby and his men—all but Jason—ran for the cars and fled.

Trey watched them run with sharp, predatory eyes, and then rounded on Jason. He bared his teeth as he stalked toward him.

Jason backed away, hands raised. His face, covered in a sheen of sweat, glowed in the light from the fire.

"No!" Kyle's voice was a cross between a shout and a howl as he fell to his knees and shifted.

The black wolf—Trey, I had to remind myself—snarled at Kyle and then turned its attention back to Jason. It crouched, like it was preparing to spring, and Wolf-Kyle lunged.

The two wolves rolled away, jaws snapping, in a blur of color. I watched with my heart in my throat, remembering how the white wolf had nearly beaten Kyle.

But Trey and Kyle seemed more evenly matched. Each time one got the upper hand, the other quickly reclaimed it.

I ran to Jason. "You have to call 911!" My voice came out a hoarse croak as the smoke from the fire burned my throat and eyes.

Jason just blinked at me. "Kyle's a werewolf?"

"Yes," I said, dropping the Taser and shoving my hands into Jason's jacket pockets. "And he just saved your life."

My fingers closed on his cell and I dialed 911. "There's

a fire at three fifty-eight Hampton Road." I hung up before the operator could ask any questions.

I saw Jason glance at the Taser and I kicked it as far away as I could. "If you even think about going for that thing, I'll use it on you myself."

Without giving Jason a chance to respond, I sprinted down the driveway, ignoring the way the muscles knotted in my side as I checked to make sure the Trackers really had left. I was terrified they had only pulled back and would find out Kyle was infected, but there was no sign of them. They had come prepared for one werewolf; Serena must have tipped the scales too far out of Derby's comfort zone.

When I got back to the yard, Kyle and Trey were still fighting. Or, more accurately, Trey was trying to get to Jason while Kyle kept forcing him back.

"Go," I coughed, inhaling a lungful of smoke. "While Kyle has Trey distracted. Just get in your car and get out of here before one of them actually hurts the other."

Jason shook his head. "I'm not leaving you with a bunch of fleabags."

I started to point out that the werewolves weren't the ones who had manhandled me, but I caught sight of a black wolf limping around the side of the house. Serena.

She shifted back as I ran to her. She huddled around herself, trying to cover her nudity as she coughed so hard it sounded like she would tear her lungs apart. "Noah's still in there," she gasped. "I couldn't find him."

Trey bolted for the back of the house, Kyle racing just behind.

"It's okay," I whispered, praying the words weren't a lie. "Trey and Kyle will get him out. Everything will be okay." I repeated the words to myself over and over: *Everything will be okay.*

We were so close to the house that it felt like my skin was blistering, and it was hard to properly draw breath. Looking up, I saw Jason staring down at us. I swallowed. "Give me your coat."

Jason hesitated for a moment, conflicting emotions playing across his face in rapid succession; then he shrugged out of his jacket and passed it to me.

I helped Serena get the sleeves over her arms and then helped her stand. She was so tiny compared to Jason that the coat practically fell to her knees. We limped away from the house, stopping in the middle of the lawn to turn and watch.

Everything will be okay. Everything will be okay. Everything will be okay.

Jason stared and Serena gripped my hand. I realized I'd been saying the words out loud, like a Hail Mary.

Serena's gaze flicked to Jason, just for an instant. "Why are you still here?" Though she was crying, her voice was as sharp and steady as a blade.

Jason didn't answer. I glanced at him, but his face didn't give anything away.

Serena suddenly let out a yelp and ran for the corner of the house a second before Trey appeared with their brother wrapped in his arms.

"He's okay," Trey coughed. "Just got a lungful of smoke."

I waited for Kyle to appear. Any second, he would come around the side of the house. Everything would be okay and Kyle would be fine.

Panic swelled in my chest.

Everything was okay. Everything had to be okay. Any second and it would be okay.

Trey transferred Noah to Serena's arms even though— at eight—he was really too big to carry. "Mac . . ."

Any second Kyle would appear. Because. Everything. Was. Okay.

Jason reached for me and I shoved him away. I didn't need him. Everything was okay.

"Mac . . ." Trey was suddenly in front of me. I hadn't seen him move.

I shook my head. "Please." *Please don't tell me whatever it is you're trying to.* The panic in my chest spread through the rest of my body until I could feel it behind my eyes and in my lungs and at my fingertips, dark and toxic and poisoning me from the inside out.

"Part of the ceiling caved in. I couldn't reach him. Kyle was trapped."

The panic swallowed me whole.

I ran for the house, making it as far as the burning porch before arms locked around my waist.

"Let me go!" I screamed as Jason dragged me back to the safety of the yard. "Lemmego!" Kyle. I had to get to Kyle. Kyle was inside that building and nothing was ever going to be okay again because part of me was burning with him and every breath I hauled into my lungs was fire and ash.

I kicked and pleaded and scratched at Jason's arms until I drew blood. But he didn't relax his grip.

I screamed Kyle's name as part of the roof collapsed, sending sparks into the night sky. One word, over and over until my throat was shredded. And when Serena told Jason to get me to his car, to get me out of there, I fought so hard he barely managed to hold on.

"You don't understand. He'll make it out. He took on Jimmy and the white wolf. He's strong. He'll make it out. Please. Just wait. I know he'll make it out. He has to make it out." I was babbling, the words tripping over each other as they rushed out of my mouth.

"We've got to go." Serena jogged to her car and eased Noah into the backseat, then grabbed clothes for herself and Trey out of the trunk.

Jason murmured meaningless words against my hair, trying to calm me enough to get me to the SUV. Trey came back and held one of my arms, making sure I didn't bolt for the house again.

"If he's dead, I'll never forgive you." I suddenly felt cold and frail and horribly numb.

Jason's reply was so soft that I almost missed it. "I won't forgive myself, either."

I tried to count down the seconds and minutes Kyle had been in the house. I held my breath and counted back and watched the flames, and when a second-floor window exploded, when a dark shape hurtled to the ground, I wasn't sure whether or not it was real.

I just stared.

Until Jason and Trey let go of me and raced back across the lawn, and then I ran so fast that my heart threatened to explode out of my chest.

The large, brown wolf shuddered, and the air around it seemed to shimmer as fur flowed back into skin, limbs straightened, and bones shrank until Kyle was lying on the grass, bloody and broken but alive.

I fell at his side as I heard the first sirens—still so far off—in the distance. My hand hovered over his cheek. I wanted desperately to touch him, but I was scared of hurting him. There had been a sickening thud when he hit the ground, and his skin was covered in cuts and burns that the shift should have healed.

"Kyle?" Drops of water landed on his face, carving tiny rivers in the ash and dirt. For a confused second, I thought it had started to rain, and then I realized I was crying.

Serena knelt next to me and pressed two fingers to Kyle's neck, checking his pulse. She frowned. "Weak but steady. I don't know if it's safe to move him."

I expected Trey to reply, but it was Jason who spoke. "You can't leave him here. It won't take the paramedics long to figure out what he is."

Trey stared at Jason for a moment and then nodded.

I gently touched Kyle's hair; it was the only part of him I was certain I couldn't hurt. "It's going to be okay," I murmured. "You're going to be fine."

He let out a soft groan, almost like he had heard me, but he didn't stir.

Trey looked at me. "Do you have his car keys?"

I nodded and wiped my eyes with the back of my hand. The Honda's keys were still in the ignition.

"You and I will take Kyle's car. Ree will follow with Noah."

"My car has more room in the backseat," said Jason.

Trey snorted. "You're not coming with us."

"He's my best friend!"

"We're going to take him someplace safe." Trey's voice came out with the edge of a snarl. "Safe means the Trackers can't know about it. Last I checked, you were a Tracker."

Jason didn't deny it, and my stomach twisted. He turned to me. "Mac?"

I stared at the tattoo on his neck. "No." My voice was cold and final. "You aren't coming with us."

His eyes flashed and he took a step back, shaking his head like he couldn't believe I'd sided with Trey against him.

I turned away. Kyle was broken and bleeding, and right now that was the only thing I cared about. I didn't have room in my heart or head for Jason.

Trey and Serena crouched down to lift Kyle. His eyes sprang open, wide with pain, and he screamed—a jagged howl that sounded like it was being ripped from deep inside his chest.

I squeezed my eyes shut against the sound, just for a second, and then ran ahead of Trey and Serena to open the back door of the Honda. As carefully as possible, they maneuvered Kyle into the backseat.

"Mac?" His voice was a barely audible rasp.

"I'm here," I said, pushing past Serena.

His eyes fluttered open and found mine. For a split second, relief flooded his face. Then a spasm of pain racked his body and he passed out.

The someplace safe turned out to be a house near Breyer's Lake—about a twenty-minute drive from town. At least it would normally have been a twenty-minute drive. Twice, Trey had gotten worried we were being followed and the route he'd taken had been so tangled that we had driven for almost an hour.

As desperate as I had been to get help for Kyle, I hadn't argued for speed. We couldn't afford to take chances.

The house was owned by a paramedic. And a werewolf. Serena and Trey trusted him—and I trusted Serena and Trey—but that didn't mean I felt safe. I wasn't sure I'd ever feel safe again.

At least I was wearing a clean T-shirt—one that wasn't covered in Tracker blood. Serena had fished it out of their trunk. It was like a discount clothing bin in there. I guess werewolves went through clothes pretty quickly.

I pulled my knees up to my chest and wrapped my arms around my legs. It was drafty in the upstairs hallway. And dark. The only light came from underneath a closed door across the hall.

I heard footsteps on the stairs, and then Serena's socks came into view.

I glanced up. "How's Noah?"

"Okay, I think . . . all things considered. He's sleeping on Henry's couch." Serena crossed her arms and shivered.

"Trey made him hide upstairs when he saw the Trackers pull up, so Noah didn't see most of what happened in the yard."

She studied my face and frowned worriedly. "Can I get you anything?"

I shook my head.

Serena lowered herself to the floor next to me. "Henry is really good at what he does. He'll know what to do for Kyle."

"What if—" I clamped my mouth shut and breathed shallowly through my nose. I couldn't make myself finish the sentence. Kyle hadn't stirred on the drive over or as he was carried into the house.

"Kyle's strong and he's stubborn. He'll be okay."

"Maybe." The word came out a choked whisper.

Serena stood and walked to the end of the hall. She was back a minute later with a box of tissues.

"Werewolves can take a lot of damage," she said as I blew my nose. "Trey was shot by a group of hunters last year. He almost gave Dad a heart attack, but he pulled through."

I swallowed. "Your dad knows?"

Serena nodded and sat back down. "We were pretty young when we were attacked. Trey was twelve and I was eleven. It was kind of hard to hide."

"What happened?"

She didn't say anything, and I immediately felt bad for asking. It wasn't really the same thing, but I wouldn't be comfortable if people asked me to tell them what had happened with Jimmy in the alley.

A blush crept across my cheeks. "I'm sorry. It's none of my business."

"No, that's not it." Her gaze flicked between my face and the closed door. I realized this was the first time I had ever seen Serena without makeup and wearing sweats. It made her look younger and a little vulnerable, like I was seeing her without the armor she usually wore. "It was a long time ago and it doesn't bother me to talk about it. I'm just not sure you need to be hearing about werewolf attacks right now."

I slowly exhaled, glad I hadn't upset her by asking. "Honestly? I could really use the distraction." Anything to disrupt the horrible litany of *what-ifs* that kept running through my head.

Serena studied my face for a moment and then shrugged. "It was when we were living in Maine. Our house bordered a wooded area with hiking trails. Trey and I were playing out back and this huge, black shape came out of the trees. I thought it was a dog at first, and then Trey yelled at me to get inside. I tried to run, but it was too fast."

She touched her shoulder and I wondered if there were scars there, like the ones Kyle had on his back. "It went after me first and then attacked Trey when he tried to help me."

"I can't believe you both survived." Children under fifteen had less than a 40 percent chance of living through their first transformation. No one really knew why. Some people theorized that it was because their bodies were still developing, that some critical change happened around fifteen that allowed the human body to survive the shift. The younger the victim, the lower their chances were.

"I almost didn't," said Serena softly. "That first year, I got horribly sick any time I shifted. The first time it happened, I ended up in bed for a month." She shuddered. "I remember feeling like my entire body was on fire and like a thousand spiders were crawling under my skin."

"But you made it through."

Serena nodded. "And so will Kyle."

I wanted to believe her. More than anything. I pressed the heels of my palms to my eyes, trying to keep from crying again. Crying felt too much like admitting Serena might be wrong.

"What about Henry?" I asked, desperate to keep her talking. "How do you know him?"

Serena smiled. "Henry's from Hemlock; he grew up here. His wife left him when he got infected. We just sort of ran into him in the woods one day after we moved to town. About four years ago. He was curious and followed us home. We've learned a lot from him. Like self-control. That thing you told Jason about Trey not being infected because he hadn't shifted? That wasn't totally off base."

I tried to remember what I had said. The previous few hours were a nightmarish blur, like a horror movie shot out of order and played backward. "What do you mean?"

"Most wolves would have shifted long before we did, but Trey and I have been taking lessons from Henry three times a week for years. Lots of meditation. Physical exercises. Breathing techniques. Some herbs and vitamins.

Henry used to be a vegan and a Buddhist and he's all about self-control."

"Sounds like *The Karate Kid*."

"It's not far off," she said thoughtfully. "We use meditation to control our shifts, to keep our emotions in check." Serena rubbed her eyes; she looked as exhausted as I felt. "It helps that Trey and I have each other and that we found Henry. I can't imagine what it would be like to go through the whole wolf thing on your own." She was quiet for a moment. "That's why Trey's repeating senior year. He got held back on purpose because he was worried about me being by myself—especially after what happened to Amy."

She twisted her hands and looked down. "Anyway, that night after the Tracker meeting was the first time I ever came close to losing control in public. That's why I got Trey to pick me up instead of letting you and Jason drive me home. If Trey hadn't been around, I would have called Henry."

"Not your dad?"

She hesitated, like she was weighing her words. "I love my dad, but he doesn't always get the wolf stuff. In bigger cities, wolves usually form packs—pockets of people who haven't registered and who help each other. Or control each other. In Hemlock, there's just Henry, Trey, and me. And I guess Kyle now."

"And whoever's been attacking and killing people," I added.

A wary look crossed Serena's face. "Trey didn't hurt Amy."

"I know." For one thing, Trey didn't look anything like the werewolf that had been terrorizing Hemlock. For another, I'd seen the expression on his face when he confronted Jason. If he had drugged Amy, he wouldn't have been so furious at Jason for hurting her.

"She must have really hated me, huh?" My voice broke over the words.

Serena wrapped an arm around me. "You didn't know," she whispered. "It's not your fault."

But it was. If I had paid attention—if I had noticed what was really going on—then maybe none of this would have been happening.

It had never occurred to me that I could lose Amy twice, but that's what it felt like. It felt like I was losing her all over again.

The door across the hall creaked open and I climbed unsteadily to my feet as Trey stepped out.

"Kyle's still unconscious, but Henry said you can go in."

I started to push past him, but he grabbed my arm. "Dobs . . . He's not in good shape." Trey's eyes were sad and serious and his face was still streaked with soot.

He glanced at Serena and then moved aside to let me pass.

Inside, Henry stood between me and the bed.

I'd seen him when we first arrived, but I'd been too shaken to really notice anything about him. The man standing in front of me, blocking Kyle from view, was only about five seven, but he was wide through the shoulders and built like a barrel. Though he had salt-and-pepper hair, he didn't look that old—midthirties, maybe.

I opened my mouth to ask how Kyle was, but the words wouldn't come out.

Henry pushed a pair of thick, horn-rimmed glasses up the bridge of his nose. "Trey and I set a few broken bones in his legs—otherwise, they would have healed badly and he would have had to shift to fix them. Which can be excruciating. The burns weren't as bad as Trey thought they were—your friend's body probably healed some of them in the car." He cleared his throat. "Werewolves can heal much faster and take more damage than humans, but there are still limits. We sometimes need to go into a sort of sleep to heal critical injuries. That's what's going on with Kyle right now. His body is keeping him unconscious while it tries to repair itself. There isn't anything else I can do for him."

"But he'll be okay, right?"

I didn't miss the look Henry exchanged with Trey.

Just outside of town, where the river narrowed, there was a suspension bridge. Amy and I used to go out there on windy days and stand at the halfway point, clutching the ropes as we swayed over the water.

That's how I felt—like I was stuck in the middle of the bridge, swaying back and forth as I stared down at the icy water below.

Serena took my hand.

"I don't know," Henry admitted, eventually. "If he jumped out of a second-floor window *after* parts of the house fell on him, then he has to have internal injuries. Not to mention damage he might have taken from smoke inhalation. We won't know if his body can heal itself until he wakes up."

"How," I swallowed, trying to get the words out, "how long until that happens?"

Henry shook his head. "There's no way to know. I'd say at least four or five hours—probably longer. But the longer he's unconscious, the greater the chance that he isn't able to heal his injuries."

The light in the room seemed to dim. "What happens then? He wakes up hurt?"

Henry didn't answer.

"Mac . . ." Serena let go of my hand and tried to touch my shoulder.

I brushed her off. "He just wakes up hurt, right? And then we try something else, like a human hospital? He just wakes up hurt." The room blurred. "Serena, tell me he just wakes up hurt."

She looked away, unable to meet my eyes.

"If the injuries are too severe to heal," said Henry, "I'm afraid Kyle won't ever wake up again."

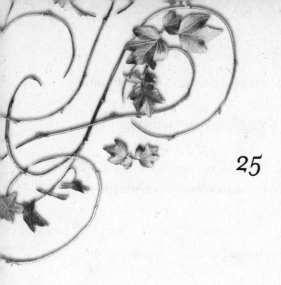

25

Henry and Trey left. There wasn't anything else they could do.

I stared at Kyle from across the room. If I didn't go any closer, I could pretend he was just sleeping. If he was just sleeping, then everything would be okay.

"Do you want me to stay?" Serena's voice seemed far away even though the room was small and she was standing right next to me.

I must have shaken my head or said something, because she left and closed the door behind her.

She left and I was alone with Kyle.

I took a step toward the bed and faltered. Tears filled my eyes, turning the room into a jumble of blurred shapes and colors. I wasn't strong enough for this. I could lose almost anything—almost anyone—but I couldn't lose Kyle. I clamped a hand over my mouth, trying to suppress a jagged sob in case he could somehow hear me.

I wasn't strong enough for this.

Anything or anyone, just not Kyle.

I wanted to run and hide. I wanted to rewind the past twenty-four hours, the past week, the past month, and do everything differently. I wanted to disappear, to be one of the shadows in the corners of the room, because shadows couldn't feel pain.

But then I remembered the way Kyle had cupped my face in the hospital, the warmth and strength of his hands and the quiet intensity in his eyes as he helped me through my panic attack—even though part of him was scared I would reject him. If I were in that bed, Kyle wouldn't be hovering across the room.

He was stronger than that.

I had to be stronger than that.

I had to be stronger for him.

Someone—Trey or Henry—had left a chair next to the bed. I forced myself to walk forward and sit down and take Kyle's hand.

A cotton sheet covered him from the waist down and his torso glistened with sweat. Bruises, burns, and cuts marked his skin like grotesque body paint. For each wound I counted, I felt an answering pain in my chest until it hurt so much that it was hard to breathe.

My brain kept insisting that it wasn't Kyle, that Kyle could never look so . . . *broken*.

What if he didn't wake up?

The thought pressed on my chest and ripped the air from my lungs and shattered any illusion of strength I had fooled myself into thinking I possessed. It tore things deep inside my body and flooded my mouth with the taste of copper and my eyes with tears so hot they burned.

"I'm sorry," I whispered, later, when my sobs had subsided enough to speak. "All of this is my fault." I was the one who had wanted to find out what had happened to Amy. I was the reason Kyle had stayed in Hemlock, the reason he had been at Trey's. It was my fault he was lying in this bed. Each thought fell like a stone dropped into water, and the ripples shook my shoulders.

I didn't know what to do. Sometimes I tried to talk—even though the words came out haltingly and all wrong—and sometimes I just cried. Once, I prayed—trying to bargain with God, even though I had never understood why people did that.

I understood now. I would have promised anything.

As the sky outside the window lightened to mauve and dawn touched the trees, the bruises and cuts on Kyle's body slowly faded. It was like one of those time-lapse videos of flowers blooming. The changes were too small to notice as they happened, but I'd glance away, and when I looked back, more of them would be gone.

But his eyes didn't open. He didn't move, and no matter how hard I searched his face, there was no sign that he knew I was there.

"Please, Kyle. You have to wake up." If he didn't, part of me would never leave this room. I'd be twenty-five and then thirty and then an old woman and I'd still be waiting for him. I'd turn down a street or walk into a room and scan the face of every person I passed, trying to fool myself into thinking that one of the faces would be his.

I walked over to the other side of the bed. It was narrow—just a double—but I stretched out on my side, careful to keep a few inches between us, scared that I would hurt him if I got too close.

I took his hand and gently pressed my lips to his shoulder. His skin was warm, like he had a fever. "You're right, you know. I do make it hard for people to love me. I don't mean to. If you had grown up the way I did . . ." I swallowed. "But I'll be better. If you wake up, I'll stop pushing people away. I'll stop being so standoffish and stubborn. Anything you want."

I closed my eyes and tears leaked out from under my lids. Voice thick and strangled, the syllables barely distinguishable from one another, I said the only words I had left. "I love you."

"God. Poor Kyle." Amy sat in the chair next to the bed wearing a men's white dress shirt that was at least three sizes too big and that hung halfway to her knees. "He had to practically die for you to admit you love him. Not that he'll remember it when he wakes up." She glanced at the door.

"So Derby thinks Trey killed me, and Bishop is sure Jason did it. You look pretty comfy considering there's a guy suspected of my murder downstairs."

I shrugged. Carefully, I let go of Kyle's hand and pushed myself to my feet. This wasn't really the kind of conversation I wanted to have lying down. "I don't think Trey did it."

Amy blinked. "And what makes you think that?"

"He has an alibi. I think Derby was setting Trey up so Jason would kill his first wolf or something."

"Sounds like a bad soap opera script."

"Doesn't mean it's not true."

"And Jason?"

"Would never have hurt you." Whatever moments of doubt I'd had after talking to Bishop had passed.

"You sound so sure." Amy leaned forward, eyes twinkling, almost like she was enjoying herself. "How well do you really know him? After all, you didn't know he was in love with you."

I blushed and pushed my hair back, using the gesture as an excuse to look away. Was that really true? Had there ever been hints that I ignored? Glances and touches and words that should have set off alarm bells?

"Busted," she whispered. "Maybe you don't want to think Jason could have done it because you secretly get off on the idea that he's into you."

I met Amy's eyes. I tried to remind myself that it wasn't her, that the real Amy wouldn't have said it, but then I remembered everything I had learned. How well had I really known my best friend? "Why don't you just tell me who did it? Was it even a werewolf?"

She shrugged. "How should I know? I'm just a figment of your imagination." She stared down at her shirt. "Gross." A red stain spread out from her shoulder and was quickly joined by a second and a third until the fabric was so saturated with blood that it clung to her.

Amy looked up at me, a bewildered expression on her

face. "I don't know why it keeps doing that."

I gasped as my body jerked back to consciousness. Against all odds, I had somehow fallen asleep.

I had a moment of heart-seizing panic when I realized that I had lost my grip on Kyle's hand. But then I noticed that he was lying on his side—not on his back, as he had been when I dozed off. And the hand I had been holding was now resting on my hip, two fingers hooked through a belt loop on my jeans.

"Kyle?" It was barely more than my lips forming the shape of his name, but his eyes opened. Warm and brown and maybe the single most comforting sight I'd ever seen.

"Sorry," he said. "You looked exhausted. I thought I should let you sleep."

My hand flew to my mouth, trying to muffle a noise that was halfway between a shout and a sob. And then I was crying—so hard and so fast that it hurt.

"Shhhh." Kyle pulled me against his chest. "It's okay. I'm okay. I'm fine."

I heard feet pounding on the stairs and the creak of the door and I stiffened.

"It's all right," murmured Kyle. "It's just Serena."

The door clicked closed and I sucked in deep breaths, trying to stop the flood of tears. I'd heard of people weeping because they were happy, but this was from sheer relief.

Kyle reached for a blanket at the foot of the bed and draped it over my shoulders. He looked perfect and whole; there wasn't a trace of the injuries he'd gotten last night.

"Out of curiosity," he said, "where are we?"

"Henry's," I gasped.

"Right. Henry's. How stupid of me." He smoothed the hair back from my forehead and then clumsily tried to wipe the tears from my cheeks. "Don't suppose you could tell me who Henry is?"

I took a deep, shuddery breath. "A werewolf Serena and Trey know. We're about twenty minutes from town, out near the lake." I closed my eyes. "You almost died," I accused, curling closer against him.

Kyle planted a light kiss on my forehead. "Sorry. Wasn't planned."

"Just don't do it again."

He chuckled, a low rumble deep in his chest. "I'll try not to."

"I'm serious." I titled my head back so I could study his face, and Kyle brushed his lips against mine.

"I know," he said, voice thick. He cleared his throat. "Is Serena's little brother all right?"

I nodded. "Trey got him out."

"Jason?"

"He's okay." I assumed he was okay, at least.

Relief slid across Kyle's face. He leaned in for another kiss.

I fisted my hand in the sheet wrapped around his waist as he gently pressed his lips to mine. I had almost lost him. He could have died without ever knowing how I felt. Without me ever saying those three stupid, impossible words.

Because saying them when he was comatose didn't count.

"Mac . . . ?" Kyle pulled back, a wary look crossing his face. "Are you all right?"

I tried to suppress the fluttery, nervous feeling in my stomach. "Yeah. There's just something you should know."

Kyle cupped my face with his hands, like I was something fragile. "Whatever it is," he said, "you can tell me." And then he kissed me again—soft and tender and a little desperate—like I was the one who had almost died, like he had almost lost me.

I heard a rap on the door, but it barely registered. Whoever it was would go away.

"Ahem . . ." Serena cleared her throat and Kyle and I froze. "I'm really sorry, but Henry's on his way upstairs to check on Kyle before he leaves for work."

I scrambled to a sitting position, trying to straighten my clothes.

Serena was studiously staring at the wall, but the corner of her mouth twitched in a grin. "I just thought you guys would appreciate some advance warning."

26

I SLIPPED OUT OF THE BEDROOM TO GIVE KYLE SOME privacy while Henry checked him over. Trey was in the hall.

"What time is it?" I asked, combing my fingers through my hair in an effort to work out some of the tangles. I sniffed a strand and frowned: it still smelled faintly of smoke.

Trey shrugged. "Around ten, I think."

I suddenly didn't care that I smelled like a forest fire.

Tess would be freaking. Even though she couldn't report me missing for twenty-four hours, it'd be a miracle if she hadn't called the cops. I reached for my pocket before remembering that I had lost yet another cell. Tess would kill me if I kept going through them at this rate. "Do you have a phone?"

A wary look crossed his face. "Who are you going to call?"

"Tess. My cousin," I said, trying not to sound impatient.

Trey studied me for a minute, then handed me his phone. "Don't tell her where you are."

I rolled my eyes and spun on my heel, looking for an

empty room as I punched in Tess's number. It went straight to voice mail. She still hadn't charged her phone.

The only other rooms upstairs were a home office and a bathroom. I opted for the bathroom. Sitting on the edge of the tub, glancing around at the blue and white tiles, I tried the apartment, followed by Ben's place. No answer at either.

I bit my lip. What if they were out looking for me? I remembered the receipt with Ben's cell number on it and dug down into the depths of my pocket. The scrap of paper was crumpled into a small ball and I had to flatten it against the edge of the tub to read the number.

Taking a deep breath, I dialed.

Ben picked up on the third ring. I could hear the familiar sounds of a restaurant in the background.

"Umm, hi," I stammered. "Is Tess with you?"

"Yeah, we're just having breakfast. Hang on—oh, and don't worry about the truck. I had it towed over to the garage."

Breakfast? They were eating out while I was missing?

There was a muffled noise as Ben passed the phone to Tess. I steeled myself for a verbal lashing.

"Hey. How'd you sleep? Are you home?"

"Huh?" Tess sounded way too cheerful and remarkably unconcerned. "You're not mad?" I asked, cautiously, wondering if her chipper tone was some sort of trick.

"Why would I be?" I heard her take a sip of coffee. "Okay, yeah, I was a little worried until I called Jason."

I broke out in a cold sweat. "Jason?"

"Yeah. He told me you guys were watching a movie and you passed out on the couch. He said you seemed exhausted and asked if it would be okay if he just let you sleep. You did look really tired yesterday morning."

"Yeah." I rubbed my temple as I tried to go along with the lie. "Jason said something about having people over later. I was thinking I'd just stick around—if that's okay?"

"Sure," said Tess. "I'll see you at home later."

I hung up and stared at the phone. Jason had covered for me?

He picked up on the first ring.

"Why'd you lie to Tess?"

"Mac." Jason said my name like a relieved, exhausted sigh. I could practically picture him leaning against a wall for support. "You're okay. Is Kyle all right?"

"Yes. No thanks to your friends." I stood and began to pace the tiny bathroom. Four steps to the door. Four steps back. Rinse. Repeat.

"That doesn't matter right now."

I stopped. "You did *not* just say that."

"Look, I'm sorry for what happened—you have no idea how sorry—but you have to tell me where you are."

"Not a chance."

He let out a strangled, frustrated groan. "They're watching the roads, Mac. The Trackers are trying to catch Trey and Serena. Trey made Derby run and now Derby is out for blood. You can't get in or out of Hemlock without passing through a checkpoint."

I sat back down on the edge of the tub and swallowed.

"How far out are they looking?"

"They have checkpoints near that motel at Morrissey Point and out by that turnoff you take to get to the old mill. I know there are others, but I don't know where or how many."

I pressed my nails into my palm. Morrissey Point was fifteen minutes farther out than we were. If there really was a net, we were caught in it. "Are you lying?"

"No." Jason's voice was low and urgent. "You have to let me help you."

Maybe it was stupid, but something in his tone made me believe him. Or maybe I was just trying to make up for doubting him after Bishop's.

"What about Kyle?" I asked, closing my eyes for a second and trying to think things through. "You said they were looking for Serena and Trey, but what about Kyle?"

"No one saw him shift," said Jason. "The cars were already gone when he went all furry." There was a bitter edge to his voice, but I couldn't tell if it was because Kyle was a werewolf or because we had hidden it from him— possibly it was a bit of both.

"Serena, Trey, and Kyle are all infected," I reminded him. "Why would you help us?"

"Because you're with them, and if the Trackers catch you with three werewolves, they might shoot first and ask questions later," he said harshly. He hesitated, then added, "And I owe Kyle for saving me last night."

I rubbed my temple, trying to think past my exhaustion. "And because Kyle's your friend."

Jason didn't say anything.

"*Because he's your friend,*" I repeated, my pulse skipping.

"Because he's my friend." The words were so soft that I only caught them because I was listening so desperately.

Praying I was doing the right thing, I gave him directions to Henry's and hung up.

I glanced at the floor. I'd dropped the receipt with Ben's cell number. I picked it up, stood, and was about to slip it back into my pocket when something caught my eye.

It was just a receipt for gas from the Chevron station on Maple Street—thirty dollars' worth of unleaded and a cup of subpar, battery acid coffee—but something about it seemed *wrong*.

I stared at the date. April fourth. The day before Amy had died.

A Tuesday.

Ben had been out of town. He'd left the Sunday before and not gotten back until Friday. He had been at his aunt's funeral in Dayton.

So why was I holding a receipt from a gas station in Hemlock with his credit card number and signature?

My head swirled. Why would Ben have lied about his aunt's funeral, and if he'd really been in Hemlock, where had he been staying? Not at his apartment—Tess or I would have noticed.

There was a knock on the door and I jumped, whacking my shoulder on a towel rack.

I shoved the receipt into my pocket and opened the door.

Kyle stood in the hall, dressed in a pair of worn blue jeans that were just a little too short and a Lakers T-shirt that clung to the muscles in his shoulders and chest. He smiled and then frowned as his gaze swept my face. "Are you all right?"

"Yeah," I lied. "I was just calling Tess." I squeezed past him and headed for the stairs. I didn't know what the receipt meant and I didn't want to give Kyle anything else to worry about—he was going be worried enough when he found out Jason was on his way over.

"Have you lost your mind?" Trey paced the bright, yellow kitchen while the rest of us sat at the four-seater breakfast table. "You had no right to tell him where we are!"

Figuring the fewer werewolves in the house the better, I'd waited until Henry left for work before telling the others that Jason was on his way.

"Trey . . ." Serena watched her brother pace.

"He helped them burn down our house, Ree. *Our house.* They almost killed Noah." Trey's voice was a deep growl.

"I haven't forgotten," she said gently.

"Derby thinks I killed Amy. A mob is probably on their way here right now."

I swallowed. With all the tension in the room, it was a little hard to breathe. "I don't think Derby really believes you killed Amy," I interrupted.

A wave of goose bumps swept down my arms as three pairs of werewolf eyes locked on me. Warm, late-morning sunlight streamed through the windows, but I shivered.

"If he really thought you had, Derby would have shown up with the police and a press corps. He would have made it an event." I thought about how last night had felt more like an initiation than an interrogation, how Derby had watched Jason like he was certain of what he'd do. "I think he somehow found out about you and Amy and was hoping it would be enough to push Jason into killing his first werewolf."

Serena cleared her throat. "No offense to Jason, but why would Derby care what he did?"

"Jason is young, charismatic, rich, and handsome. His girlfriend—the granddaughter of a senator—was killed by a werewolf." *At least everyone thinks she was*, I added to myself. "He's the perfect poster boy for them—if Derby can control him. I think he was hoping that killing Trey would bind him to the Trackers. Permanently." It was just a theory, but it made sense.

Trey stopped pacing. He towered over me, glowering. "And you just invited their poster boy over. That's just great."

"Back off, Trey," said Kyle. "She did what she thought was right."

"Thanks," I whispered, once Trey had stalked to the other side of the kitchen.

The look he turned on me wasn't happy. "I said you did what you thought was right, not that I agreed with it."

Anger I could have dealt with, but Kyle looked disappointed, and that, somehow, was worse.

Everyone froze at the sound of tires grinding up the unpaved driveway.

"Only one car," said Kyle.

"Doesn't mean there's not more on the way," countered Trey.

Serena stood and slipped out of the room. A minute later, she was back. "I told Noah to hide downstairs." Her gaze locked on mine. "If the Trackers show up, you have to look after him."

"Serena—"

She shook her head. Her eyes were wide and the expression on her face was desperate. "You're the only one of us who isn't infected. He'll have the best chance with you. You have to promise to take care of him."

My stomach lurched. I had gambled everyone's safety on the hope that Jason could be trusted. Suddenly, it seemed like too huge a risk to have taken on my own. My face flooded with warmth as I realized how very justified Trey's anger and Kyle's disappointment were. "I promise."

Kyle watched me for a moment, like he knew what I was thinking, and then he scraped his chair back against the kitchen floor and got to his feet. "Well, we can't just leave him out there."

Trey headed for the door, but Serena put a hand on his shoulder. "Let Mac and Kyle go first," she said. "*Please*, Trey."

Trey closed his eyes, took a deep, ragged breath, and nodded.

Hoping I hadn't made a huge mistake, I stood and followed Kyle through the back door.

We crossed a small, shady porch and stepped down into the warm sunlight. Serena and Trey followed us outside, but they hung back, sticking close to the house.

Jason was leaning against his SUV, arms crossed. There

were dark shadows under his eyes and a cut on his lower lip. His shoulders were rigid and his gaze swept the yard relentlessly, like he was waiting for an attack. He hadn't shaved and his clothes, under his jacket, were wrinkled. He clenched and unclenched his right hand, like he was aching to hold a drink.

He looked less like a perfect poster boy and more like someone on the run.

There was a shopping bag at his feet. Jason unfolded his arms and reached down. He hauled out a bundle of black cloth and tossed it to Kyle.

"You've got to be kidding me," muttered Kyle as he unrolled a T-shirt with a replica of a *Respect Regs, Report Wolves* poster on the front.

Jason nudged the bag with his foot and glanced up at the porch. "I've got a *Hunt or be Hunted* one for Serena."

"I am *not* putting that on," she growled.

Jason shrugged. "Fine. The Trackers have checkpoints set all around town. They know you've got a kid with you and will probably have to travel by car. Feel free to try and get past them on your own."

"And you think a couple of T-shirts will get us past them?" Kyle crossed his arms.

"I'll be with you." Jason tugged down his collar. "Whoever's manning the checkpoint will see my tattoo. They probably won't bother making us get out of the car—especially if you and Serena look like Trackers in training. Serena can make sure the kid stays down and out of sight. We drop them at some motel far enough away that they can lay low until Trey shows up, and then you and I head back in the morning."

"What about Trey and me?" I asked, a sinking feeling in my stomach.

"You're staying in Hemlock." Jason's eyes flashed and he suddenly looked every bit as deadly as Derby wanted him to be. "And Trey can find his own way out."

"I'm not staying behind," I said just as Trey leaped over the porch railing in an inhumanly graceful movement.

He landed lightly in front of Jason. "You think I'm just going to let you drive off with my brother and sister after everything you've done?"

If Jason was frightened of standing a few feet from an angry werewolf, he didn't show it. "Right now, you don't have much of a choice."

"He's right, Trey." Serena's voice was resigned—almost hopeless—as she came down the steps. She walked past her brother and took a red T-shirt from the bag, holding it away from her body like it was toxic. "We have to call Dad and tell him not to fly home tomorrow, and we've got to get Noah out. We can't risk the Trackers hurting him to get to us and we can't just stay here. Sooner or later, they'll start watching anyone connected to us. Too many people have seen us with Henry."

Trey whirled on her. "There has to be another way." His lip curled back from his teeth and the words were more growl than speech.

"Look," said Jason, "Kyle didn't shift until after the Trackers left. They don't know he's infected, so they won't be looking for him. They *will* be looking for you and Serena, but they won't expect you to split up. The Trackers at the checkpoints are pulling twelve-hour shifts. Seven to seven. We time it so we get there around six—when the first shift is almost over and the guys are tired—and then we make it through."

"How do you know all of this?" I asked, a thread of doubt winding through me even though I had been the one to call him. "I mean, the Trackers left you behind last night. Derby didn't just email you the checkpoint roster."

Jason shrugged. "Derby's not the only Tracker I know. As far as I can tell, he hasn't told anyone not to talk to me. Not yet, anyway."

Next to me, Kyle watched Jason with a thoughtful, considering look on his face. "It's not the worst plan in the world," he said, eventually.

Despite the warm sunlight beating down on me, I felt a circle of cold in the center of my chest. "You can't seriously be thinking of leaving me behind."

"I'll come back," said Kyle. "As soon as Serena and Noah are safely out of town." His hand brushed mine. "I told you I'd stay until—" He caught himself, almost as though saying anything about Amy would be like throwing a match into a gas can.

Given the way Trey and Jason were glaring at each other, I had the feeling he was right.

"You're not going without me," I insisted. Maybe I wasn't so great when it came to overpowering werewolves, but the Trackers were human. I couldn't just sit at home while the three of them risked their lives.

"Why are you doing any of this?" asked Trey, suddenly. His voice held a mixture of anger and suspicion, but there was an undercurrent of genuine curiosity.

"Isn't it obvious?" Jason's gaze darted to mine, just for a second, so scorching that I almost flinched. "I'm doing this for Mac. Because she'd be safer with all of you gone. If I can't convince the Trackers that she didn't know about Serena, or if they find out her *boyfriend*"—he said the word like it was obscene—"is infected, then I won't be able to protect her from them. I don't want her getting hurt because she cares about a bunch of fleabags."

"Jason . . ." What was I supposed to say to that? Part of me wanted to hug him, the other half of me wanted to slap him. Both options somehow felt completely wrong and utterly right, like an emotional stalemate.

"So you're all about the protection," snarled Trey. "That's great. I mean, you've done such a good job of protecting girls in the past."

All the color drained from Jason's face. "Amy was killed by a werewolf," he reminded Trey, the words cutting the air like shrapnel. "One of your kind. Maybe you even know the fleabag responsible."

In a blur of motion, Trey thrust his arms out, connecting with Jason's chest.

Jason hit the hood of the SUV with a sickening crunch and only barely managed to keep from sliding to the ground.

Before Trey could do anything else, Serena and Kyle each grabbed one of his arms and dragged him across the lawn.

There were two of them and one of him, but Trey was so wild that I wasn't sure they would be able to hold him back.

Heart thudding in my chest, I ran to Jason's side and got an arm under his shoulder. He stared at me, dazed. A small trickle of blood appeared at his temple.

His brows knit together, like he was trying to remember something. "No," he said, "that's not . . ." He took a deep breath. "Last night . . ." His voice faltered, and I wondered how much of the previous evening he actually recalled. "Last night, you and Kyle said the police weren't sure if a werewolf killed her."

He stumbled away from me, managing to stand on his own. He stared at Kyle. "Why did you say that?"

"Because they were trying to get you away from Derby," Trey growled, like Jason was the world's biggest idiot. "I went there the next night—after the police and reporters left. A wolf's scent was all over that alley."

Trey glared at me. "Tell him it was a wolf." He waited for me to say something, for me to back him up. When I didn't, confusion slid over his face and slowly turned to desperation. "It had to be a wolf. I smelled it."

I swallowed and looked at Kyle. Nothing about Amy's death added up.

"She was drugged," I said softly. "We spoke to the detective who started the investigation and he said they found GHB in her system and that it killed her. He thought . . ." I hesitated, wondering how much I could spare Jason and Trey. I took a deep breath. "There were signs that the fur they found might have been planted, that she didn't fight back."

Trey stared at me, horror-struck. "But the alley, the scent . . ." A flash of pain crossed his face as another thought occurred to him. "GHB is a date rape drug."

"She wasn't raped," I said quickly.

Trey was shaking.

"She wasn't," I repeated. "Maybe someone slipped the drug to her and the wolf just . . ." What was I supposed to say, that maybe the wolf had interrupted? That wasn't better. It wasn't better at all. Bile scalded the back of my throat and I felt perilously close to throwing up.

"Someone drugged her?"

I turned to Jason. The muscles in his jaw clenched and unclenched and his shoulders were hunched, like he was curling around a blow. Without waiting for an answer, he turned and strode away.

I glanced back at the three werewolves. Serena was whispering something to Trey, her voice so soft that all I could hear was a comforting murmur.

Kyle watched me, thoughts swirling through his eyes that I couldn't read.

Without a word, I turned and went after Jason.

Henry's house was in the middle of nowhere, his nearest neighbor at least a half mile away. If you were a werewolf, you probably valued your privacy.

As I approached the edge of the sprawling yard, the neatly mowed grass gave way to rocks and straggly weeds. The ground sloped down sharply until it met a small stream.

Jason was sitting on a large rock, facing away from the house.

I started down the hill, gravel and pebbles sliding beneath my sneakers. I cursed as I lost my footing and stumbled down the last few yards.

"You suck at stealth," muttered Jason, not turning.

"Well, you suck at hiding." I shoved my hands into my pockets and shivered, but it didn't do any good: the cold I felt had nothing to do with the weather.

"Why'd you come after me?"

There was something easier about talking to Jason's back. "I wanted to make sure you were okay. And I wanted to talk to you without everyone overhearing."

"Without Kyle overhearing, you mean."

"And Serena and Trey."

Jason let out a deep breath. "Right. Mustn't forget about Trey." Though his tone was mild, there was a poisonous tang to the words.

I swallowed. "I'm sorry about Trey and Amy."

"Don't be. I had it coming." Jason turned. His eyes held the same horrible, lost look they'd had at the funeral. "He was right, you know. I didn't protect her. I'm the reason she was out there alone that night. I'm reason she's dead."

"Jason . . ." I fumbled, not sure what to say.

He stood and crossed the few feet that separated us. "*Don't*," he said. "Don't pretend like you're not thinking it's my fault."

"Okay," I whispered, two syllables that made him flinch.

He pushed his hair back with both hands and pressed

his palms against the sides of his skull, like he was trying to keep his thoughts from tearing him apart. "Someone *drugged* her, Mac. She was mine to protect and look after and I just let her walk away. I let her walk away and I could have gone after her but I didn't. I was scared of what she'd say, and I was tired of feeling guilty for loving you, so I just let her go. I let her go and someone else found her."

A dull throb started in my chest and echoed through my head. For the second time in as many days, someone had said they loved me. Only, this time, it made everything wrong.

"How . . ." I wrapped my arms around myself and dug my fingers into my skin, so hard it hurt. "How long did she know? How long has it—whatever it is—been going on?"

Jason sighed and crossed his arms, almost like he was mirroring my position. "A while. Since last Christmas, I think." He shrugged miserably. "It's not like it happened all at once."

"What did I do?" Because I must have done something.

He shook his head. "You didn't *do* anything. It'd be like blaming a tornado for ripping through a trailer park. The tornado's just minding its own business. It can't help what it is."

A tornado. Something that destroyed everything in its path. A natural disaster. Me.

Almost at once, Jason realized his analogy might not be flattering. "That really didn't come out right."

"It doesn't matter," I said, looking away. My eyes filled

with tears. "It's accurate." I couldn't handle this. Not now. It was too much.

I started scrambling back up the slope. I heard Jason follow, but I didn't stop. I just wanted to be far away from him.

"Mac . . ." He grabbed my arm.

I jerked away, like his touch burned. "Please," I whisper-begged, "just leave me alone."

"So you can what? Pretend I never told you?"

I turned and wiped the tears from my cheeks. "What do you want from me, Jason? Do you want me to say it's okay? It's not."

He reached for me a second time. Without thinking, I pushed him, my palms connecting with his chest so hard that they stung.

He stumbled back and just managed to catch his footing.

My voice came out with the hint of a growl, almost like I was infected. "She was my best friend and you let me be the reason she was hurting and you never said a thing."

Jason tensed. "You want to talk about keeping secrets? What about what's been going on between you and Kyle? Or how about the fact that he's supposed to be my best friend and neither of you told me he was infected."

I let out a startled, tear-choked noise. "What would you have done? In case it slipped your mind, you're a member of the largest anti-werewolf group in the country."

Jason swallowed hard.

"Yeah," I said, when he didn't respond. "That's why we didn't tell you."

He stepped toward me, stopping just out of reach. "You didn't give me a chance, Mac. Either of you."

I crossed my arms. If I kept my arms crossed, I wouldn't shove him again. And I couldn't shove him, because once I started, I wouldn't stop. I would hit him again and again until my muscles went limp and love was the last thing he thought of when he looked at me.

"Derby threatened to hurt you if I did anything to talk you out of the Trackers. He acted like he'd kill you before letting you walk away from them."

The blatant skepticism on Jason's face was borderline insulting. "Did it ever occur to you that maybe he was bluffing?"

I stared at him, shock slipping through my rage. "You saw what he did at Trey and Serena's. He had a Taser pressed against Kyle's throat. *A Taser.*" A shudder swept through me. "He wanted you to kill Trey. He set fire to their house. He was willing to kill their brother to prove a point." My shoulders shook and my throat burned as I remembered the taste of smoke and the seconds and minutes when Kyle was inside the house. "Do you really think a man like that *wouldn't* follow through on a threat?"

"Yeah, well, maybe you should have let me be the one to worry about that. I could have handled it."

A laugh—strangled and bitter and dismissive—escaped my throat before I could stop it. "Right. 'Cause you're so great at handling things." I uncrossed my arms and closed the distance between us. "Tell me what you would have done?" My chest ached, like I was being pulled apart.

I thought Jason would walk away or back up, but he stood his ground.

We were so close that I could feel his breath on my face. "What would your grand solution have been?" I heard my father in my voice. Cruel. Ugly. Determined to draw blood. "You can't take care of anything or anyone. Not even yourself."

Jason's eyes flashed. "Not like Kyle, right? Kyle takes care of everything and everyone."

"He's never passed out drunk in a bar bathroom when I needed him!"

Jason glared. "At least I'm human."

I snorted. "After what I saw last night, being human isn't exactly a rousing endorsement."

I turned to leave, but Jason caught my arm, pulling me back and spinning me around. I was too surprised to struggle.

His eyes were frantic and angry. He looked a little crazy—like an addict who was climbing the walls for a hit. Before I could pull away, he kissed me like a blow.

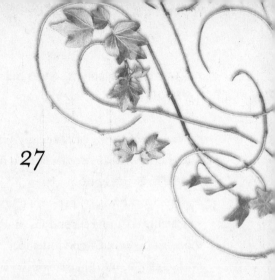

27

It was like stepping into a puddle while holding a live wire. A thousand-volt shock coursed through me, rooting me to the spot.

And that's why I wasn't pushing him away: the shock. My lips absolutely weren't parting. And I was raising my arms to shove him back, not pull him closer. And that small noise that I made deep in my throat was anger. Totally and undeniably. And . . .

Oh God.

I wrenched myself free and stumbled away. This wasn't happening. My life was *not* becoming one of those torrid teen-angst shows on cable.

But then a handful of pebbles and dirt slid down the hill and I turned toward the noise. Kyle stood at the top, staring down at us, his face a blank mask.

Something inside my chest splintered.

Without a word, he turned and strode away.

It was official: my life belonged on the CW.

"Kyle! Wait!" I scrambled up the slope and made it

halfway before Jason, who was following, grabbed my arm.

He probably just meant to stop me, but I lost my balance.

Rocks and gravel scraped my skin and the air was forced out of my lungs as I somersaulted down the hill and landed in a heap at the bottom.

The world was still spinning when Kyle lunged, moving so quickly that one second Jason was on the hill, staring at me with his mouth open in shock, and the next they were both crashing into the stream.

Kyle made it to his feet first. Jason, much less graceful, gained his a second later. The water was only waist deep, but they were both soaked.

"What the hell is your problem?" sputtered Jason, pushing his wet hair back from his face.

"Oh, I don't know. One minute you're kissing my girlfriend and the next you're throwing her down a hill."

I pushed myself to my hands and knees. Both boys ignored me.

"Girlfriend? That's cute." Some people yelled when they got angry. Jason got sarcastic. Always. "Are you taking her to the dance next month? You should probably call ahead; I'm not sure if they let pets in—even ones that are house-trained."

"Stop it, Jason." Both my voice and legs wobbled as I got to my feet.

Jason glanced at me, and Kyle took advantage of the opening to shove him.

If Kyle had used all his strength, Jason would have gone

flying. As it was, he just went under. Shivering and cursing, he broke the surface.

He splashed his way to Kyle and grinned—a tight, angry smile. Before I realized what he was going to do, he slugged Kyle in the jaw.

Last night, when Jason had hit Trey, he'd been wearing some sort of protective plate over his knuckles, and for good reason: werewolves could take a lot of damage, even in human form. Their bones were stronger than ours.

This time, though, Jason's fist was bare. He let out a howl of pain, but Kyle barely moved.

"I trusted you," panted Jason as he tried to shake the numbness out of his hand. "And all you did was lie to me. About what you were. About what was going on with Mac."

Kyle touched his jaw, not like it hurt but more like he couldn't believe Jason had actually hit him. "What was going on with Mac wasn't any of your business."

"The hell it wasn't."

This had gone far enough. I wasn't going to let them use me as an excuse to fight. I kicked off my shoes and waded into the stream. Even though the day was warm, the stream was freezing. I winced as needles of cold stabbed my feet and frigid water soaked my jeans.

"Stop it, both of you." I held out a hand, palm facing outward, like a traffic cop, to each of them. I glowered at Kyle, then scowled at Jason. "You can't blame Kyle for not telling you he was infected—not when you were in the Trackers. And I could have told you what was going on with us, so that's not all Kyle's fault, either." My teeth started chattering. "Besides, you've kept your own secrets."

Jason glared at me, the green in his eyes picking up and reflecting the sunlight on the stream. "Not from Kyle."

The cold from the water worked its way up through my body, spreading frost toward my heart. "What do you mean?"

Jason stared past me, eyes fixed on Kyle. "I've always told him everything. He knew I was going to break up with Amy and he knew why."

Shaking my head, trying to make sense of the words, I turned. "You knew?"

He didn't say anything.

Each breath I took seemed to freeze in my chest. "You knew what was going on and you didn't tell me?"

A pleading expression crossed his face. "It's not exactly the sort of thing you can just tell someone. Besides, would it have done any good? Would it have changed anything?"

The ice inside my chest shattered in a burst of heat.

I splashed toward Kyle and shoved him. It was like trying to move a boulder, but I didn't care. The gesture was symbolic—even though he barely budged.

I could have stayed away from Jason. I could have been there for Amy instead of being completely oblivious to what was happening. I could have changed things if only Kyle had told me what was going on. If only he had given me the chance.

"Mac . . ." He reached for me and I stepped away.

"The two of you can tear each other to shreds for all I care." I was done. I was *so* done. Amy, Jason, Kyle—the three people I had trusted most had kept everything from me.

I made my way to the edge of the stream, my numb feet sliding on wet rocks. I stepped out of the water and pulled on my sneakers.

Kyle waded to shore. I ignored him.

I scrambled up the hill and crossed the yard. Trey was sitting on the steps and Serena was leaning against the porch railing, still holding the red T-shirt.

Outwardly, Trey looked calm and thoughtful, but his eyes gave him away. They fixed on me with an intensity that would probably have been unnerving if I wasn't feeling so dead and tired inside.

"How much did you hear?" I asked them. We'd been far from the house, but probably not far enough to escape a werewolf's sharp ears—especially given how heated things had gotten.

"Pretty much all of it," admitted Serena. She blushed. "Sorry."

I shrugged. It didn't matter. I was too emotionally drained to be embarrassed. "Not your fault. Do you think cabs come out this far? I have to go back into town."

No way was I staying here while Jason and Kyle played a rousing game of Who's the Biggest Hypocrite.

I thought of the receipt in my pocket. I might as well try to figure out who all the liars in my life were at once. Besides, it would at least give me something useful to do. And if Ben was lying to Tess, I wanted to know.

Trey stood and stretched. "I can take you. Henry left the keys to his Jeep and I know the back roads pretty well." He

331

grinned, but it was forced. "I spend plenty of time running out here."

Serena frowned. "Trey . . ."

He glanced over his shoulder. "They won't be looking for Henry's Jeep, and it's probably safer for me to drive her than to have a cab come out here. I'll stick to the hunting trails."

Serena chewed her lip.

"Don't worry," said Trey. "I'll be back before you and Noah leave."

Kyle rounded the corner of the house. Jason was right behind him, breathing hard, like he had run to keep up.

"Mac . . ."

Emotions flickered across Kyle's face—embarrassment, guilt, worry—but I couldn't trust any of them. I couldn't trust *him*.

"I'm sorry I didn't tell you. I thought I was doing what was right."

I turned away from him, even though the unhappiness in his voice tried to wrap itself around me like a chain. Trey started for the garage, and somehow, I managed to follow.

"Maybe," said Jason. "Or maybe you were worried she wouldn't want you if she knew how I felt."

Serena snorted as Trey and I reached the garage door. "I'd say you two are lucky if she wants either of you after the way you just acted."

"So is it all it's cracked up to be?" Trey pulled onto an unmarked—and unpaved—road. Though calling it a "road" might be giving it too much credit.

"Is *what* all it's cracked up to be?" I fiddled with the Jeep's heater, trying to get a steady blast of hot air aimed at my freezing feet.

"Having two guys fight over you." Trey glanced at me, his eyes a firestorm. "Amy always made me promise not to touch Jason." His voice was bitter and serious and devoid of the cockiness I usually expected from him. "She was all about the secrecy."

I swallowed. Amy had been my best friend, but I knew how selfish she could sometimes be. She had grown up getting everything she ever wanted, and after a while she had started to take people and things for granted—especially as we got older.

"Amy wasn't always great at considering other people's feelings," I said carefully. "I don't think it was anything personal." I grimaced as I realized how horrible that sounded. Trey and Amy had been sleeping together; you couldn't get much more personal than that.

The Jeep bounced over the road, and Trey swerved to avoid a puddle the size of a small pond. Trees crowded in on both sides, providing so much shade that it looked like late evening instead of early afternoon. The rain from the day before had left the road slick with mud, and anything less than a four-wheel drive would probably have risked getting stuck or breaking an axle in the water-filled craters that pockmarked the narrow lane.

"I would have, you know," he said. "Fought Jason. I would have fought anyone for her." He stared straight ahead, not taking his eyes off the road. "Amy was the only person I've ever been tempted to tell I was infected. Ree made me promise not to. She said Amy didn't really care about me and was just using me to get back at Jason, but I didn't care."

Somehow, I thought he actually cared a great deal. I remembered Serena's warning about how I might not like some of the things I found out about Amy. "Did you love her?"

Trey didn't answer, which was, of course, an answer in itself.

I was starting to wonder if love was just the universe's idea of a Kick Me sign. Amy, Jason, Trey, Kyle, Tess, me—all love seemed to do was mess things up and hurt you. Maybe not being able to say those three words wasn't such a bad thing after all.

"Was it true?" Trey suddenly asked. "Did someone really drug her?"

The heaters were on full blast, but I was still achingly cold. "Yeah. Unless the detective was lying." I closed my eyes. "I think he was telling the truth, though. He said the GHB would have killed her with or without everything else."

I opened my eyes as we took a turn so sharply that I had to grip the door to keep from falling against Trey.

He shook his head. He was so tense that I could actually see the pulse jump in his throat, pushing at the skin like it was trying to break free. "You don't die from GHB."

"You do if the dose is big enough," I said softly.

Trey took his eyes off the road. "How big was the dose?"

The muscles in his arms began moving, like snakes writhed just underneath the skin.

All of a sudden, there wasn't enough air in the Jeep. My heart raced as I turned in my seat, frantically pushing myself as far back as I could in the small space. "Trey . . ."

The bones in his hands cracked and lengthened. "How big was the dose?" The plastic of the steering wheel groaned in protest as he flexed his hands around it.

"Stop the car!" I tried to make my voice as commanding as possible, but it was hard to sound authoritative when you were less than three feet from a distraught werewolf on the brink of shifting.

"How big was the dose?" Trey's voice was an ear-splitting howl.

The Jeep swerved, careening perilously close to the trees on the left.

I reached for the wheel, but I couldn't grab it without risking a scratch from Trey's claws. "Enough to send her into cardiac arrest!" I yelled. "Stopthecarohmygodstop-thecar!"

I screamed as the driver's-side mirror clipped a tree and was torn away from the car. Trey slammed on the brakes and the Jeep slid into a 360-degree skid on the mud-slick road.

The trees blurred together and became a solid wall of brown-green color as branches scratched the paint job.

Finally, the Jeep shuddered to a stop.

We were completely perpendicular to the road, and the front tires were in the bushes.

I flung open my door and staggered out, legs shaking like I'd been at sea for a year. The ground seemed to tilt at crazy angles as I stumbled to the nearest tree trunk and gripped it for dear life as I threw up.

After a couple of minutes, something touched my back and I shrieked.

"Sorry," muttered Trey as I whirled.

I stared at his hands, arms, and neck. They were all completely normal, completely human.

He cleared his throat. "I think maybe you should drive," he said, voice hoarse.

I nodded, too queasy to make a sarcastic remark about understatements, and followed him back to the car. The keys were still in the ignition and, miraculously, the steering wheel had survived with only a slight crack.

Still shaking, I started the car, turned off the heater, and rolled down my window. Even though Trey seemed normal again, I was feeling claustrophobic at being in a small, confined space with a werewolf. "How about we forget talking and just listen to the radio on the way back?" I suggested.

Trey closed his eyes. A slight sheen of sweat covered his face and he looked exhausted. "Sure."

I turned on the radio and flipped through the stations, trying to find classical music because I figured that would be the most soothing. Eventually, I gave up and just settled on NPR. There was something familiar about the voice coming through the speakers, even though the signal wasn't great and whoever *was* talking was interrupted by intermittent bursts of static.

"Werewolves are a real and credible threat to our nation's security and our way of life," the voice said. "The new legislation we're proposing will make it more difficult for wolves to evade internment and would also level stricter penalties—including possible jail time—for aiding and abetting any person known to be infected with lupine syndrome."

Great. I'd turned on the radio to calm down a werewolf and hit the one station talking about how dangerous werewolves were. I reached forward to find something else, but the voice suddenly clicked. "That's Amy's grandfather. It's Senator Walsh."

"Senator, how do you respond to critics who claim that the camps are inhumane?"

John Walsh cleared his throat. "The rehabilitation camps allow werewolves to live out a semblance of a normal life—albeit somewhat restricted. They are a regrettable necessity and I assure you that the conditions are adequate. The camps are the most humane way we have of restricting the spread of lupine syndrome."

"Senator, what about people who claim your new stance is the result of grief?"

Trey reached out and flicked off the radio. "Talk about a complete one-eighty."

"His granddaughter *was* murdered," I reminded him gently. "Senator Walsh was the one who pulled the strings to get the Trackers into Hemlock, and everyone's saying he's behind the reward money Derby told the students about. I bet Derby started working on him right after the funeral . . ." I trailed off as bits of information slid into place and created a horrific picture.

Amy's death had been bigger than any of the others. It had given Derby access to Senator Walsh and had resulted in the Trackers taking over Hemlock. And it had—

"The new legislation."

Trey shot me a puzzled glance.

"Before Amy's death, her grandfather supported increased werewolf rights. Her murder is the reason he switched sides. Before that, people thought he was the best chance at getting more rights for werewolves."

I pulled to the edge of the dirt lane and, hands shaking, turned off the ignition. I might not have been a werewolf, but I was still perfectly capable of wrecking a car. "Someone slipped Amy the GHB—way more GHB than they would have needed to just spike her drink. What if they did it so they could somehow leave her where the werewolf would find her?" Bishop thought a human had murdered Amy and made it look like a werewolf kill, but Trey had said he smelled a wolf in the alley. What if they were each sort of half-right? "What if someone orchestrated Amy's death so that her grandfather would drop his support for werewolf rights?"

"You think Amy was murdered for *politics*?" Trey squeezed his eyes shut. He breathed in and out in long, measured breaths.

"So if someone did kill Amy to get to her grandfather, who? Derby?" His voice was lower than normal, each word falling like a threat.

"Not Derby himself. He would never have risked getting his hands that dirty. It had to have been someone working for him. Someone who . . ." *Could get close to Amy.*

"Dobs?" Trey opened his eyes.

I dug my nails into the cracked steering wheel. "I have to go to Amy's."

"Why?"

I tried to think past the roaring in my head. "I have to talk to her parents about something. It's just an idea. It might be nothing."

Trey frowned. "What is it?" When I didn't reply, he reached out and gripped my shoulder. "Dobs, *what is it?*"

I swallowed. "It might be nothing," I repeated. The suspicion that was slowly building in my chest was too awful to say out loud. Besides, I might be wrong. I'd never wanted to be so wrong about anything in my life.

Ben might have lied about being in Dayton the week Amy died. And he'd been different when he turned back up. For a few days, he'd been almost like a stranger. And the one time I'd mentioned the funeral since—the night Ben had come upstairs to check on me and told me about his brother—he'd shot me such a piercing look that I immediately regretted saying anything. Hank had gotten like that sometimes, when he'd seen or done something really bad—withdrawn and guarded.

If someone had slipped Amy GHB, it would have been in a drink. And Amy was way too paranoid to leave a drink with someone she didn't know—she had lectured me about doing it more times than I could count.

But she wouldn't have hesitated to leave a drink with Ben while she got up to use the washroom or make a call. And there'd been a witness statement in the file—a woman had seen Amy with a blond man. The police had thought it might be Jason, but Ben was blond. And only an inch or two taller.

Ben couldn't have hurt Amy. He was *Ben*.

Thinking it—even for a second—was messed up and twisted.

But then I shoved my hand into my pocket, letting my fingers skim the receipt wedged in the bottom.

I looked at Trey, who was still staring at me with a combination of worry and frustration.

I hadn't known he was sleeping with Amy. I hadn't known that both Jason and Kyle had feelings for me or that Serena was a werewolf. How well did I really know anyone?

I reached for the ignition, but Trey was faster. He covered the keys with his hand.

"We're not moving until you tell me what's going on."

I shook my head. Given how close Trey had come to shifting, I wasn't sure standing up to him was the smartest idea. But I didn't have a choice. I couldn't tell Trey the things that were going through my head—not when I might be wrong.

I summoned every ounce of stubbornness anyone had ever accused me of having. "I can't tell you anything until I talk to Amy's parents, so, the way I see it, you have two choices. You can play keep-away with the keys and I'll take my chances trying to walk the rest of the way, or you can come with me and wait while I talk to them."

"And if I don't like either choice?" Trey glared at me, waiting for me to back down.

My heart jackhammered in my chest and I broke out in a cold sweat, but I didn't look away. By Hemlock standards, Trey was tough. But I hadn't been raised by Hemlock standards.

After three minutes, when I still showed no signs of backing down, Trey muttered a string of curses. "You know, sometimes I think you might actually be as tough as you think you are." He moved his hand away so I could start the car. "You *are* going to tell me what all of this is about after you talk to them." It was an order, not a request.

I started the car without comment.

Eventually, the narrow back roads and hunting trails deposited us behind an abandoned soccer field on the north side of town. As we headed toward Amy's, I tried to recall everything I knew about Ben. It wasn't much. I had always assumed he was like me—that he didn't talk about the past because he'd rather forget it—but what if it was because he was hiding something?

Like, say, the fact that he was working for the Trackers.

28

STANDING IN FRONT OF AMY'S HOUSE, I GLANCED AT the sun and tried to figure out how late it was. The clock in Henry's Jeep didn't work, and I wasn't sure how much time we'd lost with the two unexpected stops on the way to town. Jason wanted to make the checkpoint at six. If Trey didn't get back to Henry's by five, he might miss his chance to see Serena and Noah before they left.

My stomach twisted. I wanted Trey to get back in time, even though I wasn't sure if I was going with him.

I rang the bell and studied the carvings in the massive wooden door that I knew had been handcrafted and shipped over from Europe. I'd passed through that entryway almost every day for three years, but this was the first time I'd stood here in five months.

The door opened a crack.

"Mackenzie?" Mrs. Walsh opened the door a bit wider and stared at me, confusion and concern sliding over her face as she took in my disheveled hair and the dirt on my clothes. "Are you all right?" she asked as she ushered me into the foyer.

I blushed, guessing how awful I probably looked after everything that had happened in the last twenty-four hours. "I was hiking with Kyle and Jason and fell into a stream," I lied. It was sort of close to the truth.

Thankfully, Amy's mother had the worst truth-meter on the planet—a failing that Amy had never hesitated to exploit. I could practically see her relax as she accepted the lie at face value.

"I'm sorry to just show up," I continued, stumbling slightly over the words. Amy had gotten most of her looks from her mother and I felt a little like I was staring at the ghost of a future she'd never get to have. "I need to talk to you about Ben Fielding."

She herded me into the front living room—the room in which no living was ever to be done, Amy had always said—and steered me toward a white chair.

I sat on the edge of the seat, worried about the state of my clothes and the dirt I might leave behind, but Mrs. Walsh didn't seem too concerned about the upholstery.

"A couple of days before—" I almost said *Amy's murder* but caught myself and started again. "Around April second, Ben told Tess that he had to go to Dayton for a funeral. We thought he was gone all week, but now I think he might have been lying. I was wondering"—I took a deep breath— "if he came into work at all that week or if he told you where he was going."

Mrs. Walsh twisted her wedding ring around her finger and walked over to one of the large windows that overlooked the manicured front lawn. "That week is sort of a blur, Mackenzie."

I winced at the faraway, pained tone in her voice and felt guilty for putting it there. "I know. And I'm so sorry. I wouldn't ask if it wasn't really important."

She turned away from the window and met my eyes. "Why is it? If you don't mind me asking."

I had concocted a story as Trey and I had turned onto Amy's block, and I was ready for the question. "I think Ben's been cheating on Tess. And I think he was in town but with someone else that week."

"Tess is a grown woman, Mackenzie," said Mrs. Walsh gently. "She may not appreciate you snooping into her relationship."

"I know. It's just that they're talking about moving in together . . ."

Amy's mother frowned. I had the sudden feeling there was something about Ben she didn't like. "Ryan keeps a record of the days our staff work. It's in his study." She nodded, more to herself than to me. "He's out of town, but I can check—if you don't mind waiting."

"Actually," I said, feeling the blood rush to my cheeks as I stood. "Would it be all right if I used the washroom while you look?"

Mrs. Walsh nodded and turned to the door. "Of course." She didn't bother telling me where the nearest one was.

It might have been five months, but I still knew my way around Amy's house.

I headed for the washroom on the main floor until I was sure she was in the study, and then I crept up the curving staircase to the second floor.

Third door on the left.

My hand hovered over the knob. There was no reason for me to be up here. It wasn't like Amy had known she was going to be murdered and left a note saying *Ben killed me, see you on the other side XoXo.*

But I still found myself pushing open the door.

Inside, it was like the room was waiting for Amy to come back. Nothing had been packed away and the only difference was the absence of clothing that had once covered the floor and every other available surface. The bedroom was still an explosion of purple—purple and silver fleur-de-lis wallpaper, purple bedding, purple curtains—and the same bright band posters covered the walls. It was loud and chaotic and it should have been fun, but without Amy to animate the space, it felt sad and empty—like a helium balloon that had mostly deflated.

I walked past the vanity—trying not to stare too long or too hard at the photos of the four of us Amy had taped to the mirror—and headed for the window seat. I always told Amy it was a stupid place to hide her diary, and I was right. When I slipped my hand underneath the cushions, it wasn't there.

Part of me was disappointed; half of me was relieved. If Amy had known about Jason's feelings for me, I wasn't sure

I wanted to see what she'd written about the whole mess.

I wondered if Derby had somehow gotten ahold of the diary, if that was how he had known about her and Trey.

I started to pull my hand out when it grazed a smooth piece of paper. I slid a photograph into the light.

Trey. Sitting on a park bench and grinning self-consciously and looking very unlike his tough-guy persona.

Feeling a little like some sort of grave robber, I tucked the photo into the strap of my bra—not wanting to fold it and slide it into my pocket.

I took one last glance around the room. Any minute, Mrs. Walsh would be wondering where I was. My eyes lit on a flash of copper and silver on the dresser: Amy's lucky bracelet.

I walked over and lifted it from a tangle of bangles and necklaces, trying to ignore the way my vision blurred.

Amy had gotten the bracelet at a flea market. Someone had taken a bunch of foreign coins, drilled holes through them, and slipped them onto a piece of leather. I thought it was a waste of money—the coins weren't even that old—but Amy thought the bracelet was exotic. Like pirate booty or the coins belly dancers tied to their scarves. She swore it brought her luck and always wore it during exams.

The fact that her grades were always dismal hadn't shaken Amy's faith. After all, she'd say, it wasn't the bracelet's fault she hadn't studied.

A tear rolled down my cheek and landed on one of the coins.

Before I could talk myself out of it, I slipped the bracelet into my pocket. Someday, Amy's parents would clean out her room. When they did, the bracelet would be written off as junk and tossed.

Amy had loved it too much for it to be thrown away.

Wiping my eyes with the back of my hand, I walked out of the room, closing the door behind me. I darted into the washroom across the hall, flushed the toilet, and ran the tap while I counted to sixty.

When I came out, Mrs. Walsh was standing halfway up the stairs.

I tried to look like nothing was wrong, like I didn't have bits of Amy's life tucked into my bra and pocket.

If Mrs. Walsh thought it was strange that I had used one of the upstairs washrooms, or if she suspected I had been in Amy's room, she didn't show it. Maybe she didn't have the heart to. She just turned and headed back downstairs.

I followed, trying not to trip over my own feet.

At the bottom of the stairs, by the front door, Mrs. Walsh turned and frowned. "According to Ryan's records, Ben called in sick most of that week. But he did work Monday and Tuesday. I actually remember that. We were renovating the kitchen and the new cabinets arrived. It was one of the last jobs he did before he quit."

I grabbed the bottom of the banister to keep from swaying. The floor and the walls were suddenly at the wrong angles. They were closing in.

Ben had worked Monday and Tuesday.

He had lied to Tess.

He had lied to me.

He was hiding something. He was hiding something and he had been lying to us for months. And I had trusted him.

"Mackenzie?" Mrs. Walsh peered at me, concerned. "Are you all right? You look as though you've seen a ghost."

If she only knew how close she was. After a second, when I was certain I could speak, I said, "I was just really hoping I was wrong."

The second part of her statement hit me. "Ben never told us he quit. He said you laid off most of the work crew and put the renovation project on hold."

Confusion flashed across her face. "We didn't lay anyone off. To be honest, the renovation has been . . . a good distraction. After we lost Amy"—she faltered—"well, I was glad to have something to concentrate on." She shook her head. "Ben quit mid-April. He told Ryan that he had been offered a job with better pay and felt he had to take it."

I knew what the Cat paid, and it wasn't nearly as much as Ben would have made working on the renovation.

The whole conversation was a series of earthquakes and aftershocks, and my body ached with the strain of not letting the destruction show. Ben wasn't just a liar; he was a complete fake.

Mrs. Walsh gently touched my arm. "Maybe I should call Tess. You really don't look well."

I shook my head and forced myself to focus enough to lie. "I'm okay. I think I'm just coming down with something." I walked toward the door. "Thank you for taking the time to check about Ben."

Mrs. Walsh said something else—good-bye, I think—and I answered, but I was five months back and a million miles away.

I blinked in the afternoon sunlight and jumped when I heard the heavy door close behind me.

What if Ben had taken the renovation job to get close to the Walsh family and then quit after he had done whatever it was the Trackers wanted him to?

What if he had drugged Amy and set her up to be killed?

29

TREY WAS SITTING IN THE DRIVER'S SEAT WHEN I GOT back to the Jeep. I slid into the car, trying to quell the urge to throw up or start screaming, and handed him the photograph.

He frowned. "Where did you get this?"

"Amy's room." I pulled the bracelet from my pocket and fastened it around my wrist. I traced the edge of one of the coins and a wave of dizziness hit me. I had to close my eyes for a second.

Maybe I was wrong. It was possible, right? Maybe Ben really was just cheating on Tess—or was running drugs or had an illegitimate child in desperate need of a bone marrow transplant. The point was, there were other reasons he could have lied and I'd take almost any of them—from the sleazy to the downright criminal.

I opened my eyes and glanced at Trey. He was staring at the photograph like he was trying to remember everything about the day it had been taken. "Amy never told me about you, but she kept that photo. It was important to her."

"But she wouldn't have left Jason for me." His voice was bitter, but he carefully slipped the photo into his jacket pocket. "What did you find out?"

"Nothing," I lied.

All I had were two deceptions and a bunch of *ifs*. *If Ben was in Hemlock that night. If Ben was working for the Trackers. If Ben had slipped Amy the drugs.*

If Ben was a monster.

It wasn't enough. If I told Trey, he'd go after Ben first and ask questions later. I had to be sure before I told anyone.

Trey leaned toward me with a bleak, feral grin. "Remember what I said about you telling me what was going on after you talked to Amy's folks?"

I shook my head and tried to look as though Trey intimidated me. It wasn't hard with him grinning like that. Intimidation would excuse the shakiness in my voice when I lied. "There was this guy who worked for her parents and I remembered Amy saying he dealt drugs and she felt like he was watching her. But he was working the night she died."

Trey cracked his knuckles. "That's way too big of a coincidence. What's his name?" Maybe it was my imagination, but his canines looked sharper than they had a moment ago.

"Toby Jacobs," I replied, seizing on the name of one of my father's drug dealer friends. "But Mrs. Walsh said he left Hemlock last month."

"And you couldn't tell me this on the way over?"

"I was scared you'd snap and go after him," I admitted. "I didn't want you ripping someone's throat out unless I was sure."

It was just enough truth to convince him. Trey nodded and some of the tension eased out of his shoulders. He started the Jeep and pulled a U-turn in the wide, court-yardlike space in front of the Walsh house before heading out to the street.

"Can you drop me off at home?"

He shot me a surprised glance. "You're not coming back to Henry's?"

I shook my head and stared out the window as we passed the kind of houses I'd never have set foot inside if it hadn't been for Jason and Amy.

"Jason and Kyle aren't going to let me go with them. If I show up at Henry's, it'll just turn into a fight." That wasn't the real reason, but it wasn't exactly a lie, either. If I went, a fight was exactly what would happen.

"Dobs . . ."

"Please, Trey." I was scared to look at him, scared I'd crack and tell him the truth. The suspicion I was carrying was too big for one person; it pressed down on me and I was worried I'd be crushed under its weight. "I just want to go home. If you're worried about being spotted, I can hop out and catch the bus."

"No, that's not it." Trey turned right at the end of Amy's street and headed for the bridge. "It's just that you were hell-bent on going this morning. I didn't figure you'd give up so easy."

"A lot's changed since this morning," I said softly.

We crossed into the south part of town. There seemed to be cop cars everywhere, cruising up and down the streets in an endless patrol. More posters and flyers had gone up overnight, urging people to put regs first and report suspicious activity.

We stopped at a red light. Trey reached across me and rooted in the glove compartment until his hands closed on a Lakers hat. With a tight frown, he slipped it on.

I never should have let him drive me back into town.

"It's okay," Trey said, picking up on my fear the way Kyle could. "If I have to, I can ditch the Jeep and get back to Henry's on foot."

We pulled up in front of my building. "Be careful," I said. On impulse, I reached across the seat and hugged him.

For a second, Trey froze, and then he hugged me back awkwardly. "Careful, Dobs," he muttered. "Nice girls aren't supposed to worry about guys like me."

I pulled away. "Tell Ky—tell the guys and Serena to be careful, too." I swallowed. "And tell Serena I'm sorry I didn't get to see her before she left."

If Jason's plan worked, I might never see Serena again. She and Noah would be safely outside Hemlock and they probably wouldn't return.

Trey nodded and I slid out of the Jeep.

I didn't let myself look back as I headed for the parking lot at the rear of the building.

Ben's truck wasn't outside, but that didn't necessarily mean anything. It was probably still at the garage.

I crept upstairs to my apartment. Trying to be as quiet

as possible, I slipped my key into the lock and opened the door.

Sunlight streamed into the empty kitchen and living room.

After making sure the bathroom and both bedrooms were deserted, I picked up the phone and called Ben's place. I let it ring thirty times, hung up, waited five minutes, and then redialed and let it ring thirty more.

Heart thudding in my chest, I replaced the receiver and went to Tess's room. I got down on my stomach and reached under her bed for the crowbar she'd started keeping there after we watched a *Scream* marathon.

Then I headed for my room.

When we had moved in, Tess let me have the larger bedroom because she didn't like having the fire escape directly outside her window.

I drew back my bedroom curtains and pushed open the window, saying a quick prayer of thanks that Ben's apartment was below ours and had almost the exact same layout.

I laid the crowbar outside and then wiped my palms, which were slick with sweat, on my jeans. I couldn't believe I was doing this. Hank had always said it was smarter to go in a back window than a front door; I just never thought I'd be in a position to listen.

The rusted fire escape groaned under my weight as I crept down to Ben's apartment. The windows in the building were ancient and drafty, but each one was accompanied by an inside storm window that locked and kept out the worst of the wind and rain.

I peered into Ben's room and let out a sigh of relief: he'd left the storm window up.

I slipped the edge of the crowbar under the outer window frame and, grunting with effort, put all my weight behind forcing the window up until it was just high enough for me to slide my hands underneath. After that, it was easy to strong-arm it up until there was a gap big enough for me to climb through.

Once inside, I let out a shaky breath.

I was really doing this. I had really just broken into Ben's apartment to look for evidence that he was working for the Trackers.

I felt like I had swallowed a wasp's nest: my stomach twisted as though thousands of wings were beating against its lining and my skin itched like insects were crawling beneath the surface.

If Ben really had hurt Amy, it would destroy Tess.

And if I found anything, Kyle would leave. He was coming back only to help me find out what had happened to Amy. As soon as we did that, he'd be gone.

I started with the dresser. Socks. Boxers. T-shirts. A box of condoms—ewww! No empty vials or memos on official Tracker stationery.

The closet was similarly evidence-free.

Think. I had to think.

Where would Ben keep stuff he wouldn't want found?

Not anyplace Tess might look. And Tess was a total snoop.

I headed for the spare bedroom. There was a computer in

the corner—the screen displaying a password prompt—and a couple of cheap bookcases crammed full of paperbacks. After a few failed attempts at guessing Ben's password, I started flipping through the books, thinking maybe he had stashed things between their pages. I was shaking a copy of *The Road* when I noticed three framed photographs on one of the shelves.

There was a picture of Tess—one I recognized from a day the three of us had spent out by the lake—and a photo of a striking, slightly older redhead who smiled as she shaded her eyes from the glare of the sun. The other picture was of a boy with the same gray eyes as Ben.

They had to be Ben's brother and mother.

Something about them was vaguely familiar, but I wasn't sure why.

A key scraped in the lock and my heart jumped to my throat. When I was halfway back to the other bedroom, the front door opened.

I went completely still as Ben stepped into the apartment, sniffing like he had a cold.

His eyes locked on me and he froze. "What are you doing in here, Mac?" He looked different. Harder. Older.

I strained to make my voice sound normal. "I was looking for Tess. Your door was open."

"She went over to Jason's to see if you were there. Amy's mother called. She told Tess you stopped by and seemed upset." He shut the door and took a step forward. "She was worried about you."

"Oh." I glanced down—like I was embarrassed for

356

causing so much trouble—as I tried to buy myself time to think. "I've been missing Amy a lot lately. I was walking around and I just sort of ended up at her house."

Ben took another step forward and my head snapped up. He looked genuinely concerned, but when he tried for a reassuring smile, it didn't reach his eyes. And he was between me and the front door.

Acting on impulse, I said, "I guess Tess told you about what happened last night. At Serena's."

Ben nodded. "You could have been killed."

My blood turned to ice water as I struggled to keep my expression blank. I hadn't told Tess a thing about what had really gone on last night; if Ben knew what had happened, he had heard it from the Trackers.

Something flickered in his eyes, some realization that he had said something wrong. Before he could work it out, I turned and bolted for his bedroom.

I slammed the door shut and turned the latch. The knob rattled so hard that it sounded like Ben was trying to rip it out of the wood with his bare hands.

"Mac? Open the door! I just want to talk to you."

I ran for the window and made it halfway through before the door burst open.

Ben grabbed my legs and I desperately wrapped my hands around the metal grill of the fire escape.

He pulled so hard that it felt like my shoulders were popping out of joint. I managed to hang on—barely—and, when he loosened his grip to get a better hold, I kicked back as wildly as I could.

It didn't matter. He was two times my size and had leverage.

A nail on the window frame caught Amy's bracelet as Ben dragged me back inside. The leather string snapped and coins went raining to the ground below.

I tried to scream, but he put his hand over my mouth before I could manage a single decibel.

Ben wrestled me to the ground, pinning me so that I was flat on my stomach with my cheek pressed to the cold floor. I thrashed and squirmed, but I couldn't stop a thin line of fire from piercing my arm. A needle.

Just before everything went black, I felt Ben brush the hair away from my face and heard him whisper, "I never meant for you to get hurt."

30

"YOU REALLY SHOULD GET UP." AMY LEANED OVER me, the ends of her hair skimming my cheek. Her face seemed almost luminous in the darkness.

I blinked and weakly batted the hair away.

We were surrounded by low, rounded stones and faded plastic flowers. I was on a bench in the cemetery. "How did I get here?" I asked, struggling to sit up. I was so tired. Every muscle in my body felt like lead.

What was wrong with me?

"Ben has this whole thing about drugging girls," Amy said, answering the question I hadn't asked out loud. "You've been in and out of consciousness for a few hours. Your dreams were totally out of commission."

"Am I dead?"

Amy shook her head. "Not yet—but you will be if you don't wake up." She gripped my shoulders, her fingers digging painfully into my skin. "You have to wake up. Now!"

Like a mirror hitting the floor, the dream shattered and I rushed back to consciousness.

I was lying on my back and I could smell cedar and earth. Rough dirt scratched against my bare forearms and dampness seeped through my clothes. I was too scared to open my eyes. It was the logic of a child: if you don't open your eyes, the monster won't see you.

It took me a minute to realize that the pain surrounding my wrists and ankles came from ropes and that there was something in my mouth. I choked on the gag, my eyes flying open as I panicked. I couldn't get enough air.

"Breathe through your nose."

Ben's face gradually swam into focus. I could see the night sky and a blanket of stars behind him. What had he shot me up with? How long had I been out?

Jason and Kyle must have left Hemlock with Serena and Noah hours ago. With a sinking feeling, I realized two things: I had no way of knowing if they had made it safely past the checkpoint, and there was no one to help me. Trey might still be in town, but he would have no idea what had happened after he dropped me off.

I was on my own. Completely and utterly.

I turned my head, trying to ignore the sensation that it was splitting open. We were in a small clearing that could have doubled for any patch of forest outside of Hemlock. And we weren't alone.

Branson Derby stood a few feet away, arms crossed. "Ian, I told you to stay away from her."

Ian?

Ben opened his mouth like he was on the verge of

replying. Then he shook his head, stood, and backed up a few paces.

I breathed through my nose and tried not to surrender to the feeling of complete dread that threatened to overwhelm me. It was a losing battle. I still couldn't get enough air and spots hovered in front of my eyes, making it hard to see.

Derby walked over to me and withdrew a long hunting knife from a sheath on his belt. Moonlight bounced off the blade.

He knelt next to me and I shied away as the knife approached my cheek.

Derby gripped a handful of my hair to keep me from moving my head. "Given all the trouble you've caused, I'd be happy to let you pass out. Unfortunately, I need you conscious."

A small line of hot pain stung my cheek as he sliced through the gag. When he pulled back, the edge of his knife was stained with a thin trace of my blood.

I opened and closed my jaw, loosening it, even though the movement made the cut on my cheek burn and pull apart. My tongue felt like it was wrapped in gauze and my head throbbed in waves of pain.

Derby stood. He wiped the knife on his pant leg before putting it away.

"You didn't have to cut her," said Ben, the hint of a growl in his voice. He sounded angry, but his nostrils flared and he licked his lips—he looked like Jason did when he was itching for a drink. Even in the faint light, I could see perspiration on his forehead.

It was the blood. *My* blood.

"You're infected." The words were a raspy whisper, but Ben still cringed. I knew there was ground underneath me, but I was in free fall. Ben was a werewolf. Ben was *the* werewolf. He hadn't just drugged Amy and handed her over; he had torn her apart. Maybe he had killed all of them. "Tess trusted you. I trusted you."

"I . . ." Ben shook his head, his blond hair falling over his eyes.

"I told you not to get involved with that woman. It's complicated everything."

Ben stared at the ground. "I wanted something normal."

"You don't get to have normal, Ian." Derby regarded Ben like he was an insect: mildly interesting but, ultimately, disgusting. "You keep forgetting you're one of the monsters."

Ben raised his head. He was close enough that I could see the muscles in his arms twitch underneath his skin. "I could never forget that. Not after the things you've made me do."

"It was for the greater good," snapped Derby. "You know that. You didn't have any objections until the Walsh girl, and then your squeamishness almost ruined everything. If I hadn't stepped in—"

A shrill ring cut through the air and Derby slid a phone out of his pocket. He glanced at the display and then strode away, pressing the phone to his ear.

I'd been kidnapped and was lying trussed up like a hog and he was *taking a call*?

I took a deep breath. At least I knew I was somewhere with cell reception—though I wasn't sure what good that did me.

"So you really killed Amy?" The words came out in a shaky rush. I wanted to hear Ben say it. I needed to hear him say it. The cold from the ground seeped into my body.

He only nodded.

"She *trusted* you. She *liked* you." A wave of dizziness hit me.

"I liked her, too," Ben murmured.

Each word stung like the lash of a whip. "Don't say that." I choked with the effort of speaking. "Don't you *dare* pretend that you cared about her. You killed her. You drugged her so she couldn't even fight back!"

Ben stalked forward, and I recoiled as he crouched next to me.

His eyes bored into mine. "I drugged her so it wouldn't *hurt*," he snarled. "So that she wouldn't be scared." He shook his head. "The rest of them were so scared. I didn't want that for Amy."

"I'm sure that will be very comforting to her." I swallowed and blinked away tears. "I'll let her know when I see her."

Ben made a strangled sound in the back of his throat. Looking like he was going to be sick, he swore softly and stood.

When I had seen the white wolf on the street, it had

been Ben. He'd gone after Kyle, but he'd held back from attacking me. His words in the apartment echoed in my head: *I never meant for you to get hurt.*

Maybe he really didn't want to do this.

"It was all just so Derby could get to Senator Walsh, wasn't it? Why would you let him use you like that?"

He didn't say anything.

"Ben . . . please . . ."

He shook his head and pulled at his collar, like it was choking him.

Ben never unfastened the top button of his shirt. He was always worried the scars on his torso would show; he always thought people would stare.

The puzzle pieces slammed together with such force that I would have staggered if I hadn't already been on the ground. I suddenly realized why the woman and kid in Ben's pictures looked so familiar.

"There was never a car accident, was there?" I whispered. "The scars are from a werewolf attack."

Ben stared at me, eyes wide and gray. The same gray eyes as the boy's in the photo—the boy I had first seen in Derby's slide show the night of the Tracker meeting.

"Branson Derby is your father. That's why you've been helping him."

I turned my head. Derby had returned and was watching us, the barest hint of a smile on his face. "I wish Jason had been able to recruit you," he said, almost sadly. "It's not often someone surprises me." He walked over to Ben and placed a hand on his shoulder.

Maybe it was a trick of the shadows, but it looked like Ben flinched.

"Then again," added Derby, "I have a feeling you would have proven difficult to control."

I swallowed. "Unlike your son. How can you use him like this?" It was sick. Completely and utterly twisted.

Derby stepped away from Ben. "Ian was infected in the attack that killed his mother and brother. When that happened, I was left with a creature that looked and sounded just like my son but which was a copy of the thing that had killed my family. I had him interned the same day I buried them. As far as the rest of the world is concerned, both my sons were killed that day." His eyes glinted. "I 'use him,' as you put it, to try and stop that from happening to anyone else."

I tried to imagine Ben as a teenager. He had lost his mother and brother, and then the only person he had left had turned on him.

I willed Ben—Ian—to look at me. "You've been in the camps since you were fifteen?"

He nodded and stared at the ground. "Until he got me out."

"Until he needed you," I corrected.

Every muscle in my body trembled with disgust as I looked at Derby. I'd known the man was evil, but this was almost beyond comprehension. "You turned your own son into a killer. You're just as much a monster as he is. Probably more."

The instant rage on Derby's face was so fierce that I wished I had kept my mouth shut.

"I did what was *necessary*." He crossed the few feet that separated us and glowered down at me. "I mourn those deaths more than you could ever know."

Those deaths. Plural. Derby had been behind them all.

"You couldn't just kill Amy," I said, piecing it together. "On its own, her death would have been suspicious. But since she died in the middle of a string of attacks, everyone wrote it off as an ironic tragedy." My stomach churned with revulsion. "You had your own son kill and attack all those people so you could use them as window dressing."

"This is a war, Miss Dobson, and wars are not without casualties." There wasn't a trace of guilt in his voice. True devotion to the cause he had established. "At least their deaths weren't wasted. They served a greater purpose—as will your's."

Derby crouched down and sliced through the bonds at my ankles. "It will be too messy to undo these after you're dead," he explained, ignoring my struggles as he pulled me to a sitting position and worked on the ropes around my wrists. "Besides, we need it to look as though you fought back. We don't want a repeat of what happened with Amy Walsh. If the police don't find anything beneath your fingernails, some of them might become suspicious."

It was the wrong thing to say. I curled my fingers and gouged Derby's cheek with my nails.

His face twisted into a sneer as he drew back his arm and slapped me.

My head rocked to the side and the world tilted. "I thought you controlled the police," I said, as I tried to blink away the illusion that the nearby trees were dancing in a circle. "Or is someone besides Bishop catching on?"

"Ian," snapped Derby, ignoring my taunt and standing.

Ben shook his head. "I don't know if I can."

Derby's voice sliced through the air, so sharp it made me wince. "This is your chance to repent for what you are. Remember why you agreed to do this—to help put an end to infections, to make sure no one else dies like your mother and Scott, and so no one else has to endure what you did inside the camps."

I pushed myself to my feet, swaying slightly. "Ben . . ." I reminded myself that Ben wasn't real; he was an illusion. "Ian, he doesn't care about you. What he's doing doesn't even make sense. No one can put an end to infections."

A flicker of doubt crossed his face.

I didn't hear Derby behind me until it was too late. He grabbed a handful of my hair and yanked me back. I cried out as he drew his knife along my arm, splitting my skin from elbow to wrist. He shoved me so hard that I went flying.

My shoulders collided painfully with dirt and rocks a nanosecond before the side of my head bounced off the ground. I blinked up at the stars and then glanced at my arm. Thin rivers of blood were running down my pale skin.

And I was lying in a heap at Ben's feet.

I scrambled unsteadily away as he stared, transfixed, at my arm. He licked his lips, almost like he could taste the blood.

I kept moving backward, too frightened to take my eyes

off him long enough to gain my feet. It felt like a dozen fishhooks were hauling my heart and lungs in different directions and it was hard to breathe.

"You don't have bloodlust," I said, desperately seizing on what Bishop had told Kyle and me about the other victims and how they had been killed. "You don't have to do this."

It was like he didn't hear me. "No . . . no. No. No. No." He said the word over and over, like a refrain.

"Ian doesn't have bloodlust—not in the traditional sense," said Derby, almost like he couldn't resist talking right up until my bitter end. "But, with each attack, he's had more and more trouble controlling himself. It's almost as though he's developed some form of it after repeated exposure to blood. It's rather fascinating."

Derby really had turned him into a monster.

Ben fell to his knees, the movement strangely graceful and inhuman. Slowly, with horrible cracking sounds, his arms lengthened. His fingers stretched, growing oddly jointed as his spine shattered and reknit itself. With each pop and splinter of his body, he slowly advanced.

He kept saying, "No," under his breath, and I had no idea if his transformations were always like this or if it was taking so long because he was trying to fight it.

But just as that thought gave me the faintest glimmer of hope, the recognition slid out of his eyes, leaving them unfamiliar and inhuman. Ben was no longer home, and the thing that was left didn't care about me.

My shoulder hit something and I chanced a glance

behind me. Just a tree. When I turned my attention back to Ben, I was facing a white werewolf.

The wolf sprang and I had nowhere left to go. I threw my arms up to protect my face as its weight crashed into me. I smelled its hot, rank breath as bits of saliva dropped onto my hand. I whimpered and the wolf let out a low growl of pleasure.

Its fur brushed against the gash on my arm, white soaking up red, and I screamed. *Please let it be quick*, I prayed. *Please don't let it hurt too much*.

A shot rang out across the clearing. The beast above me let out a roar of pain just as something lodged itself in the tree next to my head. Flecks of bark hit my skin as the wolf reared up and away from me.

I lowered my arms and tried to force air back into my lungs; I had forgotten how to breathe.

Jason stood at the edge of the clearing, a gun clasped in his hand, a massive black wolf at his side.

He swung his arm, training the gun on Derby. "Call it off."

31

THE WHITE WOLF FROZE. ITS GAZE DARTED BETWEEN Jason and me, and then it slowly backed away.

Shaking so hard that my muscles ached, I curled my arm against my chest and pressed the cut to my shirt in an effort to slow the flow of blood.

The wolf licked its maw and stopped its retreat. An involuntary gasp escaped my throat as it took a small step back toward me.

"Call it off or I swear to God I will shoot you." Jason's voice echoed off the trees.

I had never heard him sound so strong or certain of anything in his life. I clung to that certainty even as I stared at the thing that used to be Ben.

"Jason, you don't understand what's going on." Derby's voice was calm, almost paternal.

"I don't need to. Call it off."

The placating tone in Derby's voice slipped. "It could tear her throat out, you know. Before you could squeeze off a single shot, she'd be bleeding her life onto the forest floor."

Jason's eyes flicked to mine, and then locked back on Derby. "You'd still be dead."

A low growl trickled out of the black werewolf's throat and Jason shook his head. "I don't think he's too happy about what you pulled at his house."

The moment stretched out like a rubber band. Everything was hyperclear and crisp. Then Derby reached for something at his belt and time snapped back.

There was the sound of gunfire—so loud in the small clearing—and I screamed as the white wolf leaped at me. But before it could connect, before its claws could shred my skin like paper, a dark shape hit it from the side, knocking it away in a blur of fur.

Kyle.

I struggled to my feet as he placed himself between Ben and me. The white wolf took a step to the side, and Wolf-Kyle mirrored the movement, snarling.

Pulse pounding, I looked around for a fallen branch or a rock. Anything so that I wasn't completely defenseless.

There was nothing.

Across the clearing, Jason dove behind a thick elm and I lost sight of Derby and the black werewolf. Trey, I reminded myself. The wolf was Trey.

Motion pulled my attention back to the two wolves in front of me as Ben lunged and sank his teeth into Kyle's back.

Kyle managed to shake him off, but the white wolf's face came back stained with blood.

I knew Kyle couldn't keep this up. He hadn't been able

to stop Ben in the Meadows, and he wouldn't be able to stop him now.

This time, I didn't have a Honda I could just aim at Ben, and I was the only person on two legs who *wasn't* armed.

Kyle was going to get himself killed. He was going to get himself killed and there wasn't anything I could do to save him.

A hand locked around my wrist and I lashed out before realizing it was Jason.

He dragged me deeper into the trees.

I stumbled along behind him, trying to plant my heels into the ground, desperate to go back. Branches scratched my arms and face. "No! We can't just leave Kyle and Trey!" I tried to wrench my arm free, but Jason's grip was like a steel manacle.

"Come on," he panted, pulling me forward as though my struggles didn't have the slightest effect. "I promised Kyle I'd get you away."

Ignoring my objections, Jason forced me farther and farther from the fight. I kept trying to make him stop, kept trying to break free, but I barely slowed him down. Dimly, some part of me realized that I was still weak from the drugs, but that fact didn't matter.

All that mattered was that Kyle was facing down Ben and he was going to lose if we didn't do something.

I tripped on a tree root and nearly went crashing to my knees, but that wasn't what finally stopped Jason.

He let go of my arm and stared down at his palm. In the scant moonlight filtering through the close-crowded trees,

I could see that his hand was covered in something dark, almost like he had pressed it into a tray of paint.

Jason's other hand still clutched the gun. He shoved it into the waistband of his jeans and I had the brief, slightly hysterical thought that I hoped he had remembered the safety.

He grabbed my arm and turned it so that he could examine the cut.

"We have to go back."

"What"—Jason swallowed—"what happened to your arm?"

I shook my head. My arm didn't matter. "We have to go back," I repeated. "We can't leave them."

Jason gripped my shoulders. "Did it scratch you?" His voice was low and urgent, almost frantic. I remembered the morning he saved me from Heather, the fear on his face when he thought she might have infected me.

"No. Derby did this." I touched the edge of the cut and then wiped my fingers on my jeans. "He was trying to set Ben off with the blood."

Jason let go of me. The relief that slid across his face was overwhelmingly palpable, and for a horrible moment I wondered what scared him more: the idea of my death or the thought of me becoming a werewolf.

Ben.

I gasped, realizing I hadn't told Jason. "It's Ben. He's the wolf. He killed Amy."

"I know." The two words were a threat. "Trey called Serena. He smelled the wolf when he dropped you off. He was nosing around the building when Ben dragged you out the back door and into Derby's car."

Jason hauled out a pocketknife and, before I could ask what he was doing, cut away a strip of his black T-shirt. He put the knife away and lifted my arm. "He followed them out to the nature preserve—which is where we are, by the way—and called us from the road."

Jason wound the cotton around my arm, binding the cut. "He lost them once they were inside. It took a while for him and Kyle to pick up the trail."

He stepped away and I bent my arm, testing the make-shift bandage. "We have to go back. We have to help them."

Jason shook his head. "I'm going back. You're staying here."

"Not a chance!" I was aching, bleeding, and terrified, but I wasn't going to stay behind. Not when everyone else was risking their lives.

Jason reached out and brushed the hair back from my face. "Please, Mac. Just for once, do what someone asks you to." His eyes were so fierce that my legs trembled.

I opened my mouth to object, and he pressed his fingers to my lips. His skin smelled faintly of gunmetal and blood.

"Please," he repeated, the fierceness in his eyes turning to something haunted and desperate. I wondered if he saw Amy when he looked at me.

A low growl echoed through the trees and I whirled.

Relief surged through me as I realized it was Kyle.

And then Jason swore.

Heart in throat, I turned.

Derby stood a few feet away clutching a black handgun and pointing it squarely at my chest.

I froze. Everything around me dimmed until all I could see was the barrel of the gun.

Jason must have made some movement, because Derby suddenly said, "Toss it away or I shoot her."

I tore my gaze from the gun.

Kyle was crouched a few feet away, teeth pulled back in a snarl. I had the horrible, lonely thought that if Derby did shoot me, I wouldn't get a last chance to look into Kyle's eyes—his beautiful, human eyes.

Next to me, Jason cursed and tossed his gun a few feet to the left.

Derby had a strange expression on his face, almost like a grimace. "You ruined everything," he said, voice hoarse and eyes glinting. "Years of planning."

Before Jason realized his mistake, Derby squeezed the trigger.

I closed my eyes and held my breath. Instead of my life flashing behind my closed lids, I saw Amy.

And then something slammed into me. Something larger than a bullet. Something that sent me flying through the air.

The breath I'd been holding was forced from my lungs as I hit the ground and rolled onto my back. A heavy shape landed across my chest and I cried out as the crushing weight caused pain to explode across my torso. Something soft brushed my face. I opened my eyes. Kyle, still in his wolf form, was on top of me.

A second gunshot echoed through the trees, and a bullet lodged itself in the dirt just inches from my face, sending up a small spray of black earth.

Kyle rolled off me as Jason and Derby struggled over the gun. Jason's hands locked around Derby's wrist, trying to make him drop it.

Kyle raced for them as I scrambled to my feet and dove toward the cluster of bushes where I thought Jason's gun had landed.

I heard a low growl and another gunshot followed by a high-pitched, animal whimper, but I didn't turn to look. I pawed through the bushes, cursing under my breath and ignoring the pain in my body, until my fingers skimmed something cool and hard.

I whirled, gun in hand.

Derby was lying on his back, his throat a mess of torn tissue, his eyes staring sightlessly at the sky.

Jason pushed himself to his feet, swaying like he'd taken a blow to the head.

The white werewolf had reappeared and had Kyle pinned, its jaws buried in Kyle's side.

I swallowed. I knew how to shoot—Jason's father had taken Amy and me to the shooting range with them a few times—but there was a world of difference between shooting a paper target and shooting a living creature. Especially one that was inches away from Kyle.

And it was Ben.

I blew my breath out slowly and aimed for the white wolf's hindquarters. It wouldn't be a killing wound, but maybe it would make it back off long enough for Kyle to get away, long enough for me to work up the nerve to take a second shot.

I squeezed the trigger and the gun recoiled in my hand. CRACK!

The wolf let out a howl of pain and fell away from Kyle.

A dark patch of blood spread along its white fur, but I was pretty sure I had just grazed it.

I wrapped my finger around the trigger, holding my breath as I tried to squeeze down a second time. My hand wouldn't stop shaking. I remembered Ben—standing at the stove as he made pancakes, hugging Tess and kissing her forehead, trying to teach me a Johnny Cash song on his guitar after the three of us watched a biopic on TV. The wolf watched me, but all I could see were a year's worth of moments with Ben.

Taking advantage of my hesitation, it tossed its head and spun. It raced through the trees, a streak of white splitting the shadows. I trailed its movement with the barrel of the gun, trying to work up the courage to shoot. Suddenly, a black shape bounded past me, almost knocking me over.

Trey. There was something off about his gait, like he had been hurt, but he still went after the white wolf.

Wolf-Kyle let out a whimper of pain as he got to his feet.

Though obviously wounded, he tried to follow the path Ben and Trey had taken. He made it only a few steps before collapsing and shifting back.

Jason tore his eyes away from the spot where the two wolves had disappeared. Looking as though something inside of him was breaking, he slid a backpack off his shoulders, rummaged inside, and then tossed Kyle a pair of jeans and sneakers.

Looking for injuries, I scanned Kyle's back and chest as he hauled on the clothes. The shift seemed to have healed all of his wounds. "Better?"

He let out a shaky breath. "Much." He walked over to Derby and stared down at the lifeless body. After a moment, he glanced up and met my eyes, the expression on his face a mixture of horror and revulsion.

Before I could assure him that he hadn't had a choice, he stumbled away, looking like he was on the verge of throwing up.

Trey, in human form, limped back through the trees, his dark skin covered in a sheen of sweat. He didn't say anything; he just went for the bag of clothes and quickly got dressed.

I took a step toward him. "Trey . . . ?"

"He got away." The three words were like a dam breaking. Trey didn't cry, but his whole frame silently shook as he sank to his knees and laced his fingers behind his neck.

Uncertainly, I walked over and crouched at his side. I gently put my hand on his shoulder, half expecting he would brush me off. He didn't.

Jason was the first to speak. "What do we do now?"

I didn't have a clue.

I'd wanted so badly to find out what had happened to Amy—to find her murderer—and he had just escaped.

32

EARLY-MORNING HEMLOCK WAS A GHOST TOWN. THE sky was starting to lighten, but even the die-hard, predawn joggers weren't out yet.

"Do you think Jason's all right?" I asked. It was almost five thirty. Almost seven hours since we had left Jason in the woods. Almost seven hours without word.

Trey parked Henry's Jeep in front of my apartment building and turned off the engine. "He's fine. He has that tattoo on his neck and he's a Sheffield."

In the end, it had been Jason's idea to call the police and tell them Derby had asked him to meet in the woods. He said he'd give us two hours to get back to Henry's, and then he would call 911 and report finding Derby's body.

Derby had obviously been killed by a werewolf and no one—no one besides us, anyway—knew Kyle was infected. Jason thought calling the police was the easiest, and safest, way out of the mess Derby's death had created.

Trey hadn't been convinced. He claimed there was noth-ing to keep Jason from turning around and pinning the murder on him or Kyle, but in the end, it was three against one.

Jason had even found a clump of Ben's fur and slipped it into Derby's hand.

Poetic justice, he'd said.

It may have been poetic, but it didn't feel like justice. Not with Ben still out there.

After Henry had patched up my arm and Serena loaned me another set of clothes, Trey and I had gone to the Stray Cat to keep an eye on Tess in case Ben showed up. Kyle had gone home to check on his parents and change into something that would properly fit his tall frame.

Luckily, Kyle's mom and dad were the world's heaviest sleepers; otherwise, he would have had to explain why he wasn't camping with Jason like he had told them he would be.

After Kyle had met back up with us, Trey asked him to take over watching Tess so he could go check out Ben's apartment.

He had insisted, actually. And I had insisted on going with him.

Trey reached for the car door handle and then paused. "Maybe you should wait here while I see if it's safe."

"Oh, please." After everything that had happened, did he really think I wasn't up to checking out a probably empty apartment?

I stepped out of the car and tried to hide the shiver that crept down my spine as I stared up at the apartment building. Tess and I had lived here for two years. We had agreed on the place together. We'd cleaned and decorated and lugged dozens of cardboard boxes up three flights of stairs. It was home. It should feel safe. But looking up at the painted wooden trim and dark windows, it didn't feel safe at all.

I slid my hand under the cuff of my borrowed shirt and touched the new stitches on my arm—Henry's handiwork—then trailed my fingers upward until I hit the small, invisible spot where Ben's needle had pierced my skin.

"Let's get this over with," I muttered. I wasn't going to be scared of my home. I wasn't going to let Ben take that from me when he had already taken so much.

Despite my determination, I had to keep fighting the urge to turn and bolt.

Inside the apartment, my bedroom window was still open and the curtains fluttered in the breeze. A bead of sweat rolled down the side of my face and a knot formed in my stomach as Trey started to climb out onto the fire escape.

He glanced over his shoulder. "Last chance to stay here," he said, voice surprisingly kind.

It was so tempting to say I'd stay upstairs while Trey climbed down in search of the big, bad wolf. But if I did that, Ben and Derby won.

Heart beating triple time, I followed Trey. Ben hadn't bothered closing his window, and Trey ducked right inside.

I was about to climb in after him when my sneaker caught on something. Glancing down, I saw the crowbar— right where I had left it. I wrapped my hand around the cold steel and, gripping it tightly, slipped into Ben's bedroom.

Trey flipped on the overhead light and I blinked.

The furniture was gone.

He walked to the closet and tugged open the door. Empty.

We checked the other rooms. Everything was gone. Right down to Ben's toothbrush and the food in the fridge.

Someone had even cleaned. The smell of bleach and Pine-Sol hung thick in the air and clung to the insides of my nostrils and the back of my throat.

Sometime during the past seven hours, every trace of Ben had been wiped away.

I wrapped my arms around myself, trying to keep from shaking. Amy's killer had disappeared.

Trey cursed and punched the wall, hitting it with such force that bits of plaster fell to the floor and revealed the brick underneath. If the building had been newer—if the walls had been drywall—his fist probably would have gone straight through.

"He's gone," Trey muttered, his voice empty. Dead. "I should have stopped him. I shouldn't have been so slow."

Ben may have outrun Trey, but I'd been the one standing there with my finger wrapped around the trigger and unable to shoot.

It was my fault Ben had gotten away. At least as much as Trey's. Probably more.

I opened my mouth to say so just as Trey suddenly spun and stared at the door. A second later, I heard footsteps.

The doorknob turned as I gripped the crowbar, raising it slightly in front of me.

The door swung open.

Kyle. Jason.

"It wasn't locked," said Jason with a small, weary shrug as they crossed the threshold. "I ran into Kyle out front."

I set the crowbar on the kitchen counter and walked over to Kyle. I wrapped my arms around his waist and pressed my forehead to his chest. "Ben's gone. The whole place is empty."

My stomach lurched. "Where's Tess?" I asked, pulling away.

"She's here," said Kyle, giving my shoulder a small squeeze. "She just went upstairs. She left work and came straight home."

Trey glanced at Jason. "How'd you make out in the woods?"

Jason shrugged. "Lots of questions about what I was doing out there in the middle of the night. I just kept saying Derby wouldn't tell me over the phone. It helps that he has—had—a reputation for being paranoid."

He leaned against the wall, right next to the dent Trey had made. "Honestly, I think they were less concerned with the body and more upset that it'll be harder to pin the checkpoint mess on a dead guy."

Trey and I stared.

I cleared my throat. "Checkpoint mess?"

"They've been running bulletins on the radio every half hour." Jason shook his head. "Didn't it occur to any of you to listen for news?"

Trey scowled and I felt the blood rush to my cheeks.

"This, ladies and gentlemen, is the team that brought down Branson Derby's cunning plan . . ."

"Oh, shut up," I muttered.

"A group of Trackers got overzealous at one of the checkpoints and beat a couple of reg hikers," said Kyle, shooting me a sympathetic glance. "Someone in the car behind them caught the whole thing on their cell and posted it to YouTube. Thirty minutes later, it hit CNN. The police department is claiming the checkpoints were set up illegally and that they didn't know anything about them."

I guess Kyle had actually been checking for news.

"The radio's been running bulletins telling people not to stop their cars for anyone other than marked police cruisers and asking them to call in any roadblocks they see," added Jason. "I called a couple of guys who joined when I did, and they said the Trackers are pulling out of Hemlock. They're in full damage-control mode, which for them means get out and lay low."

I reached for Kyle's hand. "At least now you don't have to leave."

With the Trackers gone, it would be safe for Kyle to stay in Hemlock. Everything was still completely messed up, but that one thought was like a light in the dark. I remembered what he said before—about how the Trackers weren't the only reason to leave—but surely he didn't still feel that way. Not after everything we had been through since then.

I glanced at Jason. He was staring at my hand as it held Kyle's. He looked tired and sad and oddly . . . resigned.

Trying to make the movement seem as natural as

possible, I let go of Kyle's hand and put a fraction more distance between us. I didn't want to hurt Jason.

I turned to Trey. "If the police are acting like they didn't know about the roadblocks, does that mean they won't come after you? Can you guys stay?"

"I don't know. It's probably a wait-and-see." Trey shrugged and a flicker of pain crossed his face. "But it's not like we have a house to go back to." His gaze swept the empty apartment and he pressed his knuckles to his palm, massaging his hand. I had the feeling he was resisting the urge to punch things again.

"Anyway, it's getting late—or early, depending on how you look at it. I don't like leaving Ree and Noah on their own—even with Henry around. And until I know whether or not the police or the LSRB *are* looking for Ree and me, I don't want to hang around town during daylight hours."

I was suddenly struck with all the things that were impossible to say without them sounding inadequate. Trey had saved my life. "Thanks for, you know, *everything*. The woods. Coming with Kyle and Jason to save me. All of it."

Trey glanced at Kyle. "Given what happened at my place, I'd say we're even." He opened the door and stepped into the hall. A second later, I heard his footfall on the stairs.

"I should head out, too," said Jason, not really looking at either of us.

"Jason . . ."

He met my eyes. "I'll call you tomorrow. There are things we should talk about."

A flutter of foreboding filled me; I didn't want a repeat

of our conversation out at Henry's. But before I could say anything, he was gone.

And Kyle and I were alone.

"Are you okay?" he asked after the door had swung shut.

I glanced toward the bedroom and shivered. I closed my eyes, fighting off the memory of Ben's weight on top of me as he pressed me to the floor.

"As okay as I can be, all things considered." I opened my eyes. "How are you?"

Kyle shoved his hands into his pockets. "Been better," he admitted.

His face was pale and drawn and covered with a shadow of stubble. There were circles under his eyes so dark that they looked like faint smudges of ink. I noticed, absently, that he was wearing jeans with a hole over the left knee and his gray Arcade Fire T-shirt.

The corner of his mouth quirked up in a small, mirthless smile. "Guess I'm officially one of those werewolves they always warn people about."

I stared at Kyle, confused, not getting it.

"Derby," he said. "I killed him."

I shook my head. "You didn't have a choice. One of us was going to have to do it—Jason or me or Trey—he wasn't going to let us walk out of there alive." I wondered if I could have pulled the trigger; thanks to Kyle, I would never have to know the answer.

I reached up and gently touched his cheek. "This doesn't change who you are."

He let out a low breath. "Promise?"

I was reminded of Jason staring into my eyes and asking me—a lifetime ago—if everything would be all right.

"I promise," I whispered.

A floorboard creaked above our heads, and I lowered my hand. "I should get up there before Tess realizes I never came home last night."

Kyle nodded. "Okay."

I bit my lip. After everything that had happened, I didn't want to be away from him.

There was a muffled thud upstairs. I held my breath, listening. The thud was immediately followed by the sound of breaking glass.

Without thinking, I ran for the third floor, taking the stairs two at a time, not checking to see whether or not Kyle followed.

Tess glanced up as I hurtled into the apartment. Her eyes and nose were both extremely red. "Men are scum and I'm joining a convent."

33

TESS WAS CROUCHED DOWN, THE BROOM CLUTCHED in one hand. She stood and wiped her eyes with her sleeve. "It'll be great," she said, voice choked with tears. "I look killer in black and I can sing on a hilltop like Julie Andrews in *The Sound of Music*."

I walked over and glanced down at the mess she had been sweeping up. Twin images of Ben stared at me from beneath a blanket of shattered glass and cracked plastic. The piggy bank he had bought her as a joke was broken in half, a few quarters and dimes glinting among the debris.

"What happened?" I asked, taking the broom and propping it against the wall before gently steering her away from the mini-wreckage.

"Ben broke up with me." She sniffed loudly. "He called me at the Cat. Collect. From a pay phone. On his way to Ohio. Who does that?"

I swallowed. Who, indeed. What kind of murderer took the time to break up with his girlfriend as he fled town? "Did he say why?" I asked, dreading the answer.

She shook her head, but then nodded. "He said he ran

into an old girlfriend when he was in Dayton and that they've been emailing. The jerk was cyber-cheating on me. For months."

I wrapped her in a hug. "I'm so sorry, Tess." I had cared about Ben and trusted him, but Tess had actually loved him. The fact that Ben Fielding hadn't really existed—that he'd just been a costume worn by Ian Derby—didn't make Tess's pain any less real.

But as hurt as she was now, I couldn't tell her the actual reason Ben had ended things. It would destroy her if she found out the man she'd been kissing at night had murdered four people—including Amy.

I heard a small creak and tensed. Kyle opened my bedroom door a crack, relief sliding over his face as he realized everything was all right. He must have gone up the fire escape.

He stepped back before Tess could spot him.

"It's like I didn't know him at all." Tess pulled away and frowned, studying my face. She reached out and tilted my chin. "What happened to your cheek? And why weren't you in your room?"

Right. Derby had sliced me when cutting off the gag. Henry hadn't thought the cut needed stitches and I'd almost forgotten about it. I glanced down. Thankfully, the black sweatpants and red hoodie I'd borrowed from Serena covered the gash on my arm and the dozens of bruises on my limbs.

"I fell when I was over at Jason's," I lied. "By the pool. And I was downstairs, in the laundry room." Luckily, Tess was too preoccupied to question why I would be doing laundry at dawn on a Sunday morning.

I forced myself to act like it was a normal breakup so she'd never suspect otherwise. "Do you want me to go out and get a tub of rocky road?" My sleep-deprived body practically cried out at the thought, but I ignored it. "We can eat ice cream and make a list of all the things that were wrong with him."

She shook her head. "Actually, I think I'm going to go lie down. I just want to turn off all the lights and crawl under my comforter and sleep for, like, forty-eight hours."

I frowned. Tess's breakup ritual always included ice cream and making what she called "The List of Judgment." I'd seen her through the disintegration of five relationships before Ben. The guys and the circumstances changed, but the ritual stayed the same.

Until now, apparently.

Worried, I watched her walk slowly to her bedroom and shut the door.

I tried to tell myself that she would be okay, that Tess bounced back from everything.

With a small sigh, I quickly swept up the pile of broken mementos and dumped it in the trash so she wouldn't see it when she came out.

When I walked into my room, Kyle was standing by the window with one hand wrapped around the frame.

"I should go," he said softly as I closed the door behind me.

My heart sank. "You're not staying?"

"Better not. Tess."

I reached behind me and turned the latch. "She'll have to knock."

The sun was coming up and the dawn light made Kyle's hair look like it was shot through with strands of copper. I stared at his shirt, and despite everything that had happened, the ghost of a smile crossed my lips. We had driven three hours to catch Arcade Fire play. We hadn't told Jason or Amy or Heather about the concert—we'd just taken off. Just the two of us.

I crossed the room. A breeze stirred the curtains around us as I gently brushed my lips against his—the first time I had kissed him since that morning at Henry's. How was it possible that was only yesterday? It felt like years had been crammed into the past twenty-four hours.

After a moment, Kyle pulled back. "I figured you'd still be mad at me—you know, about the stuff Jason said. At Henry's."

I shook my head. "I'm too tired to be mad. Plus, I figure knocking me out of the way of a bullet gets you about a million bonus points."

A shadow crossed his face, gone so quickly that I barely had time to register it.

I opened my mouth to point out that he couldn't stand by the window indefinitely, but the words were lost in a yawn.

Kyle reached out and gently traced the curve of my cheek, his fingers grazing the shallow cut Derby had left there. "You're exhausted. You should get some sleep."

"I'm scared to close my eyes," I confessed, the words barely a whisper. "I'm scared I'll end up back in the woods." The thought of those lost hours between the needle slipping into my arm and the moment I regained consciousness terrified me. It had been too close to being dead, too close to what had happened to Amy.

And God only knew whether or not Amy herself would show up in my dreams. I'd been certain the nightmares would stop if I could solve the riddle of her death. But finding out it had been Ben and letting him get away . . .

I shuddered.

Kyle frowned and ran his hand along my arm, stopping his fingers when they were just over the pulse in my wrist. He looked serious and a little sad. "Could you sleep if I stayed?"

I nodded. I didn't trust myself to speak.

He let go of my wrist and turned toward the fire escape. For a horrible second, I thought he was going to leave, but he quietly closed the window and shut the curtains.

I stepped back as he kicked off his Vans and pushed his hair away from his face.

"Bet you think I'm a total wuss," I said. I bit my lip and blinked away tears. I hated being so afraid, hated that Derby and Ben had made me scared to close my eyes in my own bedroom.

"Shhhhh," murmured Kyle, taking my hand and pulling me gently toward the bed.

I lay on top of the covers, facing the wall, and Kyle

stretched out behind me, putting his back to the room. He draped his arm over my waist and threaded his fingers through mine.

After a while, I closed my eyes. Nothing terrible waited for me in the darkness, and I eventually felt the thick pull of sleep.

"Kyle?" My voice came out a mumble.

"Yeah?"

I struggled to speak before I was completely sucked under. "I love you."

He squeezed my hand. "Me too."

For the first time in weeks, I didn't dream.

I opened my eyes and blinked. My thoughts were sleep-sluggish and it took me a moment to remember why I had been sleeping, fully dressed, in the middle of the day.

The events of the previous evening came rushing back, and I rolled over to curl against Kyle.

He wasn't there.

Confused, I sat up and rubbed my eyes. I was completely alone. Someone had covered me with a blanket, but my bedroom was empty and the window was open.

I caught a glimpse of white out of the corner of my eye and glanced down. A folded piece of paper was next to me on the bed. My name was written on the front in Kyle's familiar, looping scrawl.

Mackenzie.

Not *Mac* but *Mackenzie.*

Nothing good ever came of anyone using my full name.

Hands shaking, trying to ignore the queasy feeling in my stomach, I unfolded the sheet of paper.

Mac,

I'm sorry I didn't wake you. I knew you'd try to talk me out of leaving and I was scared I'd let you. By the time you read this, I'll be gone. My stuff's already in the car—I just couldn't leave without seeing you and making sure you were okay.

What happened in the woods was a warning. You said I got bonus points for saving you from a bullet, but I could have scratched you in the process. I wouldn't have been able to live with myself if that had happened.

I'm too dangerous to be around anyone I care about. And there's nothing to say the Trackers won't come back or that someone won't figure out what I am. If they do, and you're with me, you'll be at risk. So will my parents. I can't take that chance.

I know you'll be angry and hurt, but I also know you'll be all right. You're always all right. And after enough time has passed, you'll realize this was for the best.

Kyle

PS: Keep an eye on Jason. He messed up, but he tried to fix things. We probably wouldn't have made it out of the woods without him.

I tried to read the letter a second time, but the words blurred together.

He'd known. Downstairs, in Ben's apartment, when I said he didn't have to leave with the Trackers gone, Kyle had already made up his mind to disappear.

When he had stood by the window, his bags had been in the car downstairs. When he had wrapped his arm around me—when I told him I loved him—he'd just been waiting until I fell asleep before slipping away.

Choking back a sob, I crawled across the bed and grabbed my iPod from the nightstand. Fumbling, I hooked it up to my portable speakers and hit shuffle, hoping music would drown out the strangled noises trying to fight their way free of my throat.

I didn't want to explain to Tess why I was crying. I *couldn't* explain to Tess why I was crying. Not without explaining everything, and I couldn't do that to her.

Like a cruel joke, "My Body Is a Cage" by Arcade Fire started to play.

Something inside of me broke. I knew I should reach out and skip to another song—anything that wasn't loaded with memories and connotations—but I couldn't do it.

I pulled my knees to my chest and listened to the entire thing. All four minutes and forty-seven seconds. Despite the tears coursing down my cheeks, when the last note faded, I reached out and skipped back, listening to the song again as I tried to figure out what I was going to do.

Epilogue

I CLUTCHED MY TICKET AND ADJUSTED THE STRAP OF
my backpack.

I could have waited inside the bus station, but there were
only a dozen plastic chairs and most of them had been occupied. So instead I waited outside, leaning against the brick
building in the twilight and waiting for the bus to Denver
to pull in.

I flashed back to the motel parking lot where I'd waited
for Tess after Hank split town. Standing outside the bus
station in Hemlock, I felt almost as lonely as I had then.

Maybe it would be different if I knew what I was
doing—if I could be certain Kyle actually was headed for
Colorado—but all I had were a handful of facts and an edu-
cated guess.

Kyle had asked Serena about packs during that afternoon they'd spent out at Henry's, and she said he'd seemed
particularly interested when she mentioned Colorado.

Denver was within a day's drive—provided you didn't
mind driving long hours and drinking lots of coffee—and

it was rumored to have one of the largest werewolf packs in the country. More importantly, Kyle had lived there until he was six.

My stomach knotted at the thought of school and how far behind I was going to get—especially since I'd been a less than stellar student over the past couple of weeks—but I pushed the worry away. I'd get caught up.

I thought about work and how there had been a message on the apartment voice mail telling me I was on probation for missing my shift yesterday—a probation that might turn into a termination since I hadn't shown up tonight.

But it wasn't like I could wait for a more convenient time to go chasing after Kyle. The longer lead time he had, the harder he'd be to find. I'd learned that much from years with Hank.

The worst part of this whole thing—other than the possibility of not finding Kyle—was knowing how worried and hurt Tess would be when she found out I was gone. She had come out of her room midafternoon and tried to pretend that she was fine, that this was like any other breakup. But she'd barely touched the pizza I ordered, and she got someone to switch shifts with her at the Cat so she could crawl back into bed.

I swallowed, throat suddenly tight. I hated myself for running out on her—especially with what she was going through—but I couldn't think of any other option. There was no way she would have just let me go, and the alternative—letting Kyle slip away forever—was too horrible to contemplate.

I couldn't lose anyone else I cared about. Even if it meant not being there for Tess when I desperately wanted to be.

She thought I had gone into work—which would at least buy me a few hours. She wouldn't start to worry until midnight, and by then I'd be far enough away from Hemlock that I could call her from one of the bus stops and try to explain.

If I couldn't convince Tess over the phone that I'd be back and not to panic, Serena would try to talk her out of calling the cops and reporting me as a runaway.

I was really hoping it wouldn't come to that.

"So this is what a bus station looks like. Kind of underwhelming."

I turned. Jason stood five feet away.

"How did you know I was here?"

"Serena." He crossed his arms. He was wearing a black leather jacket over jeans and a black T-shirt. The light from the bus station sign illuminated half his face and the tattoo on his neck, leaving the rest of him in shadow. "You didn't really think she'd let you leave town on your own, did you?"

I stared at him, blankly.

"I'm going with you. Preferably in my car, since it has heated seats and satellite radio, but I'll take the bus if you insist on slumming it. It can be an experience. Like daytime television."

I shook my head. "I don't need your help."

"Yes, you do. Denver is a big place, Mac. You won't find him on your own." He uncrossed his arms and walked toward me, stopping when there was less than a foot of space between us.

"Denver is the werewolf capital of the West," I countered. "What do you think will happen to you if you go walking down the street with that thing on your neck?"

Jason shrugged. "I'll cover it up. I'll wear shirts with ridiculously high collars or I'll put a bandage on it or I'll swipe some of your makeup—you know, all those cliché things girls do to hide hickeys. Besides, this isn't about me. Or you. It's about Kyle. And I can help."

His green eyes glinted and he was suddenly serious. "I know I've spent all summer screwing up, but I haven't touched a drink since that night at Trey's."

I wanted to point out that the night he was talking about was Friday and that this was Sunday and that two days wasn't exactly an eternity of clean living—but the expression on his face stopped me. It was earnest and a little desperate.

I reached out and touched my fingers to his neck. A black dagger but without the red letter that made it complete. "You never did get the whole thing, did you?" I murmured as I dropped my hand.

Jason shook his head. "No." He reached into his pocket and withdrew a small, glittering bundle. Looking slightly embarrassed, he handed it to me.

Amy's bracelet.

"How did you—"

"I heard you tell Kyle about it in the woods. I went to your place and found the pieces. Most of them are there, I think."

I stared down at the bracelet. The leather string was new and there were a few less coins, but it was still achingly familiar.

"Thank you," I whispered, closing my fingers around it.

"Let me help."

I handed him my backpack.

"Where are you going?" he asked as I turned and walked away.

"To see if I can get a refund on my ticket."

Twenty minutes later, I settled down into the passenger seat of Jason's SUV. He was oddly quiet—almost like he was worried I'd change my mind if he opened his mouth.

The truth was, even though I had told him I didn't need his help, I was glad he was coming with me. Kyle, Jason, Amy, and me. It had always been the four of us. Even with Amy gone, it felt right that Jason and I were going after Kyle together.

I yawned and slid farther down in the seat, trying to ignore the way Jason kept sneaking worried glances at me when he thought I wasn't looking.

We'd find Kyle, and Tess would be okay while we were gone, and somehow, eventually, things would go back to some semblance of normal. Even though Ben—Ian—was still out there.

I knew things couldn't be that simple, but that didn't stop me from lying to myself. Sometimes, lies gave you more strength than the truth.

Eventually, somewhere just over the state line, I fell asleep.

"This was so going to be my prom dress." Amy twirled, the white, beaded fabric flaring out around her. It was a completely 1930s flapper look.

She came to a clumsy stop and collapsed in a dizzy heap.

I turned in a slow circle. We were on a small square of neatly mowed grass—a patch of green so bright that it almost glowed—in the middle of what looked like a cornfield.

I felt completely underdressed in my jeans-and-T-shirt combo. "You're going to get grass stains all over it."

"It doesn't matter," Amy said, lying back and lacing her hands behind her head. "Not anymore."

The cornstalks rustled, like something was moving through the field. Hiding in it.

"Amy . . ."

She sighed and sat up. "It's not over—you know that, right?" She shook her head, looking unhappy, her delight in the dress apparently forgotten. "I'm sorry, Mac, but it's not. Something's coming."

I stared into the field. "What's in there?"

"If I told you, it wouldn't be a surprise."

I turned to ask Amy if she could be any less helpful, but I was completely alone.

Acknowledgments

So many people have contributed support and guidance throughout this adventure that naming them all would probably be a book in its own right. That being said, special thanks go to:

Emmanuelle Morgen, my fantabulous agent, who picked my query from the obscurity of her slush pile and who wanted to see more of Mac, Jason, and Kyle. Her unwavering support and faith mean the world.

Claudia Gabel, my amazing editor, who stuck with me, who pushed me to stretch myself, and who encouraged me to think big. This book would not be what it is without her guidance, input, wisdom, endless patience, and replies to emails sent at 2 a.m.

Katherine Tegen, for her input and support, and for running such a fabulous imprint. *Hemlock* could not have found a better home.

Thanks, also, to Editor-in-Chief Kate Jackson and Publisher Susan Katz.

Barbara Fitzsimmons, Amy Ryan, Joel Tippie, and Torborg Davern, for making *Hemlock* look so gorgeous. Lauren

Flower in marketing and the publicity team.

And a huge thanks to everyone else at KTB and HCCB who had a hand in getting *Hemlock* onto shelves and into hands.

Thanks to Debra Driza, Jamie Blair, and Laurie Devore (aka the original Jason fangirl), for beta reading early drafts.

Kate Hart, Jodi Meadows, and Debra Driza (again), for keeping me on track those days when I worried this whole crazy adventure was going off the rails, for reading random snippets, and for providing advice at all hours. I am blessed to call such talented and kind writers friends.

Nancy and Susan, for their friendship, endless support, and cheerleading.

Very little would be possible without the support of my family. Huge thanks (and much love) to my parents for passing on their love of books and for raising me to believe I could do anything—no matter how farfetched, impractical, or magical. To Justin and Sarah, for remembering my dreams when I misplaced them. And to Krystle, for making sure I stepped away from my laptop and didn't become a crazy hermit.

And thank you, whoever you are, for reading.

Mac thought her nightmares would end,
but the truth is that they're only just beginning.

Read on for a sneak peek at *Thornhill*,
Kathleen Peacock's thrilling sequel to *Hemlock*.

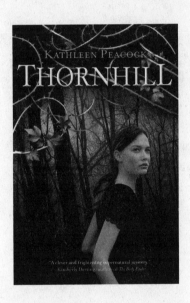

1

SOME ROOMS LOOKED BETTER IN THE DARK. THIS WAS definitely one of them.

Neon light slipped around the curtains, muted flashes of red as the vacancy sign blinked on and off. I shifted my weight and the mattress protested with a chorus of groans and squeaks.

"Are you okay?" Kyle's voice was still rough around the edges as he tightened his arm around me. "Was it okay?" He had done this before; I hadn't.

I pressed my lips to his bare shoulder. "It was perfect."

The muffled sounds of a fistfight drifted in from the parking lot, and Kyle made a skeptical noise in the back of his throat.

"Okay," I admitted, a sleepy smile tugging at the corners of my mouth, "so it's not the most romantic place to deflower a girl."

"Deflower?"

My cheeks flushed. I shrugged and my skin brushed his, sending a wave of sparks racing down my spine. "That's what Tess calls it. Any time she tries to give me a serious sex talk, she turns into the mom from a sixties sitcom."

"Bet none of her talks covered werewolves." A somber note crept into his voice, one that hinted at the reasons he had left.

"No," I said, struggling to keep my voice light, "but she did say all teenage boys were ravenous beasts. Plus, her last boyfriend was a mass murderer. Compared to that . . ." I shivered and cursed myself. I didn't want to ruin what we had just done with thoughts of Ben and everything that had happened in Hemlock.

Silence filled the spaces where our bodies didn't quite meet.

"You shouldn't have come after me," he said, finally.

"I had to." I couldn't remember finding him or how we had gotten here or who had kissed who first, but I knew there had never been a choice. We were inevitable. "You know I did."

"I know."

"You can't just run away."

More silence.

"Kyle?"

"Yeah?"

"It's still kind of perfect."

He pushed the hair back from my face and traced the line of my cheek with the pad of his thumb. "I love you, Mackenzie."

I opened my mouth to tell him that I loved him, too, but a particularly loud thud from the parking lot made me jump. "Okay, the setting could be a *lot* more romantic," I said, looking over my shoulder. "The back of your car would at least be quiet."

I turned to kiss him, but he wasn't there.

"Kyle?" My throat was sandpaper dry, my voice thick with sleep. Soft snores came from across the room, and Jason's shape—a tangle of blankets and skin—shifted in the dark. Outside, the fight in the parking lot was going strong.

I skimmed my fingers over the other side of my bed. The sheets were cold. Reality sank in: I hadn't found Kyle; he had never been here; we had never done . . . that.

It had all been a dream.

For a moment, it was like losing him all over again, and I put a hand over my mouth to smother the small, strangled sound that lodged in my throat and fought to get free. I wouldn't cry. I *couldn't* cry.

Jason was sleeping seven feet away. If he woke, he'd put his arms around me and whisper that everything was going to be all right.

Part of me wanted the comfort and the lie—wanted it badly—but it wouldn't be fair. Not to Kyle, who had walked away from everything to keep us safe. And not to Jason, who thought he loved me and who belonged to my best friend even in her death.

Burying the desire for comfort, I stood and made my way to the bathroom, ignoring the way the carpet crunched under my feet. The North Star Motor Inn—cash up front and no questions asked—was a step above a total dive, but it wasn't a very big step.

I should know.

Home isn't a permanent address—not for people like us. My father's words drifted back to me as I flicked on the bathroom light. Hank had seen motels as the way stations between cons and as dumping grounds for things he no longer wanted. Things like me.

I ran the water in the sink and scooped up a drink in my palm. It tasted of chlorine and brine and did nothing to dislodge the lump in my throat.

Rat-tat-tap.

Three glistening drops of red hit the porcelain. They mixed with the water, tingeing it pink.

My heart jackhammered as I glanced up.

Amy—my best friend and one of Ben's victims—stared at me from the other side of the bathroom mirror.

I scrambled away so quickly that I tripped and had to grab the towel rack to keep from falling.

"Easy, tiger." Amy leaned forward. Her ink-black hair fell around her like a curtain and her eyes were shadows that shifted and swirled like smoke.

I hadn't seen her in days—not since the night Jason and I had left Hemlock. Foolishly, I'd begun to think maybe I had left her behind.

"Just because you didn't see me didn't mean I wasn't here," she said, reading my mind in the unsettling way she sometimes did. "Don't you remember what I told you?"

I shook my head. Amy had said a lot of things—both before and after death.

She pressed her fingertips to the glass, her manicured

nails making the same rat-tat-tap sound the blood had made when it hit the sink. With each tap, fault lines spread across the mirror. "Something's coming, Mac." She sounded oddly sad. Almost apologetic. "It's not over."

A large crack split her face in two and the mirror exploded outward.

I woke—really woke—gasping. Soft yellow light filled the motel room, and I was lying, fully clothed, on top of my bed.

I struggled to shake away the fog of sleep.

Jason and I had come back to regroup. I remembered lying down—just for a second—and . . . nothing. I must have passed out.

A ball of lead settled in my stomach as I realized I was alone.

I checked the bathroom—empty—and then pulled my phone from my pocket. Ten p.m. I'd been asleep for over three hours. Pacing, I dialed Jason's number. The call went straight to voice mail.

"Where are you? I woke up and—"

My foot hit something smooth and solid. I glanced at the floor and then crouched down.

"GoddamnitJason." I breathed the words in a rush as I straightened, one hand still pressing the phone to my ear, the other holding a half-empty bottle of Jack Daniel's.

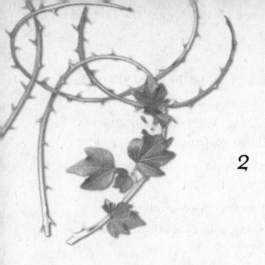

2

THERE WERE FIVE BARS WITHIN STUMBLING DISTANCE OF the motel, but in the end, I found Jason right back where I had started.

More or less.

We were in room eleven. He had made it as far as number seven before slumping to the pavement, bloody and battered, beer and whiskey riding his breath. He'd forgotten the room number. And his key.

That had been thirty minutes ago.

Now he leaned against the bathroom door frame, shirtless, blond hair still dripping from a dunk in the sink. Two cuts crossed his chest—just over his heart—like the *X* on a pirate's map. There was a third gash on his upper arm. *A broken bottle,* he had promised. *All three. Not claw marks.*

I thought he needed stitches, but he had refused to go to the hospital.

He reached past me and set a bloodstained washcloth on the edge of the sink. "You can't give me the silent treatment indefinitely." The slur had left his words, but his voice was slow and cautious.

I stared at his tattoo in the mirror—the black dagger on his neck that marked him as an initiate in the largest anti-werewolf group in the country—before dragging my eyes upward.

Jason's gaze was brilliant green and bloodshot.

"Are you hurt anywhere else?" The words—the first I had spoken since he told me where he had gone—sliced my throat like razor blades.

"No."

I glanced at the floor where his shirt lay in a crumpled heap. Torn and stained red, it was beyond saving. The cuts were bad, but they weren't *that* bad. I'd had enough practice patching people up—my father and, more recently, Jason—to know that much.

"Not all of the blood is yours." I closed my eyes and gripped the edge of the sink.

"It's Tracker blood." There was an undercurrent to Jason's voice that was as dark as the stains on his shirt. "All of it. We ran into a fleabag and his reg girlfriend. He tried to throw a guy through a wall while she came at me with a busted bottle. Tiny, but fast."

I tightened my hold on the sink, clutching it so hard that I cut off the circulation in my fingertips. "You could have been killed." Another thought occurred to me. A group of Trackers didn't just happen onto a werewolf by chance.

"They were hunting." Hunting wolves. Hunting people

7

like Kyle. "They went on a hunt and you went with them. Did you . . . did they . . ." I sucked in a deep breath. "What happened to the reg and the werewolf?"

"They got away. Both of them." There was a faint rustle of denim and then Jason was behind me. I could feel the air he displaced and the heat radiating off his skin. If I turned my head, I'd smell the alcohol on his breath. "I wouldn't have let them hurt her. The reg."

"And the wolf?"

He hesitated. "I don't know," he admitted. "It almost killed a man. . . ."

"A man who was hunting him." Jason didn't deny it. "What if it had been Kyle?"

"What if . . . ? Jesus, Mac. Kyle's my best friend."

I opened my eyes. I wanted to say I was sorry and I knew; instead, what came out was, "You promised to stay away from them."

Jason held my gaze in the mirror. "The local Trackers are the best way to figure out where a wolf in Denver might go. You know that."

I did know, but if Jason got sucked back into the Trackers, if they ever discovered the part he had played the night their leader had been killed . . .

I had almost lost him to them once.

"I didn't have a choice, Mac. My father's going to report the car stolen and Tess is going to report you missing—sooner rather than later. We're running out of time to find him."

"And the drinking?"

Jason was standing close enough that I felt him flinch. He reached for me, but I pushed past him and out of the bathroom.

I stopped when I was halfway to the motel room door. I wanted to storm off, but I'd have to come back here eventually. Jason was all I had. I crossed my arms and waited, half hoping, half dreading he would try to talk to me.

He didn't.

The bathroom door clicked shut. A moment later, the shower clanked to life.

Kyle had once told me that I needed to have faith in people instead of expecting them to let me down. But putting my faith in Jason's promises had almost gotten him killed.

I couldn't lose anyone else. Not after Amy.

I pulled my phone from my pocket and punched in a number. A familiar, melodic voice answered on the third ring.

"I need a favor."

The Denver Bus Center wasn't hard to find. My hands tightened on the wheel as I pulled off the street and up a ramp marked Public Parking. After today, I would well and truly be on my own.

"I thought we were getting breakfast." Jason flipped open the glove compartment and dug through a rat's nest of paper and plastic.

"Lunch," I corrected as I turned off the ramp. "It's past noon. And we are."

He paused his search just long enough to shoot me a

skeptical look over the top of his shades. "Week-old sand-wiches from a bus station vending machine wasn't what I had in mind."

"I'm surprised you want to eat at all, considering you felt too hungover to drive." I bit my lip and backed Jason's SUV into a space as he located a small bottle and popped two white tablets. "I just have to do something. You can wait here. I'll crack a window."

"Right. Because I'm a child or a puppy." He followed me out of the car and downstairs.

The inside of the bus terminal seemed unnaturally dark and dingy in contrast to the bright morning outside. A tired-looking woman hauled a screaming toddler toward the restrooms while a junkie rocked back and forth on a bench. A few security guards wandered through the crowd, their yellow shirts the only spots of color.

"Middle America at its finest," muttered Jason. The corners of his mouth twisted down as he watched a cleaning lady mop up a puddle of vomit. "Want to explain why we're here?"

I pushed back the coins on the bracelet I wore—Amy's bracelet—to peer at my watch. I hadn't factored in traffic and we were a few minutes late.

"You can't seriously think Kyle's been hiding out in a hole like this." Jason made it sound like we were standing on skid row. To someone as rich as he was, maybe the distinction didn't seem that big.

I fingered the edge of a coin and swallowed. I had rehearsed what I would say all morning, but now that we were here, all my practiced words deserted me.

Before I could recapture them, the crowd shifted and someone squealed my name. I caught a split-second glimpse of dark skin and bright fabric before I was tackled by five feet and one inch of enthusiasm.

"Human ribs," I gasped. "Can't. Breathe. Se—re—na."

A flicker of embarrassment crossed Serena Carson's face as she released me. "Sorry. I forgot." She raked a hand through her shoulder-length curls and scanned the crowd to see if anyone had noticed her minuscule slip. Serena was usually very good at hiding her condition. She had to be. Like Kyle, and thousands of other werewolves living underground, she'd be sent to a government rehabilitation camp if anyone found out she had lupine syndrome.

She turned back to me and frowned as she catalogued the bags under my eyes and my rumpled clothes. "Don't take this the wrong way, but you look like hell. And I'm saying that as someone who spent the night on a Greyhound listening to the life story of a guy called Murray the Rat." She slipped a backpack from her shoulder and tossed it at Jason.

He caught it effortlessly, his eyes impossible to read behind the sunglasses. "Carson. Fancy seeing you here."

I shot Jason a nervous glance, then flashed Serena a small smile. "Not all of us dress like every day is a casting call for *America's Next Top Model*."

She glanced down at her outfit—a turquoise bomber-style jacket over a belted pink shirt and gray capris—and grinned. "The shoes don't really work," she said, gesturing to the blue Chuck Taylors on her feet, "but I figured flats would be better for pounding pavement."

"They look good. Tess has a pair just like them." Guilt flooded me at the thought of my cousin. "Is she okay?"

Serena nodded. "Upset and worried, but okay. At least you're providing the mother of all distractions from Ben. No sign of him," she added, before the question could leave my lips.

I exhaled. I still wasn't sure how—or if—I should tell Tess that Ben was the white werewolf who had terrorized Hemlock and killed Amy. As far as she knew, he had dumped her and skipped town to hook up with his ex. I wanted it to stay that way until I figured out what to do.

Serena glanced at Jason and arched an eyebrow. "Speaking of distractions, I told everyone at school that you went to Vegas on a bender. Mac and Kyle are supposedly tracking you down before you marry a hooker and sign away the family fortune."

Without a word, Jason turned and headed for the parking garage, striding through the crowd like he expected them to clear a path for him. Most of them did.

Serena shot me a bewildered glance. "Okay, since when does Jason Sheffield care about his reputation?"

I sighed. "It's not that. I sort of didn't tell him you were coming."

The look on her face slid from bewilderment to reproach. "So he doesn't know why I'm actually here? Oh, this is going to be fun."

"I just couldn't figure out how to tell him."

"Well, you'd better think fast," she said, falling into step next to me as I started after Jason.

"Did you really tell everyone we were in Vegas?"

She nodded. "Figured it was either that or say you had a pregnancy scare and ran away because you didn't know which of them was the baby's daddy."

"Soap opera much?"

Serena shrugged. "We do live in Hemlock."

Truer words had never been spoken. I shook my head. "Thanks for coming."

"Are you kidding?" She grinned. "Denver is like the ultimate werewolf hot spot. I've been dying to check it out for years."

We reached the stairs to the upper parking level. Jason was almost at the top. The set of his shoulders was stiff and he dangled Serena's backpack by one strap, gripping the fabric so tightly that his hand shook.

"Jason?"

He kept walking.

I jogged up the stairs. Serena didn't follow, trying to give us the illusion of privacy even though she'd hear every word. Werewolf hearing.

"Jason? Would you stop for a second?" I grabbed the other strap of the bag.

He turned and slipped off his shades with his other hand. His expression was carefully blank as he slid the glasses into his jacket pocket, but his eyes glinted like pieces of broken glass. The backpack dangled between us, each of us holding a strap like it was the prize in a tug-of-war. "You want to tell me why Serena's here?"

I swallowed. "I thought she could help."

"So you called her without telling me?"

"You like Serena," I reminded him. "At least you used to." The *before you found out she was infected* hung heavy and unspoken.

"Sure. For a—" He caught himself. "—for what she is, she's great." He ran a hand over the light stubble on his face. "That's not the point. If you think Serena can help, fine, but you can't get pissed about me meeting the Trackers without telling you and then call her behind my back."

"It's not the same thing."

"It's exactly the same. You never trust anyone."

The idea of being lectured about trust by Jason was so ridiculous that only the look on his face stopped me from laughing. "I trust people who deserve to be trusted." I wasn't sure what else to say.

"Like Kyle? Leaving you a Dear John letter and slipping out before you woke up is really deserving of trust." Almost at once, Jason realized he'd gone too far. His eyes widened and the expression on his face softened. He released his grip on the bag and it thudded against my legs. "Mac . . . I didn't . . ."

I set the bag down and crossed my arms, using them like a shield even though the words had already hit. What Kyle had done, he had done to try and keep us all safe. That had

14

to make it better, didn't it? "It doesn't matter," I said, even though it did.

I glanced over my shoulder. Serena was at the top of the stairs. I sucked in a deep breath and turned back to Jason. "Serena's here to help us find Kyle, but if we don't have any luck by morning, the two of you are going home. I'll stay here and keep looking, but you're going back to Hemlock."

"You've got to be joking." Jason stared at me, incredulous. "I do one thing you don't like and you want me gone?"

I was pretty sure meeting the Trackers and falling off the wagon counted as two things, but I didn't point that out. "I can't look for Kyle and worry about you at the same time."

"You can't force me to leave." Jason's voice came out with the edge of a growl, almost as though he were infected.

"You're right." Serena was suddenly beside me. She flexed her hand and muscles shifted under her skin. "Mac can't force you, but I can." She didn't look happy when she said it, but she flashed him a wolf's grin, showing teeth that were a little too long and a little too pointed.

Jason swore under his breath and walked away. When he realized we weren't following, he turned. "Are you coming?"

I hesitated and he pushed a hand roughly through his hair. "Look. I want to find Kyle. You want to find Kyle. We can argue about everything else"—his gaze darted to Serena and a thunderstorm played out across his face—"later. The Trackers said Montbello was fleabag friendly. It's one of the few parts of Denver we haven't checked."

15

"You're still going to help?" Serena asked the question before I could.

"It's not like I have a choice."

I followed him to the SUV. "Jason, you've always had a choice."

"Kyle's my best friend and you . . . you won't come back to Hemlock without him." He pulled open the driver's-side door and slid behind the wheel. "Choice doesn't factor into things."

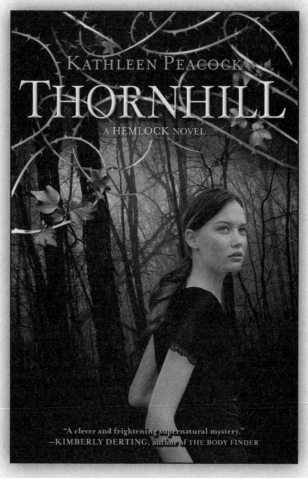